The Heart of Yonkers

A Novel

by Patricia Vaccarino

Modus Operandi Books • New York

Published 2020 by Modus Operandi Books
www.modusoperandibooks.com

ISBN: 978-0-9963494-6-8
Library of Congress Control Number: 2020905910
Printed in the U.S.

Praise for Patricia Vaccarino's The Heart of Yonkers

The predecessor to this work by Patricia Vaccarino was entitled **YONKERS Yonkers!** This book, **The Heart of Yonkers**, might just be *Yonkers Redux*. Yes, there's a not-too-subtle Updike reference there. The story telling, the characters, everything about Yonkers and its characters, are all seen once again through the eyes of protagonist Cookie Colangelo (Vaccarino's Rabbit).

There's a lilt in the writing; to read it feels like music and dance. The characters are older. We see growth, more teenage angst as hormones rage. Perspective and worldview evolve, as Cookie experiences life events in her family, school, neighbors, and the wide circle of schoolmates, some of whom are friends, many of whom are those tertiary characters that play an occasional but significant role in one's life.

New characters arrive who are at the heart of the story. A Vietnam vet and his mother, and a nun with a heart of gold. Yonkers, of course, remains both the backdrop and plays a lead role throughout. It is Vaccarino's way of giving the characters and the city of Yonkers a warm and loving kiss.

—Dean Landsman, Author, Digital Strategist

I'm glad to see the character Cookie Colangelo again! Only this time, she's a little older but not necessarily wiser. In fact, in **The Heart of Yonkers**, Cookie is a fool for love! This story captures working-class heroes of a bygone era. Much more than a love story, great characters will touch your heart and make you feel good about what it means to be a human being. You might even remember your own first love.

—Wali Collins, Comedian & Author

The Heart of Yonkers is a deep dive into the turmoil of a city in transition during the years of the Viet Nam war, seen through Cookie, a teenager experiencing the torments and excitements of becoming a woman. Every character is illuminated with empathy. We watch with trepidation and bated breath as Cookie matures and grows, finding her unique way forward. This is a masterful and fully rendered story.

—Susan Alice Bickford, Author

The Heart of Yonkers is a revelation. Patricia Vaccarino's prose combines lyrical narrative with a practiced ear for dialogue, for an authentic portrait of ethnic, blue-collar Yonkers. Cookie Colangelo is a fresh face and a welcome new voice in the world of modern literature.

—Manny Frishberg, Author, Editor

My early family was in America before the American Revolution and dates back to the 1600s. My mother was a Dutch Jew whose family came to America from a village outside of Amsterdam back when Yonkers was a Dutch colony. They worked as coopersmiths, (workers of wood), some worked on sawmills to make barrels and shipping containers, others made clocks and furniture.

My era of the 1960s and 70s is the same time period that Cookie Colangelo grows up in the Yonkers books. As a hippy guy who grew up in east Yonkers, I know where the bodies are buried. In **The Heart of Yonkers**, Patricia Vaccarino vividly captures the way we lived, loved and came to age in Yonkers during one of the most turbulent times in the city's history. I love the way she captures the soul of the Hudson River and shows how important it was in our lives. Patricia Vaccarino's Yonkers books will live on for generations to come.

—Larry Frumkies, lifelong Yonkers resident

Patricia has vividly created an amazing coming-of-age story in a time of great turmoil and change. The characters are so lifelike and the grit of the neighborhood so seemingly familiar, you can smell the bus exhaust from the 2 Tudor Woods in front of Morsemere Market. For all of us who grew up *Down the End*, this is *our story*.

**—Tim Phelps, Former Yonkers resident,
Chef-Instructor/Educator**

In her newest book **The Heart of Yonkers**, Patricia Vaccarino takes us back to a much more innocent time—to 1971. I spent many years living in Yonkers and knew people just like the ones she so vividly describes...people that come to life in the pages of her book. Patricia has such a descriptive way of writing that you really feel you knew Cookie Colangelo, the protagonist of this novel, as well as Johnny, Kitty, Stanley, Debbie and all the other wonderful characters.

The book truly captures a moment in time of Cookie's young life as a teenage girl, experiencing the confusion of coming of age at a time when kissing a boy could label you a "slut," and "going all the way," whether you actually did it or whether it was just a rumor, didn't really matter. It was still whispered about behind your back to everyone in the neighborhood.

The book left me wondering what Cookie would be like as a grown woman, so I hope this is just part of an ongoing series that takes her into adulthood, because I already want to read the next book!

—Jeffrey Gurian, Best Selling Author on Amazon

ACKNOWLEDGEMENTS

Thank you for the historical memory of many wonderful Yonkersites: Sarah Barysauskas, Karen Conroy, James Del Bene, Larry Frumkies, CindyLou Kempkes, Tighe Nolan, Barbara O'Connell, Timothy Phelps, Charlie Piersall.

For my husband Joseph M. Puggelli

and

In memory of my family and friends

with love

ONLY MOTHERS WAIT FOR THUNDER

No woman shall ever quite compare,
Stanley, because your mother leaned
out of a window from the fifth
floor of a brownstone tenement
encasing your dark, one room flat,
that had no running water. She
never complained the window
faced carbon monoxide streaked
brick walls, and the stench of
squalor and urine drifted up from
the streets, like steam rises heavy
in air, producing catharsis in breath,
as she shook crumbs, and dust, and
varmints from the ragged mop bearing
woolen, methuselah locks.
She was big and robust, red-faced
from the heat, odor, and the toil.
She made meals from chicken necks,
backs, and oxtails, scrimping for
Sunday sauerkraut and pig's feet stew.
She drew the juice from cartilage and
bone when there was no meat.
She wore faded pastel house dresses
without sleeves and stiff oxford shoes.
She had only one pair of nylons
and cried when they ran. Her arms
were freckled and fleshy, and gyrated
when she beat rugs and pounded flour
into dough on wooden boards. Her hair
fell in her eyes, matted and coated

from smoke in the kitchen. You didn't
like her kisses, with breath that smelled
of empty stomach and rotted cabbage boiled
pale from the day before. She embarrassed
you in front of your friends with her
thick accent tripping over *What's so funny?*
You always ran from her outstretched arms
into open fire hydrants spraying on city streets.
It wasn't until things went bump in the night
from thunder to nightmare that you longed
to be enveloped in her thick, fleshy arms,
and drawn to her breast in a knot,
until you could slip away again,
so no one would ever have to know.

—Concetta *"Cookie"* Colangelo, 1972

"Yonkers, where my story begins, and where it ends."

—*Anonymous*

One

The River

Close to the river's edge, the air was swollen with the scent of dead fish, raw sewage, waterlogged grass, cast-off rubber tires, tar, and mud. There was always a hint of salt in the air too, which could be strong or faint, depending how the currents ran on a given day, along with the heat, and the sun, and the wind and the phases of the moon; all of these elements worked together to course the flow of the water and the intensity of the scent of salt. There were fresh and saltwater portions of the river, and it made no sense to call the water brackish when some tide pools swilled with salt and other shallow coves and wetlands were full of clear fresh water you might want to dunk your body in to cool down or take a swim on a hot summer day. The presence of salt was as strange and as fleeting as the sound of silence in her heart.

It was hot enough to take her clothes off and think about jumping into the river. Except the water was filthy, swarming with oily blue sewage. Haze shrunk the sun, making it the same pale shade as a banana unsheathed from its skin. Smog shrouded the skyline of Manhattan to the south. You wouldn't know New York City was so close unless you had seen it from the river's edge on a clear day. Yonkersites called the Hudson "The River" the same way the original inhabitants of the area, the Iroquois tribes, had also named it "The River" *Cahohatatea (Ca-ho-ha-ta-te-a).*

Cookie Colangelo expected to see someone she knew down here. Carbon monoxide streamed from two cars parked near the Kennedy Marina. People were in the cars, with the motors racing, ready to squeal out of the lot in case the cops showed up. From what she could see, the action going on down here had more to do with sex than drugs. She didn't recognize the two cars.

Her eyes fixed on a marine green 1966 Oldsmobile Cutlass Supreme. Aside from a few dents around the hubcaps, the car was in great condition. The driver's side of the car was buttressed against railroad ties, a makeshift retaining wall staving off water from the river. At first, she did not know who was in the car, but soon the driver made his presence known. He propped open the car door and stuck his head out. "Aren't you afraid you'll get mugged down here?" His forehead screwed up with the intensity of a smartass remark. "Or worse?"

He got out of the car and looked at her. "You're a Catholic schoolgirl." Appraising her school uniform, he smiled. "Don't you care about what happens to yourself?"

What a creep, Cookie thought. She did not remember seeing him before. He looked older than the usual crew of kids who hung out down here and didn't seem to be a stoner. He had thick blond hair twisted into a single braid clinging to the middle of his back like a question mark. He wasn't wearing a shirt. His beaded metal necklace with two medals flashed in the sun. He was lean with powerful arms and a massive chest, not a trace of body hair. His two pink nipples were round and too hard looking to look at for long. High cheekbones, a fine line of a mouth, his face was a chiseled work of art except for his nose that came to a too sharp point. She felt like a hot blade had stabbed her in the back, cutting so deep it pierced her heart in two. She could not stop looking at him.

When he stepped into the sun, his eyes were indigo blue, until a shadow flitted across his face; then his eyes darkened to the shade of grey stone dug up from the Yonkers quarries a half a century ago. He was drinking a bottled beer, Pabst Blue Ribbon, *the beer that made Milwaukee famous*. She estimated he wasn't a regular Yonkers guy, just someone passing through. She thought he could see inside of her if he cared to do so, but he didn't seem to be interested in going that far.

Her face flushed and her legs knitted together, locking up like spiny sewing needles. Shocked by the intensity of the heat she felt, she was simultaneously repulsed by him, surprising herself because she had not felt this way before, not with a real guy. Her repulsion was usually reserved for Yonkers boys. Exuding raw masculine energy, this guy had an edge, like he had been in combat and won.

"Where'd you score the car?" Cookie asked him. "Looks brand spanking new."

"I'd ask you to get in, so I could drive you home, but I have company." He looked like he was trying to be nice to her, but she knew he wasn't sincere. Then she figured it out. He was trying to get rid of her.

The blond head of a girl popping up on the driver's side gave away his true intentions. He had no use for Cookie and wanted to get back to whatever he had been doing with the girl in the car. The blonde started squawking, "I know her. I know who she is. I didn't say to let her in. I don't want her in this car with us. Why'd you say something so stupid, Stanley!"

"Stanley? Nice name." Cookie was kidding him. Normally, she would have felt sorry for a guy who had a name like Stanley, but there was no feeling sorry for this guy. He was too sure of himself to let his name stop him from getting whatever he wanted.

The guy shrugged and smiled. "Haven't I seen you before?"

"Fuck, Stanley, you don't have to go and get personal with her. Everyone in Yonkers has seen everyone else somewhere before! Will you just get rid of her," the girl said.

Stanley shrugged. "Debbie Ochiogrosso. Know her? She seems to know you."

"You didn't have to tell her my name!" The blond girl yelled out the window.

Cookie figured she had interrupted whatever was going on between them inside the car. Obviously, Stanley was the kind of guy who didn't want to be caught with his pants down. He seemed to be a decent sort of fellow who wanted to spare her from potential embarrassment. Himself too.

Cookie shook her head apologetically, turned away from Stanley and spoke under her breath, "Be careful."

She didn't tell Stanley Debbie had already had three babies. None of which she had kept. By Cookie's reckoning, every other year, Debbie went on a solo vacation. Her trips weren't fun-filled jaunts to Florida or to the Jersey Shore. She took regular trips to a convent for unwed mothers where they had babies in hushed secrecy. The babies were given up for adoption soon after birth. Debbie, the youngest daughter of Fran Ochiogrosso, wasn't a nymphomaniac; she was just dumb.

Debbie got out of the car and kicked the door. Wearing red short-shorts and a tie-dyed midriff top barely covering her breasts, she teetered on skinny brown platform shoes. "Stanley, I'm so sick of this! Will you stop talking to her!" She put her hand on her hip, tossed her cigarette to the ground and stamped on it. "Let's go now!"

"Never liked it down here anyway," he said, responding to the girl but looking at Cookie. "Aren't you too young to be down here alone?"

Cookie really wanted to get away from them and backed away, until she hit a moment when it was okay for her to completely turn her back to them and walk off. Parting was a mutual decision. She heard them get back into the car, slam the doors, and drive away. By the time she looked back, the Oldsmobile was gone.

She didn't know what to make of Stanley and didn't want to care. He made her feel funny inside and stirred something up. But unless she saw him again, she didn't have to deal with it.

Some couples don't notice they're making a spectacle of themselves. In parking lots, side streets and parks, she had seen plenty of kids doing all kinds of things in cars. Sex in all its phases and incarnations was practiced in a fugue-like state. Kids might be unconscious and unaware they were having sex; it was a vague part of growing up.

Sex came in musical spurts, a brief melody or phrase in a song: a girl might make out with one guy, let another guy feel her up, still another would get to finger her, but she reserved going all the way for the guy she was actually going steady with. No one wanted to be an unwilling spectator. There was great pressure to have sex in short lyrical bursts with an infinite number of partners. Sex was everywhere you went in Yonkers; kids were pumping and balling in basements, attics, in abandoned buildings, and in the back seats of cars.

Even after the Oldsmobile was long gone, the image of Stanley festered like an open wound and would not go away. She would love to have a boyfriend, walking there beside her on the bank of the river. But this Stanley guy was no ordinary boyfriend. She didn't want to like him. Thinking of him was like being in the dirty water over her head and drowning.

No one seemed to care about the river that had become a dump-off site for hazardous waste, industrial garbage, and chemicals. The sharp scent of metal reminded her of the hydrogen peroxide she had used to clean the scrapes and bruises on her knees. She wrinkled her nose to be certain, but the scent had already drifted away. Too bad about the river. It still looked like it was a wonderful place to swim. She scuffed the tip of her new patent leather, navy blue Mary Janes against the dried-out grass and pushed it into the soil made hard from shale and limestone. The sun glittered along the surface of the water like a thousand small diamonds courting the prayers of sinners who could not be saved.

She sat on the crumbling curb on the edge of the riverbank, not thinking about anything in particular. She pulled a Marlboro out of her hemp sack, lit it and tossed the match into the water. The river was a jewel in the late afternoon sun. For a moment, she considered taking her shoes off to let her feet skim the surface of the water as a way to cool her body.

Her father used to swim in the river with his friends. Johnny Colangelo used to say, "I always gotta go and take a dip in the river and cool off. It's free, you know, I used to swim in the river for free."

In the 1940s Johnny used to sit on the Alpine Ferry Dock and fish. He caught bluefish and striped bass; Johnny called them *stripers*. He also trapped small crabs. Johnny used to say, *the Marina...the way we remember it, we used to fish, we used to swim, and we made a lot of good friends...too bad it's changed.*

Working-class kids were no longer free to enjoy the Hudson River. Those days were gone. Beneath the shimmering surface, the ever-present sludge of toxic waste was a mighty deterrent to jumping in for a swim. The garbage companies and the politicians could care less about ruining the river.

Cookie had trouble thinking about what it was going to be like when she grew up. It was sad to think about her father swimming and fishing in the river with his friends. Then they took it away from him. They took it away from everybody. Growing up meant you had to spend a lot of time fighting off people who were trying to take something away from you.

She stood up, tossed her cigarette butt into the water and turned her back on the river as if she was saying goodbye for good, even though she knew she'd be back. She walked across the lumpy thatches of flattened crab grass and weeds. Only one car was parked on the bank on what had once been a grassy knoll and was now used as a public parking lot. If she had a boyfriend, maybe she would park there too. They would hold hands, kiss, hug, and do other things. She wanted to have a boyfriend, but her goal was just not possible—she didn't want to be with a guy for the sake of having a boyfriend. The guy had to be different, meaning there was no way he could be from Yonkers.

Wondering if the Stanley guy was from Yonkers, she picked up a chunk of rock covered with dirt, but underneath she could see it was rose quartz. Something was off and she felt like she wasn't quite right in the head, like she had been hit by the big rock and was suffering from a concussion. She heard music and did not know if it was coming from the last car left in the lot or if a song was playing inside of her head. She could care less about rocks and the currents of salt and silt deposits humming a sad song through this dirty and tired, old polluted river. She tossed the rose quartz into the water and watched it sink.

Two

The Café Trento

From the time she was six years old, Cookie Colangelo walked from Untermyer Park in the north, marching straight south though Getty Square and South Broadway and Riverdale to Van Cortlandt Park, hovering on the edge of the Bronx. In the summers, she walked east to Tibbetts Brook Park to swim, or shuffled her sweaty body in slow motion down to the Kennedy Marina on the banks of the Hudson River. Her childhood tendency to walk all over the city now seemed to belong to a fleeting time, one of innocence.

Most adults had looked out for her, and policemen gave her a friendly nod, sort of a pat on top of her head like she was a puppy. Then the generosity and good will stopped. Now she saw signs of frailty setting in—her feelings could easily be hurt and then other times she had no feelings at all. Cookie was a sturdier child back then than the young woman she was now becoming. She knew deep down in the silence of her heart that all promises were meant to eventually be broken. She was a full-fledged teenager now, and a nasty one at that, a dangerous force in the world, but, in her estimation, a beautiful sight to behold.

The heat on this mid-September day made her remember the death of the lead guitarist of Canned Heat, *Blind Owl* Alan Wilson. He had died on a day like this, full of muggy air too hot and heavy for a fan to move. It took effort for her to slog through the streets. She caught sight of the red-headed busybody Fran Ochiogrosso just as she got to the corner of North Broadway. Cookie tried to avoid her, but it was too late. Fran had already seen her and gave her a gregarious hello. Cookie thought of everything she could do to avoid an encounter with her and broke into a run.

She called out and waved, "I'm late for my bus!" Fran Ochiogrosso had made a lifetime career of being the neighborhood gossip and had a reputation to maintain. For years, she had been the school crossing guard between P.S. #16 and Christ the King elementary school and had committed the name of every man, woman and child in the 'hood to her monumental memory. She never forgot any detail, inconsequential or not. And if you needed to tap into an obscure fact about Yonkers, you went to Fran for instant recall. She was a living history book. She knew who was doing what to whom and reveled in prying into the affairs of the spicy Colangelo family.

Surprisingly, Fran paid her no mind, actually dodging cars to avoid Cookie, and walked to the opposite side of Broadway. It was uncharacteristic for the woman not to pummel Cookie for tantalizing tidbits. Instead of walking toward her home, Fran turned right and walked north on North Broadway. Even from across the street, the wake of Fran's perfume clung to the humid air and brought attention to what she was wearing. Fran was all dressed up. Her rather large behind had been snugly stuffed into a fancy floral skirt and her white cotton top looked freshly starched, a far cry from her usual stodgy brown crossing-guard uniform or her slinky, see-through pajamas.

Even though Cookie didn't need to run to get away from Fran, at least not this time, she continued to charge toward the bus stop, managed to board the Number 2 bus in the nick of time, gave the driver a big smile, a huge fake hug in-the-air, and intentionally walked on without paying.

The bus driver immediately yelled, "Ain't you forgetting something! You need to pay, Miss!"

She returned to the front of the bus, dropped thirty-five cents into the cash box, and gave the bus driver a big smile. "How come it always works for my mother?"

The big balding fellow looked disgusted and muttered under his breath. His thighs were huge and spilled over the sides of his seat. Cookie didn't bother to explain how her mother, Kitty, made it a game to get by without paying for anything, especially a bus ride to Getty Square. Yonkers girls knew if they were good looking enough, they could get away with anything. Kitty Colangelo might have been crazy, but she had confidence in her beauty.

Cookie was looking for love but not having much success at finding it.

All Yonkers girls wanted to find a boy to love. Cookie was feeling this desire, enough to explode. She really wanted to kiss a boy, and do much more, except there was a problem. She didn't like any of them, not even the one who glanced at her from the corner of his eye, said hello, looking down to the floor of the bus while he sat across from her. Instead, an image of a clamshell pastry popped into her head.

Sfogliatelle, pronounced so-fee-uh-tell-ay, was a traditional Italian pastry with a flaky shell filled with creamy soft ricotta cheese and a tart bit of sugary citron. Cannoli was also filled with ricotta crème, but when she bit into one, its crispy fried shell crunched in her mouth. She was torn between cannoli and sfogliatelle. Licking her lips, she kept one eye on the boy's sneakered feet while she imagined the first bite of a pastry. Maybe she'd order iced coffee too. She'd make up her mind when she got to the Café Trento.

All the way in the back of the bus, the long banquette had enough room to seat five people. Cookie remembered her kindergarten teacher Mabel having to sit in the back of the bus because she was black, but things had changed. Now white girls sat in the back of the bus so they could be bad ass: smoke, curse and chew gum.

The boy across from her wouldn't look at her directly, but she felt his eyes watching every move she made. Not bad looking. He had curly dark brown hair parted in the middle and had let it grow long without giving thought to an actual style. He wore loose-fitting bellbottom jeans, frayed on the bottom, and a sleeveless orange t-shirt showing off his taut arms and torso. His face had a dark shadow, making him look a bit rakish, and while she liked the look, she wasn't going to let it get the best of her. Cookie remembered how her father, Johnny, had been sent home from school in the eighth grade because the nuns said he had a five o'clock shadow.

The boy on the bus spoke fast. "I've seen you before. Don't you go to *The Heart?*"

What a lame thing to say, she thought and rolled her eyes. "Don't most girls around here go to *The Heart?*" Cookie didn't know why she was being so mean to him. Maybe she just felt like it. She didn't like boys, especially Yonkers boys. She wasn't going to let him think he had a chance with her, when he had none.

"My name's Cookie. Cookie Colangelo." She pulled out a Marlboro, lit it and flicked the match out the window. "Got a name?" she asked. *Like I care,* she thought.

"Darrell Ricci." He seemed to be put off by her smoking and looked down at his hands a lot, on the verge of biting his fingernails. "I thought for sure I'd seen you before and you were wearing a uniform."

Wow, that's really deep and meaningful, she thought. She gave him a standoffish look. She was letting him know he was too young for the worldly, deep and introspective Cookie Colangelo. She studied his face and imagined what it would be like to kiss him. The outer edge of his ears had tanned from the summer sun, and his lips looked shiny, as though he had been biting his lower lip. She couldn't see the color of his eyes but guessed they were brown because if they had been blue, they would have immediately gotten her attention.

Ever since she had fallen for the Blind Owl Alan Wilson, she had a thing for blue-eyed men. She estimated Darrell Ricci was about sixteen and while he seemed nice, she could care less. She had nothing to say to him even if she found him to be attractive in a boyish way. Maybe he had just grown on her. The thought of kissing him, though, was a no-go.

She sat in the back of the bus with her arms crossed, skulking and smoking, until the bus reached the bottom of Palisade Avenue, where it flattened out and intersected with Ashburton Avenue.

She pulled the cord to get off the bus. "See you." She got up and without looking back at him, jumped off the bus at the next stop. She would never forget his face. She never forgot anyone's face, but there was no way she'd be stuck kissing a sixteen-year-old Yonkers boy. She shuddered at the thought of pressing her body up against his in a slow grind.

Walking on Ashburton Avenue, Cookie had to admit to herself she did not like the way she had treated the boy. She was so unhappy with her life and didn't know what to do about it. When she got this way, Johnny called her a pill and said she was being moody, as if her emotions were best explained by the fact she was a girl. She hated her father for making dumb assumptions, but what could you expect? Her father was dumber than a slab of granite fresh from the Yonkers quarries.

Cookie was in crisis! What do you do when your body is flooded with red hot flames pricking your skin inside out and you can't find a way to vent the heat? There wasn't anyone she wanted to touch her or kiss her delicious mouth. Small fires ignited in her heart and she did not know how to put them out. She could not pretend everything was okay no more. Something was really wrong with her!

Reenie Ruggiero turned around in front of the Yonkers General Hospital and walked across Ashburton Avenue. Her hair had grown into a sumptuous gnarl of wooly curls cascading down her back, stopping for a pause above her rotund bottom. If this was her idea of an afro, then it was the most gorgeous, shiny mess of curls on earth. Reenie stopped walking and was waiting for Cookie in front of the Café Trento.

"I've got a big surprise for you." She ran up to Cookie and put her hands over eyes. "Guess who?"

Cookie tried to shirk off her hands, but she enjoyed the prospect of a surprise. "Stop it, you'll smear my makeup."

Reenie examined her hands for streaks of black mascara. "Since when did you take to wearing so much makeup?"

Cookie brushed her fingers under her eyes to erase any traces of black.

"Don't look until I tell you to." Reenie pushed Cookie through the front door of the Café Trento where cool air fanned her face.

Cookie smoothed the front of her peasant blouse and got her finger stuck in an unraveling thread of embroidery. She yanked the thread and pulled it tight until it squeezed the pattern of what had been a flower into a squat-shaped snake. "What am I looking for?"

"No! Told you not to look." Reenie put her fingers to her lips to keep Cookie quiet. "Close your eyes!"

Cookie tried to focus on a lazy ceiling fan.

"Now look!"

"Yes!" Herman Lynch leaned up against the first pastry case, standing on one leg. He started rocking, moving from side to side, too excited to stay still. Rushing, almost knocking each other over, Cookie and Herman locked into a crazy I-love-you-forever embrace.

"Yo, Cookie girl, do you see what's inside here? At first, I thought it was crazy that Reenie said you wanted to meet in a bakery. But mmm mmmm mmm," Herman intoned. "Wow! Look at all this stuff!"

The scent inside the Café Trento conjured waves of fresh baked bread, sweet almond croissants and a heady blast of cinnamon buns, poppy seed, cardamom, butter and anise. There were high notes and low notes as fragrant as any otherworldly perfume, a plum cakewalk through sugar, custard, and flaky crusts.

"Don't ever think I saw a cake looking so good." Herman pressed his fingers along the glass display case.

The lady behind the counter looked hot and menacing. The nametag on the top of her apron said Bertha Sokól. She really should have been named *Big Bertha*. She came from behind the counter to the front of the pastry case with a white rag to rub away Herman's fingerprints. "All day long I try to keep the glass clean. Then you guys come in and make marks all over the counter."

Cookie heard Bertha's accent and guessed she could have been Russian or German. "Try not to make so much work for me," the woman told Herman. "You can only come in here if you wanted to buy something!"

"Man, look at those cakes! Yummy!" Herman nudged Cookie and whispered in her ear, "What's gotten into you, girl?"

Cookie traced her finger along the glass pastry case and began pointing. "I want that and that and that. I want a taste of everything. I want so much that I'm going to start drooling."

The upper shelf held Cassata cakes, round sponge cakes soaked in a fruit-flavored liqueur and layered with ricotta crème. Two Ciambelle cakes, Italian Bundt cakes, were tucked into a corner of the first shelf, dwarfed by the trays of bombolini, Italian donuts filled with custard and apricot marmalade.

"Don't make me hungry, man." Herman tapped his taut muscular stomach. "I could be wrong, but is that an éclair that I see?"

Not-so-Italian éclairs, napoleons, and two Charlotte Russe cakes made from ladyfingers were filled with chilled custard and topped with mounds of whipped cream and fresh strawberries. The glazed apple strudel, cinnamon buns, and French crullers looked tempting and inspired desire, but none of these treats were a match for the grandeur of the marzipan iced cakes—too beautiful to eat or even touch.

Bertha, who had gone back behind the counter, leaned forward. "We have customers who come in every day." Then she eyed Herman. "If you have the money to pay, then you can order anything you want."

"Come again? I don't know," Herman said. "I'm a dancer and if I ate stuff like this all the time, then that would be the end of me."

Bertha frowned at him. "Then why you bother me coming in, in the first place?!"

Reenie and Herman both pointed at Cookie.

"It was my idea. I'm trying to decide what I want."

Bertha rested her fleshy arms on top of the counter and placed her face in between her two hands. "I'll be here when you're finally ready." Her eyes followed Herman as he sat down at a small table. The bakery had a café area resembling an ice cream parlor, where customers could sit at small tables and eat treats. The chairs had wrought iron legs, metal backs sculpted in floral patterns, and soft round pastel pink cushion seats. They were the sort of chairs found in a girly powder room.

Cookie thought she wanted sfogliatelle or a cannoli, but now she wasn't so sure. Apple, peach, and blueberry tarts nestled in the front row, and were flanked by a sheet of angel wings shaped into twisted ribbons and sprinkled with confectionary sugar. The second shelf from the top displayed Panforte, full of fruits and nuts, resembling a sultry fruitcake. Two different kinds of miniature cannoli sat on a long metal sheet. One type of cannoli was coated with chopped pistachio nuts on each end of its fluted shell. The other cannoli's two fluted ends were topped with tiny chocolate chips. Looking like the last girl to be asked to the prom, only one sfogliatelle sat alongside the full tray of cannoli. It was a tough decision.

Bertha placed her hands on her hips. Under her stained white apron, a sleeveless loose cotton blouse ballooned up around her waist and tucked carelessly into her faded pink drawstring pants. "Speak up and tell me what you want."

Cookie told Bertha, "I'm thinking about the sfogliatelle, but I haven't made up my mind yet."

"I've only got one left, so you better make up your mind in a hurry."

"I'm deciding. Would you stop pressuring me?"

Bertha rolled her eyes and stared at Herman. She might have been staring at his harelip, or maybe she didn't like Herman coming into the Café Trento just because he was black. She never said anything to him directly to make her true feelings known.

"People just don't walk in off the street to grab something to eat, like it's a slice of pizza." Reenie tossed back her hair in a manner reminiscent of the Hollywood legend Rita Hayworth. She even had a glowy-red tint going on. "There's usually a special reason for being here. A holiday or something. You don't have nothing like that going on, do you?"

Cookie eyed Reenie cannily. "Every day's a holiday to me."

Marzipan was everywhere in the shape of fruits, vegetables and small animals. The bottom shelves of the pastry case held sheets of colorful cookies of many different sizes and shapes in pinkish red, green, yellow and chocolate brown. Almond fla-vored biscotti in white and chocolate—some glazed with white frosting, some full of nuts—and lemon and orange crocette lined the trays like proud soldiers, waiting to take a last stand. A lone tray holding lady fingers, the sponge fingers used to make tiramisu and Charlotte Russe cake, was only a quarter full.

"Made up your mind yet?" Then on second thought, Bertha looked at Cookie as though she thought she could read her mind. "I don't have no free samples today. Not one for you, or your friends!"

Bertha's way of saying she would not give them a free taste meant she wasn't happy about them. Dealing with Bertha made Cookie feel confused. Bertha wasn't being very nice, but she wasn't overt about it. And there was too much temptation, too many treats to choose. One treat cancelled the other. She wanted to try everything, or eat nothing, run from the Café Trento, and never come back, so long as she lived.

Herman patted his hand on his stomach. "Cookie, if I eat any of this stuff, I'll get so fat, I won't be able to dance."

Reenie draped her arm around Cookie. "Not her. Not this girl. She'll eat rich pastries day and night, just because she can."

"That stuff is good but nasty," Herman said. "Looks so good, but I don't want to pay the price."

Doing her best to stop herself from saying something she'd be sorry for later, Bertha closed her eyes.

"She'll get something soon," Herman promised Bertha. "She likes sweets. How do you think she got a name like Cookie, anyway?"

Bertha gave Herman a smile of mild amusement and lit a cigarette. The gap between her two front teeth made her look more friendly. She clenched the cigarette between her teeth and said, "Call me when you make up your mind." She left the front counter, muttering under her breath, and went into the kitchen.

Cookie drifted to the side of the pastry cases to see into the kitchen. Bertha had set her cigarette down on the counter, and let it hang off the side. She took a round of dough and flattened it with a rolling pin. Pounding dough on a wooden board, her powerful hands and fingers worked without pause. Kneading the dough in pointed taps, prods and pinches, her rhythm slowed as though she was playing a musical instrument. Flour covered her arms all the way above her elbows, and flew everywhere, dispersing a small dust storm across the wooden board. Scrunching her shoulders, she brushed away the spatter of flour nearly reaching her eyes.

Bertha swept the loose flour toward her, then spread it over the board, and slammed down a new round of dough. She repeated the process until she formed six loaves. She took two eggs and broke them. Separating the whites from the yolks, she added them to two separate bowls, whisked them until foamy, then set them to the side. She dipped a basting brush into a small glass jar and dabbed the tops of the loaves until they were lightly coated with drops of milk. Placing the loaves onto a metal baking sheet, she took her arm, brushed back her hair to stop it from falling into her eyes, and pushed the tray into the oven.

She picked up her cigarette, took a long drag, held it clenched between her lips, while smoke poured out of her mouth and nose. A fiery ash from her cigarette dropped onto the wooden board, blended in with the flour, and extinguished its spark.

Loaves she had baked earlier sat cooling on racks. Bertha touched one round loaf, then ran her hand over its slightly brown surface, tapping her fingers, checking it to see if it had cooled. She took this loaf and many others, adding them all to a larger tray. She never once looked up to see if anyone was watching. A few ashes dropped on to the wooden board. Bertha brushed them away then dropped the cigarette butt on the floor and stomped on it to make sure it had gone out.

Cookie had never seen anyone make bread. What Cookie's mother, Kitty, had in the way of beauty, she lacked in culinary skills. Her idea of cooking was to remove the tin foil from the top of a Swanson's frozen TV dinner.

Cookie didn't think Bertha knew she was there until she spoke to her without bothering to look up. "I have some good rolls," she said. "Kaiser Rolls. You don't just have to have something sweet to eat."

"Thanks." Cookie backed away from the kitchen, riveted

by a tub full of penuche. The fudge-like candy, made from brown sugar, white sugar, heaps of butter, milk and pure vanilla, was formed and turned golden from the caramelization of the sugar, making it taste like pure caramel. A bin full of pastel-colored Jordan almonds sat on the counter behind the cash register. Stacks of small blue boxes full of white Jordan almonds were tucked in an alcove next to a six-tier, decorative wedding cake and two large catalogs. Cookie opened the catalog, turning pages with pictures of cakes. Encased in plastic sleeves, the photos of the cakes had yellowed and grown brittle with age. How weird to think of weddings when she didn't even know how to kiss! She thought kissing would come naturally, maybe.

Reenie came up to her side and peered over her shoulder. "Oooh, wedding cakes," she said. "Think you'll get married some day?"

"No way," Cookie shot back. "Think I want to end up like my parents or half the people in this city? They say they love each other, but they sure don't act that way."

"I never knew my father and my mother's dead. Don't even know if they were married very long," Reenie said.

Bertha heard Reenie. "You're lucky to have your grandmother," she yelled from the kitchen. "Not all of us are so lucky. "I never had nobody take care of me," she said. "Not one. In the war, I lost everybody."

Bertha's comments were lost on Reenie. She looked at Cookie and rolled her eyes. Bertha's prattle did not qualify as a bonding moment. The girl had enough suffering of her own to worry about and didn't need to hear Bertha's tale of woe.

Cookie flipped the pages of pictures and let the cover fall to the right and drop shut. There, she had closed the catalog and had no reason to think of kissing boys, or wedding cakes.

A blond guy burst into the café, instantly catching Cookie's attention. She was sure he was the same guy she had seen in the green Oldsmobile down by the river. His eyes followed the trail of Reenie's hair and stopped where her mane made the point of coming to an end. He seemed to know Cookie was watching him and nodded as a show of respect. He moved with the stealth of a wild animal, rounded the corner away from the front pastry cases, and went into the kitchen.

Cookie stopped breathing and could barely ask, "Who is that guy?"

"Delivery guy? Never saw him before," Reenie said. "Not around here. He's white."

"Damn," Herman said. "He looks like he can out-dance me."

Cookie rolled her eyes. "Sure," she scoffed, "no one can out-dance you." Then she whispered, "He's hunky…not a paunchy Yonkers guy. What do you think he does to look that way?"

"He was born that way," Herman said, ribbing her. "You're sweet on him, aren't you?"

"White," Reenie said. "Too white to be good looking. I'm bored," she said, yawning and tossing her curls. "Let's get out of here. What are we doing in a bakery, anyway?"

Swept away in a daze, Cookie had been overwhelmed by the scent of sweet rolls and warm almond cake. Looking to see where the blond guy had gone but trying not being too obvious, she remembered Debbie cursing at him and calling his name. Stanley. She lost track of what she was doing and did not realize she left the keys to her house on the counter by the wedding cake books.

Bertha carried a tray of freshly baked bread and slammed it down on top of the counter. Full of oblong loaves of Pugliese, Ciabatta, Focaccia, and finger-shaped breadsticks, the tray put out heat from the oven.

"Are you staying or leaving? If you're staying, then you need to order something. Just tell me what you want."

Then she looked at Herman as though she had a change of heart. "We're taking out the café soon, son," she said. "You can tell all of your friends. We don't want no kids hanging around here like it's some kinda joint. From now on, it's strictly counter service. Cash and carry!"

"Man, is she cold," Herman said.

"Allow me to translate." Reenie spun around and gave big Bertha a dirty look. "What she's trying to say, we don't want no darkies coming here and hanging around."

"I've got nothing against the blacks," Bertha said. "The neighborhood's changed. It's a sign of the times and we've gotta change with it."

"They're taking out the dining café?" The blond guy, Stanley, stood in the entrance of the kitchen. He placed his hands above his head and rested them high on the door frame. His underarms had the faintest trace of blond hair. His face looked sad in a way Cookie could not define. She noticed his eyes were very blue. His face stunned her. He looked so raw it hurt to look at him for too long. His eyes, seeking hers, turned serious.

"Stanislas, stay out of this," Bertha said. "It's none of your business."

"What kind of name is Stanislas?" Herman asked. "Never heard of that one before."

"It's Stanley to you!" Bertha boomed. "My son's named Stanley de Falco."

Stanley looked at Cookie and smiled, shaking his head, making an apology for his mother.

Bertha gave Stanley a stern look. "I'm sorry! Can I talk to you? In the kitchen?"

Stanley didn't respond; ignoring her seemed routine. He walked out the front door without looking back. "Later," he said.

"My son," Bertha said, "since he's come home, he hasn't been acting right. He never talks to me. I'm worried about him."

Cookie looked at Reenie, giving her the cue that they should leave.

"Best to get our stuff and go," Reenie said.

"That's right," Herman said. "It's take-out only, order your stuff and carry it out in a box."

"It's bad luck to take the last sfogliatelle," Cookie said. "I don't want it."

"I've got more coming out of the oven. It's not the last one." Bertha lunged inside of the back of the pastry case, grabbed the lone sfogliatelle, stuck it into a slice of waxed paper and handed it to Cookie. "Here, take it, just go. Eat it or you'll end up as an old maid." She shoved the pastry forward on the counter and motioned for Cookie to take it. "No need to pay me nothing, just go."

"I don't want nothing," Reenie said. "I'm not patronizing someone who's going to be nasty to black people."

"Good things come in threes," Reenie told Herman and Cookie. "What do you say we mosey on out of here?"

Stanley no longer stood in the service entrance to the kitchen. Cookie strained her neck to see if where he had gone, then looked back at Bertha. "I don't want nothing from this place."

Bertha gave her a funny smirk. "Come on, give me a break."

Cookie snatched the sfogliatelle from the top of the counter and tore it into three pieces. The featherlight crust summoned the buttery texture of a croissant, releasing the ricotta crème into her mouth with such sweetness she sighed.

Reenie didn't want her share and shook her head. "Okay, let's get out of here."

Herman ate Reenie's share, plus his own, and saved one last bite for Cookie. "Now that's good."

Bertha shook her head and shrugged with confusion. "Okay, then be about your business."

Cookie remembered Johnny used to take her here when she was little. He'd pick miniature pastries, mostly cannoli, enough to fill up a pink box. The Café Trento also sold small individually wrapped boxes of La Florentine Torrone, an almond nougat candy in vanilla, orange or lemon. The small boxes were decorated with images of men *Ferrante* or women *Ippolita*. Wrapped with thick foil, each candy took time to tear open. Coated with a papery wafer, the candy tasted like a Catholic communion host. She'd eat the Torrone in small bites, savoring each sweet crunch of almonds.

And it tasted good.

Three

First Kiss

Do you remember your first real kiss? Cookie Colangelo talked into the tape recorder. Powered by a thick electric cord, the Grundig TK141 - Four Track Reel-To-Reel Tape Recorder had a large microphone and three levers to set the volume, bass and treble. Too large to be deemed portable, the tape recorder could not be stuffed into a case and carried onto a bus.

She puckered up her mouth on the microphone, pretending it was the mouth of a boy. Trying to flick her tongue onto the metal was a futile pursuit and she worried about getting an electric shock. She confessed to the tape recorder she hadn't done much kissing. There weren't any guidebooks or TV shows on kissing. Even movie stars kissed with their mouths shut on the big screen. At least, they did in 1971. Kissing was one of those things you had to do to become any good at it. *Kissing takes practice*, she said aloud. *Lots of practice.*

She spoke into the mic, wondering if some people were born naturally good kissers. Setting the mic down, she debated whether to erase her mad tirade about kissing, and then Herman Lynch came to mind. She wondered if it was harder to kiss when you had a harelip. She made a point of remembering to ask him and knew he would tell her the truth.

Summer ended with a critical shortage in Yonkers. The shortage had not been among three Yonkers staples: pizza, hoagies, or chocolate egg creams. The shortage had not impacted summer fashion: platform shoes, skimpy halter tops, or hot pants. The shortage had not affected popular music. Mind numbing songs about death and heroin addiction from the Rolling Stones *Sticky Fingers* Album—"Wild Horses" and "Sister Morphine"—steadily climbed the charts.

Nor was there a shortage of body bags coming home from Vietnam. In 1971 two thousand Americans had died in Vietnam so far. The number had dropped from over sixteen thousand dead in 1968. Of those who had died in Vietnam, the overwhelming majority had been baptized Roman Catholic and most had died at age twenty. Only second to California, New York State suffered the highest number of deaths.

In Yonkers, everyone seemed to know at least one family who had lost a son in Vietnam—the war had become the scourge of the working-class, ripping apart the social fabric of the city by dividing families, schools and churches, and, in no particular pattern, pitting brother against sister, mother against father, grandfather against grandchild, teachers against students, and blue-collar workers against themselves. (Yonkers guys argue out loud even if no one is listening.)

And there had been no shortage of anger, humidity, or sex. Only one shortage had a major impact on Cookie's life— marijuana was in short supply. So, she had made good use of her hash pipe. For some strange reason, hashish, called hash, usually Moroccan Red, could be found everywhere. Then a rumor circulated throughout the North End that Moroccan Red was really goat dung laced with potent hash oil. So if you were a cool Yonkers girl, you dropped acid.

Then Cookie's interest in drugs just stopped. Except for maybe dropping acid. Given the opportunity, she would drop acid again. The greatest thing about being a teenager was freedom. There was no burning compulsion to make the latest obsession an unyielding, inflexible and destructive addiction. Something can be tried once or even twice and dropped, as if it never happened. Do it once and never do it again—was Cookie's new motto. Now she was all about sex. Kissing. Making out. Beyond.

Feeling so hot inside and out, her body rumbled like the first thunderclap before a storm broke. Blistering strikes of lightning whipped through her body and smacked her in the head. There was no end to the fires being lit and blowing a deadly hot wind through her heart. Only kissing could satiate her desire. *Kissing!*

Cookie propelled her body into the most energetic jerk dance she could summon. Her dance was a wild free for all, a waterfall rush of waves leading nowhere and directed to no one in particular. Dance like Crazy. Head, hair, arms, hands, legs, torso, and hips, her movement flowed in synchrony but surged with the pulse of out-of-control energy. Rocking in rapid gyrations, flailing her arms, stomping her feet hard on a concrete floor, she snapped her fingers, swung her head in a swivel turn, spun in tight concentric circles and pitched into a high-stepping frenetic shrug. She turned around and around, fancying herself as hard and as swift as the steel blades in a rotary fan. Her hair fell away, covered her face and shot through the air with the force of a cheerleader's streamers.

Driven by the red-hot emotion underlying every small thing happening in her life, her dance became passionate, a whirling dervish inching toward the promise of eternal youth, which she knew to be *so not true* because nobody lived forever. Alone in the basement, no one could see her revving up for a secret jam session, a private affair between herself and a pro- fessional quality tape recorder. *Take that and that and that!* Only a Yonkers girl could pull off this wild dance. Intent on being as bad as bad could be, only she could dance this fast and wild. Too bad no one could see her. She opened her mouth and kissed the mic with wild abandon.

She wouldn't mind dancing with a boy, but she didn't like anyone enough to kiss—and found that exasperating! What a terrible ordeal to have this much passion with nowhere to channel it! She came to an abrupt stop and collapsed into an exuberant heap on the floor. Odd feelings confused her. She was only aware of her tiny aqua bikini and the mad desire to rip it off. The bikini's bra and bottom were fastened together with ornamental metal bars that dug into her skin. She stepped out of her bikini and let it drop to the floor. The bikini's metal bars left red welts on each side of her hips and in between her breasts. Her body had flushed, making her sweaty and hotter still.

Thank God, Johnny wasn't home. If her father saw her carrying on like a go-go dancer, there would be no telling what he would do!

Johnny Colangelo used to bring home pink cardboard boxes full of miniature cannoli, but now he was too busy chasing gigs and squeezing whiskey glasses, a polite way of saying he was never home. Drinking? Chasing gigs? With whom? Everything had to do with him and had nothing to do with his family. Johnny had been spending all of his time in the city, playing in jazz clubs, hanging out with the guys, doing his thing.

Cookie often thought of following him around Yonkers, Harlem and the Bronx to learn the inner workings of his secret life, but that would be too much trouble. Frankly, she didn't care what Johnny was doing so long as he stayed out of her way. Her father was a nuisance, like a pet dog needing to be trained. An Italian Yonkers guy, a goombah, he was totally dumb when it came to women. Most men too. She was intent on growing up on her own terms, without suffering any interference from him.

Recording what she said while two reels of tape spun on metal spindles,

Testing one, two, three...

She stood up with the mic and took center stage. *Allow me to introduce myself. I'm almost fifteen and I would like to learn how to kiss. I would like to find the right boy to kiss. The problem is he cannot be a Yonkers boy. What does a girl do when she can't find a boy to like in the place where she lives?*

Cookie had intended to use her words to turn this dilemma into a story, but for some reason she could not fathom, she had lost her ability to write, and there was nothing she could do about it, except wait for her words to return.

Then the unthinkable happened. Kitty stood there with her hands on her hips. Cookie did not know where she had come from. Upstairs? The basement door leading to the woods? Kitty wore frosted, pale peach lipstick. Her lips looked ripe but bruised. A thick black headband pushed hair away from her face, making her unquestionably as beautiful as the movie stars on the big screen who kissed with their mouths shut.

Kitty's head swiveled, like a nervous finch getting ready for flight. "I saw and heard everything," she said. "You've got it bad."

She walked toward Cookie but purposefully looked away to avoid seeing her naked body. "You've got a really nice figure," she said. "I was wondering when you were going to finally mature. For most girls, it's around twelve or thirteen, but you're late."

Her voice became husky, quavered a bit and trailed off. "Sometimes when you mature later, it's like getting hit by a bolt of lightning. You get the hots really bad, and that's all you can think about."

Kitty turned off the recorder and for good measure pulled the plug. "I've heard anything plugged into an outlet still draws electricity even if it's turned off. With the way Johnny complains about the bills, especially the light bill, I don't want him getting mad. I have a hard time enough with him as it is."

Cookie watched her mother walk away. She might be

certifiably insane, but she wasn't completely crazy. She knew the slightest annoyance could set Johnny off. He didn't want to live with them *no more* but put up with them. *A father has responsibilities*, he'd say, thumping his chest. *And I'm Italian.*

She shoved the recorder back on top of the wooden workbench, clutched her damp bikini to her chest, jumped off the concrete platform, and landed in a squat so tight Herman Lynch would be proud of her. She hadn't seen Herman every day since he started taking his dance classes in the city. She ran for the basement door and closed it behind her.

Tiptoeing up the steps away from the basement to the main floor of her house made her body tingle. Naked and alone, for the first time in her life she felt free, a wild thing on the verge of abandoning every part of herself. Trying to make as little noise as possible, she took small measured steps up the stairs leading toward her bedroom. She didn't worry about running into her mother. Kitty would stay out of her way to avoid having to look at her naked body. No signs of Donny. These days, Cookie's younger sister had created her own world away from everyone. The two sisters coexisted in the same house in an uneasy relationship of mutual avoidance. The little girl didn't want to run into Cookie any more than Cookie wanted to see her.

In her bedroom, her small portable Remington typewriter looked lonely where it sat on top of her dresser. She didn't have a desk or a chair to go with the typewriter and had taught herself to hunt and peck type while standing. But now, she couldn't write *no more*.

Throwing open her dresser drawer, she searched for her ragged blue jeans with the seventeen patches and the American flag on the seat. Not there, not under her bed, not on top of her bookcase or in the back corner of her closet; she threw mismatched socks and mislaid shoes, short shorts and halter tops into a heap on her bed, but the jeans were gone. She sat on the floor in the middle of the room and thought if she stayed calm, the jeans would magically come to her. She closed her eyes and visualized the jeans, faded and worn, holes, ripped seams, as soft as an old blue dust cloth. But they did not appear. The jeans were gone. Lost. Without them, she would never be the same person ever again.

Four

Queen Bee

On the river the sun hung low in the sky like a smoldering fire-brand. Cookie was getting nowhere, padding through the outer edge of trashed-out, fenced-in Trevor Park. Heading south on Warburton Avenue, she walked the same path Herman Lynch took to avoid the solidly white North End. She was sure she would avoid running into any of the Italian girls from *The Heart*. With boarded-up windows and doors, some buildings bore resemblance to scared and angry people who were under attack in a war zone. Piles of wood, stucco, steel beams and girders took on the form of misshapen faces and looked like a dump site instead of the shards of what had once been a building.

She was looking for something but didn't know what it could be, aside from trouble. She didn't want to run into anyone from *The Heart* because she was experiencing mixed feelings about having been expelled. One part of her was proud, but another part was embarrassed. She did not know what to say to anyone. It was best to steer clear of the Italian girls, who swarmed the school like a plague of wanton buzzards. These Italian girls went on an aggressive prowl after boys. Did they want to have sex with boys or attack them? One could never be sure.

Some of the buildings on Warburton Avenue looked as though they were still standing after being bombed in an all-night air raid. Once grand old homes now had grey stone retaining walls holding back weed-infested knolls. Take away those walls and a huge movement of soil and debris would erupt into a landslide and tumble down the hill. In between large, rundown homes, three-story, wood-frame apartment buildings had rusted fire escapes blocking the windows; and it looked dark inside like the people who lived there didn't ever want to see the sun again.

In the alleys between the ravaged buildings, there was a clear shot to the river. Walking down the bottom slope of Palisade Avenue, flattening out onto School Street, she was shouting distance to where Herman Lynch and Reenie Ruggiero lived. She had not seen them since the Labor Day Weekend. Reenie was still at *The Heart*; Herman went to Gorton High School; and Cookie had started up at a new school, Blessed Sacrament Academy (*BSA*), where the nuns were cloistered and not allowed to leave the convent except to teach. After her expulsion from *The Heart*, BSA was willing to give her a chance. All-girl. Girls. Gross girls. Hanging out with a bunch of girls was the last thing in the world she wanted to do. Regardless of where anyone went to school, the marijuana shortage had affected everyone.

Late afternoon at the end of a school day, it was humid but not hot enough to break open a fire hydrant to cool off kids on the street. The streets fanned with the rhythm of late summer. People looked hot, tired and fed-up. Cars chugged up Palisade Avenue with windows rolled down low and music cranked high as if they weren't sure they could make the climb. Cookie was certain she would not run into any of the Italian girls from *The Heart*; it was too far off the beaten track. There were too many blacks down here to suit their lily-white desire to be separate from them.

She saw herself in the storefront window, dressed in her

school uniform: a teal blue jacket with matching culottes. How she hated her uniform! At least when she went to *The Heart*, she wore a woolen skirt she could roll up at the waistband, show some leg and look sexy. The culottes were the brainchild of evil nuns so girls could not hike their skirts! As she walked, she grew warm and took off her jacket. Her short-sleeve cotton blouse clung to her back. She examined her jacket more closely— new, it had not yet achieved a crumpled look. The color resembled a cadet blue Crayola crayon. She imagined a big blue stick chasing her down the hill until she ran out of breath and could run no more. She didn't know if she was exercising her powerful imagination or if she was having an LSD flashback.

She pulled a fountain pen from her knotty hemp bag and thought if she held it long enough, she would have a story to tell. Maybe not. These days, stories were hard to come by. The pen felt empty and forlorn in her hand. Her words were fleeting and not flowing like the polluted currents of the Hudson River. Toward the end of the summer, she had been dropping plenty of acid. It had been fun until she realized acid could warp her brain and she'd wind up schizo.

Goodbye, Timothy Leary. The famous freak of a psychologist who advocated dropping acid once said, "The universe is an intelligence test." Obviously, he had never met a Yonkers girl!

She imagined her pen as a divining rod, straight from the ball of fire now turning pink and dark orange, setting in the western sky over the river. Her pen shot magic sparks of ink, stamping letters as hard and as deep as the strokes of an ancient printing press. And even though she had never seen a printing press, she had read about one somewhere. What did she know about these things? She barely saw the sky now because it had been overtaken by the New Jersey Palisades. Tall and flat, a line of steep cliffs formed a plateau, cutting the western horizon in half. Dense with carbon monoxide, the air smelled like the burnt soft pretzels sold by old men in outdoor stalls on Main Street. The sky looked ember-bright on the river until she reached the flat plane of Larkin Plaza and realized the sun had sunk behind the buildings of Getty Square. She had succeeded in not running into any of the Italian girls from *The Heart* and was almost home free.

She tugged on her silver hoop earrings and was reassured to find them intact. Ever since she had started BSA, she kept losing her earrings. Two pairs gone. Since she had quit dealing drugs, she couldn't afford to keep replacing them. BSA had a lost and found in the principal's office where a cardboard box stashed gloves, mittens, eyeglasses, and an assortment of single earrings: hoops, nobs and studs. But none of them were hers. She began to call BSA the school of the missing earrings—the last stop for lost girls.

As she passed a Chinese laundromat, a blond girl stepped into the street directly in her path, almost blocking her. The girl acted like she wanted to tackle her to the ground. Cookie paid her no mind. Aside from blocking the sidewalk, the girl gave no other indication she wanted to fight. Her hair wasn't really blond but an awful shade of gold, brassy blond.

The girl's appearance didn't give a clue to her identity; it was the way she smelled. Yardley lip gloss, Wrigley's spearmint chewing gum and a strong spritz of the maddeningly offensive perfume called Tabu by Dana. Of all cheap drugstore perfumes, this one had a disgusting dose of patchouli. When combined with other chemicals, Tabu could have been released into the Hudson River as toxic waste.

The girl stuck her foot out in front of Cookie, intending to trip her. "The least you could do is say hello," she snarled.

The reigning Queen Bee of Italian girls was last person in the world Cookie expected to see so close to Ghetto Square. No longer surrounded by her pack of gal-pals, Toni Ferlinghetti was alone. She wore a clingy, peach-colored sleeveless blouse, magnifying her large breasts. The waist of her low-slung bell bottom jeans nipped her skin a half-inch above her crotch. On her arm, she held the textbook *Gregg Shorthand*. She was studying to learn how to take notes so she could become a secretary! Cookie chuckled to herself. She couldn't help it. Toni Ferlinghetti had been expelled from *The Heart*! Only Toni had not been expelled for being a gangster and a hippie. She had been expelled because she was dumb.

Out of breath, jittery, not happy about running into Cookie, Toni plumped her fingers through her bold blond tresses. "I never expected to see you down here. What are you doing? Looking to score drugs?"

"Does Arky know that you did that to your hair?"

"What's the big deal?" Toni brushed her bangs out of her eyes. "It will grow back. I'm trying something different because I'm going to a new school. I'm going to Commerce now! But I'm still me!"

"And you're all by yourself?" Cookie put her hands on her hips and stared at Toni with disbelief. "Did you get kicked out of *The Heart?*"

"Oh my God, I can't believe you would say that to me! No! There's no use hanging around Sacred Heart studying that stuff when all I want to do is get married."

Toni stared hard, trying to make her point known and also trying to intimidate her. A face off.

Cookie would have none of it. She knew the truth. Yonkers kids had to decide by the end of ninth grade if they were going to stay on an academic track, and maybe go to college, or go to a trade school. Trade schools like Commerce High School offered programs to become a secretary, a beauty operator, or an office clerk. Mostly girls went to Commerce and only boys went to Saunders to learn a trade like plumbing. Back then, they didn't let girls become an electrician or a plumber, but they did let boys go to Commerce if they wanted to cluck around like foxes in a hen house. The boys at Commerce High School were outnumbered by girls a hundred to one.

The Queen Bee glommed onto Cookie and would not let

go. She dragged Cookie into her arms and made a big point of hugging and kissing her. "I always liked you! Remember that kiss I gave you? I meant it! I think you're really cute. I love your hair. I love you."

Cars passing by slowed to watch the girls turning the corner onto New Main Street. Toni knew she was being watched. Craving attention, she was indiscriminate about responding to the slightest show of admiration even from total strangers, especially men. Turning her head slightly to see each passing car, she gave everyone a big white smile.

"Why are you still wearing that uniform? Can't you see that no one will ever ask you out when you're wearing those ridiculous culottes. They make you look fat, frumpy. Disgusting!"

Toni turned to see herself in the glass of a passing storefront. "I don't have to wear a uniform no more. At Commerce, they let you wear your own clothes and there's hardly any dress code. You have to wear a bra and your jeans can't be ripped, torn or patched. I like it so much better. You should really get out of Blessed Sacrament and go to Commerce with me."

Toni had latched onto Cookie and would not let go. She had left behind her brood of acolytes at *The Heart*. Put into the impossible position of having to start up a whole new clique at Commerce, she actually had to be nice to girls and charm them until she could get them under her spell and suck them into her game.

She hooked her arm into Cookie's arm as though they were best friends. "I'm only telling you for your own sake," Toni went on. "You're not very popular. I doubt you'll ever go to college anyway. You should transfer over to Commerce while there's still time."

Cookie broke her arm away from Toni and told her, "I'm heading to the library. Would you like to go with me?" She thought for sure, the prospect of going to the library would rid her of the bee-stinging energy of the world's most vicious Italian girl.

But Toni surprised her. "Okay." She smiled, squinting her sultry eyes tight. "But don't ever tell anyone I went to the library. It will ruin my reputation."

A portly man, swarthy and scowling, walked by on the street. His few frizzy strands of hair poked out above his bald head. Dandruff dusted the tops of his shoulders. He held his leather pouch tightly against his hip. The entire time, he never once made eye contact with the girls. His eyes were unwaveringly focused on Toni's breasts.

"Disgusting pig! Look, he's looking at my tits," Toni said, but she gave the man a generous smile.

From Toni's perspective, he had paid her a huge compliment. Italian girls were so in need of attention they became willing victims to allow men to do anything they wanted, even things totally disgusting and rude.

"Look at his car! Look!" Toni jabbed Cookie in the ribs as the man got into a red convertible. "He's rich. Look, he's gotta Thunderbird! Know how much that costs?!"

The cranberry red Thunderbird slowed to a crawl on New Main Street but didn't stop. "Too bad," Toni sighed. "I wouldn't mind going out with a guy who had a Thunderbird."

Cookie had made a terrible mistake by asking Toni to go to the library.

"Look, look." Toni nudged her in the arm. "Look, but don't look right away, so she'll see you. Don't let her see you looking at her. Turn your head away, like this." Toni showed her the move, a quick flick of her head turned away from the target, while her eyes were still fixed on the object of prey. A side-eye glance. And while it was a difficult maneuver for most people, Toni Ferlinghetti had turned it into high art. She shrieked, "And then look! I can't stand the stink! Will you look at that! It's disgusting! How does she live that way!"

Cookie didn't have to look or make a weak attempt at mimicking Toni's side-eye glance. Everyone knew Angie the bag lady. She sat on a broken milk crate inside of a fenced-in concrete stoop on the corner of New Main Street, across from a florist shop. Close to where Angie sat, a lone sparrow fluttered to the ground in pursuit of an empty junk food wrapper.

"She's a streetwise bird," Cookie said.

"You're talking about a bird for Chrissakes! Everyone thinks you're weird." Toni rolled her eyes. "Including me!"

Angie rubbed the soles of her filthy feet and talked to her callouses as thick as tire tread. All ankle and swollen calves under layers of ragged clothing, she bore a stoic expression vaguely reminiscent of the bad cases of lockjaw depicted in medical annals. Cookie tried to think of what life would be without shoes. After all, she knew what it was like to lose things.

Lately, Cookie had lost lots of things but not the things she wanted to lose. Held captive by the Queen Bee of Yonkers Italian Girls, Cookie considered the plight of Angie the bag lady. What could be worse? Sitting there in the same spot on the same burgeoning load of excrement, day after day, night after night, or having to suffer at the hands of Toni Ferlinghetti. Both choices made a person a prisoner in her own land. Self-contained and eminently self-controlled, the bag lady seemed complete, so full of harmless intention, and at peace with herself. Toni Ferlinghetti had no other purpose in life than to be perpetually on the prowl and ready to swoop down upon unwitting, helpless prey.

Five

Eyes Like Mine

The Yonkers Carnegie Library could see the far corners of the
world, beyond the Hudson River, and understood that Yonkers
hovered in an undefined limbo, blurring the distinction among
urban, suburban, and rural; the rich, working-class and ghetto;
and the people, black & white. Yonkers had no choice but to
relinquish its unique place in this world because it shared its
border with one of the largest cities in the world, New York
City. Sadly eclipsed by its neighboring cosmopolitan mecca,
Yonkers was dismissed as a small city on the river with a
funny-sounding name.

Yet the library stood on the hill, keeping close watch
over the city to protect its inhabitants. More than a splendid
beaux arts style building, the library took on human char-
acteristics, and opened its arms in a graceful hug to all who
entered here. A knowing nod, a welcome prayer, a pat on the
back, the library was a woman who brought out the best in
people because she had hope in all things. A gospel singer
who could belt out a spiritual aria taking your breath away,
she moved you to a higher level in your own humanity you
did not know you possessed until you heard her song. Old,

kind, and black, the library was as wise as Mabel Kerry, who worked here.

In the final years of the library's life before being destroyed, this fine old woman had begun to show her years. The library's exterior walls greyed with age the same way Mabel Kerry bore a few grey streaks in her hair. For now, though, the library held its own and maintained a safe distance from unfairness and corruption. Its walls housed a trove of books like body armor to protect the city's inhabitants from harm. Things did go wrong out there, but the library took care of everything wrong with the world. The library did not change because it did not need to and remained steadfast in its loyal promise to be the one thing in the city everyone could count on. Greater than any one person, the library represented hope and a window to the future. This library had been built to stand the test of time. Other than its greying walls, the building showed no signs of decay or neglect, inside or out, until the day the wrecking ball came and blasted off its head.

Even if people in Yonkers hadn't used the library since they were kids, they were aware of its presence as a beacon of hope, sitting on top of the hill next to City Hall. Not Toni Ferlinghetti. She looked nervous and uncomfortable.

Cookie asked her, "Have you been here?"

Toni threw her head back and scoffed at Cookie for being so out of line to suggest such a thing.

She squawked, "My hair's gotten frizzy." She smoothed the sides of her hair, pressing two orangey-blond brillo pads. The top of her head had a thick black stripe, revealing her natural hair color. "It's not even raining, and my hair's gone way big. I feel like Bozo the clown."

"You look like Bozo the clown."

"Thanks, bitch. I owe you one."

"Bitch, everyone owes you," Cookie snarled.

Grinning, Cookie held open the front door for Toni and said, "After you, milady."

The moment Toni walked into the hall, she wrinkled her nose with disgust. "What's that smell? It smells funny in here, like everything's old." She crossed her arms to protect herself and looked around the room at the standing fans. She shivered as though the air from the fans made her cold. "I'm really sorry that I let you make me do this." Still flattening the sides of her hair, she put her head down and spoke from the side of her mouth. "I shouldn't let you do this to me. I'm going to get back at you. You do know that, don't you?"

The chief component of Toni Ferlinghetti's persona was revenge. She thrived on jabs, digs, and barbs. Any time she felt wronged, she kept track. She had a calculator in her brain tracking the number of times she had been hurt, adding points every time she took personal revenge and got back at you.

Two librarians were sitting at the front circulation desk, but only one knew Cookie by name. Mabel Kerry stood up from her desk and smiled warmly. "I see you brought a friend with you. You've barely started school! What a nice way to spend the afternoon!"

Toni whispered under her breath, "What's she doing here? She's black! Libraries should not let blacks in."

Cookie felt her cheeks get warm and was sure her face had turned red. Her palms felt like they had begun to sweat. A small fierce knot formed in her stomach. Her hands felt unsteady. If she put them out in front of her, they would begin to shake. She walked away from Toni. She had to get away from her or she would kill her.

Mabel Kerry must have sensed something awkward between them. Then she eyed Toni with more than curiosity. "I could swear that I've seen you before, but you had dark hair. My, my, tell me that isn't so, and I've made a mistake."

"She's in disguise," Cookie offered.

"Stop that." Toni cracked her gum in five defiant pops. "I wanted to find out if blondes have more fun."

"I see." Mabel leaned forward. "As far as I recall, you were having plenty of fun being a brunette." Her black-framed eyeglasses hung from an amber-beaded chain around her neck. She lifted her glasses, adjusting them so they sat on the bridge of her nose. "What can I help you find?"

Toni emitted a nervous peep, a crass giggle, conveying how uncomfortable she felt about talking to Mabel. "I don't read much unless I have to." She held up her *Gregg Shorthand* textbook. "I have to know all this stuff by the end of the year... if I'm going to pass and get a job someday."

Mabel's eyes brimmed with laughter. She wasn't laughing at Toni but looking for a way to make a connection. "You remind me of my daughter," Mabel told her. "And how much I miss her."

"What happened to her?"

"She's no longer with us." Mabel closed her eyes for a few moments as though she was saying a prayer and finding a way to forgive something or somebody all over again.

Toni stared at her but had nothing to say. Her face bore a blank expression; she did not know what was happening and did not know how to react.

When Mabel opened her eyes, she smiled at Toni. "Tell me what you like to do, the things you like to do when you're not at school."

Toni shrugged and cracked her gum, making two small pops. "I don't know. I haven't thought much about it. I don't do much of anything, except hang out."

For a moment, Cookie thought Mabel would suggest books for Toni to read, but she didn't. Cookie really wanted to see if the library might have a book about kissing, sort of an instructional guide, but felt too embarrassed to ask.

Mabel walked from inside of the circular reception area, opened a small swinging wooden door and walked to the front, where there were two magazine racks on one side of the circulation desk next to a case filled with record albums. "I can't suggest books to you unless I know what you're interested in.

It would be unfair for me to make assumptions of what you might like to read. Tell me a little about yourself."

Toni backed up a bit away from Mabel. She looked toward the ceiling where four rectangle-shaped fluorescent lights were hung by thick rope cables from the ceiling. She turned back to Mabel and spoke to her condescendingly. "Don't you understand? Someday, I'm going to marry a rich guy and get out of Yonkers. I'm going to live in Larchmont!"

"I see. I wish you a very good chance with that, and all of the happiness in the world. A young woman such as yourself will be very happy in Larchmont." Mabel swept her arm along the standing magazine racks. "*Ladies Home Journal, Family Circle.* Any of those interest you?"

Toni gave her a mock laugh as though Mabel didn't get it. "Those magazines are for old ladies!"

"How about *Vogue*? It's the fall fashion issue." Mabel thumbed through the magazine, but Toni showed no interest. "I can't afford that stuff anyway. Why should I bother to look at the pictures! Besides, I don't even have a library card."

Mabel slipped *Vogue* back into a display slot on the stand. "You don't need a library card for the magazines, but I'll get you an application, just in case. You never know when you might need to check out a book." Mabel gave Cookie a quick, wry wink, turned away from the girls and headed behind her desk.

Toni pulled Cookie away from the front circulation desk and into an alcove where oversized reference books stocked the shelves. "What was that look she gave you all about?"

"You're being rude. I don't like the way you're treating Mabel. Before she was a librarian, she used to be a teacher. My first teacher in school. In kindergarten! She's also Herman Lynch's grandmother."

Toni looked shocked. "That explains it."

"Explains what?"

"Why're you're such a N-lover. Know what I mean? It's just like you suck up to them darkies. They're disgusting!"

Toni never saw it coming. Cookie pulled her arm back and crunched her hand in a tight fist. She had every reason in the world to punch Toni, but before she did, Toni put up her arm to block her, stopped the blow, but felt its impact in a big way. "Okay, I got it," Toni said. "I'll shut up, but I'm entitled to my opinions because I know what I believe is true."

"I'm not going to have you showing disrespect to Mabel Kerry."

"Look, I'm sorry," Toni said. "But all of this is just too much for me. I'm in a new school with no friends. And I'm in this funny smelling building with too many books." She stomped her feet on the ground in a tantrum. "I really don't want to be in here! I really don't want to be anywhere! My whole life has been a mess since I started going to Commerce! I hate it." She popped her gum until her face looked red and swollen.

Toni backed against the bookshelf, twisted her face up into a series of contortions that could have been unexpected grief, righteous indignation or the fake maneuvering of an unheralded drama queen. "You really need to find a boyfriend, so you stop wasting away in a frigging library," Toni whispered. She pointed toward the circulation desk. "And she smells like the library. Or maybe the library smells like her."

Too late to quiet Toni before she caused further embarrassment, Cookie leaned into a rack of bookshelves and closed her eyes. Mabel Kerry had returned and stood there looking at the both of them. If she heard everything Toni had said, her face betrayed little. Neither angry nor hard, if anything, she looked sad. Noble too. Toni's outburst did not stand in the way of the work she knew she had to do.

"I've brought you an application." She handed Toni two sheets of paper. "Let's go into another room where we can talk, and I will help you to fill it out."

Toni pulled up her shoulders and shrugged. With no polite way of getting out from under Mabel's good intentions, Toni cracked her gum. "Oh my god, I can't believe I'm doing this."

She followed Mabel dutifully; she had regressed to a young child who no longer wanted to misbehave.

"I find that noise very distracting. If you don't mind, toss the gum here." Mabel held up a small wastepaper basket for Toni to dispose of her gum. Amazingly, Toni obliged her request, but gave Cookie enough of a nasty look to know she would have to pay the price.

Cookie's mission to the library had been thwarted the moment Toni had decided to tag along. Too embarrassed to ask Mabel to search for a book on kissing, she stalled, debating what to do. If she found a book, how would she carry it out of the library and avoid Toni's scrutiny? Feeling strangely sullen and depressed, Cookie knew no guidebook existed called *Good Kissing*. If there had been such a book, everyone would have read it by now, and passed it around until the pages became torn, mangled, and stained with small smudges.

She told herself, if she could love a boy, then the kissing would come naturally to her. One thing would lead to another. Their souls would kiss. Their eyes would kiss. Then their lips would come together. Kiss. Pucker up, baby, and do the thing to me no one else can do. Pow! Knockout! The fire came back in a string of red hot musical notes. Raging, pulsating, her flesh craved love, a bump and a grind. Her legs, liquefying to jelly, made her want to throw herself onto the cool marble floor and spread open. The total reflex action took her by surprise, and she did not know what to do to extinguish the fire. *Oh my God, why do I feel this way?*

Reverting to childhood would take her out of this mess. Cookie climbed the steps to reach the children's reading room on the second floor. No matter how hot Cookie felt, the children's room could quench her fire. Hearing the octaves and highest alto verses of *Stairway to Heaven* by Led Zeppelin, her heart stopped skipping beats and the marble steps cooled her.

The murals on the wall reminded her of the first time she had met Herman Lynch here. He broke into a soft-shoe shuffle to demonstrate how well he could dance. She half expected to see Herman, but today he was nowhere to be found. She wandered around, scanning the books left on the tables. Seeing what children had recently read inspired her to go into the secret part of herself no one could touch and no one could break.

The book *A Hole is to Dig* by Ruth Krauss struck her fancy and she looked for a place to sit down. Made for little kids, the chairs were small. She thought if she sat on one, it might collapse. She circled around the room until she found a tight corner behind a reading table, sat on the floor, and burrowed into *A Hole is to Dig*. She knew if Herman saw her there reading, he would kid her because the book had been written for little kids. But there was no denying how she felt, and, right now, digging a hole was one way to recede from the earth, to retreat, rest like an owl, and calm the heat within.

Cookie did not immediately recognize Bertha Sokól, but Bertha soon saw her. She wasn't wearing her bakery whites or dredged in flour. Not dressed real fancy, she wore a crisp blue corduroy dress and a pale-yellow sweater looking as though it had once been a bright color but had faded over time. Her simple brooch gleamed with a polished silver, sculpted heart, a blue bird, and a flower as tiny as a buttercup. Each part came together to tell one story. Her brooch, actually a fastener, allowed her to draw her sweater to close without buttons.

Bertha picked up a large-letter-sized black leather pocketbook pocked with splotches of white powder.

"You're the girl who left the keys at the bakery," Bertha said. "I've been waiting for you to come back, but you never did. I didn't know where to find you. Today is lucky for you. That I find you here by accident."

She opened her large pocketbook and took out the keys. "I've been carrying them everywhere, looking for you."

Pressing the keys into Cookie's hand, she smiled, showing the gap between her two front teeth. "You left them by the wedding cake books."

Soon joined by a skinny old man who had abundant grey hair, a large droopy moustache and a kind smile pouring from his heart, Bertha Sokól smiled, again showing the gap in between her front teeth. He said hello to Bertha, as if he had long been looking forward to seeing her. A much younger man came to join them. His round, rosy face made him look Irish. His thatch of brown hair had been swept back and piled high on top of his head. He must have been new to the group because he told them with a distinct Irish brogue his name, Francie. Bertha greeted him and invited him to join them. The old man introduced himself as Ivan to the newcomer Francie. They spoke softly in their different accents. Immigrants who had come to America, they were working on their pronunciation. Bertha seemed to be in charge of the group and picked the book to read. Each one opened the children's book *Goodnight Moon* and passed it around, taking turns to read out loud.

Six

Lennon Park

Warped from too many hot summers and cold, harsh winters, the fading green siding on Toni's ramshackle clapboard house was sloughing off its wood like grey bark on an old tree. Toni lived with her mother Fern on Convent Avenue, next to Sacred Heart High School. The houses on the block showed neglect, not because people were necessarily slovenly. The families who lived here struggled to make ends meet. Working hard at jobs barely paying a living wage, they didn't have time to fix their homes and couldn't afford to pay someone to do it for them. White and poor, people lived in boxy little houses covered with bumpy asbestos siding and speckled shingles. Convent Avenue led to the back entrance of Lennon Park. Reenie Ruggiero still went to *The Heart* but didn't hang around here. Cookie never remembered seeing a black person in this 'hood. She and Herman had never thought about walking through Lennon Park.

The park was named after James Lennon, who had grown up working at the Alexander Carpet Mills, and later became a successful businessman and Mayor of Yonkers. All of the city's parks shared one thing in common: they were safe havens to do drugs, drink alcohol, and hang out. If you were young and hot, Lennon Park was where you went to kiss.

In later years, when Cookie thought about it, thousands learned how to kiss in Lennon Park; it was unofficially known as the *kissing park*.

Right next to the park, Toni's front door had a window with grey, tattered loosely-knit lace curtains and no doorbell. Timidity was not Cookie's style, but, somehow, she sensed danger. Before she could knock, Fern swung open the rusted screen door and propped it ajar with her knee.

"I hear you're a big troublemaker from *Down the End*. I don't want none of those people coming around here." Fern shook her finger at Cookie. "I don't need no trouble for my Antoinette!" Then she called inside, "Antoinette, that troublemaker Cookie Colangelo is here to see you! Better come now or forever hold your peace! Swear to God or help me." She made the sign of the cross and looked at Cookie like she was a vampire.

In all of this time, Fern had never made eye contact with Cookie. One of the few women who worked, Toni's mother's given name was Fernanda, but everyone called her *Fern*. The most famous counter person at the Hoagie Hut, Fern had a reputation for putting together killer meatball wedges and the best sandwiches, with an inch of pastrami on rye. Fern's pointy chin poking out between her fleshy jowls made her face sink and bob like a buoy. With her voice oozing a sweet lilting sing-song, she gave the impression of being good, kind and friendly. But she wasn't.

Fern slammed the door shut in Cookie's face and made her stand outside on the concrete front stoop. Beyond the door and in the interior hall, junk was stuffed into a rusted metal umbrella stand. Broken umbrellas with fabric coming undone from the shaft looked like they had been battered by the wind. A lone ski pole had been stuck in the stand looking as though no one knew what else to do with it. The floor of the hall was cluttered with winter boots, rubbers, a rolled-up door mat, a plastic polka-dot poncho and dozens of cardboard boxes overflowing with clothes.

The sun had disappeared from the sky. Close to the entrance to the park, four round metal trash cans overflowed with garbage. Cookie did not know what she was doing here, other than following up on Toni's entreaties to *please come over to my house so we can hang out together*. Cookie touched her ears, checking for her silver hoop earrings.

Fern opened the door again and looked at her. "Still here! I'm surprised you're still here! Don't you have nowhere else to go! The last time you were here, you made a mess of my kitchen in the basement. You blew up the oven and those disgusting brownies were everywhere, on the walls, on the floor. And they didn't even taste good! You don't know how to cook. Did you ever think your mother should spend some time teaching you the things girls need to do!"

Cookie moved away and lit a Marlboro. She could tell Fern had a mean streak, but she was the kind of bully who never got caught throwing the first punch. Early nightfall cast a grey pallor on the front door curtains and Fern's fleshy face.

"Don't give my daughter no ideas about drinking or taking drugs! I know all about you! Everyone from Hastings to the Square knows about you!"

According to local lore, Fern came from the Italian neighborhood Arthur Avenue in the Bronx. For a lot of people from the Bronx, moving to Yonkers meant climbing a notch on the social ladder. The move uptown, into the suburbs, owning your own home and not living in a matchstick tenement walkup, was a come-up—the realization of the American dream.

"Shut up, Ma!" Toni squeaked open the screen door and kept her head down. Since she had made the change to Commerce High School, her new habit of being discreet about her comings and goings had been concocted to avoid her former gal-pals from *The Heart*. From Toni's bedroom window, she could have tossed a stone into the school's parking lot.

"What do you mean, shut up!" Fern sniffed the night air. "Fall is coming, I can smell it. Crisp and cool. Don't see no leaves on the ground yet, but they're coming. Then I'll have to be out here spending all my time raking! Those trees down there shed a lot of leaves, 'specially when the wind blows, like it's gonna do all this winter."

Fern was as noisy as a broken tea kettle rattling on the stove as soon as the water got hot enough to boil. "Don't even know where the rake is..." She produced a large gold lighter from her apron pocket and lit a Viceroy. "I'm not used to having leaves pile up so quickly." Fern talked and acted tough; she could prattle knowledgeably about almost anything. "I smell that other stuff out there too! One of these days the cops are going to come and take everyone away in a paddy wagon!"

Letting the front door slam behind her, Toni bounded out of the house. Since Toni had dyed her hair blond, she took on a keener resemblance to Fern, who wore a blond fall wig that she teased into a soft bump onto the top of her head. Her wide fringe of bangs covered her dark eyebrows and always stayed the same length—that's how you could tell for sure her hair was fake. Fern tried to hand Toni a laundry sack, but Toni shucked off the bag and turned away.

"Forget it, Ma, I'm not doing nothing of the kind." Toni already had black roots growing in on the crown of her head, belying her true hair color. It took a lot of upkeep to be blond.

Fern begged Toni to take their clothes to the laundromat on Lake Avenue, but Toni would hear nothing.

"I'm not going to that place. Enough said! What do I look like? A Chinese laundry! Yeah, I'm a blond chink!" Toni linked arms with Cookie and headed toward the park. She gave Cookie a shiny smile. "She's so embarrassing. I don't know why she does this to me!"

From upstairs, Fern opened the window and yelled out, "You're not going to have clean underwear if you don't do it!

See if you like that! See what kind of boyfriend you get if you don't have clean underwear! Go on, be my guest!"

"Oh, please! Is your mother like this?" Toni's brown eyes grew large, taking on the look of feigned shock. In a fake dramatic display, she held both hands to her mouth. "Oh, I forgot, your mother's crazy. Sorry! Why do I always forget that! Then I remember it at the last minute when I've already mouthed off and made you think of something awful. How weird! I don't know why I do things like that."

Cookie did not know what force on earth had prompted her to come to this awful place to be with Toni. She resolved this would be the last time. Toni's house was last on the block and marked by a dead end sign. Even though the street was a dead end, sooner or later, everyone passed through Lennon Park.

Staring at the ground, Cookie intentionally dragged her heels. "Where are we going?"

Toni raced ahead, pretending she hadn't heard her. The flat plane of the walkway gradually sloped down into the main playfield. Not too familiar with Lennon Park, Cookie caught sight of a dogwood tree set at the farthermost edge. The branches of a bushy willow tree sprang forth in the night, swaying in the shape of a water fountain. Some leaves had begun to turn a yellowish green.

"Come on!" Toni implored her. "Can't you walk any faster?"

Turning around to stare at Cookie, Toni stopped walking for a moment. "Come on! Why are you walking so slow?"

The tone of Cookie's voice dipped low and sullen. "Yeah, I'm with you."

"We don't got all night," Toni shrieked. "All of the good ones will be taken!"

The thought of meeting boys did not automatically register heat. Cookie thought for an instant if she kissed a guy, her fire would be quenched. But then she remembered they were Yonkers guys. Her heat rose and fell along the same mysterious arc as the Yonkers weather. She had been feeling hot, but now her temperature dropped, and she began to shiver.

The first grove of trees in the park had not yet turned color. Strong straight trunks spaced far apart gave each tree its own place to reach for the sky. The tops of oak trees formed a dark silhouette in the shape of a single green leafy mushroom-cloud. In the encroaching night, only a few shards of red touched the outer fringe of leaves. The air had chilled, but the trees held onto the decaying flush of late summer's bloom. The trees had the aura of a certain loneliness and Cookie longed to be one of them. Instead, she had allowed herself to be held captive by Toni who was shrieking and keening about meeting boys. Yonkers boys.

The shortage of marijuana in Yonkers no longer held true in Lennon Park. As Cookie and Toni walked under the protective cover of oak trees, the air reeked with the sweet acrid scent of marijuana.

"I'm so excited," Toni keened. "Aren't you?"

Nodding her head, Cookie pressed her lips together and tried to force a smile.

Clusters of kids lolled across the playfield in an encampment of intense social mayhem. The groups varied in size; some were small with three kids; others sprawled down through the thickets and under the trees in loose gangs. Dense smoke invaded the brisk autumn air and made it hard to see where one large gang ended and another began. Sheaths of an indifferent haze drifted through the rays of fluorescent light and illuminated sections of the park. Not everyone smoked cigarettes or pot. Bottles and cans in brown paper bags were being passed hand to hand; some held onto bags too long, drinking too much, staggering, and slurring their words. Scattered about in no particular pattern, kids were paired and heavily making out in the open.

"Look at all of them!" Toni's eyes blazed with scathing accusation. "Which one would you pick to kiss?!"

Energized by the sight of so many guys who seemed to be looking for a girl to like, Toni shrieked, "I'm so excited!" She nudged Cookie in the stomach. "Look at all of these guys. I've never seen these many guys out on a Friday night in October!"

She nudged Cookie in the stomach again. "Pick one."

"Which one?"

"There are so many! Can't you find just one to like!"

Cookie could not identify exactly what she felt, and it made her wonder if she had turned into a turnip. "I don't like any of them."

"What's wrong with you!" Toni's voice accused her of an offense akin to crime. "There's gotta be something wrong with you!!"

"There's nothing wrong with me! I just don't like any of them."

"What about that one? There!" Toni pointed to a boy on the outer fringe of a larger gang of mostly guys with three girls. "He keeps looking at you! See him! He's cute."

"I don't see no one."

"Look, he's right there. There. There!!" Pointing right at him, she said, "He's really cute!"

Now Cookie remembered him. Seeing him made her feel hot and cold at the same time. It was the boy she had met on the bus. "Darrell Ricci."

"Know him?"

"Sort of."

Darrell nodded and waved. Cookie waved back. "Not really," she said. "I don't really know him."

"Look how cute he is!" Toni nudged Cookie on the arm. "He likes you. Look at him looking at you. Why don't you like him?"

"I don't have to have a reason." Cookie sought a way out. She would run as fast as her legs could carry her. Just thinking about running made her start doing deep knee bends and shallow lunges. She had been consistent about keeping the muscles around her kneecaps strong. No more trick knees. She wore brown granny boots laced all the way up her leg.

"What are you doing?" Toni narrowed her eyes. "Do you have to go to the bathroom?"

"I'm exercising." Cookie picked up momentum and sprang into the air, doing small jumps. Her legs were getting so strong she could jump high even wearing boots. She ran in place to stay warm.

"Weird." Toni looked at Cookie as though she had lost her mind. "It's all because of your mother. Everyone knows being crazy goes directly from the mother to the daughter."

"So does meanness." Cookie eyed her. "Your mother's a bitch."

Toni rolled her eyes. "Don't be talking about my mother that way."

"Everyone knows your mother's a real piece of work, a whack job of the first degree."

Toni cracked her gum as if she was firing off a round of ammunition. Pointing her finger at Cookie, she said, "Let's go hang out with him."

"I don't want to." Cookie stood firm.

"Come on!" Toni implored her. "What's wrong with you?"

"Nothing."

"No wonder why you don't have a boyfriend. I think there's something wrong with you. You probably have never even gone out with a guy." Toni walked away from her and stepped into the shadows. "Coming?"

A smaller grove of three oak trees provided protection from the sun, the rain, and from being seen kissing. On the outskirts of the trees, Darrell Ricci stood alone.

Cookie looked at her feet, where she had slight scuff marks on the sides of her boots. The more she thought about Darrell Ricci, the more she decided he wasn't too bad to look at. She told herself she should probably give him a chance. Toni was right about Darrell. Cute guy. She began to warm up to the notion of going with Toni to hang out with Darrell, but her so-called friend had disappeared. So had her heat, often rising mysteriously and without warning and then going away with even less warning. Darrell just didn't do it for her. She was trying, really, she was, but a roiling welt of warmth did not come.

In the dark, Cookie could see everything, even things she did not want to see. The trees were scary, throwing out unexpected shadows with each passing gust of wind. Two girls came from behind the grove of trees where they had been hidden from plain sight. She remembered their faces from *The Heart*. Both girls wore their school uniforms, which meant they had not yet gone home. Noreen DiOreo had white blond hair and longish rabbit teeth but none of Toni Ferlinghetti's panache as an Italian girl. Devoid of Italian girl curves, her tiny body ran straight up and down like a cork. She passed a bottle in a brown paper bag to Anna Maria Scarpino, who took a chug. Through glassy eyes, they stared at Cookie and giggled. They were obviously drunk.

Cookie searched around the park, looking for Toni's orange-blond head but could not find her. Her nose tickled. She felt an itch coming on, along with simple foreboding. Kiss a fool or get into a fight. She had a deep suspicion even the trees did not want to be here.

Shoving the bottle back to Noreen, Anna Maria came forward, zeroing in on Cookie. "What did you say, you crazy bitch?" Her black hair had been chopped to below her ears like an unformed bush. Her skin and hair took on the blue tone from fluorescent light and shadows drifting through the trees. "You want to say that again to me, bitch!"

"You're drunk!" Cookie put her hands on her hips in defiance. "Real drunk." Cookie knew it was two against one. She told herself nothing was going to happen, not so close to *The Heart*, and especially not while they had their uniforms on. But they were also drunk, which meant all bets were off.

Anna Maria began weaving on the walkway. Every time she took a step, she looked as though she might fall. "What did you say to me?" Her words slurred. She spun around in an attempt to steady herself. Nothing she said made sense.

"What trouble? Are you calling me trouble?!"

Anna Maria charged as if she meant to butt her head into Cookie's chest, but clumsily, she missed. Noreen stepped to the side. "Come on, Anna, you'll get us both in trouble!"

The girl almost fell to the ground but caught herself and grabbed on to a mulberry bush to pull herself up for support. Not quite making it, she fell face forward into the bush. "You bitch!"

Cookie's heart raced, but she never raised her voice. "You drunk bitch, don't you ever fuck with me again. You fuck with me and I'll kill you." Even though her words were brutal, her voice remained contrite and to the point. Whatever anger she had seething inside of her, she held in check. Even though her adrenaline had pushed her over the edge and made her jumpy, she walked away from the girls. Not thinking for a minute they'd ever come after her, she didn't even bother to look back. She checked to see if her earrings were still there. Amazed to find them intact, she thought for sure she would have lost one in the fray. Having to work so hard to stop losing things made her sad. Deep down inside, something troubled her, but she did not know how to define it.

Walking on, she didn't bother to turn around to see what had happened to Anna and Noreen, or Toni Ferlinghetti. Cookie didn't like alcohol and found it made people stupid and sloppy. She much preferred pot and acid, but these days even her love affair with drugs was coming to an end. She knew she was changing but didn't know exactly how, or who she would become.

Fern stood shrieking at the top of the park, where it opened up into Convent Avenue. "Antoinette, come home, you come home now!"

Fern pounced on Cookie. "Where's my daughter?"

"I don't know."

"Don't tell me you don't know! Did you do something to her?" Fern talked right in her face. Cookie tried backing away. Fern pursued her. "You left here with her, where'd she go? You tell me now or I'll call the cops!"

Fern reached for Cookie's sweater, but Cookie brushed her off. "Leave me alone! I said don't touch me!"

Fern looked confused. No one had ever talked to her with such disrespect.

Cookie must have looked scary to Fern because she backed off. "Touch me again and there'll be trouble!" If Fern laid a hand on her again, Cookie would have no choice but to hit her.

"Look, Hon," Fern's voice softened to mild exasperation, "I'm just so upset with Toni because she doesn't listen to me no more." She pulled out a Viceroy and lit it. In the absence of light, her eyes seemed to recede into her head and turn into two ebony stones. Fern tried to pedal herself away from Cookie's rage, without having much success. "Cat got your tongue, Cookie? It's hard to believe you don't know where Toni went when you both left here together, and you didn't have no fight or nothing like that."

Cookie turned away from Fern and walked back into the park.

"Come on, don't be like that. I'm just worried about her."

Blowing smoke into Cookie's face, Fern said, "Let's go look for her."

Fern carried the laundry sack she had earlier tried to hand off to Toni. They walked down the footpath. The groups of kids had grown larger and would hang out in the park until sun-up. All of the conditions were right. It was clear and brisk but not too cold. A splatter of chunky vomit marked the spot where Anna and Noreen had been staked-out with their bottle in a bag.

Beyond the grove of oak trees, an ancient dogwood tree with a thick, grey and twisted trunk had not yet shed its leaves. Spanning across its many branches, a flaming barrage of fall foliage yielded burgundy, orange, coral and blood-red leaves. The tree's vivid color was a reminder of how quickly time flew. The glow of the dogwood's leaves eerily transcended the cycle of the seasons. Not only was autumn rapidly passing through, but soon spring would return. Come spring, hundreds of fragrant pink flowers would bloom. The field would be teeming with the Blue Jays Little League. After practice, kids would head down to the Hoagie Hut on Lake Avenue to order sandwiches from Fern, who knew every kid by name.

"That's my tree," Fern said.

"Then why don't you just pee on it," Cookie said.

"You've always had a fresh mouth. It's because you don't have no mother or nothing looking out for you."

Cookie was adamant and shrugged. "It's everyone's tree."

Before Fern could heighten the conflict, something moving caught her attention. "Looky there…"

Around the corner from the base of the tree, two bodies had taken on the swaying rhythm of wind. Facing toward the park's interior, the couple huddled together like small trees hiding from the stores and taverns on Lake Avenue. The glare of yellow streetlight, broken by intermittent flashes of green neon, exposed the pair in the shadows. The couple had lodged themselves up against the dogwood tree like two saplings. His face was shiny with perspiration. Pressed against the tree, she could hardly be seen. His hands gripped her shoulders for support. His tongue slid in and out of her mouth. Fern and Cookie had stumbled upon the terribly awkward moment when you have inadvertently interrupted two lovers.

Yet a complete absence of embarrassment prevailed. Everyone had their clothes on. And they were not on the verge of taking their clothes off. Everyone made out in Lennon Park. This was their moment, one more phrase in the fugue-like existence of Yonkers kids coming together in an impromptu jam session or in the communal passing of a joint, sharing a bottle of booze or a cigarette. Hooking up was the same kind of thing.

It was also Cookie and Fern's moment. Fern shook her laundry bag at Toni and yelled, "You gotta go to the laundry mat! You gotta get this done now!"

Cookie had been trying so hard to force herself to like Darrell Ricci, and almost succeeded. Just when she had gotten used to the fact she might like him, Toni snatched him away.

Even though Cookie didn't say anything, she felt a strange pang of regret. It was like losing something you didn't know you might want until it was gone.

Toni might have had an inkling about what Cookie felt and snapped at her, "You said you didn't like him!"

She trailed after Cookie, yelling at her while Fern stayed two steps behind, forever the chaperone to her daughter's mischief.

Fern sniped as she swung the laundry bag against Toni's backside, nudging her to get down to the laundromat. "I hope that boy comes from money and he's not just some punk from Lake Avenue!"

Without saying goodbye, Darrell Ricci had disappeared into the shadows behind the hedges flanked with heather, conifer and camellia shrubs. His parting had not been at all awkward. Toni didn't even notice he was gone. She wasn't into Darrell Ricci or any other boy. Her brief encounter with him was meant to show off her sexual power. Hookups were a game for her and a way to keep score. Casual hookups could mean anything from making out to going down to Lake Avenue on a spontaneous date for a slice of pizza.

The most popular stores on Lake Avenue were the Hoagie Hut and Busy Bakers, which was known for its fluffy crumb buns, jelly donuts and feathery-light Kaiser rolls sprinkled with toasted poppy seeds. The Hoagie Hut had the best meatball wedges around! Even though it was called The Hoagie Hut, they didn't call meatball sandwiches meatball hoagies; they were meatball wedges! Fern was known to slice a long hard Italian roll in half. She'd put the top of the roll to the side and dig a canoe-shaped moat on the bottom half. Then she ladled tomato sauce made from sun ripened plum tomatoes into the moat, drenching the wedge without making it soggy. All of this was preparation for the grand moment when the juiciest meatballs were dropped into the moat and left floating on top. Mozzarella glazed the underbelly of the top half of the crusty bread, and clung to the tender meatballs, creating a seamless and extraordinary sandwich, meant to be eaten so quickly it never had a chance to fall apart.

Seven

The Valley of Lost Earrings

Catching the Number 2 bus on Palisade Avenue was a lucky break. The bus barreled down the hill over potholes and slim ruts in the road. The night had cast shadows from the trees lining both sides of the street. The trees were swollen with leaves, catching light from the streetlamp to create a burgeoning umbrella of orange, russet, and red. Yellow leaves looked as pale as an old moon. Some green leaves had not turned color, mottling and shriveling into the shape of grey ghosts. An open window above the side seat in the back of the bus let in the soft sound of crunching leaves, crumpling paper, smashing beer bottles, a flick of wind, the sound of a car starting up, another car speeding up and passing the bus, and the noisy cough of the bus engine. Voices from kids burst into the bus in the form of stray words, an occasional curse, and laughter. These were the sounds of a late October night in North Yonkers.

Cookie turned her head to look out the window and drifted to another time, when she saw a man with a long blond ponytail, the hunky guy named Stanley de Falco. She had not seen him since the Café Trento. Then she remembered where she had first seen him—down by the river. He had been there with the incredible expanding baby machine Debbie Ochiogrosso. They had probably been kissing in the car. Maybe doing other things too. Baffled by how things just popped into her head without an obvious trigger to jog her memory, she had no idea why Stanley had sprung to mind.

The Number 2 bus stopped by a strip of stores on Palisade Avenue. Ever since Cookie could remember, this 'hood had always been called *Down the End*. She almost missed her stop and jumped out of her seat. Fortunately, other passengers were getting off at the same stop in front of Peter Reeves' Grocery Store. Jumping out of the back-of-the-bus exit, she landed squarely on the pavement and moved along quickly, darting across the street to avoid the guys standing in front of Donaghey's Pub. She didn't want to run into anyone she knew and have to stop and talk. Worse, she didn't want to face rejection. None of the guys would want to talk to her. Most were older and not wanting to get caught out on the limb with prime jailbait. She felt for her earrings to make sure they were firmly in place.

A shortcut through the parking lot led to a narrow alley behind the National Bank of North America on Roberts Avenue. As she approached the corner of North Broadway, traffic was light for a Friday night. Of the few cars cruising by, an Oldsmobile caught her attention. Even in the dark, its marine green color radiated a metallic sheen indicating it had been waxed and polished with care. The car turned down Roberts Lane, trundled up Argyle Terrace and was soon out of sight. Walking in the dark, she lifted her arms to the sky. She wanted to catch a ride on a shooting star to streak away from this bleak place. She heard a dog barking and fancied it was Blackster—the dog she and Herman had given to Louie Santamassino. Sure enough, Blackster lumbered down the street. Wagging his tail, he sidled up to her and sniffed her hand. Blackster had become everyone's dog and watched over the 'hood. Satisfied Cookie was okay, Blackster retreated toward the wall of the Calvary Baptist Church and picked up his stride onto the sidewalk of North Broadway.

At the bottom of Arden Place, she scuffed the top of her brown granny boots into a heart-shaped pond of fresh earth. The rough pavement walkway had big uneven chunks of broken concrete. In the underbelly of a hedge and in the midst of camellia shrubs, she spotted a bouquet. Short-stemmed flowers, round and pale, gleamed on the dark ground. Showing signs of a florist's skill, pastel poms were tethered close together by wire covered with flat green floral tape. Tiny white flowers and long sheaths of fern-like leaves were strung in between the poms. Covered with specks of dirt, the poms looked like someone had violently shoved their heads into the soil to bury them.

Cookie felt for her silver hoop earrings again, but this time one was gone. She panicked and let out a small cry. So tired of losing things, there seemed to be no end to her losing streak. She looked around on the ground and actually got down on her knees and began to crawl. The earring could have dropped anywhere. She thought of retracing her steps back to the bus stop. She did not know how long she scrambled along the sidewalk, searching for anything glinting under the streetlight. No matter. She lost one more thing she had cared about.

Between the discarded bouquet and the loss of her earring, Cookie began to cry, and really cry. It felt good to cry. Shut down all of the time, she never had a chance to cry. If someone caught her crying, she would be dubbed as a crybaby, and that notion made her cry all the more. The tears poured out of her. The bouquet had been tossed as garbage. Someone had a chance at happiness and threw it away.

A car slowed on the road as it came down the hill. Vaguely aware of her surroundings, and certainly not focused on the car, she ran her hands through the planting strip covered with fine moss and newly fallen leaves. Getting dirt under her fingernails, she dug under the leaves and clawed them up from the ground. Her earring wasn't there. She crawled almost to the bottom of the hill, where a small patch of woods camouflaged the secret shortcut leading to Gilbert Place. Racked with sobs, her body shook, and tears covered her cheeks. She cried and cried, but she could not stop. She did not want to stop. Losing her earring was the last straw.

A green Oldsmobile idled on the side of the road by Rock Lane. The driver got out of the car and called to her. "Are you okay? Did you fall?"

She didn't recognize him at first. He wore a black suit, very formal, the kind Johnny used to wear sometimes when he played music for a wedding. His blond hair was pulled tight in a long braid. It was Mr. Trouble. Stanley. Blood pumped into her wet cheeks making her face grow warm. She knew she had turned red and could feel raw sensation in her skin worsening like a sunburn. She brushed away her tears with the back of her hand and prayed her nose wasn't running.

The air became fragrant with him as he grabbed her by the shoulders and lifted her from the ground. She picked up the strong scent of the earth and his warmth as he huddled closer to her against the wind. "Is everything okay? I saw you on the ground and thought you had fallen." He looked at her more deeply, scrutinizing her for telltale signs. "Have you been drinking?"

She shook her head but would not look at him. "Stanley, right?"

He looked at her and nodded to be certain. "You're not drunk?"

She turned her head away, so he would not be able to see the last of her tears. Her embarrassment made it difficult for her to breathe.

"Drugs? Do you need to go to the hospital?"

This time she closed her eyes tight and tried to find the right words to explain to this strange guy, Stanley, why he had

found her crawling along the ground. "I lost my hoop earring."
Then she took a deep breath. "And lately, I've been losing too
many things."

"I know what you mean. I've lost a lot of things too." She
could tell he meant to be sincere by the way he looked at her.
"Maybe your earring has gone to the Valley of Lost Earrings."
He chuckled and looked concerned. "It's not far from the Gulch
of Lost Socks. And I've been there, once or twice. I've been
there too many times and it's not fun."

She realized she didn't make a very good impression on
him. For a moment, she wished she could be anonymous
and free from his scrutiny. She had to think fast and say
something.

Surprising herself, she blurted, "I've lost my words. I used
to be able to write about my feelings and now I can't."

He nodded and studied her face to assess the gravity of her
situation. Then, his attention drifted nowhere. He didn't focus
on the trees or a house, his car or the road. He blanked out
and became lost in thought. He had gone to some other place
in his mind. He did not appear to be visibly distressed, but he
did not seem to be aware of her or the world around him. He
forgot he was standing there talking to Cookie.

Cookie watched him carefully. It was starting to become
awkward. She did not know what she should say. More than
a few seconds passed. Maybe a minute. She heard her heart
pounding in her chest. Suddenly, he shifted his weight from
one standing leg to the other. He resumed making eye contact
with her, but he looked dazed.

"What did you write about?" he asked her.

"Everything."

"Everything?" he nodded.

His blue eyes had turned cold and roughhewn in the dark,
a grey stone wall. The stubble on his face gave him an edge,
strong and masculine. As he stepped into the streetlight, a
subtle dimple on his chin appeared like a divine afterthought.

She estimated him to be in his mid-twenties, maybe a year or two older.

Down by the river, he had been with Debbie Ochiogrosso, who lived on the same block. "Why are you around this part of town?" she asked him.

"I had to drop someone off."

The tone of his voice made him sound defensive. Cookie didn't want to push him, but she wanted to know more. "Is Debbie your girlfriend?"

Stanley shook his head no. "Not anymore. We broke up."

"I saw you down by the river with her. I just figured."

"Why do you ask?"

"Just curious."

She hoped he might bend down and hug her, but he retreated, backing away a couple of steps, giving them both space.

"Everything will be okay," he told her. "Don't worry. I can tell things about people, and you're going to be alright."

She knew he wasn't lying. He spoke the truth. Unlike most of the people she had known, Stanley talked to her as though she was grown up and not a kid. In a funny way, he was wise, sort of like Mabel Kerry.

He walked back to his car. His blond braid looked too heavy to carry all the way down to the middle of his back. She thought if he had to run fast with his braid, it would slow him down. Just before he got into his car, he turned around and looked at her again. "You're going to be okay."

He wasn't giving her the brush-off or patting her on the head like she was a little kid. He seemed to know something about her, and that made her want to know more about him.

She watched his Oldsmobile cruise toward North Broadway and turn right to head south. Stanley had not grown up in this 'hood, otherwise she would have seen him around long before now. Stanley! What a name! Something had happened to her. She kept thinking about the way he had looked at her

and said everything was going to be okay. And as quickly as
he had appeared, he was gone. She wondered what he would
have done if she had jumped up and held him tight. Maybe
he would have bent down and kissed her. She had boarded a
runaway roller coaster, the Dragon Coaster at Playland! No
way to get off. No way out of here. She had no choice but to
stay the course, riding the highs and lows, through the tunnel,
through the body of the Dragon, until she reached the end. In
the final leg of the journey, she hoped she would be able to find
her way out of the Valley of Lost Earrings.

Eight

A Kiss is Just a Kiss

New notions of Stanley crept into her consciousness each day. Stanley conjured emotions in her similar to ones inspired by the Blind Owl Alan Wilson. But these new emotions were different and unsettling. Stanley presented grave danger, one she did not know how to define, at least not yet. She still did not know where he lived or where he had come from. She had not seen him since the night she had gone crawling for her earring. Since then her fifteenth birthday came to pass. No phone number. No school. No place of work. She did not know how to track him down except by going to the places where she had seen him before, hoping he'd be there again. The Café Trento. Down by the river. She looked for him everywhere she went.

The thought of seeing him again thrilled and excited her, making her knees feel weak. Unlike the trick knees buckling from under her body due to some malformed genetic predisposition, her knees were weak and trembling with the anticipation of seeing him.

And if she did see him, what would she say?

The words Cookie uttered into her tape recorder focused on Stanley. She spoke the truth as though she was writing a poem.

The heart knows of many types of kisses, from a chilly peck on the cheek to starved, maddening desire. The kisses I want to give you will linger on your lips, as our lips lock together in an urgent embrace. Taste my lips. Feel my breath. If we could die here in this very moment, it will have been worthwhile to have our lips locked in an eternal kiss, an embrace outlasting death. Our kiss will live until the end of time. You are mine and I am yours.

In a million years, she could not imagine saying something so corny to a guy. Saccharine nonsense made her gag. Her chit-chat into the tape recorder was pure fantasy. If word got around, she'd be the laughingstock of the North End and this was not fun to think about. She felt sure if she talked aloud about Stanley long enough, then her words would return, and she would no longer have to put up with this clunky tape recorder.

There were voices upstairs in her house. It had not occurred to her anyone could be home. Her musings on tape could be overheard. She did not want anyone to know about her secret recordings. Most suspicious. Who could be in her house? Kitty was in the nuthouse again. Early afternoon, Donny was at school. Cookie had cut out of school in the morning, right after second period. Still the voices persisted, and she guessed the stray sounds to be friendly banter taking place between a man and a woman.

The woman laughed, a silly, flirtatious giggle.

The decision to go inside the house would be fraught with complication. Gaining entry from the basement meant climbing makeshift wooden steps into the laundry room. The voices, especially the woman's laughter, seemed to be coming from the main floor, the living room. Walking undetected into the house was not possible. Another way meant exiting the basement, walking around the house and entering through the front door the way she would if she was coming home from school. She wondered if the house was in the midst of being burglarized. Thieves could be lying-in-wait, ready to jump an unwitting spectator. The criminals might have murderous intent. Hippies from Untermyer Park might be searching for Kitty's ludes, Johnny's liquor, or money.

Of all the scenarios she imagined, it was best to alert the intruders they were not alone. She turned off the tape recorder, pulled the plug and pushed it toward the far back wall behind the workbench. Exiting the basement, making as much noise as possible, she slammed the door shut, bounded down the steps, found herself stalled in front of the house and looked up. The bay window's two curtains had been drawn. It was very strange.

Kitty never drew the curtains. Facing west, the window caught light from the sun as it coursed the sky over the Hudson River. One of her mother's small pleasures in life was watching light change. Kitty sat in her armchair, sewing, darning socks, patching holes and fixing hems. A true seamstress, she was not. Her flair for sewing didn't expand to creating clothing, but she was good at fixing things and could do alterations. Far from being a domestic goddess, Kitty couldn't cook, rarely took the trouble to go to the grocery store and had most of her groceries delivered. Cookie used to do most of her grocery shopping, but those days were gone.

Movement disturbed the curtains in the bay window. The curtains were pushed apart, and a glass vase was knocked off the shelf. In the window, a woman appeared with blond hair styled in a page boy. She set the vase back onto the shelf and closed the curtains.

Johnny's red Buick Skylark was parked in front of the house. If he was home this early, trouble had to be brewing. Something was happening she might need to know about. Cookie had no trepidation about proceeding up the steps. She opened her hemp sack to look for her keys but could not find them. Lost again! The thought of losing her keys made her feel frantic. She had no idea where she had left them this time!

She tried the doorknob. Fortunately, the front door was

unlocked. Pushing open the door, she walked into the house and took a look around. Johnny sat in Kitty's armchair as though he had taken over her spot for good. Covered with clear plastic to protect the fabric, the chair had special upholstery in blue satin stripes. If Kitty had been there, she would not have allowed Johnny to sit on her chair. It was her chair, where the rhythm of watching the changes in color and light on the river soothed her and kept her voices at bay.

Johnny didn't bother to introduce the blond woman. She smiled at Cookie and said hello in a tiny voice.

"What's she doing here?"

"She's my friend," Johnny told her. "What am I, not allowed to have friends?" He looked at the woman. "Right, Joanie?" Then he turned to Cookie. "Joanie's my friend."

The couch did not have a plastic cover like Kitty's blue striped chair. The blonde sat there as uncomfortable as all hell, pulling her knees to the side of her body. Her bare feet poked out under her long bellbottom jeans. Her bangs were too long, almost covering her eyes. Sallow skin, lots of black eyeliner, dark circles under her eyes, the woman was a mess. The couch looked rumpled as if two people had sat on every square inch as many times as possible.

Johnny asked her, "Aren't you supposed to be at school?" Then he shook his shaggy head. "You know you're a real pisser."

"That's my daughter, Cookie," he said to the blond woman. "She's a real pisser."

"Where's Donny?" Cookie asked.

"What the hell do I know? She's still at school. Isn't that where she's supposed to be?! Aren't you supposed to be at school too?"

Whenever Johnny was wrong, he made a habit of not apologizing. Instead, he went on the offensive and attacked the person he had wronged. Unbeknownst to Johnny, Cookie had become truant and rarely went to school. Cookie did not know what he had done, but he was hiding something and not doing a very good job. She stared at him, letting him wallow in discomfort.

Cookie did not know exactly what they were doing. Or did she? She had not been privy to sex up close and personal. A certain moisture in the air reeked of two people physically coming together. Neither pleasant nor foul, the scent in the room smelled like the blond woman's cheap perfume and her father's sweat. It punctuated a tryst. And it was really disgusting. It was so horrible, seeing Johnny caught with a woman who was not his wife. Not Cookie's mother.

She threw her head into her hands. *Oh god, what do I do now?*

No one wants to imagine their parents having sex. What's far worse is having to imagine your parents having sex with other people who are not your parents. It's almost like laying witness to a devastating car wreck. She did not want to be there. She did not want to watch. But she did not have the strength to turn away from the carnage. She needed to take one more glimpse of tragedy, committing it to memory, to have and hold for all time, so it would never happen to her, or anyone she knew, ever again.

Johnny would have hell to pay and he had no idea how bad it would be.

"I think you ought to leave," Cookie told them.

"Hey," Johnny said, "that's not nice."

"I said to get out of my house!"

Cookie looked at them with the most intense form of hatred she had ever known. She did not need to say anything to Johnny. He caught her gaze and looked away, ashamed. Deep embarrassment made his face red.

She went to the bay window and opened the curtains. Johnny did not stop her, and the woman had nothing to say. The colored glass in the bay window caught jagged shards of afternoon light. Across the river on the New Jersey Palisades, clusters of trees glowed with red and yellow leaves. The radio tower resembling a skeletal metal ladder shot up to the sky above the Palisades. At night, a small red light blinked on top of the tower. So far away, the small red light was the first thing to catch your eye when you looked out at night. It was a touchstone for Kitty. Cookie too.

Cookie looked around the room as though she was seeing all of her mother's things for the first time, noticing *how beautiful*. Even if Kitty could not live in reality, the world she carved out for herself was not too bad a place to be.

Joanie sat on the couch examining her fingernails. Above where she sat, a framed woodblock Japanese print depicted cresting waves, stillness in motion, rising and falling. One large wave, more prominent than the others, could be a tsunami or maybe what sailors call a green one, a sudden freakish and terrifying wave as large as a hundred-foot-wall coming from nowhere, having the power to take whatever it wants, living or not, away from the shore and drag it out to sea. Another print posed two lovers, a samurai warrior who lays his sword on the ground beside his lover while she bends and arcs her body toward him in an aching song of love. Johnny had bought the prints when he was stationed in Japan before shipping out to Korea.

Next to the couch where the woman sat, two bronze wild mustang sculptures climbed into the air above a side table as though they were protecting their right to be unbroken and free. Kitty's aesthetics were not ordinary for a woman who had been raised as a Yonkers girl. She had the sensibility and charm of a southern belle, albeit one who had traveled no farther south than New Jersey. Even if Johnny had bought the prints in Japan, nine out of ten Yonkers girls would not have wanted them in their living rooms. But Kitty was different. So different. Strange but wonderful.

Cookie did not recall if Johnny had said anything during this passage of time. She had stopped hearing altogether. And if she had her druthers, she would stop seeing too.

She turned to her father and spoke softly but firmly. "Get off my mother's chair."

"I paid for the thing." Johnny stood up and put his hands along his sides as though he was hiding something. "It's my home too, you know!"

"Not really," Cookie said. "You built this house, but you never made it a home. You're never here." She waved her hand toward the couch where the blond woman sat in awkward silence. "And now this!"

Johnny turned to Joanie. She caught his eye and gave him a nod, *Let's go.*

Cookie planted her hands on her hips to stop from shaking. "Johnny, you know, I've always wanted to tell you this, so I'll tell it to you now in front of your friend," she emphasized. Taking a deep breath, she said. "You're a lousy father."

Johnny made a weak protest sound, a clicking *tsk tsk*, but he didn't dare look at his daughter. He was afraid of her. And he had good reason to be. Cookie felt as though if he said one more stupid thing, she would take one of the bronze mustangs and crush it against his skull. The blond woman jumped up from the couch, scrambling to find her shoes and handbag. Cookie didn't bother to look at her. She was the worst form of a Yonkers girl. She had no respect for anyone, not even herself. She was probably someone Johnny had cozied up to at the Italian American Club on Lockwood Avenue, which seemed to be his latest hangout when he wasn't playing music in the city. Neither one had the balls to say anything and they left through the front door.

Cookie sat on her mother's blue striped chair and looked out the window.

Kitty called it her picture window and worshipped the light filtering in, illuminating her many-colored glass objects. Each piece of translucent glass had a base no wider than two inches because it had to be narrow enough to sit on the shelf. Reed-thin vases, dainty baskets, miniature pitchers and orbs, clear

Steuben glass animals, and concave mirror domes inverting the imagery of light and glass, all of these things spoke to Kitty in a way only she could understand. More than a place of light, glass and color, the window was a tribute to Kitty, and told the story of her life.

The light in the October sky flared forth multiple tones of red, igniting the glow of fire on leaves still clinging to branches, and trembling as though they were holding on for the last vestige of life. She watched the leaves falling, dropping to the earth in the rhythm of a song. The leaves sang loud and intensely. The leaves landing on the ground crunched as though they were inflamed, burning up in a raging bonfire, making a sizzling sound. Whether they had fallen to the ground or clung to the trees, the leaves seemed to emit sound and could speak or sing, taking on the cadence of musical notes, an expression of pure poetry, the brushstrokes hidden and not readily apparent in a magnificent painting. These leaves were a form of art, transcending life and making all things possible. If only she could find the words to describe what she was experiencing. And she could not. Her words were stuck, caged in the back of her throat.

Nine

Killing Johnny

Killing Johnny was the right thing to do. Cookie climbed the steps to her parents' bedroom, seeking some way she could vent her fury. She pulled on the banister so hard it unhinged from the wall. The force had loosened the bolts and flecks of white plaster fell onto the step. She smacked the banister back into place. She fully intended to defend her mother's honor. Hers too. Ditto Donny. The more she thought about what Johnny had done, the more furious she became. The anger came in waves, rising and falling in no particular pattern. Every time she thought she had recovered from what her father had done, a fresh swell rose and took her breath away.

A philanderer, a bad boy, one of the guys in the band, never home, Johnny spent his entire life on the run, in pursuit of playing music in the city. Floozie women and booze were natural companions to the life he led. This was his life! Philandering away from home was somewhat acceptable, but rubbing it in their faces was more than she could take. Although Kitty had been betrayed, Cookie also felt betrayed and tried to understand why. Johnny wasn't her husband.

But as her father he had broken her heart. Their family was already messed up and he had made it even worse.

He had not come back home since he had been found with the blond woman. Imagine leaving two young daughters home alone! This was nothing new. For years, Johnny had left them on their own to raise themselves and babysit Kitty. Cookie wondered if he had walked out of their lives for good.

Donny followed her into their parents' bedroom. "What are you going to do? I know you, Cookie, and I get scared when you get like this. Please don't hurt something!"

Cookie searched around the room for something to harm but could not find a specific target. "I'm going to kill him."

Donny threw herself at Cookie and sobbed, "Please don't kill him, Cookie. Then, you'll go to jail and I'll have nobody."

Cookie put her arms around Donny. "Maybe he hasn't come back home because he knows I'm going to kill him."

"Please don't kill him, Cookie!"

Cradling her arms around Donny, Cookie realized she was no longer a frail little girl. Ten years old, solidly built, Donny stood toe-to-toe with Cookie, and clung to her as though she would never let go. "I don't want that Joanie woman to be my mother, even if she's not crazy," she sniffed.

"She's gotta be crazy to go out with Johnny," Cookie snapped.

"Yeah," Donny said, wiping back tears, "I know, but he's crazy too."

Cookie could not take much more. As much as she wanted to kill her father, she hesitated for a moment and thought what would happen. If Cookie went to jail, Donny would have to fend for herself.

He wasn't worth killing.

Not much in the way of family could step in to help. Cookie thought about going to see Grandmother Delia, but the old woman had become a shut-in since Grandpa *Old Jack* had died. Besides, Delia wanted no part of Kitty or Johnny. She constantly referred to Johnny as being a crazy eye-talian and cursed the day her beautiful Irish daughter had married a wop. Good looks were prized by Kitty's side of the family. And even though Johnny was very good looking, no one liked him very much and often referred to him as being too hotblooded. While the Italian and Irish complained about each other and hurled wild aspersions composed of exaggerated claims and insults, they always ended up marrying one another.

"Everything's gonna be alright?" Donny asked. "Right?"

"We just have to get through it, that's all." Cookie examined the room as though she had never been here before. Johnny's clothes were loosely draped over a vanity chair. The bed had been made, but its quilted coverlet was not properly tucked into four corners. Whoever had made the bed did not care how it looked. On the rare occasions when Johnny slept at home, he did not put any effort into making a bed. The sight of the made bed offered a small measure of comfort. At least he had not brought the blond woman into Kitty's bedroom. The open door to Kitty's side of the closet showed her Jackie Kennedy-lookalike wool suits and wrap dresses. Her hatboxes, pocketbooks and shoeboxes were neatly stacked on the shelves. Kitty's favorite perfumes were displayed on a gold-plated mirrored tray. She favored Chanel No. 5 and My Sin by Lanvin.

Cookie picked up a small oval-shaped stone knick-knack from her dresser. "Remember this?" she asked Donny.

Donny nodded. "It looks nothing like the owl we saw in the park."

Minus ears and a pointy beak, the misshapen grey blob could hardly be described as an owl, but Cookie had given it to Kitty. She told her mother as long as she kept the owl close to her heart, she would always get well again and return home.

Donny took the owl from Cookie and turned it around in her hand to inspect its face. "It's the saddest owl I've ever seen. Look at his expression."

"You'd be sad too if you were an owl with no ears. At least none that we can see." Cookie took the owl from Donny and held it with reverence and carefully set it on Kitty's dresser. "He looks like he wants to fly away from here. And I can't say that I blame him."

Donny leaned forward to give the owl a kiss. "Even though I've only seen one owl, I've seen enough pictures in books to know a sad owl."

"Kitty will come home again," Cookie reassured her.

"I hope so," Donny said. "I miss her and don't want a different mother."

As furious as Cookie was, the more she thought about it, she didn't have to actually kill Johnny. There were other mean things she could do. She looked around the room and took inventory. She could take one cufflink from every set he owned and drop them down the sewer. She could cut off one sleeve from every shirt he owned and slice his ties in half. She could put itching powder in in his boxer shorts and add a touch of Nair to his hair pomade. She wanted to box his ears and punch his nose. She could do all of these things and kill him too. He had no right to do what he had done to Kitty. She was willing to fight for her mother's honor.

She walked out of the bedroom without doing anything but left the door open in case she wanted to return. Donny came down behind her, taking two steps at a time, making a thud every time she landed. Then she started to hiccup, but it was too dramatic to be an involuntary reflex. She seemed to be playing a game according to her own private rules. Cookie walked through the kitchen and considered the liquor bottle left out on the kitchen counter with two empty rock glasses. Johnny had offered the blond woman a drink. The glasses and the bottle had been left there. Cookie didn't want to touch them and catch their cooties. Suddenly, she had a bright idea—she could spike his Beefeater Gin with acid and send Johnny on the trip of a lifetime. Nice.

On second thought she nudged the two glasses off the counter and into a trash can. "There, don't have to look at it no more."

Donny opened the refrigerator door. "I'm sick of grilled cheese sandwiches," she said. "Can't we get something else?"

Cookie hated when Donny whined, making it out like Cookie was in charge of her life and could make good things happen. Most of the time, Cookie struggled to get by and to make the best out of a bad situation. She had no idea if she was right or wrong, good or bad, rotten, indifferent, or something in between. She hovered between the best and the worst in life, struggling to make the best decision for the both of them.

Cookie looked in the refrigerator and saw a half-eaten block of cheese. They had been living on bread, butter and cheese. When dinner time came, she fixed grilled cheese sandwiches and warmed a can of soup. She wished she had more to offer Donny, but she was in no mood to go to the grocery store. She asked Donny to go instead to fetch some tomatoes and lettuce, so she could make a salad.

Donny pressed her hands together in prayer and implored, "Please no more cheese sandwiches."

"How about if you buy some chuck chop? Just a half a pound? And I'll make hamburgers for a change?"

Donny wrinkled her nose. "Do I have to?"

"Either that or I'll make chuck chop out of Johnny."

Donny balked at having to go shopping, but they had an account at Peter Reeves Grocery Store *Down the End.*

"Chop, chop." Cookie motioned with her hand.

Donny took forever getting dressed and nagged Cookie about how to order meat. She should have known how to shop by now. She was ten, old enough to figure things out on her own. Cookie gave Donny a handwritten note for the butcher at Peter Reeves and practically pushed her out the front door.

Now she could see why Donny didn't want to leave the house. Fogged-in with fine mist, not quite turning into rain, soon it would be dark. Even though it was the end of October, the days were growing shorter, but not yet colder. The weather had been unseasonably warm with temperatures hovering in the low seventies. Cookie would have called it an Indian Summer day, but the fog dispelled her notion. A true Indian Summer day would be sunny and hot.

Once Donny left, she thought about Johnny and the blond woman kissing, which seemed strange. Johnny didn't seem to be big on kissing. In fact, Cookie had never seen him kiss Kitty. He grabbed her bottom, squeezed her and nuzzled her like an animal burrowing into a cave, but he had never actually kissed her. And on more than one occasion, she had heard them making strange noises while they rocked their bed. But kissing? The thought of Johnny kissing anyone, even her mother, made her shudder.

For weeks Cookie had been consumed by the notion of kissing and wanting to learn how to do it. Now she had been forced to deal with her father kissing another woman. Life wasn't fair, she protested inside. More than unfair, the life she experienced was tragic, full of furies, horrible winged creatures who had flown in straight from a Greek tragedy and sought to torment her—straight out of *Antigone*, the girl who had been forced to go at it alone and destined to die young. What's worse, Cookie might be destined to die young and sadly unkissed.

She went outside and sought a weapon from the garbage shed on the side of the house next to the woods where Johnny had murdered the Sumac trees. It seemed like only yesterday when he had bludgeoned the trees because he mistakenly believed they had caused Donny's allergic reaction to poison sumac.

"You killed all the trees!" She yelled into the void where trees once stood. Weeds and moss covered the stumps left to decay like headless corpses strewn on a battlefield.

She took the pickaxe from the shed and swung it against the side of the house and left a gash in the wood siding. "Look at what you did to Kitty! To Donny! Look at what you did to me!"

Working herself into a bit of frenzy, she wailed the axe against the first tree stump where it lodged into the damp wood. The force pitched her body forward and she almost fell over. "You still think that the trees made Donny break out in a rash! Don't you! That's how stupid you are! You don't listen to reason! You don't listen to common sense!"

The fog made many stumps clustering together look surreal on this unruly terrain. In her capable hands, her angry axe hacked debris. Sinking into the damp earth, the blade of her axe scattered wood chips, sheaths of bark and weeds. Panting for breath, she dropped the axe. This land did not resemble a forest, or even a small grove of woods. Low-hanging boughs had once belonged to the living trees. Now craggy twine and tangled branches cascaded over the land, making it look like a swamp. Fog distorted her vision. The headless trees seemed to be full of growth, steeped in signs of new life. The new life seemed to spring from the return of the Sumac trees, but she could not be sure.

"You're as dumb as a brick!" she yelled out. "There's no hope for you! You've destroyed everything that's good in your life! You destroyed the trees. You destroyed our family! It's because of you that Kitty is sick!"

The land of stumps might be laden with growth only because it had been forgotten and intentionally neglected due to the shame borne by Johnny in the aftermath of its destruction. Over a year had passed since the trees were cut down, but no one walked here. There was no need to be here. No one wanted to remember. Now in late October the sun did not want to visit here. With the changing position of the sun in the sky, not even scant diagonal rays of sunlight shone in between the stumps.

And on this day in the fog, when there was no sunlight at all, a labyrinth of gnarled roots had become tangled with brown fibrous cords. Broken trunks, stump-like and hollow-shaped, were no longer living trees but a home for seedling plants and yellow-green moss, kelly-green lichen with tendrils resembling slime, or the heads of cabbage, and human matter, or brains. Some brown spiraling spores took on the look of stalactite crystals or twisted hemp and knotted clumps of hair on an old, homeless woman. Some tree stumps lay on their sides, flattened by wear and time, appearing to be makeshift bridges crossing to nowhere. There were insects too, mainly beetles and centipedes with as many legs as the roots of trees. The centipedes' legs moved rapidly and as sharp as piano keys.

She grew calm and kicked the axe she had allowed to slump to the ground. She could end up like Johnny if she wasn't careful! And the notion terrified her. "You're a destructive coward," she called out.

Red-faced, Johnny Colangelo stood there watching her. He might have been standing there for some time. If Johnny had been listening to her, he didn't care to comment. For once his mouth wasn't moving.

"I lost my keys to the house," she said. "You need to make me another set."

Johnny nodded. "How'd that happen?"

"What business is it of yours!" Cookie felt her face screw-up in anger. She knew what she must have looked like to Johnny. She had practiced the look a million times in the mirror back when she was trying to be a gangster. She thought she looked like a lion about to tear off the head of its prey. "Why'd you show up? Don't tell me... Is it time to pay the bills and complain about your rotten luck?"

Johnny looked at her cautiously, trying to assess her mood. He kept an eye on her while he paced a small patch of what had once been the woods. "You don't have to tell your mother, you know. I love your mother and I don't want her to know. She'll get the wrong idea. There's no way she'll ever find out unless you tell her."

Cookie knelt on the ground and inhaled the air full of humus. Rich fertile soil and fermenting leaves had been unleashed from the earth. She picked herself up from the ground and shook off stray bits and pieces of wood from her sweater and pants. A few weeds were caught in her hair.

Johnny's voice was a booming intrusion. "I know you love her too." His hands stayed in his pockets and he looked at the ground. "Joanie means nothing to me," he said. "All I did was kiss her."

Those words became permanently etched in Cookie's mind. She turned her back to him and tried to pretend he was no longer there. When she turned around, he had actually left, but his Buick remained parked in front of the house.

Stumbling through her neighbor Bert Rosner's yard, she threw her arms out to steady her balance. The fog had crept in and formed a blanket over the neighboring yards, hushing sound, including the cars driving by on North Broadway. She barely saw the opening to the Owl Hole.

Night was falling and gave the fog an added incandescent dimension to the darkness. No movement here. Hardly any sound. She had walked this route many times throughout her childhood, and she remembered to close her eyes to avoid branches and tangled vines from hitting her in the face. Even in the dim light, she uncovered the narrow opening into her secret hiding place. Camouflaged by the massive overgrowth of weeds, bushes and hedges, the entrance to the deep stairwell had not been used in years. Twenty concrete steps led down to the basement of the Calvary Baptist Church. At the bottom of the steps, the basement landing had become a small natural enclosure flanked by fern and tall grass where anyone or anything could be concealed. A place of refuge—her *Owl Hole.*

For a brief expectant moment, she thought Herman Lynch would show up. Maybe Reenie Ruggiero too. In the past, the three of them had come to know and treasure this secret hideaway. Reenie had always been Cookie's link to keep tabs on Herman; they lived in the same building. But things had changed since the school year started, and she did not know if anything would ever be the same. They were drifting apart. She experienced a stab of pain like a buzzard tearing a hole inside her heart.

Still, she felt grateful for small things. She could come here and hear only her own thoughts. This Owl Hole is where she came to worship stillness, the silence of her heart. And even if she had lost her words, and she would never be able to write again, she felt she had already come to know much more in her short life than most older people would ever know. She heard the song of a bird, knowing the rapid beats of its heart were faster than her own. She wished she could perch herself high on a bough on the ledge of a mountain, where she could see everything, and no one could see her. Like an owl, or a rare bird of prey, she was not scared of the silence. This is where her heart was buried in the detritus of all of her bad feelings. And it is here where she came to lay them to rest.

Ten

Not Even A Kiss

The slight nip in the November air made her breath fan out in front of her face. She walked east on Ashburton Avenue, where a deeper chill blew up from the river. This stretch was open and more exposed to the wind from the river than other parts of the city. The river was always there, a reminder of its prominence as a major waterway to move cargo and people to other places. At the turn of the century, the river made Yonkers a hub for manufacturing and a magnet for immigrants. Those days had come and gone. Many of the earlier waves of immigrants had moved away. In this part of South Yonkers, every day another old building was torn down. Now too many vacant lots gave rise to a fiercer wind coursing up from the river.

Restivo's Florist, Café Trento and Gene's Pizza came into view. The Henry Bedard Drugstore had an old-fashioned soda fountain counter. She headed to the Café Trento. Aside from being known for their rum cake, and the best sfogliatelle and cannoli, there was also a possibility she might have a chance encounter with Stanley.

The trees had dropped their leaves, leaving two large piles as tall as a fortress on the corner of Ashburton and Palisade

Avenue. Cookie felt like jumping into piles of leaves, but her new-found maturity battled with her childish impulses and won the duel within. The child inside had been killed long ago. Every so often, though, a mischievous notion would pop into her head and she would act on it just to show the world she could do whatever she felt like doing.

Tomorrow would mark the four-year anniversary of when Fangs had pulled her out of a line during a fire drill and savagely beat her, leaving her with a bad concussion and a dim memory of what had happened. After school, she changed into rust corduroy pants and a matching wool sweater with dark brown patches on the elbows. She had lost her jeans with seventeen patches, the ones boasting the image of the American flag on her ass. She didn't know where she had lost her jeans and no longer cared, considering it to be one more loss in the musical composition of her fugue that was full of low notes, bad breaks and minor calamities.

Her new school was much different than *The Heart* or Christ the King. The principal of Blessed Sacrament Academy, Sister Mary Eau Claire, encouraged Cookie to enter writing competitions and participate in public TV production projects made for high school kids. But Cookie would have none of the nun's suggestions. It was just a grim reminder that, for the time being, she had lost her words. Sister Mary took an interest in her girls above the call of duty; and as much as Cookie could plainly see the nun had a heart, it did not make up for the dreadful beating she had suffered at the hands of Fangs. Unlike Fangs, Sister Mary belonged to the Sacramentine order of nuns and did not wear the traditional Dominican high-hat habit. Sister Mary's veil was truncated in length with a thick headband revealing some of her hair.

Once school had ended for the day, she saw Sister Mary Eau Claire leaving the building with Carole Zukowski. Carole's flawless skin had an unnatural pallor, as though she had been born with good skin but was lacking something essential in her diet. Under a bob of shiny brown hair and shock-blue eyes fringed with long dark lashes, Carole Zukowski moved gracefully, held her head high and tilted her face expressively with the composure of a classical dancer. But when she opened her mouth, her teeth were rotten. Every single tooth had turned black with decay.

How would she ever be able to kiss anyone with a mouth like that? Cookie knew the girl's teeth had gone bad due to neglect. All that gum chewing had taken its toll. The same thing had happened to the teeth in the back of Cookie's mouth. She had not been to a dentist since she was eight. Fortunately, her front teeth had not decayed.

For no explicable reason, and despite the desire to act older, she threw herself on top of a mound of russet maple leaves, spreading her arms and legs wide, making the shape of a drunken snow angel. You can't keep a good kid down. She knew she was making a fool out of herself, but she did not care. She had endured too much the last few days and tumbling through a pile of leaves made her feel free.

"Aren't you getting too old for this?"

When she looked up, Herman Lynch struggled to hold back his grin. "I've been wondering about you, Cookie girl. Now I know what you've been up to. There you go, acting like a little kid again. Bet you're still reading those little kid books too."

Herman held out his hand to help Cookie up from the ground. Leaves stuck to her pants and sweater. "I didn't expect that to happen," she laughed. "I don't know what's gotten into me."

Herman helped her brush off the leaves. "I mean, why are you messing yourself up?"

"I was heading to the bakery," she told him.

"Which one? I see three bakeries right here."

Yonkers was known for having almost as many bakeries as there were pizzerias. Yonkers had the world record for more pizza places per capita than any other city in the world, or so it had been rumored. The number of bakeries came in second. Fleabag dive bars were number three. Could be true, or not true; it did not matter because people in Yonkers believed it anyway.

"Ashburton Bakery's got great crumb buns and rolls. There's the National Bake Shop by Orchard Street and down in the hollow there's the German bakery, Mengers. Looking for cannoli, Cookie girl?"

A touch of afternoon light crossed her eyes and she lifted her face toward the sun. She felt a fleeting touch of warmth despite the cool November air. It was a fall day in Yonkers like no other and yet the same as so many she had experienced in the past. They darted around an alley next to Edgar's Pub. A nearby gun shop had the head of a dead animal in the window. Cookie wasn't sure what kind of animal. She still had not seen a cow or a horse up close.

"Why do they have a dead animal in that window? I mean it's not like anyone's hunting around here."

"There aren't any animals on Ashburton but go down to Nepperhan Avenue and you'll see wild animals everywhere."

"No way," Cookie said. "You're pulling my leg."

"It's just us black folk," Herman said. "Believe me, if they could hunt us for sport, they would."

Herman stuffed his hands in the front pockets of his blue jeans. "Last time I saw you was up at the Café Trento. What's with the bakery thing?"

Cookie reached into her back pocket, pulled out a crushed pack of Marlboros and lit up. She took a long drag, then handed the cigarette to Herman. He took a long drag and leaned forward and picked a twig out of her hair. "Cookie, it's that blond guy, isn't it?!" He handed the ciggie back to Cookie.

Cookie clenched the cigarette between her teeth and came behind Herman. "Close your eyes." She held her hands over his eyes. "What do you see?"

"I see nothing."

"That's what I want. The blond guy's nothing." She released her hands, exhaled a long stream of smoke away from Herman's face and looked into his eyes just to make a point.

"Cookie, what's going on with you?"

"Nothing."

"Cookie?" He looked at her and raised his brows. "I know you better than that. I can tell when something's going on in that brain of yours. You have a mighty fine understanding of life and think about things no one else seems to care about."

For Herman, her smile came easily. He was her owl, more tender and wiser than her Blind Owl Alan Wilson. The Blind Owl had died, but Herman Lynch was here and very much alive. "I was hoping to run into you," she told him. "I knew you would understand what I'm going through."

They both stopped in front of the Café Trento. "I'll treat you," she said. She took two more short drags, dropped the cigarette on the ground and stubbed it out. A fleck of hot ash flew up and landed on top of her boot.

As soon as they entered the bakery, a rush of bread fresh from the oven flooded her senses. Undercurrents of nutmeg, cinnamon, and butter also permeated the air. The fragrant note of almonds and the sweetness of Italian cookies came in waves.

From behind the cash register, Bertha Sokól smiled at Cookie and Herman. A crowd of people pressed up against the pastry counter. Two girls wore the teal blue BSA uniform, but Cookie did not know them. She had not been at school often enough to tell what grade they were in. Most of the small tables in the café area were taken by girls wearing candy striper uniforms, who volunteered at Yonkers General Hospital.

Three elderly women talked quietly, eating cookies and sipping small cups of coffee. Every so often, Bertha yelled loudly to them in a foreign language like they were hard of hearing. They responded by laughing and saying something in their own language.

But all of this was lost on Cookie.

Because Stanley stood behind the counter in the far corner of the bakery. His eyes flickered as if he remembered her, and he nodded. He gave Herman a once-over that appeared to be curiosity more than anything. He folded his arms and moved toward Cookie as though he was trying to figure something out. "Did you ever find your earring?"

He kept coming toward her but stopped just short of making physical contact. He looked like he meant to say something but could not remember and hesitated. He reached forward to pull a twig from her hair and smiled. Then, he walked away.

The power of speech left Cookie. Not only had she lost her ability to write, but she became mute, unable to make any sort of sound. And she couldn't breathe. Heat inflamed her cheeks. Her response was pure, physical and raw, a stab in her heart, an ache in her mind and a palpable loss of being. Herman nudged her, but it made no difference.

Bertha leaned over the counter. "Don't pay my son no attention," she said. "He's different now that he's come back home. He's not the same as when he left." She grimaced and squinted her eyes. "It's going to take him time to be okay. You understand what I'm saying, don't you?"

Stanley didn't seem to like Bertha talking about him but did not care to comment. And his face betrayed so little emotion. He held himself apart as though he was intent on removing himself from any potential conflict and left without saying anything.

Bertha leaned over the counter and whispered, "He's getting over what happened to him over there."

Cookie nodded and pretended she understood but she had no idea what Bertha was talking about. "What do you mean?" she whispered.

Bertha ignored her question and stiffened to attention, ready to take an order. "What do you want?"

"Coke. Two cokes."

Bertha shook her head. "You don't want to try no pastry?"

Cookie didn't see where Stanley had gone, but Herman had caught the entire interaction. He leaned in and whispered in Cookie's ear, "You're sweet on that blond guy, aren't you?"

Bertha set two bottles of coke on the counter with straws. Herman handed Bertha two quarters, then tugged on the sleeve of Cookie's sweater, prodding her to a café table.

"I don't know if I want to stay here," she said.

"Just tell me what you want to do," Herman said. "I'm fine staying or leaving."

She could feel the eyes of everyone in the café turn to look at them. Herman sipped the coke through a straw from his thicker upper lip on the right side of his mouth. She thought for sure fizz from the soda had gone up into his nose. There were too many onlookers to talk privately. Without saying a word, they both had the same idea to leave.

Outside on Ashburton Avenue, standing in front of Restivo's Florist, they began to talk freely.

Herman nudged Cookie for the fifth time. "I'd be sweet on him too. He's mighty fine looking."

Cookie shrugged. She didn't know if she should say anything. She still hadn't admitted to herself she had a crush on this guy.

"Isn't he kind of old for you?"

"I guess. I don't know."

"I know you liked Blind Owl Alan Wilson, but it wasn't real."

"What do you mean it wasn't real? It was very real to me."

"Cookie, you know what I mean. This guy is right here! In Yonkers! And just now he was right in your face! I mean, who is this guy? What is he doing with his life? He's hanging around at a bakery in the afternoon checking out high school girls! He's a loser, if you ask me!"

"He hasn't tried to pick me up! He hasn't tried to do anything. Not even a kiss!"

"Just wait!" Herman's eyes jumped, increased in intensity, getting more dark than green. "You just wait!"

They huddled into a doorway in a dark corner where the streetlights did not reach. Cookie pulled out a Marlboro and lit it, handing it to Herman before she took a deep drag. Restivo's Florist had closed for the day. The store lights were off, but the refrigerated cases displaying floral arrangements, carnations, and roses were shining with white light. White buckets full of gladiolas stood tall in the bottom of the refrigerated display case. Halloween had passed but the decorations stayed up. Jack o'lanterns, some carved, some painted by hand, sat on top of the check-out counter, and in every nook and cranny. Black paper witches on broomsticks were strung on a wire across the front of the storefront window as though they were flying through a night sky. Orange and black letters spelled out Happy Halloween.

Herman handed the cigarette back to Cookie. "What's gotten into you?"

"I don't know." She stared through the florist window at a bouquet of miniature pink rosebuds and baby's breath. "I guess I should tell you what happened..."

Cookie saw a stream of smoke coming out of her mouth and the gleam of her teeth in the florist's window. Her front teeth looked good. No one could tell her molars had crumbled. She suffered from small toothaches, surging pings of pain, eventually going away on their own. Sadly, she had stopped trying to crack her gum.

"I caught him red-handed with another woman," she told Herman.

"The blond guy?"

"Will you forget about the blond guy! I'm talking about my father," Cookie said, looking away. "I don't know where to go or what to do. I can't completely run away because Donny's stuck there too."

"Man, I'm sorry, Cookie. Can't you find someone to help? Isn't your grandmother still alive?"

Cookie nodded grimly. She had not seen her grandmother

in nearly three years. She didn't have a grown-up to share her story. And what was worse, she had lost her words. Then she thought of the one thing really bothering her. Kissing.

Seemingly out of the blue, she asked Herman, "Are you worried about kissing?"

Herman shook his head with confusion, quickly turning to shock. "Man, I can't believe you would ask me such a thing. Cookie, that is so cold! I mean I live with my mouth every day and the way people stare at me. Kissing! I guess I'll get to that, eventually, but right now, you saying that to me feels cold. Cruel! I don't know why. I just didn't expect it, I guess."

"I'm sorry," she told him. "Herman, I didn't mean it...I don't know why I said that." She put her hand on his shoulder, but he shrugged it off and put his hands in his pockets, hunkering down to protect himself.

Even in the midst of her apology, she knew she had made a terrible mistake. Whatever she had discussed with Herman in the past, and despite the depth of the bond between them, the sanctity of their friendship had been called into question, and maybe even broken beyond repair.

Herman did not resume his easygoing banter. Mentioning his deformity within the context of kissing was the wrong thing to do. All along he might have been worried about the same things as Cookie, except he had a stigma—whenever people looked at him, they noticed his color first and then his mouth.

Cookie thought his harelip made him more endearing. She had not considered Herman did not feel the same way. He no longer cared to talk to her about the world, or about anything. He grew quiet and remote. Cookie could not reach him. She tried to back pedal and undo what she had said, and why it mattered to her, but the damage had been done and sometimes things cannot be fixed.

Eleven

Kissing Jack Goodbye

Cookie wore an earphone so she could listen to music on her robin-egg blue transistor radio and not have to talk to anyone on the bus. The news break droned a tribute to Jack Kennedy. Eight years later, on Monday, November 22, 1971, no one knew for sure who was behind his murder. Oh, there were theories, more than you could shake a stick at, but nobody had gone to jail.

Small slivers of pain pricked Cookie's heart, just thinking about the slain President. Yonkersites never forget anything. They will talk about someone who died forty years ago as if the death happened an hour ago. And even now, it still seemed as though the big event, his death, had just happened.

Women of all ages took to the streets weeping, balling their eyes out, moaning, clutching their chests and sobbing. Men were crying too. Young, old, age didn't matter, men were fighting back tears or collapsing into heaps. You had to be there to witness the spectacle. What a sight—so many people crying in the streets! It had been eight years since President John Fitzgerald Kennedy had been killed in Dallas. They might call it an assassination, but the plain fact of the matter is most of the back of his head had been blown off. Someone killed him and got away with it.

Eight years had passed since Cookie had been told to kneel on the floor beside her school desk and say a prayer because the President had been shot. She prayed fervently with all of her heart. And in the next instant, even before the shock had set in, she was told he was dead. The prayers had done no good. Cookie knew, most of the time, prayers didn't work.

No one in Yonkers would ever forget President Kennedy because he had not forgotten them. In 1960, while campaigning for the presidency, the young Senator from Massachusetts came to Yonkers and rode in an open car through Larkin Plaza in Getty Square. Old timers called him Jack Kennedy. He didn't just belong to them; he was one of them. People still talked about the day young Jack Kennedy had put Yonkers on the map.

William Manchester's book *Death of a President* had come out in 1967. Kitty Colangelo read the serialized chapters published in *Look Magazine*. Then Kitty bought this book determined to know what had happened to Jack Kennedy; and it was funny to see Kitty reading the book because she never read anything. Irish Catholic, she regarded the Camelot kingdom of Jack Kennedy to be far greater than the second coming of Jesus Christ. Devastated by Kennedy's death, Kitty often fussed someone was hiding the truth from her. She didn't know the truth was being hidden from everyone, not just crazy people.

One of the best things about Kitty was that she admitted she was crazy. Kitty often said, *they used to call people like me queer. I am a little odd, different you might say*, then she would giggle.

Wearing an earphone made Cookie oblivious to the world and she felt immeasurably happy, sort of smug. The song *Wild Thing* played by the English Band the Troggs screeched in her ears. She'd mouth the lyrics but hated to mimic other people's words because they were not her own. Going through a stubborn phase in her life, she didn't want to listen to any other words unless they were her words. She hated when the radio stations belched old music, and especially this song *Wild Thing*, because now she had grown too old to be a wild child. Cookie felt like she was all grown up—fifteen, but who's counting?

It had been over two years since she had gone to Woodstock. By now, every girl she knew had lost her virginity. Not Cookie. She was so not like other girls. Every time she thought she liked a boy, she found something terribly wrong with him and froze up like a block of ice from the old Yonkers icehouse. Grandpa Jack had worked there as an iceman. He used to drive a truck, delivering ice all over the city, back in the day, before refrigeration. Years later, when every home, flat, or walkup had a refrigerator, Grandpa Jack was out of a job. He only had a fourth-grade education and little training. He became a night watchman at a Catholic children's orphanage in the city, working there for forty years. Too bad. Now he was dead.

Everyone in the family called Grandpa Jack *Old Jack* as a way of distinguishing him from *The Jack*, the number one Jack, Jack Kennedy. For a long time, family members called them *The Two Jacks*. Things could be confusing in a crazy, Irish Catholic household.

The Number 2 bus stopped in front of Louie's Italian restaurant on South Broadway, where she got off and turned the corner to walk up Herriot Street, going west up a small sloping hill. Herriot Street was a modest hill in a city priding itself for having many impossibly steep hills. Like Rome, some called Yonkers the city of seven hills: Nodine Hill, Park Hill, Church Hill, Cross Hill, Glen Hill, Ridge Hill and Locust Hill. What were they thinking when they came up with the name Locust Hill? Cookie wondered if there were lots of locusts there, biting poor people on the ass to make them work harder.

Up the hill, down the hill. Up the hill, down the hill. Let me tell you something: Yonkers ain't no Rome. Never was and never will be. As much as Yonkersites liked to exaggerate and romanticize the past, more often than not, people here were small-minded and mean-spirited—the progeny of hardscrabble immigrants who came over to America, clawing their way out of vermin-infested squalor to move up a notch.

Herriot Hill was nowhere as steep as Park Hill, but she prepared herself for a terrible climb. Overlooking magnificent views to the Hudson river, Park Hill lorded over southwest Yonkers as though it was a city of Greek gods looking down at the working-class slaves who toiled away one step up from poverty. The great unwashed masses did not venture up to the gilded Victorian and Georgian Colonial mansions of Park Hill. The neighborhood had hit its stride in the 19th century, when Yonkers had earned its reputation as the *city of gracious living*.

Making her way up Herriot, she caught a whiff of the food from the exhaust fan coming out of the kitchen of Louie's Italian restaurant. The scent of warm Italian food hitting the cold air made it more tempting and mouth-watering. Her stomach rumbled at the thought of Louie's eggplant parmesan sandwiches, which were known to be the best in the city and called wedges, not hoagies or heros. Louie's also had the best baked lasagna. She thought the aroma wafting into the air from restaurant kitchens always smelled more acute in cold weather.

A light mist straddled on the edge of becoming freezing rain. The radio said today's low of 35 degrees was almost freezing, but tomorrow, it would get really cold, dipping down into the twenties. By then the rain would stop and there would be no snow. Weather forecasts were not always accurate, and tomorrow a sneaky snowstorm could take everyone by surprise.

During the long winter, snow and ice on the hills of Yonkers created traffic problems. Cars often got stuck on the ice, spun out of control and slid broadside down hills, stopping at nothing until they hit something hard or bottomed out. People would get out of their cars and just leave them there, hoping a thaw would come by morning. Traffic backed up behind stalled and abandoned vehicles, blocking snowplows. The salt trucks avoided the steepest hills for fear of skidding to a certain icy demise. Dents, wrecks, and fatalities dotted the news briefs and obituaries in the *Yonkers Herald Statesman*. A popular urban legend claimed Elisha Graves Otis chose Yonkers to build the first elevator because he had been inspired by the city's many treacherous hills.

The aroma of Italian food flooding the air from Louie's reminded Cookie the Irish did not know how to cook. Even their funerals served up bad or mediocre food. Cookie realized she had not eaten since the morning. She had cut out of the last two periods of school and walked to Ashburton Avenue and beyond, almost to Nepperhan Avenue, before circling back up toward Broadway, where she could catch the bus. The light drizzle dampened her skin and left a fine mist on her jacket. She needed the cold air to keep her alert and felt grateful that a hard rain had not yet begun to fall.

Old Jack had ten grandchildren, and among the pack, Cookie was the only grandchild who had not gone to the hospital to pay her respects before he had died. She didn't know he was dying. Neither did he. He had never been to a hospital in his entire life. He only went this time because his stomach hurt a lot. When the surgeons opened him up, they found he had a blockage and said it was inoperable. He died two days later. On both sides of Cookie's family, no one went to a hospital unless they absolutely had to, and within days of being admitted, death arrived like an old, welcoming friend.

Old Jack had always lived with Grandmother Delia on Jackson Street. The quiet street in front of the old clapboard tenement was deserted. The whole neighborhood had become mixed. The 'hood used to be predominantly Irish, with a sprinkling of Polish and Jewish families. Now it was black and Puerto Rican. Many of the old-timers had passed on or moved away. Delia's neighbors on both sides were black, and the two families directly across the street were Puerto Rican. Color didn't matter much to Delia. She spent many summer afternoons dancing to her neighbor's boom box cranked high and perched on the sidewalk in front of her front stoop. Everyone on the block knew this old woman liked to dance.

Cookie pushed open the chain link gate in front; it squealed grating metal, and the bottom of its frame dragged a bit on the concrete ground. She closed the gate behind her and pushed its latch down to lock it in place. She didn't bother to knock on the heavy outer door and pushed it open. Both sides of the door had been heavily varnished with olive green oil paint, and for as long as Cookie could remember, the door had always been the same color. The narrow hall led to a first-floor apartment where Old Jack had lived. Metal tread steps were sized differently, uneven in height, stacked in the pattern of a jigsaw, and covered with faded turquoise linoleum. The steps led upstairs to second floor apartment, but no one lived there.

Cookie knocked on the inner door leading to her grandmother's apartment. At first no one responded. She put her head against the door and listened, but she couldn't hear anything. Then the door flew open quickly, knocking her off balance, and snapping back her head. Grandmother Delia gave her a faint smile. Her eyes were pale and blue and could have looked as bright as Donny's eyes before they had dimmed with age. She didn't invite Cookie inside and simply stepped away from the door to make room for the both of them.

"I was just fixing some tea." Delia wore a faded blue housedress and soft slippers snugly fitting her feet, complementing her petite steps. She reminded Cookie of her mother, except Delia wasn't as seriously deranged as Kitty. Delia was prone to intermittent bouts of melancholy, which were unavoidable; she was Irish Catholic and the personification of the Virgin Mary, a martyr living on the outer edge of sainthood.

Delia walked over to the refrigerator where she took out a white box labeled *Entenmann's*. She raised the lid and showed Cookie an iced chocolate cake. About half of the cake was gone. "I'm going to have a bit of cake. I know you like to have your cake and eat it too." She gave Cookie a peculiar smile, suggesting a wink.

Cookie felt like lighting up a Marlboro, but the strong odor of gas lingered in the kitchen and seemed to permeate the walls and furniture. It could have been a low-grade leak, but all of these tenements smelled the same. Gas could be leaking all over South Yonkers, but no one ever mentioned it or seemed to mind.

She watched her grandmother move around the kitchen. She lifted a latch and opened a cupboard in the dry sink where she took out a box of Lipton tea. Everything in her kitchen was a relic from an earlier time. A massive dry sink had two cabinets on the upper half and two below. Chipped and scarred around the edges, a white lacquered countertop exposed its black metal frame. Before indoor plumbing, everyone had dry sinks. The large sink constructed from cast iron had been built as a modern improvement generations ago. Above the sink, two tall built-in cabinets bore faint cracks in the wood, and paint peeled in a few spots. Everything in the kitchen needed to be replaced. It would never occur to Delia to make a change because everything still worked. The white GE refrigerator had stood in the same place since the 1930s.

The phone in the kitchen began ringing. Delia moved toward the black rotary dial phone mounted to the wall but not quickly enough and it stopped on the third ring. "They'll call back," she said.

Delia pulled a small pot out from the oven and filled it with water. She didn't own a tea kettle and preferred to boil water in a small aluminum pot shaped like a saucepan, only it did not have a cover. Striking a match, she turned the dial on top of the stove and lit the gas burner. An erratic blue flame ignited under the pot. She sat down across from Cookie but didn't look at her for too long. Her eyes wandered around the room. She seemed to be searching for the words she wanted to say.

"Too bad you had to leave Sacred Heart. Sacred Heart was a nice school."

"No big deal. I go to Blessed Sacrament Academy now. You know, BSA."

Her grandmother seemed only mildly interested. "Oh yeah, what's that like?"

"We call it the Bull Shit Academy. Get it? BSA."

"You always were a card," Delia said in a strained, fey voice.

"I don't know," Cookie said. "BSA girls used to wear hiked skirts like everyone else, but not anymore. Now I have to wear this rag!"

Cookie stood up and yanked at her teal blue skirt. "This is not really a skirt." She tugged on her hem. "This skirt has secret compartments. Culottes!" She pulled the big fat pants and fanned them wide. "These culottes cannot be hiked! Wearing this skirt is like wearing a chastity belt."

Delia avoided looking at Cookie. Scanning the surface of the kitchen table, she said, "So long as you're at a Catholic School, everything will be alright."

"This skirt is a way to protect our *hooches* from men!"

Delia looked mildly amused. "I don't think I've heard that term before."

"I don't know what it means either," Cookie confessed. "I just thought I'd put it out there."

"You've always had a way with words." Delia looked toward the stove to see if the water had come to boil yet. She was very obviously not having the time of her life.

"I've lost my words too," Cookie said. "I don't know what to say any more and I can't write."

"I'm sure you're exaggerating," Delia scoffed. "What are you going to do with all of those big words anyway?" She pushed forward the box cake, offering a piece to Cookie. "They say the Irish have a way with words."

Cookie was hungry but didn't feel like eating chocolate cake and pushed the box away. She had never noticed before how cold her grandmother's eyes looked. She wasn't cruel, but she didn't seem to have much in the way of feelings. The way she chattered incessantly about things seemed shallow. She'd fuss about the neighbors having visitors coming and going in the middle of the night but hardly noticed when the city shut off her water for two days because utility crews had accidentally broken a water main.

Delia filled up her bathtub with water and let it stand for days until it turned grey. She had developed this habit during the Great Depression when water and soap ran scarce. Delia didn't have a washing machine because there was no room for one. She washed her clothes in the bathtub and hung her lingerie out to dry on the shower curtain rod. Delia belonged to the generation of women who didn't shower, and only occasionally took full-body immersion baths; her daily regimen consisted of sponge baths with a plain white washcloth.

She ate her cake, pausing in between each tiny bite. "I don't have much food in the house. I haven't gone shopping everyday like I used to since Jack died."

"He's been gone for three years," Cookie said.

"I know," Delia said. "It still seems like yesterday. Maybe I'll go shopping tomorrow after mass is over."

When Cookie was four, Kitty was sick and had gone to the nuthouse; Johnny had to work, so she lived with Delia for six months. Cookie was closer to her grandmother than all of the other grandchildren, but Delia did not get too close to anyone. Cookie felt as though a wedge had come between them. Ever since Old Jack had died, Delia became trapped in the past. And yet, Cookie felt she owed her grandmother an apology of sorts.

"I came to tell you I'm sorry I didn't visit Grandpa Jack. I didn't know he was so sick."

"No one did." Delia turned around and checked on the water. "But he's gone and he's not coming back."

Cookie stared at her grandmother, trying to see if she could feel her sadness, her pain, but she just felt emptiness emanating from the woman, as if she had been laid bare, nary a stitch of clothing, underneath her full suit of armor. The sensation made Cookie feel empty inside. She had nothing to give. Neither did her grandmother. Delia had come to closure with something only she knew about. Her husband had died, her children were long grown, and she had so little emotion. No tears. No sadness. Nothing.

There was no way her grandmother could handle a conversation about what should be done about Johnny and the blond woman.

Cookie repositioned herself, drawing in her breath, to pursue a different reason for visiting Delia. "Mind if I ask you a question?" Cookie covered her hand over her mouth, suppressing laughter, but it was a fake gesture. "What I have to ask you could be embarrassing."

"What's this about?" Delia's face was full of mischief. Jack had been full of piss and vinegar too; the two of them, overgrown toddlers in spirit, always playing pranks like twin leprechauns who had red hot hearts.

Cookie could barely talk and fumbled for the right words. When she started to say something, her voice became winded. "I never saw Grandpa Jack kiss you. Did he ever kiss you?"

"Oh that." Delia waved her hand, giving Cookie a brush off. "Oh that," she said again and laughed. "There was none of that. I was a virgin when I met Jack."

"A lot of men don't know how to kiss." Cookie knew her grandmother well enough to know she didn't like being put on the spot. "Was Jack a good kisser?"

"You don't need to kiss to get pregnant! But it does help to be wet!"

Cookie raised her eyebrows. "Come on, you're pulling my leg."

"You ask the wrong questions and you get zinger answers. How do like them apples?"

Delia had stiffened in her chair and she looked at Cookie with a touch of venom. "Before they closed his casket, I kissed Jack when he was dead. His lips felt cold."

Delia scrutinized Cookie's face to see if she had succeeded in shocking her granddaughter, but she hadn't. Cookie didn't even blink.

"What's all this stuff about kissing, for god sakes?" Delia stood up and helped herself to a larger piece of cake. "You always did have big dreams, bigger than anyone else I know. You're too big for your britches."

Turning off the stove, she poured water from the pan into a fragile hand-painted porcelain teacup with a tiny chip on the handle. Delia preferred her tea black and let it steep good and long. "Too bad Jack's not here. He always liked to take a small piece of cake and he'd make you eat some too. Remember how he'd always give you something sweet to eat?"

Cookie saw his cane leaning against the wall under the black rotary dial phone. She picked up the cane and started walking around the room with it, hobbling as though she was too old to walk without assistance.

"That's really not funny." Delia took on the airs of a somber child. "You should leave his cane alone. He had a bad foot."

Cookie put the cane back. "Grandpa Jack could be very funny. Do you remember how he pulled out his own teeth when they went bad and kept them in a jar? Then he used to pull out the jar and show us how many teeth were inside. The jar was full of teeth! And he used to shake it. He'd rattle the jar the way skeletons rattle their bones. He'd scare us all to death."

Delia looked up and gave Cookie a small smile, but she didn't laugh, which was sad, because Cookie was trying to get her to laugh.

"You always used to tell him to stop scaring the children. But he never did. He never listened to you." Cookie leaned in closer to her grandmother. "He always gave you a hard time. He liked to get a rise out of you."

Delia didn't say anything. She didn't have to. There had always been an uneasy tension between them. Cookie thought of her grandmother's world as small and stifling; Delia rarely ventured farther north than Getty Square or farther south than St. Peter's Church on Ludlow Street, unless she had to visit relatives. She hardly ever came to visit Kitty, and Cookie resented her, the matriarch of the family, for not helping out and acting more grown-up.

"Think I'll have a beer." Cookie got up and reached to pull down the door handle to open the refrigerator.

"Oh, no, don't do that. That's Jack's beer."

"And he's not coming back." Cookie eyed the contents of the refrigerator, searching for beer. She pulled out a can of Ballantine, took a can opener from the side of the refrigerator and opened the can. She took a long chug and burped. "I just had to do something to show I'm still the same bad kid that I've always been."

Delia let go of a hearty laugh. "I've never had any doubt," she said, motioning with the sign of the cross. "You've always been a troublemaker." Delia was starting to sound like her own self.

"I hate beer. Always have. Always will." Cookie emptied the can into the sink. "I'm just trying to be a show-off. I can do anything I want to do."

"You always were wild."

"I just came by to see how you're doing." She came up to Delia's side and kissed her lightly on the cheek. Her grandmother smelled like strong soap, the old-fashioned kind made from lye. "I'm sorry I don't come by more often."

"Jack didn't last long. I wish he had more time." Delia dropped her hands into her lap and began to brood. "I wish we all had more time. Who knows where the time goes?"

Becoming pale, she looked up at Cookie, and her shoulders sagged as if all of her energy had fled from her body. "Today's the day Jack Kennedy was killed."

"I know," Cookie said. "Losing your husband the same day Jack Kennedy died is just too much for any one person."

"It's been three years already. Three years for my Jack and eight years for Jack Kennedy..." Her voice turned meek, childlike. "Seems like yesterday. We had a handsome President. The first Irish Catholic. And my Jack was still alive."

Delia didn't bother to look at her granddaughter and seemed to focus on her hands in her lap. She certainly did not cry, not even a sniffle. "I just wish I had more time with him. He's the only man I've ever been with."

Cookie sighed to herself. She couldn't imagine being with only one guy. A Yonkers Guy. "What a horror!" she cried out.

"Aren't you fresh!" Delia didn't look happy. Her lips pressed together in a tight grimace, belying her true feelings; she had always been stingy with her emotions, unable to care much about anyone.

"Here's more than a penny for your thoughts," Delia said. She pulled a five dollar bill out of her faded black leather change purse covered with scratch marks.

"Cookie, don't tell nobody that I gave you money, and it's not even the holidays," she whispered. "Next thing I know they'll be wanting something from me and get jealous if I don't give it to them."

Delia was referring to the other nine grandchildren. Delia had a long-standing habit of giving each grandkid ten dollars for holidays and each birthday. She didn't have a checkbook, so on special occasions, she went to the bank and had money orders drafted.

Stuffing the five-dollar bill into Cookie's hand, a look of mischief sparked in her two pale blue eyes. "Don't say nothing about this, that I gave you money."

Delia reminded Cookie of a doll. She acted like a girl who had suffered from an event so traumatic she had been prevented from growing up. And this much was true. She had experienced great tragedy.

"You do remember what happened to Tiny Ten Pint?" Delia reminded her. "The same thing could happen to you if you're not careful with the beer."

Cookie scoffed and shook her head.

"You mark my words," Delia said, pointing her finger as an admonition. "Don't ever tempt God or the Devil, which is really the same thing. God can be a devil and the devil wants to be God."

The story about Tiny Ten Pint had been passed down in crude oral tradition. When Delia was two, both of her sisters had died. Mary was four, Josephine an infant. A doctor came to the house to examine Mary and left his gloves on the bed next to the baby. Mary was sent to the pest house to be quarantined and died there. Josephine had been accidentally infected by the doctor's gloves and died at home. Great Grandpa Tynan O'Toole, known as *Tiny Ten Pint*, was driven to the drink and became a binge drinker. As it turned out, the Great Influenza killed Mary and Josephine, and so many other children. Everyone said Tiny Ten Pint had a curse on him until the day he became cured from the drink.

Of the three girls, Delia was the only daughter who had survived the Great Influenza. Delia's mother, Cookie's Great Grandmother Mary, treated her surviving daughter like a precious doll and smothered her to keep her safe from illness and harm. As a result, Delia never grew up, a young girl forever frozen in time.

Delia's story was only one among many making Yonkers tragic and sad but hopeful and human too. The city had grown to become a refuge for the immigrants who came to America and were looking for a chance. Every block had a church for every denomination and a synagogue. There were community centers, dance halls and neighborhood restaurants. Men could find work, and the women took care of their families. Every 'hood had its own bakery, bar, grocer, hardware store and cobbler shop. Then the Vietnam War came, dividing the country, and Yonkers became a city torn in two.

So many years had passed since President John F. Kennedy had died. The time would come when people Cookie's age would forget President Kennedy's nickname Jack. There was something crazy about the Irish because they had to give everybody a nickname. And there was something much crazier about a country unable to find out the real reason why Jack Kennedy had died and who had really killed him. Right now, people still cared about what happened. But maybe someday they would not, and his memory would be gone, and he would no longer be in our hearts. And you have to wonder if Jack Kennedy had lived, whether we would have gone to Vietnam in the first place.

Twelve

Soldier Boy

Cookie moved about the basement as a reporter or a news anchor, posing questions while she spoke into the mic of her tape recorder. *After the Tet Offensive, couldn't they see a lot of our boys would not be coming home? Maimed, wounded, killed by the truckload, and look at what they're doing to the Vietnamese people! Why are they turning our boys into war criminals?*

The war continued in Vietnam. It had been six months since the Pentagon Papers had been released, revealing all along the U.S. government had been secretly escalating the war, sending more troops, and launching massive air strikes.

Fed up with the Vietnam War, she thought it had little to do with the tragic circumstances of her own life. She was weary of seeing the live coverage on TV and exasperated with the protesters whose activities were either childish or violent. Most of them were rich kids who didn't have to go to Vietnam. Everyone knew about the rich boys who got out of going to Vietnam. Money bought deferments and cooked-up medical excuses. But in Yonkers, working-class white boys and poor brown and black boys had no choice but to go. Some of them didn't come back.

Cookie stopped her tour around the basement and stood in front of the workbench. This place had once been covered with tools: hammers, screwdrivers, clamps, pliers, wood lathes, several saws, a drill, and many sizes of nails and screws. Shoved into Dellwood Dairy milk crates, the tools were of little consequence, and not organized but a messy hodgepodge of hammered metal and steel. The tools had belonged to Johnny, but he had forgotten about them. This workbench had become Cookie's sound studio, private and sacrosanct, where she could use her words to create the rhyme, image and rhythm of silly poems in ways different from putting her pen to paper or hunting and pecking keys on her old portable Remington typewriter.

She pressed the deck of the tape recorder and erased her report about Vietnam.

She had so little time to get to the heart of what was troubling her. On the other hand, being a teenager seemed to go on forever. She wanted to be grown up and living on her own, and at the same time she wished she could put the brakes on time and make it stop going forward so fast. It was a conundrum from which she had no hope other than to recover and push her confusion to the farthest recess of her mind.

She'd rather think about killing Johnny.

Since Kitty returned from the nuthouse, my parents' lives have gone on as usual. Their marriage is a sorry excuse for each of them to blame the other for their own shortcomings. That's too mild a way to describe Johnny and Kitty! My loving parents are total failures as human beings! And I feel like putting a hole in my father's snare drum!

"You shouldn't let anyone hear you talking like that, Cookie! I paid good money for that drum. Next thing, they'll come and lock you up in the nuthouse, just like your mother."

Johnny had been listening to her record her secret words. Ever since she caught him with the blond woman, he followed her around and tried to talk to her. She hated having him in her face.

She took off her headset, turned off the recorder, and pulled out the plug for good measure. "I have nothing to say to you."

"Cookie, come on, don't be like that. What's the matter, can't your father have friends?"

The tone of Johnny's voice was plaintive—as close to an apology as he could offer. "I don't mean no harm to nobody," he said, "especially not your mother."

"Go away," Cookie told him. "I no longer consider you to be my father. I consider you dead."

Johnny's grimace twisted into pain. It was the first time she had ever seen him look like he had been mortally wounded. "How could you say that? I'm your father, for Chrissakes! Know how many kids in this world don't even have a father to look after them?"

Johnny put his hand in his pocket to steady himself, took a few steps backward and leaned against the cellar wall. "I could have been dead, you know. How'd you like that! Then you wouldn't even be here today!"

He looked like he wanted to say more. Cookie knew he avoided talking about his past. As soon as he got close to talking about Korea, he beat a hasty retreat. Chances are he had never told anybody what had happened there.

Cookie felt a little sorry for him but not much. Whatever happened to him in Korea was no excuse for the blond woman. She set her headset on top of the tape recorder and dragged her worsted wool coat away from where it had been hung on a thick galvanized steel pipe. The basement was unfinished. Pipes and girders were exposed in the walls and ceiling. Patches of pink fiberglass insulation were randomly affixed to the rafters above Cookie's workbench.

"What the hell are you doing, Cookie? And why do you keep talking about this Vietnam War stuff? We're defending our nation against the communists! You act like you're a communist! What is it? Are you a communist?"

Cookie zipped up her coat but didn't bother to clasp the gold metal button bar close to her throat. The blue midi coat came down below her shins, almost covering her new white vinyl lace-up boots.

"Too bad that coat's not red, then you'd look like Little Red Riding Hood in that thing," Johnny said. "You should have gotten red! You want a red coat too? I'll buy you a red coat, or maybe some new boots. How about black boots? Come on, you like those go-go boots and I've gotta admit they look good on you. Jesus Christ, you're a pip. You've always been a pisser."

He worked hard to be nice to her, but the sound of his voice stung her ears. Cookie drew her hood up over her head to mute her father's voice, leapfrogged away from him and bounded out of the cellar door.

"Where are you going?" Johnny called after her, but Cookie did not look back.

"Try to figure it out," she said to herself.

She ran up the steps and burst through the front door of the house. She saw Johnny coming down the side steps, heading for his car. This game of cat and mouse had begun. He was going to follow her to see where she was going. She outwitted him by not going anywhere and returning to the house. She was a thousand times more cunning than her father.

She heard her father's Buick start up and careen down the hill, squealing slightly amid two short knocks, which could have been the sound of a fan belt as loose as the screw in his brain. She stood on top of the steps, lit a Marlboro and laughed.

Kitty opened the front door and when she saw Cookie laughing, she laughed too as a spontaneous reaction. "Your father said you're doing real nice at your new school. It's good that you're going to a new school. I'm so proud of you, honey. I know you have your stories to tell."

Cookie didn't have the heart to tell her mother she had lost her words. She came up to her mother and kissed her on the cheek. Kitty responded by patting Cookie's hand. This was as close as the two would ever get at making a connection. As far as Cookie was concerned, reaching Kitty, even in a small way, was a profound accomplishment. Kitty had allowed her to take the tip of her toe to tap open the front door into her inner world.

Her mother was the most beautiful woman! Her skin hinted of a slight flush and her lips, made red by Elizabeth Arden lipstick, parted in a playful pout. Her hair had been freshly coifed into a shining mane streaked with natural auburn highlights made apparent by the December afternoon sun. When she smiled at Cookie, all was right with the world. It was hard to believe a month ago she was as mad as a shad.

"I like your coat, too. Did you get that at Korvettes, honey?"

The chain store Korvettes sold everything, from clothing and cosmetics to washing machines and lawn mowers, at a deep discount. Its real name was E.J. Korvette but everyone called it Korvettes for short. Everyone said the name came from eight World War II Veterans, who were Korean, but it wasn't true. The store had been named for its founder Eugene Ferkauf, who was a Jewish veteran of World War II and not Korean.

Kitty patted her sleeve like she was petting a dog. "It looks so nice on you and that clasp around your neck makes you resemble a bellwether leading your flock in the right direction."

Cookie wondered how her mother had come up with a bellwether leading your flock in the right direction. She thought to ask her, but quickly decided against it. It took too much effort to probe the inner workings of her mother's brain, only to learn everything made sense to her but not to anyone else.

Hell's Bells, Cookie thought to herself. Bellwether made her think of the expression Hell's Bells she had heard in a 1940s movie. It was the same as saying Hell if I know! Cookie leaned forward without stepping into the house. Donny sat on the olive-green carpeted steps and gave Cookie a big grin. Everything was okay. For now.

By the time Cookie finished her Marlboro, she figured Johnny had gone around the block and traveled *Down the End* a few times looking for her before turning back. Sure enough, she spied his red Buick at the bottom of the hill, cruising slowly on Roberts Lane. The turn onto Argyle Terrace was one-way and it would take him about three minutes to travel around the block. By the time Johnny returned to the house, Cookie would be gone.

On Park Avenue, frigid air blew open the bottom of her long coat. She was grateful for the coat's warmth and the hood covering her head. The temperature had sunk into the low twenties. With the wind chill, it felt a lot colder. A row of trim trees clustered together on a lawn as hard looking as frozen tundra. The tops of the trees trembled in the wind. A small stone white-washed bench was partially hidden in the hedges.

Everything looked dead at Whalen's Funeral Home, and rightfully so, because a funeral was taking place. The small crowd looked mostly Irish, with skin predominately pale and freckly, or red and ruddy. Some faces were familiar from *The Heart* and *Down the End*. Short, red-headed Pinky O'Hearn made a career out of being a Yonkers guy—for years, he had hung out at Donaghey's Pub *Down the End*, or at Jimmy the Midget's Bar on Nodine Hill. But today he wore a suit and helped to lift the casket out from the back of the hearse. Draped with an American flag, the casket undoubtedly carried the last remains of a soldier boy. Flag draped caskets were not an unusual sight in Yonkers. A couple of other guys were helping too. Pallbearers heaved the casket up onto their shoulders.

She recognized one of the pallbearers. A shimmer of light cascaded the length of Stanley de Falco's long blond braid. He looked uncomfortable dressed in a dark suit. Surprised to see Stanley in the company of Pinky O'Hearn, she wondered what had brought the two of them together. They were as different as two guys could be. Pinky, the Yonkers guy through and through, would never leave and ultimately die here. Stanley looked like he was just passing through. Heat came to her face like sudden sunburn. She knew the sensation did not come from the wind and the cold. Every time she ran into him, she drifted into a fugue-like state. Some unseen sexual spark she did not understand smoldered beneath her own skin.

An old man with a pink bubble face and a few wisps of light brown hair stood next to Pinky's sister Peg O'Hearn, who would be a senior by now at *The Heart*. Out of uniform, Peg was almost unrecognizable except she wore a black lace mantilla over her hair, as red and as curly as Pinky's but much longer.

Whalen's Funeral Home served the Irish Catholics of Yonkers. Three years ago, Grandpa Jack had his funeral here. A gust from the river lifted Peg O'Hearn's mantilla and caused the lace to flutter around her pinched white face. The American flag flapped up from the casket and almost blew off, but Pinky held it down. The boy, man, whoever was in the casket, had come home.

No one cried. The Irish tended to be stoic about loss and suffering, a bit maudlin but only when they take to the drink. No use crying about it, Cookie thought. *Get over yourself and move on. Goodbye, Soldier Boy.*

Thirteen

Nodine Hill

The sky had begun to lose light. Cookie felt grateful for her long coat and hood because they concealed her identity. In the winter, she could walk about anonymously. Just south of Getty Square, she walked up the front steps of the library. It was the last place in the world Johnny Colangelo would think to look for her. She smirked to herself, thinking of how many times he would cruise the North End or her old haunt, Untermyer Park.

Almost closing time, hardly anyone was in the library. Mabel looked at Cookie and immediately sensed something was wrong, or maybe Herman had told her. Mabel came from behind the circulation desk and motioned Cookie to follow her upstairs. The Children's Reading Room was empty, except for a broad-shouldered woman hunched over a children's book.

"Come here, Cookie." Mabel led her to the alcove behind the stacks of books, inviting her to sit.

While she felt the warmth and grace of Mabel's presence, Cookie could not bring herself to let down and cry or show how sad she felt. Angry too. "Did Herman tell you what happened?"

Mabel nodded. "Boys will be boys. And I don't mean Herman, I mean your father." She looked up from her black-frame glasses and removed them where they fell around her neck, dangling from an amber-beaded chain. "But it doesn't mean it's right. Sooner or later, the chickens will come home to roost. That's what's happening here. Your father needs to grow up, but I'm not sure he's capable of it. No fault of his own. Everyone's different and we all expect different things from life."

"I don't want to live at home," Cookie said, "but I can't leave Donny there. And I can't take her with me."

"Give him a chance. He's probably very sorry about what happened. Maybe it's the right time for him to take stock of what's important. Wait and see."

Mabel talked about what Johnny had been through in Korea. What the war had done to him. And how he never had a chance to talk about what had happened. "I see these boys come home from Vietnam and they're a mess, so torn up from what they've seen and what some of them have had to do to survive."

"Everyone goes through pain," she said, "but not everyone knows how to grow from it." She patted Cookie on the hand and held on, but it felt different than when Kitty patted her hand. Sometimes Kitty tried her best to bring Cookie into her world. Mabel offered her the world—comfort and a prayer to hold in her heart.

In the far corner of the room, the woman stood up as though she had heard an alarm signaling closing time. When the woman turned around, Cookie recognized Bertha Sokól, the woman who worked at the Café Trento. Stanley's mother.

Bertha tied the scarf under her chin tight, turning it into a hooded kerchief. She wasn't wearing her fancy clothes like the ones she had worn the last time Cookie had seen her here. Her wool grey coat looked old and dusty. Between the ratty coat and her kerchief, she resembled a babushka. Bertha pushed her chair into the small table and headed out of the room. Before she reached the top of the steps, she turned back to look at Mabel and gave her a formal bow and a look of gratitude. Bertha gave Mabel every sign of respect she could show without having to talk. This was a much different side of Bertha than the woman who talked loudly at the Café Trento, hawking pastries and pounding bread. Her every move was subtle, almost tentative, as though her large body harbored a sylph whose feet barely touched the ground.

As soon as Bertha left, Mabel smiled at Cookie and told her, "I always know when she's been here. She leaves little traces of flour on the books. It's like following breadcrumbs to see what she's read."

By the time Cookie ventured outside, night had fallen. The sudden darkness obstructed her vision and made her feel bleak. It took a few moments for her eyes to adjust from the bright white light of the library to the dark, uncertain traffic on Nepperhan Avenue. In recent years, the crime rate had skyrocketed here, and everyone blamed it on the blacks— the encroachment of Ghetto Square. No one knew about the money changing hands among greedy real estate developers and corrupt politicians who were turning South Yonkers into a wasteland but whitewashing it under the guise of urban renewal.

On the street, her sight adjusted to the dark, and she saw Bertha Sokól trudging up the hill, breathing heavy. Having a hard time taking the hill, Bertha stopped every so often for a second to take a break. Looking like a wooly old bear, she pushed her body and pushed some more. By Cookie's reckoning, the woman was brutally strong and looked like the pictures of peasant women she had seen in the movie *Dr. Zhivago*.

Bertha gave up on the hill, parked herself on a bench in front of a bus stop and lit a cigarette. Cookie thought it might be interesting to see where she lived, but, of course, it had nothing to do with Stanley. She didn't want to get too close to Bertha to let her know she was considering following her home.

What better way to get to a guy than to make friends with his mother?

On the other side of the bench, Cookie sat across from Bertha and smiled.

"What do you smoke?"

Bertha had smooshed the end of her unfiltered cigarette right into her mouth. Her hand fanned open while two fingers pressed against the cigarette to keep it in her mouth for an extra-long drag. Releasing snorting plumes of smoke into the cold air, she eyed Cookie with suspicion.

"I smoke Pall Mall." Smoke shot out of her mouth and nose as she held up her maroon colored pack for Cookie to see.

"What's it to you?" The way she said *What's* made her sound funny. She used a V-sound *Vats* instead pronouncing *What's*.

"Where'd you come from?" Cookie pulled out her own Marlboro and lit it.

"Nodine Hill," Bertha said.

"No, I meant before that."

"The Bronx."

"I meant another country?"

Bertha had enough of her questions. "Shouldn't be smoking so young." Bertha eyed her as though she could see through her. "Do that and the boys won't want to kiss you."

"Unless they smoke too," Cookie shot back.

"My son doesn't smoke." She smiled. "And he doesn't like girls who do. He's always after me to stop, but I don't want to. It calms my nerves."

She looked at Cookie with such exquisite scrutiny she had to know Cookie was sweet on her son. "I don't smoke at home because Stanley doesn't like it," Bertha offered apologetically.

Bertha said something else, but Cookie couldn't hear her. The Nodine Hill bus let go of a steel belch and cranked to a stop, leaving a black puff of diesel exhaust. Smoke and street smells seemed sharper in colder temperatures. Bertha dropped her cigarette to the ground and stepped on it once, obviously an expert at snuffing cigarettes in one shot. One of the older buses in the fleet, the blue and white Nodine Hill bus had an oval-shaped body, rounded edges and a sloping chassis. Newer city buses were clean looking, green rectangular boxes with sharp angles.

Bertha smiled at the bus driver and called him *Joe*. The driver looked to be about eighty and wore an ivy wool cap. The driver knew Bertha and gave her a nod of recognition without saying anything. She dropped a quarter and a dime into the cash box. Cookie stayed right behind her and punched her money through the coin slot, so it dropped into the box with force and bounced on the bottom. Other people were getting on, but Cookie didn't focus so much on them. She paid attention to the side bench seat, closest to the driver, where Bertha plopped herself onto the worn red leatherette cushion.

"Sit here by me. Come and talk to me," Bertha said, patting the seat of the bus. "I never had no daughter, so maybe you can be the daughter I never had."

A minute ago, Bertha hardly seemed to notice Cookie. Now things were happening too quickly in Cookie's estimation. She didn't know what the hell she was doing on this bus going to a strange 'hood. Bertha spread her legs apart, planted her sensible black shoes firmly on the floor of the bus, set her worn black pocketbook on her lap and sat erect. Her posture was more than physical. She took pride in her strength.

The bus had an old standard shift transmission. Every time the driver shifted gears, the grinding noise made it hard for Cookie to hear Bertha.

"What's your name? I see you in the bakery where you left your keys, and in the library. I don't know your name or that colored boy you always seem to be with. Don't your parents mind you hanging around with the colored?"

Cookie shook her head. Normally, the question would make her mad, but she did not detect that Bertha was prejudiced, just that she was curious about Herman Lynch. "My name's Cookie."

"Cookie!" Bertha smiled, then laughed, clearing her throat from the smoke with a small cough. "No wonder why you like the bakery!" Then she leaned forward and whispered, "Come on, tell me. Is the colored boy your boyfriend?"

"What difference does it make?"

Bertha leaned further forward and looked at her closely. "Because you're pretty. I never was that pretty and I'd like to know what it's like."

"No, Herman's not my boyfriend. But I love him and he's my friend."

"That's nice." Bertha raised her eyebrows in confusion. She stared at the girl for a while, not smiling, not saying anything, as though she was making her mind up about something. She couldn't figure Cookie out, but that made her like her even more.

"I'm the next stop," she said. "Want to come home with me and have something to eat?"

"Where are you getting off?"

"Oak. Close to Maple Street."

Cookie debated going with her. She thought of staying on the bus and riding the full route, getting a transfer and then heading back to Ghetto Square to take the Number 2 bus home.

The bus climbed the steep hill of Maple Street, where the Yonkers Water Tower came into view. They were on the crest of Nodine Hill, passing row houses, tenements constructed of brick, wood or stucco. Most of the dwellings were over a hundred years old and had been built before World War I. The lower echelons of the working-class lived in tiny walk-up flats, one on top of the other. A social step below the North End, Nodine Hill was known as the *'hood of tree streets*. Flanked by Poplar, Beech, Oak, and Maple Streets, Nodine Hill had always been the toughest part of town.

People didn't have a yard and had to go to the laundromat to wash their clothes or do it in a tub in the kitchen sink because no one had washing machines. The neighborhood had always been a Polish, Ukrainian, and Slavic enclave that shared a block with the Park Hill section of Yonkers, where the Italians lived who didn't want anyone advancing on their turf and made their feelings known in street fights.

Bertha nudged her whole body against Cookie. "Next stop."

Cookie stood to pull the cord to let the driver know. Bertha hunched her shoulders and spoke confidentially, "He knows me. He knows where I get off. You don't have to do nothing but sit there and wait for him to stop."

Sure enough, the bus stopped by a row of three red brick buildings and one mustard yellow brick tenement, all three-stories.

"That's my house," Bertha said, pointing to a wood frame walkup with freshly painted dove white trim. Streaked with soot, the walls of the building were sorely in need of paint, and it was impossible to guess the original color.

A group of guys stood in front of a small red brick building on the corner of Oak and Maple. "That's the Midget Bar," Bertha told Cookie. "Those guys are waiting for Jimmy to open up. They're wild and only want to get drunk. They're not very nice to girls. Stay away from there. I wish my Stanley didn't go there. Since he come home, he goes there too much."

The boys in front of the Midget Bar didn't seem to notice Bertha, and if Cookie caught their attention, they didn't let on. There were no signs of Stanley. The stucco row houses came in rainbow colors: lime-colored concrete blocks, blunt burnt umber porticos hanging over short concrete stoops, dark red concrete cornices jutting out like bay windows, and thin strips of bright orange trim. Each bay had three narrow windows instead of a single pane of glass. Some windows were stuffed with portable air conditioning units. The windows were small and looked like they were painted shut; no one would ever be able to look out.

Bertha took small cautious steps but did not seem to be afraid of falling. Her purposeful foot movements continued to conjure a dainty woman. The sidewalk was darkened by soot and stained with dark spots from splattered oil and industrial waste. Jumbles of thick electric cables and spider-web strands of wires ran beneath the windows, or up the porticos in a fine tangled mess of utility lines.

Cookie committed the address, 98 Oak Street, to memory, while Bertha fished through her black pocketbook for her keys. Cookie's eyes followed the trail of her breath. The night had grown cold. Before she entered Bertha's building, she hesitated for a moment and saw his car, the marine green Oldsmobile Cutlass Supreme, parked farther up the hill on Maple Street.

"This place is a lot nicer than where I lived in the Bronx," Bertha told her. "There I was up on the fifth floor. Here I don't have to climb the steps so much." In the hall, Bertha checked her mailbox and stuffed two envelopes into the pocket of her coat without looking to see what they were.

Cookie nodded with uncertainty, not fully understanding what had brought her here. Bertha had already moved ahead and didn't see her. Two tin wall sconces masqueraded as candles. Tear-shaped bulbs cupped by patina leaves barely lit the dingy slate-blue walls of the hallway. Cumulative cooking odors permeating the hall were reminiscent of no food or cuisine in particular. Anything people cooked in their small flats had built up over time and left an indelible aroma as banal as cooking grease.

On the third floor, Bertha had her keys in her hand. Her keys were attached to several key chains, one a set of green tumbling dice, another a black & white photo of President Kennedy encased in clear plastic. The third key chain held an exquisitely carved miniature violin. Bertha pushed open her apartment door into a dark living room. Tiny but neat, the place smelled like strong vinegar and honey. She switched on the dome light that hung suspended above a square-shaped roughhewn oak table.

"I'll give you supper, then you can be on your way. Okay?"

She barely knew Bertha and now she was about to have dinner with her. Having a chance encounter with Bertha was not unusual for Cookie. She made a habit of attracting strange people. Being here had nothing to do with Stanley!

Bertha turned up the flame, making a blue flash pop under a large soup pot. She hummed to herself in a foreign language. Cookie didn't know any of the words, but they were melodious and suggested an ethnic folk song.

"What language is that?" Cookie asked.

"I'm Polish," Bertha said. "I thought you knew that." A large wooden washboard sat in a white cast iron sink fastened to the wall. The washboard had a riveted metal surface to scrub clothes clean. The sink had an unusually deep basin and a spotlessly clean drainboard countertop. White porcelain had chipped and worn away enough to reveal its black wrought iron frame.

Cookie worried about Donny but knew since Kitty had returned from the nuthouse she tried to act like a normal mother. And Johnny had glommed onto being an instant family man. He was like the perpetual odor in the hallway of this building.

In between the kitchen and the living room, Bertha hung her coat in the closet, clacking hangers as she shut the door. Bertha hadn't offered to take Cookie's coat. In this one room flat, no walls separated the living area from the kitchen. On further observation, Cookie decided the flat wasn't so neat but had the look of too many things crammed into too small a space. It looked like one person lived here, but someone new was camping out. Cluttered piles of clothing and overflowing bags stood in between the furniture. Clothes spilled out of a squat dresser. A trundle bed and a couch formed an L-shape against the chalky apricot-colored walls in the living area of the flat. A tall stack of newspapers sat by the front door.

Bertha took off her shoes and scuffed her feet into black & white, velvet, pointy-toed slippers, the kind with tassels. Cookie had only seen tassels on formal curtains and draperies in fancy magazines. Although Bertha had been previously light-footed, now she shuffled into the kitchen with an unexpected slow gait. She seemed tired. Cookie felt the same way.

But Stanley might come bursting through the door any moment! An exciting possibility, making her heart palpitate. His image and likeness rose to the top of her mind like a smoky apparition she could not shake off. She wondered if his hair would be in a tight braid or brushed back in a loose ponytail. She'd like to run her fingers through his hair and pull his face close to her face. Just as she imagined the first kiss between them, one of many to come, steam shot into the air with the force of an explosive cloud.

Bertha had lifted the lid on a heavy gauge dull aluminum pot. "I let my soup cook all day. I always have soup." She turned to Cookie. "Want some soup?"

Cookie didn't like the way it smelled but unbuttoned her coat and draped it on the back of a chair. She sat at the country-style farm table. Bertha ladled the thick soup into two earthenware bowls and set the steaming brew onto the table.

"It's called Kapuśniak," Bertha said. "Ever hear of it? It's good for your heart and your liver. It's got cabbage and sauerkraut. And the dumplings too. Let it cool." She blew across the surface of her soup with a heartfelt dramatic gust and offered to do the same for Cookie. Cookie was not willing to let Bertha breathe all over her soup. It was bad enough she had to eat this stuff.

Bertha had not noticed Cookie recoil, or maybe she had but did not care and continued to blow on her soup. Bertha struck Cookie as not caring what people think and doing whatever she wanted. Her way. If Johnny met her, he'd probably belt out *My Way* by Frank Sinatra. Johnny could be funny. He could look at a person and assign a signature song to fit with someone's personality. And even though she had the first good thought about her father since she had found him with the blond woman, she still wanted to kill him.

"The dumplings in the soup have potato in them. Pierogi," Bertha explained. "And this," she said, pushing forward another larger bowl, "this is my Golonka."

Two thick chunks of meat swam in a cloudy brown broth.

Cookie wrinkled her nose. "What is it?"

"Pork knuckles." Bertha spooned a hunk into Cookie's soup. "Try it," she said. "It's good for your skin. If you want to get the boys, you gotta have good skin. You've got to be rosy without the rouge."

Cookie took an ornate silver spoon and tried to take a taste. Too hot and it smelled sour. She took her time blowing on the broth while Bertha greedily ate, leaving little splashes of soup around her mouth.

She looked at Cookie and smiled knowingly. "My soup will also make your breasts grow bigger."

Cookie jerked her spoon, spilling soup on the front of her blouse. She looked down and saw three brown splotches.

"So sorry," Bertha said. "I didn't mean to make you nervous. Are you gonna need that blouse for school?"

"It's okay," Cookie said. "I have another one."

"When you're finished, I'll wash it for you.

Cookie nodded as though she agreed but said, "No, really, it's okay."

"I'll make it cleaner than anything you've ever seen."

Bertha slurped every spoonful of soup until she reached the bottom of the bowl. Then she picked it up, held it with two hands and drank every last drop. Cookie thought for sure she would belch. The woman wrinkled her nose as though she began to detect an unpleasant odor. "What's that funny smell?"

"I don't smell nothing," Cookie said, "except sauerkraut. Lots of sauerkraut."

Bertha leaned close to Cookie and sniffed. "It's you," she said. "I smelled it on the bus and almost didn't take you home. What's that stuff you're wearing?"

"Patchouli," Cookie offered.

"It stinks! Don't wear it no more. You're never going to get any boyfriends, if you wear that stuff." She pounded her fleshy arms on the table to emphasize her point. "I see all these girls do these things to themselves that aren't going to get them what they want. I know better. All I had was myself and I got what I wanted."

She picked up the two bowls from the table and went over to the kitchen sink, where she scraped the remnants into an unlabeled tin can. "I got the man I wanted," she said. "But he died. He died too young. He worked for the Otis Elevator company. One day he had an accident and he died. He left for work in the morning and he never came home that day or any other after that."

Cookie took the larger bowl from the table and stood by her side at the sink. "I'm sorry," she said.

"You never eat like this before? So, you like the food?" Bertha eyed her to see if she could tell the truth, no matter what Cookie might say.

Cookie evaded her question and walked away. She wondered if Stanley slept on the trundle bed or on the couch. Maybe the couch had a bed like a Castro convertible. She couldn't tell by looking at it. She found herself in front of the couch where Bertha had dropped her keys in a bowl on a coffee table. The third key chain with the miniature violin caught her attention.

"Do you like music?" she asked Bertha.

Bertha set the two bowls onto a dish rack to drain. She didn't say anything at first. Then she turned around and faced Cookie, giving her a somber gaze. "I have a beautiful violin. I used to play it in Poland. I don't play it here so much no more. People complain about my music. I'm not as good as I used to be. I'm out of practice. But I used to play like an angel."

She brushed her hands on the sides of her plain frock to dry them and gave Cookie a look, both tender and forlorn. "Someday,

I'll show you my violin, and maybe, I'll play it for you."

"Instead, I got this to play." She held up the old-fashioned wooden washboard and perched it precariously on the edge of the sink. "If you give me that shirt, I'll wash it for you."

Cookie looked down at the small stains on her blouse and shook her head. "That's okay, I'm fine."

"Sure?" Bertha asked.

"Sure." Cookie nodded. She was in no mood to take off her shirt. Unless…Stanley showed up, she mused to herself. Then she'd take off her shirt.

Bertha moved the washboard back into the sink basin. "This is all I got to play." She spoke wistfully, looking away from Cookie and toward the window. "Someday when I get a washing machine, I'll have time to play my violin again."

Walking backward, Cookie made her way out of the apartment. Bertha gave her a gap-tooth smile and closed the door behind her.

Up the hill, on the corner of Linden and Waverly Street, the Yonkers Water Tower beamed in the night sky like a rusty flying saucer. In the 1930s, the original water tower had burst at its seams, causing major flooding. Torrents of water washed down Elm Street, collapsing houses, displacing anything in its path: bicycles, garbage cans, cinder blocks, insulated milk boxes, radio flyer wagons, and trees.

Yonkersites are prone to exaggerate mightily and claim the bursting of the water tower is how Nodine Hill, 'hood of the tree streets, lost all of its trees. They also talk about the great flood barreling down the hill as the equivalent of Pennsylvania's Great Johnstown Flood in 1889. A new water tower was erected in the wake of the old one, where it stood as an attractive magnet for Yonkers kids to say, *I dare you to climb to the top*, and climb the tower as a rite of passage.

A lot of kids climbed. No one got killed or hurt. Not to anyone's recollection. If they had, the talk would have never stopped.

On this cold winter night in early December, though, high up on the hill, the water tower looked as lonely and as battered as a person who had endured too many beatings and had suffered too much. The tower was a frigging person. Getting beat up and showing no pain. Leaning into a fight, getting bloody, but never backing down to concede defeat—this was the Yonkers way, the only way.

Cookie waited for the bus across the street from where she had gotten off at the stop with Bertha. Other than seeing Stanley's car parked on the street, there was no sign of him. And if he was inside of the Midget Bar, she had no intention of walking into the bar alone. Not yet.

Fourteen

Grand Funk

A cold wind from the north flattened the Hudson River. The water looked icy and hardly exuded scent. Only diesel and carbon monoxide clung to the air. The late afternoon winter sun provided little light and no warmth. Cross currents of salt and fresh water surging through the pockets of dense marsh and tar needed warmth from the sun to rise and fill the cold air, in much the same way soup is warmed and brought to boil in a pot on an old gas stove. Heat made all of the difference in many things and especially in human relationships.

Down on the Kennedy Marina, boys and girls were in parked cars, with the motors racing, trying to stay warm, steaming up the windows. It was three days before the Winter Solstice, but no one called it a solstice. That concept was heathen-sounding and foreign to the Roman Catholic ethos of the Yonkers working-class culture in 1971.

On this Sunday afternoon, close to the shortest day of the year, the sun was about to go down. Soon there would be no light left in the sky. Cookie did not feel like walking home in the dark.

The steamy car windows could have been caused by warm bodies smoking, drinking, or heavily engaged in amorous activity. Small patches of ice had settled into an intricate pattern of lattice work on the ground. Cookie looked for Stanley's marine green Oldsmobile but didn't recognize any of the cars in the lot. She was in luck, though.

Toni Ferlinghetti pushed open a car door and stuck her head out. Her forehead screwed up in a snarky question mark. "Don't you have nowhere else to go?"

Cookie had not seen Toni since she had hooked up with Darrell Ricci at Lennon Park. Toni's orangey-blond hair had been dyed back to black, close to her natural hair color. Arky Lovato put his hand out the window and raised it high in a salute. He had snagged himself a 1962 Dodge Dart as grey and as muddy-looking as the river. Cookie intentionally bypassed Toni and went over to the driver's' side. Smoke hung like a curtain inside the car. Cookie tapped her toe against the rear door. "How about a ride?"

"Get in," Arky said. "It's cold outside. Don't want to let no more cold air in the car."

"I didn't say to let her in," Toni snapped. "I was just having some fun with her."

"Too late." The car door squealed as Cookie pulled it open and climbed into the back seat. She was relieved to find warmth. Her eyes traveled back to the old Kennedy Marina, where the ramshackle wharf was a deteriorating eyesore, a rotten mess of uneven boards, tarred rafters, chunks of wood and gaping holes. "I'm not ever walking on that thing again."

"Too bad you didn't fall in." Toni laughed and turned around to look at Cookie. "Remember that time I pushed you into the reservoir?"

"Did you have to bring that up?" Arky looked genuinely annoyed. "I had to jump in and get her."

Cookie turned away, looked out the window and lit a Marlboro. She cracked the window just a tad to let the smoke out.

"Still mad at me?" Toni gave her a big smile.

Cookie eyed her warily, waiting for the next barb, prod or poke. She didn't understand what made Toni so mean and wondered if it was worth her time to figure the whole thing out. She didn't want to be in the smoke-filled car, but it beat walking home in the dark.

"You coulda smoked the rest of my cigarette, you know," Toni chided her.

Cookie flicked her match out the window. "Don't want your germs. Might catch something bad, like the nasties."

Toni stuck her tongue out. She rolled down the window and threw out a half-smoked cigarette. She didn't care where it landed. A few ashes blew back in through the window she hastily rolled up. "Hope I didn't get ash in your eyes."

Toni gave Arky a smile loaded with charm, grounded in erotic promise and reeking of malevolence. "Let's get the hell out of here. Never liked it down here anyway."

Arky released the brake and gunned the motor of the car. They were going somewhere; anywhere was better than straddling the banks of the cold river. The car cruised south on Warburton Avenue, bouncing and thudding over potholes. Every time the car came to a stop, it squeaked. They hit every red light on Warburton Avenue. After so many stops, Cookie swore a family of rodents was chewing the brake lines.

"Not so fast," Toni said. "I didn't tell you where to go yet."

Cookie recognized an opportunity to scout for Stanley. She felt far too self-conscious to walk into the Midget Bar alone. If she had an entourage, then she'd have cover. While she had always been brave about going anywhere, this was a much different situation. The thought of chasing after a guy made her feel flustered. She had it in mind she'd like to get closer to Stanley but had to be cagey about it and make Toni think it was her idea to try something new and fun. "What's going on down near the square?" Cookie asked.

"What's happening?" Toni's voice warbled in the car.

No shocks, squeaky brakes, the Dodge Dart seemed as

reliable as a tin bucket of bolts, but it did have a good radio. Grand Funk Railroad's *I'm Your Captain/Closer to Home* blared, inspiring Arky to pound on his steering wheel as if he was playing the drums.

"Remember last year around this time?" Cookie yelled above the song. "Remember who came to town?"

Arky rocked hard in his seat. "Man, do I remember! Grand Funk Railroad!"

"That's cool!" Toni chirped.

"Were you there?" Cookie slyly asked her.

Toni didn't say anything. She began fidgeting with her hair, tossing her head back and then throwing it forward, fluffing her tresses up from the bottom. Without a comb, a brush or hairspray, she worked hard to make her big hair even bigger.

Cookie blew a plume of smoke toward Toni. "Did you get to see them, Toni?"

"No. So! What's the big deal!"

"I was there," Arky said, taking his hands off the wheel.

"Keep your frigging hands on the wheel," Toni yelled, turning down the volume on the radio.

"Stop picking on him! He's not doing anything wrong!" Cookie yelled. "Don't you get tired of her picking on you all the time?" she asked Arky.

Arky's grin slid to one side of his face and looked lopsided. "Grand Funk," he shouted. "We were at the RKO Theater! It was great! It will go down in history."

"We just happened to be watching a local band at the RKO," Cookie offered.

"The Headstones," Arky said. "They were outta sight."

"There was this guy who was a local promoter. He worked with all the bands in Yonkers, but he had connections! Pete Bennett was his name." Cookie expressively waved her hands in the air as if she was showing his name up in lights. "They call Pete Bennett *Mr. Entertainment*."

Arky might have been driving, but he turned away to look at Toni. "Pete Bennett kept coming out and telling us that Grand Funk was on their way. Nobody believed him. But nobody left either. Everybody hung around and waited to see what would happen."

"And it turned out to be true!" Cookie cracked open her window and flicked out her butt. "We were so hyped-up that when they finally came on stage, we were screaming our heads off! No one could believe Grand Funk Railroad showed up! For a brief moment in time, Grand Funk Railroad put the city of Yonkers on the map!"

Arky gesticulated his hands, leaving the steering wheel free. "The group shows up, stands on the stage, looks out at the screaming audience, bows...Then," he said, taking a deep breath, "then they just walked off."

"Do I have to drive the car for you!" Toni shrieked.

"Get that!" Arky said. "They walked off the stage!"

"I don't get it," Toni said. "What's the big deal?"

"Grand Funk Railroad left the stage without playing a single note. It was the weirdest event I've ever gone to." Arky turned around to look at Cookie in the backseat. "Remember, Cookie?"

"That's a concert I'll never forget. The crowd starts chanting 'Grand Funk, Grand Funk' at exactly the time as the band starts coming in from the back of the theater. The audience didn't even see it was them. Then all of a sudden, they're up there on the stage! That stage was made of rough wood and covered with strands of little white lights."

Toni rolled her eyes. "I can't believe you're talking about how the stage was made." She cradled her head into her hands. "I've got the weirdest headache coming on and it's all because of you."

"The theater was jam-full of people," Arky yelled. "We thought they were going to play a set!"

"Then nothing!" Cookie said. "Grand Funk just walked off the stage!"

Arky stepped on the gas too hard and the car lurched forward. "The place went crazy," he yelled.

"Like I'm going crazy," Toni seethed. "We're going to get into a car accident. I just know it."

"Worse than that," Cookie said. "It was love turned to hate! There they were, Grand Funk Railroad, in the spotlight before their adoring fans. Being in the spotlight has its ups and down. Once you're in the spotlight, you become responsible for everything that's gone wrong. One day fans could care less that you are even alive. Then the next day the focus is so intense that you are responsible for every single thing that has gone wrong in the world. Then the next day it's over and the feeling is gone—again. It's a cycle. Love turns to hate, and hate turns to love. Then it starts all over again."

"What is she talking about?" Toni asked Arky. "I am so sorry that you let her into this car." She turned around and looked at Cookie. "I think I've heard enough."

"The crowd went berserk and turned against Grand Funk because they didn't play. I remember that," Arky said.

The conversation came to an abrupt halt. Only sounds from the road and the mechanical realties of Arky's Dodge Dart persisted: doors rattling, brakes squeaking and a loud fan from the defroster that was not removing the condensation covering the windshield. From under his seat, Arky pulled out a rag to clean the window.

Cookie leaned forward and whispered in Toni's ear. "I hear tonight something cool's going on at the Midget Bar."

"Yeah, I know Jimmy." Arky nodded. "Really cool guy."

"Who asked you, Arky? I was talking to Toni." Cookie leaned forward even further. "Something real cool. Jimmy the Midget knows some musicians. Rich musicians," she whispered into Toni's ear. "Rich."

Toni raised her eyebrows. "How do you know?"

Cookie sat back, tilted her head to an angle, and looked

up at Toni. She gave her the sweetest smile she could muster. "Rich," she whispered again.

Toni shrugged. "If you say they're rich, then they're rich."

Arky took his eyes off the road to look at Toni. "Are we going?"

Toni nodded and shrugged. "Rich."

Cookie sat back in her seat and folded her arms. She had Toni just where she wanted her—believing a solid line of bullshit. Aside from being a dumb Italian girl, she was more gullible than Arky. Hard to imagine anyone could be dumber than Arky Lovato, but the Queen Bee had him beat, hands down.

The two of them sat in the car quibbling like an old married couple, while Cookie felt adrenaline rise from her heart to the back of her throat. Her stomach churned in knots and made a low grumble. She rubbed her clammy palms on the sides of her stiff blue jeans. Her feet had begun to sweat. Getting all choked up, her heart raced. Operating on a keener edge of exhilaration, she tried not to think about what would happen next.

If Stanley was there, what would she say to him?

On Nodine Hill, Arky pulled into an open space on Maple Street. It was bitterly cold and clear; the temperature had sunk to the low twenties. Car doors slamming shut in the cold made the sound of popping tin.

A walking poster for a 1940s sweater girl, Toni wasn't dressed to be outside in December. Her black cashmere sweater clung to her jumbo breasts and tiny waist. She made an arresting image; anyone who touched her, would be sure to get a shock of static electricity.

Even though Toni didn't own a washing machine, her mother had scavenged most of her clothes from a handful of second-hand stores in Manhattan (where rich women from the upper east side dumped off last season's smocks). Fern Ferlinghetti was grooming her daughter to snag a rich husband and made sure Toni dressed to fit her ambitions.

"I'm freezing." Toni clutched her arms around her breasts. Arky opened his drab olive army coat and moved to draw her close, but she shoved him away.

Cookie's fingers felt numb. Although it wasn't windy, the temperature felt colder than the low twenties. It was a whole lot colder a year ago when Cookie, Reenie Ruggiero and Arky Lovato had trudged off to the RKO Theater in South Yonkers and saw Grand Funk Railroad.

According to Arky, other than the Beatles, Grand Funk Railroad was the only rock band to fill Shea Stadium. Until they came to Yonkers, Grand Funk had been the biggest American rock group in history. The band's folly in Yonkers turned into a long-lasting unlucky spell. Mysteriously, they fell out of favor with fans far beyond the Yonkers city limits. In cities across America, everyone suddenly hated Grand Funk Railroad and booed them from the stage. Messing with people from Yonkers was known to tempt the intervention of the devil.

"If you want to know the truth, mess around with a Yonkers person, the devil will come right after you," Arky yelled. "Ask anyone, they'll tell you!"

Halos formed around every streetlamp on Maple Street. The fog rolling in and wafting in blanket waves meant a major cold spell would be around for a while. On the hill a straight line of yellow lamplight was upstaged by red and green strands of Christmas lights, a herd of reindeer, an opaque Santa Claus, and a herky-jerky trio of choir boys. An occasional small tree and little fences twinkled with colored lights. Chain link, threadbare wrought iron, and a dash of white pickets, all of these fences were threaded with gold and silver garland intertwined in spirals of rope with strands of twist-in colored light bulbs. A two-story red brick building sat tight and compact on the corner of Maple and Oak Street. It looked like any other building on the hill, except this place was different. A popular bar owned by a family of little people, midgets, most people called it Jimmy's (the official name), or *Jimmy the Midget's*, but it was also always affectionately known as the *Midget Bar*.

Fifteen

The Midget Bar

Drenched in black light, the Midget Bar had the ambiance of a bat cave. Black curtains covered the only window to the outside. No one could see in and no one would bother to look out. Cookie didn't know then what she came to know later—as an after-hours joint, the Midget Bar didn't start rocking until all of the other bars had closed. Things went on here and were meant to remain here, unspoken, never talked about and only whispered among Jimmy and his friends until such time they were banished from mind but never completely forgotten. Opening the door and walking in did not guarantee instant admission.

Jimmy the Midget jumped off a Dellwood Dairy milk crate, landing squarely in front of the door like a nose tackle, greeting the newcomers with an effervescent burst. This was one happy-go-lucky guy.

Recognizing Arky, Jimmy nodded to him, but the two girls came under quick scrutiny. "Are they legal?" he asked Arky.

In this regard, Arky moved fast on his feet. "I'm sure," he said, pushing both girls forward for Jimmy's inspection.

Jimmy nodded approvingly toward Toni but Cookie? Jimmy eyed her skeptically, putting his hands on his hips. "Got I.D.?

"She's good," Arky said.

Cookie huffed with irritation. "What kind of cheap joint is this anyway?" She dug into her hemp sack and produced a school I.D. card. Jimmy scanned the card and smiled. "You look younger," he said. "I would have guessed you were at the most, fifteen, not nineteen."

"Your I.D?" Jimmy asked Toni.

Toni's face turned cross like an angry crow. "I didn't know I had to bring my I.D.!"

"I'll vouch for her," Arky insisted. He squeezed her side just under her breasts. He intentionally copped a feel and for the moment she was letting him get away with it.

"Okay," Jimmy said. "They're cool."

Arky immediately relaxed, but as soon as Jimmy jumped over the counter and behind the bar, Toni violently yanked herself away from him. "Disgusting asshole," she hissed. "Touch me like that again and I'll smack you in the face."

Cookie knew Arky had opted to lie to Jimmy rather than raise Toni's disfavor. He had been totally swept away by Toni. So had Jimmy, apparently. On the other side of the bar, his eyes looked level with her breasts. Much to Cookie's horror, Toni's breasts had taken on a life of their own. Under the distorted illumination of the black light, Toni wore a white bra under a black sweater. Her massive orbs were magnified and appeared to be floating in the air. But Toni didn't know and if she had, she probably would not care. She flashed Jimmy a smile glowing whiter than white.

The black light bestowed a form of aesthetic benevolence upon everyone in the bar, making them appear surreal and beautiful. Offering Toni a free beer, Jimmy came out from behind the bar, gleefully placed his arm around Toni's waist and led her to the best seat. With an effusive smile, he paraded her before the three guys sitting at the bar, who promptly took note of the floating orbs traveling through space, making their rounds as casually as a new friend. Toni still had no idea she was causing a minor sensation. Neither did Arky.

Toni's harsh whisper tickled Cookie's ear. "Where'd you get the fake I.D?"

"I made it," she said.

Toni was indignant. "And you didn't make one for me!"

Arky spoke to them both in a confidential tone. "About a year ago, this place was busted for serving minors. A major bust. Police were crawling everywhere, and paddy wagons hauled off a whole bunch of people to jail because they were underage. Jimmy had to close for a while. What a mess! That's why he's being careful now. I should have known better and told you before we came."

Cookie knew two of the three guys sitting at the bar. Pinky O'Hearn enjoyed the stir created by Toni's arrival. He freed a bar stool. Patting the seat, Pinky tried to coax her to sit next to him, but she treated him with disdain. Red-headed, Irish Catholic, working-class, too short—not exactly a show piece on her arm: Toni had no use for him. Cookie remembered seeing him at Whalen's Funeral Home and recalled the image of the flag blowing off the casket. Somebody close to Pinky must have died in Vietnam. If the war went on much longer, all these guys here, except Jimmy the Midget, would end up there too.

Toni leaned in toward Tommy Parrello, who received her with open arms. "Long time, no see, Toni Ferlinghetti, where've you been?"

Toni gave Tommy a quick smile but pulled away from him. She had already had him, made it plain he was real good at kissing, but she didn't want him no more. "Who's that guy you're with?" Toni wanted to know. "What's his name?"

The other guy with Pinky and Tommy called himself *Eddy*. Prematurely balding, Eddy would look the same at forty-five as he did in his twenties. His big brown eyes drooped, making him look tired and sad like an old hound dog. Eddy gave Toni the once-over. "I'm not going to say nothing," he said, looking directly at Toni's breasts, then away toward Arky, giving him a *you're a great guy* slap on the back.

"No one's here," Arky said. "I thought there would be more people hanging out."

Toni grabbed Cookie and spoke harshly in her ear. "Where's the rich guys? I don't see no rich guys."

Behind the bar, Jimmy stood on top of a milk crate and poured beer from the tap. "It's early," Jimmy said. "No one ever comes this early on Sunday. It used to be that bars couldn't be open at all on Sunday. Count yourself lucky for being here!"

Cookie watched Jimmy alight from the milk crate with the deft agility of a trained dancer. Carrying two drafts of beer, he never spilled a drop.

"So, you want a rich guy?" Jimmy asked Toni. "I'm rich! I'm rich in spirit. Be careful what you wish for, you might get it. Then you'll be sorry for wishing in the first place."

What the midget lacked in stature made him tall in his ability to accurately size-up people. He climbed onto another milk carton behind the bar but in front of where Toni stood. "I'll tell you what. When you get yourself a rich guy, tell him to come back here and pay me for all of the free beer that you're gonna be drinking tonight."

Toni turned to Cookie. "He's cute. I like him. He's a leprechaun. The leprechaun of Nodine Hill."

"Be careful what you say," Eddy cautioned.

"Don't be calling him cute." Tommy put his arm around Toni. "I remember one day at lunch he went flying over the cafeteria table after some kid that was a lot bigger than he was. He didn't like what the kid was saying. Jimmy doesn't care how big you are, he'll get right in your face. He's not afraid to fight."

"Just don't get Jimmy mad," Eddy said, setting his mug on the bar. "Jimmy's one of the toughest guys I've ever known."

"Don't get me started," Arky agreed. "Jimmy and me go way back."

Jimmy's talent for turning a band of everyday guys into a comradery as tight as combat troops in a foxhole was fueled by cheap beer and nothing but talk. Jimmy puffed himself up behind the bar and yelled, "What time is it?"

All of the guys yelled back, almost in a chorus; all of their voices repeating and resounding in an echo, *It's time to party! Party! Parteeee! Party time!*

Tommy Parrello nodded to Cookie as if she was mostly invisible, a mild annoyance. They hadn't seen each other since the day Louie Santamassino had roughed him up to teach him a lesson on account of the mean things he had done to Herman Lynch.

"Where's your little black boyfriend?" he asked.

Cookie turned away from Tommy. She was not going to get into this type of conversation with the likes of him.

"What, are you into white guys now?" His voice whined in a nasal tone as he heckled her. "Tell me the truth: you're a girl with a past sucking up to black hineys, but now you've decided you want to be friends with your own kind. Let me think about it and I'll see what I can do for you. Call me in the morning."

Cookie walked away from Tommy and the bar. She heard his laughter follow her toward the back of the room, where she walked around a pool table set low-to-the-ground, a comfortable height (for children or midgets) to play pool.

Cookie did not immediately see him. Stanley de Falco sat at a small table toward the back of bar next to the jukebox. His beer mug was more than half full. He had probably heard what Tommy Parrello had been saying to Cookie and his ears had pricked up. The attention he gave the situation made him more noticeable than if he had kept to himself and remained aloof. Suddenly, he stood up, tall, lean and gorgeous. She did all that she could to stop from swooning. And she hated herself for it.

She could start by saying hello, but words failed her.

Wobbling on her legs, she prayed she wouldn't suffer a relapse with her trick knee. What a time to be thinking of falling. She tried to calm down. Almost knocking over the chair and rocking the table, she sank into her seat and lit a Marlboro as a reflex action. She felt her hands shaking. If he noticed her nervousness, he didn't say much. "You okay?"

Her nervousness had nothing to do with Tommy Parrello and everything to do with Stanley. She had always been a tough Cookie, a cross between a gangster and a hippie. She watched Stanley head to the bar, where he gave Tommy Parrello a hard look. Tommy had no reason to believe he had done anything wrong and turned away from Stanley. Neither of them said a word. No one at the bar said anything to Stanley. Pinky caught the action between Stanley and Tommy. Nodding to Stanley, Pinky's smile weakened, and his pale blue eyes watered up. Hanging out at the Midget Bar meant being part of a family.

Jimmy the Midget didn't mess with Stanley a whit and gave him the high-five. It was clear, though, Stanley was a regular there but not part of the tight social fabric stitching them together. Stanley did not enjoy the easygoing banter of their Yonkers guy small talk. He set them all on edge.

Stanley grinned at Cookie. His faded jeans hardly creased as he sat down at the table. All muscle, taut and well proportioned, strong and so sure of himself, she could not stop staring at him.

"I know you're not nineteen," he said. "I've seen you in your Catholic girl school uniform. I'd place you at sixteen, going on fourteen, max."

She wasn't going to tell him how old she was. What did it matter? Clearing her throat, trying to make her words fluid, she asked, "Mind if we talk?"

Stanley folded his arms across his chest and leaned in closer to hear Cookie. "What do you want to talk about?"

"You're not a Yonkers guy?" In her heart, she pleaded with him to say yes.

"I was born in the Bronx," he said. "Why do you ask? What difference does it make?"

"I don't like Yonkers," she said. "I'm going to leave here someday." She looked across the room at the bar where the guys, including Jimmy, were talking in hushed voices. Toni turned around and looked at Cookie, trying to mouth *let's go. What's up with you? Come on!*

"What's your name?" Stanley asked. His arms were folded across his chest.

Cookie giggled because she did not know what else to do. "Cookie."

"Cookie," he said, looking surprised.

"I go by Cookie. My real name's Concetta."

"With a name like Concetta, I hope you're Italian."

Cookie nodded. "Half."

Then he leaned closer and spoke softly. "I'd buy you a beer, but I know you're not really nineteen."

"I don't like beer anyway."

Stanley didn't say anything, but he stared at her intently as though he was curious, amused too.

Cookie gave him a grown-up smile. "I'd rather do drugs."

"How far do you think that'll get you? Do you really want to get out of Yonkers?"

"I said someday. Someday, I'll get out of Yonkers."

"I can see that," he said. "You're coming here on a Sunday night instead of doing your schoolwork. I can see you're well on your way out of here."

After seeing him so many times, she could not believe she was actually talking to him. It seemed like a dream. Is this what it feels like to want to kiss someone who makes your knees shake?

She felt like collapsing on top of him in a heap of long loose hair and limbs, pressing her flesh against his chest and sinking into his lap. This is where she wanted to spend the rest of the night, maybe the rest of her life.

"You know," Stanley said, "Jimmy's family is from Yonkers. His father started the bar. His mom's not a midget. He has one sister who is a midget and the other one is normal height. His family is a combo of midgets and non-midgets, all of them Yonkers folk. It's funny how things work."

Stanley might have thought he was causing her to become confused, but she was trying to hold onto her seat, keep her hands from shaking so much, and prevent herself from collapsing into a heap.

"What I mean," Stanley said, "the cards you're dealt with begin from birth. What you're going to look like. Sometimes even how smart you are or whether you're going to be a lefty or right-handed."

Even though the bar was overheated, his dark cotton t-shirt made him look underdressed on this cold December night. A fine touch of blond hair peeked out from the v-neck of his shirt. Light stubble shadowed his chin around his mouth and under his cheeks. Being unshaven in the dense black light made his face glow.

The bar had perked up, getting crowded with people flooding in the front door. Jimmy the Midget's voice rose above the rest. Stanley got up and walked over to the jukebox. It didn't take him long to pick a song. He knew what he wanted to hear. He plugged a quarter into the slot and pushed a silver button to make sure the coin had dropped. The song he played had been popular in the sixties, *We Gotta Get Out Of This Place* by The Animals.

Smiling at Cookie the whole time, he sauntered back to the table, and said, "Sometimes, the gifts you're given don't matter. You could be in the wrong place at the wrong time and all the lemons line up. Sometimes, you have all of the right stuff and you do all of the right things and you end up being another one of life's casualties."

His eyes grew darker and sad. "You could be in a car going down Elm Street and an oncoming car crosses the line and there's a head-on collision. Just like that," he said.

Twisting a long strand of her hair into a curl, she tossed it behind her shoulder, and asked him why he was so serious, to which he did not have an answer. Finally, he said, "Life isn't fair."

The thought of revealing himself to a young girl, or to anyone, seemed to make him uncomfortable. On some other level, though, she piqued his interest. He moved his chair closer to the table, and, coincidentally, closer to her.

"Did you ever find your earring?" His long braid fell over the top of his shoulder and slithered down his chest like a snake. She wanted to pull on his braid and draw it close. She knew if she did, he would belong to her. She touched the tip of his braid, lifted her head toward his face and spoke slowly. "I keep losing things. It's been this way for a while."

"That's been happening to me, too," Stanley said, flipping his tail behind his head as though he meant to stay in control. "It means your mind is on other things and you're not thinking about what you're doing. It's not the end of the world. You need time to figure things out."

I think I really like you and I want to be with you, she wanted to say, but it mortified her to be so bold with a guy.

With the rapid approach of Toni Ferlinghetti, saying anything further to Stanley became impossible. Toni arrived, a noisy phantom in the night with her monstrous breasts and her mouth full of shining white teeth.

Stanley never stood a chance. Immediately mesmerized by the orbs of the night floating above his head, he never took his eyes off of them. Not once. Even when he spoke to Toni, he didn't retreat from the grand spectacle of her breasts. "So, you're nineteen too, I take it."

Toni didn't sit at the table. She placed her right hand on her hip and scowled. "Are you rich?" she asked.

"Am I what?" Stanley's face screwed up with mild confusion. "Rich?" He couldn't believe what he was hearing. "Is this a trick question?"

"What kind of car do you drive?" Toni asked. In her world view, his car said it all.

Stanley put his feet up on the chair where Toni could have sat if she had wanted to. "No, Ma'am. I'm just back from Vietnam."

Toni turned to Cookie, looking frantic. "Would you go to the bathroom with me? Like now!" She pulled on Cookie's shirt, trying to get her to move. Cookie twisted her body, fending her off.

Then she leaned and whispered. "He's a crazy whacked-out Vietnam Vet. You should not be anywhere near a guy like that. He's shell-shocked. That's why no one here will talk to him."

Toni eyes grew disproportionately huge in the black light. "Everyone stays away from him. You need to stay away from him too." Toni prodded her arm, "Come on, let's go."

Toni gave Stanley her wicked *I know all about you* smile, which she meant to be snide enough to inflict a mortal blow. She came up behind Stanley. Pretending she had scissors, she snipped the air close to his long braid. Stanley must have felt her presence behind his back and turned around to see what she was doing.

She lashed out at him, "I'm just admiring your hair! I wish I had hair this long and blond. Snip Snip!"

Giving Stanley the peace sign, she walked backwards away from him and called to Cookie, "We're waiting for you! Not long, or we'll go and leave you here!"

Cookie stood and looked at Stanley. "Is it true? Were you in Vietnam?"

He nodded. "Yes." This was the first time she had seen him register emotion, and it was caustic and raw.

Cookie rose from the table. "I'm trying to think of what to say...."

"Then it's best not to say anything," Stanley said. "When in doubt, say nothing."

He withdrew from her, stood and walked away from the table. He stopped in front of the jukebox looking like he meant to stand there a long time. This time he did not put in another quarter. Fluorescence poured from the jukebox and cast an aura around his body. He stood over the jukebox, glowing in the contours defined by the black light. He didn't do anything, except stand there. Cookie didn't hang around to hear what song he eventually played. She knew she had overstayed her welcome.

On the way out of the bar, Jimmy enthusiastically waved goodbye and blew kisses. *See you. Hug. Hug. Love you girls.* She glanced back and saw Stanley standing in front of the jukebox, where she had left him. He had not budged an inch. Eddy and Pinky headed for the jukebox. As soon as the guys saw Stanley staked out, they turned around and went back to the bar. Crushed by so many newcomers straggling in, Cookie fought her way through the liquor-soaked crowd so she would not get trampled. She heard the song playing again, *We Gotta Get Out Of This Place* by The Animals. The foul breath of alcohol flooded her nostrils. Most of the people coming in had already been drinking somewhere else. The Midget Bar was their last stop. Cookie squeezed herself out of the bar. As the cold air from the street hit Cookie, the walls of three-story tenements and black steel fire escapes closed in on her. Trapped in this harsh working-class ghetto, she knew there was no easy way out.

Sixteen

Super Bowl Sunday, 1972

Winter in Yonkers meant going down hills on sleds or flying saucers. Wheels too. And when you had no money, the metal lid of a garbage worked just the same. Cars were a different matter altogether. Since the first of the year, Arky Lovato had been teaching Cookie how to drive. Three driving lessons had taken place behind the H.L. Green department store in the Getty Square parking lot next to School Street. Every Sunday, Arky came by to take Cookie for a challenging joy ride. He never brought the same car twice and did not explain where any of his loaners had come from.

Arky was good at giving instruction. Although the fingers on his right hand seemed to be permanently stained yellow from smoking (Marlboros and marijuana), he had cleaned up a bit. Under Toni's tutelage, he regularly washed his hair and brushed his teeth. He also puckered up his lips a lot, ready to steal a kiss.

The silver Pontiac Bonneville interior was two-tone with burgundy and orange-red, plush bucket seats. A pair of spongey tumbling dice dangled from the rearview mirror. Cookie sank into the deep seats and liked the feel of the hard steering wheel. She gunned the gas and whizzed down a lane in the parking lot. She gave the car far more gas than it needed to travel between School Street and a soot-stained brick wall. Open windows blew in air saturated with carbon monoxide from buses and trucks passing through Getty Square. Cookie liked the feeling of the cold air whipping through her long brown hair, turning it into a bed of natural curls. She had no time at home to fiddle with her hair.

Despite his entreaties of "Whoa, Nellie," Arky remained calm. "Don't step so hard on the gas," he told her.

He was saying "Whoa, Nellie!" the same way he said it when they rode the Dragon Coaster together at Playland, except now when he said it, his voice was not hysterical, just cautious and alert. She took her foot off the brake, then tapped the gas pedal with the pointed tip of her granny boot.

"Give it a little more," he said.

She revved the gas and grinned. "I like that sound."

"Keep your foot steady," Arky told her, "and stop jerking it around so much."

Cookie turned toward him. "I'm not even sixteen yet and I'm learning how to drive. I'm getting pretty damn good too."

"Cool." Arky smiled and leaned in close to her for a minute. He seemed intent on giving her a kiss.

"Don't even try," she cautioned him.

"I never said I wouldn't try," he said. "But don't look at me so much while you're driving."

She was never going to kiss him. She had seen the inside of his mouth before he had started brushing his teeth so darn much. No matter what Arky did, he was still the same gross guy.

"Pay attention to what you're doing."

Cookie turned the steering wheel to the left and overcorrected to avoid the wall. While it seemed as though she had narrowly averted crashing the car, she knew what she was doing. Above the buildings ahead, a large billboard ad for Viceroy cigarettes read *Travel With Taste*.

Cookie slowed down, pulled a Marlboro out of her hemp sack, and pushed in the cigarette lighter in the deep burgundy and chrome console. Learning how to drive and smoke at the same time was a blast. So far, she had learned everything, even parallel parking. Only one lesson had been omitted. She had not yet learned how to drive a car on the hilly streets of Yonkers in the winter.

Through all of the lessons, Arky Lovato was clear in his instruction and helpful. He nudged the wheel ever so slightly to the right to help her make a correction. "You're getting the hang of it."

Cookie never had to say, "I want to try one more time." Arky came knocking on her front door without being asked. He was very encouraging, and she wasn't sure why. Once she knew how to drive, he would be out of his job as her impromptu chauffeur.

On this Sunday, Arky's driveway was empty of cars, and he was nowhere to be found. Arky could be here one minute and gone the next. Cookie opened her mother's white lace curtains and looked out the bay window. Across the street, his house still leaned to one side like the Leaning Tower of Pisa.

Today the temperatures had plummeted well below freezing. Everyone was staked out in front of the TV watching the Super Bowl. She had taken Johnny's Buick before without his permission. If Johnny had an inkling, he didn't let on. He was doing everything possible to make amends with her.

Flopped flat on his back on the couch watching the game, he rooted for the Dallas Cowboys. Johnny was not watching his keys, minding his money or worried about his car. Plus, these days, Cookie had a permanent get-out-of-jail-free card. She could kill a nun in broad daylight in the middle of Getty Square, and he'd say the penguin probably had it coming. He'd call Cookie "the kid"— "The kid is alright. She's a pisser!"

The grey skies of Yonkers had churned rain for the past six days. Along with the rain came a terrible mask of fog, gripping the city in a chokehold that would not let go. Then the temperature plummeted from the mid-forties to six degrees. All of the elements of snow, ice, sleet, and hail welled up from the river to dump a nasty winter storm.

The urge to take Johnny's Buick for a joy ride in the freezing rain was an act of deliberate desperation. She had not forgotten about Stanley and concluded he must be awfully upset with her. He was like one of the guys she had seen on TV, a cowboy jumping out of helicopters and shooting up old Vietnamese women and children. As shocked as she was to learn he had been an Imperialist Baby-Killer, she was more intrigued with learning about what he had experienced in the war. She would soon come to find out asking him about Vietnam was a mistake.

She was also convinced the sooner she became a full-fledged driver the closer she'd be to leaving Yonkers. Taking Johnny's Buick up to Nodine Hill seemed like a good thing. Her second mistake.

There were other mistakes too.

She thought she might see Stanley at the Midget Bar, but she never made it there.

As much as she enjoyed driving fast, she drove Johnny's Buick at a crawl. She wasn't entirely confident, driving on her own. When Arky had been in the car with her, he acted as a ballast against the intemperate forces that allowed her to be wild and crazy. Alone, she had to rely on her own good judgment and exercised extreme caution.

There weren't many people on the road. The defroster was set on high, windshield wipers beating, heat turned all the way up, she thought of singing to herself *We Gotta Get Out Of This Place* but could not belt out the tune because she had trouble breathing. Also, she knew she could not sing very well.

Whenever she was scared, she tended to hold her breath, taking in bird-like hiccups of air. Her hands had begun shaking so hard she could not let go of the steering wheel long enough to light a Marlboro.

Halfway up Maple Street, she realized the hill had turned to ice. Maple Street was one-way, going east up a fairly steep hill. The car slipped and slid. The wheels spun and the car got stuck. She had to keep going. The more she stepped on the gas, the faster the car's wheels spun, and began slipping backwards. She searched frantically, but there was nowhere to turn around. She tried turning the steering wheel rapidly from side to side as a way to use the tires as ice cutters, giving them more traction. But nothing worked. A lump formed in her throat. She did not know what to do. She took her foot off the gas pedal. The car started slipping backwards down the steep hill at a high speed. It was a joy ride. But not pure thrill. Going backwards, the car began to skid. No clutch. No way to power down.

Arky had taught her how to use a clutch, useless now. The Buick didn't have a clutch and was out-of-control. Two cars coming up the hill behind her pulled to the side of the road to get out of her way. Her car continued to slide down the hill just as another car came from behind. This is precisely when she decided to step on the brake. Another mistake and huge. The Buick could not stop on ice. The car spun, turning into a hairpin turn, spinning like rotary blades on a helicopter, and began going sideways down the hill. She was going to crash, and there was nothing she could do to stop it.

Her hands gripped the steering wheel, but she could not stop it from turning on its own. Spinning. Spinning faster. Spinning too fast to see where the car was going. The car spun three times. It was best to close her eyes and let the car take her to another dimension. The song *We Gotta Get Out Of This Place* flitted through her mind but did no good.

She covered her hands over her face, put her head down and braced herself for impact. She felt the force of the skid and sheer inertia like a wind-tunnel pulling her downward faster than she ever thought she could go. She dared not open her eyes. Not even when it seemed the car had reached a flat plane and began losing momentum, leveling out. She pressed her eyes shut even tighter, praying to a non-virtuous and invisible god who would decide whether she would live or die.

The Buick sideswiped a car parked on the side of the road in a nasty grating crunch of metal, jarring Cookie's spine. The impact bludgeoned her senses and made her dizzy with fright. Unable to swallow or think about what happened, she thought of looking into the mirror to see if she was cut or bruised. She looked at her hands to see if they were still there. Her body was in one piece. She did not know what damage had been done to the car. The Buick had come to a stop, short of jumping the curb and hitting a fire hydrant. Even through steady snow, she saw street signs—the intersection of Maple and Linden Street. She was afraid to get out of the car to see what she had hit.

Within moments, a guy tapped on her window. She didn't look up or roll down the window. She decided to ignore him. Maybe he would go away. Snow and sleet unleashed from the grey sky, blanketing sidewalks, the front stoops, the row houses, and the road. It would not be too terrible to leave the Buick here, until she could get Arky to bring the car home. There was no way she was going to drive. She had no choice but to leave the car. She would wait until the guy walked away. Then she would make a break for it and walk to wherever she could catch a bus. Johnny would never know.

She needed to find Arky fast. In the worse-case-scenario, she could claim the car had been stolen and put the keys back where she had found them. Hot-wired! The car was hot-wired, she'd tell Johnny. Someone stole his car and took it for a joy ride. Her sorry-assed story was plausible. Except for one inconvenient detail: she had a witness. The guy who had tapped on her window had not gone away.

He stood on the corner of Linden Street flapping his arms to stay warm. He tapped on the driver's window again and banged on the door. "Are you okay?"

She was not going to get out of the car to talk to him. She slid across the front seat to reach the passenger side. She thought if she pushed open the door, she could make a getaway. But when she went to push open the passenger door, it would not budge; it had been damaged in the accident. Trapped, she had no recourse but to open her own door. She slid back across the seat and thought maybe she could get out and run fast to get away from him. The guy seemed concerned and wanted to know if she was okay, but she wanted nothing to do with him.

She heaved open her door. Cold air and pencil-thin shards of ice stung her face. Dry, cold air made sharp flakes; the most dangerous sort of snow; this type of snow accumulated, turned to ice and stayed on the ground for days.

"Are you okay?" she heard him ask again.

A frigid wind blew up the hill, making a thin whistling noise. The snow lashed her eyes making it difficult to see. The streets were empty now. No cars on the road. No people walking on the streets. The only two people in the world seemed to be Cookie and this guy.

He wore a heavy hooded parka, the kind you buy in a military surplus store. His fur-fringed hood had been pulled over the top of his head. His lashes were flecked with snow and his nose was as aquiline as the image of a Roman general on an antique coin. Then she noticed the car she had hit. Even covered with snow, the car was undeniably green. She could not see the make or the model, but those details were not important. The man jumping on the street and flailing his arms was someone she knew. She had wanted to run into this guy on purpose, and not because of a stupid car accident.

Stanley de Falco.

She experienced a choking sensation in her throat. A knot formed in her heart. Her heart felt engorged; and it had become the new home for her throat. She knew it was going to be hard for her to talk; she'd choke up. He extended his hand to steady her as she trudged through the snow from the road to the sidewalk.

"How does it feel to walk? You're not hurt? It's just a fender-bender. You should be okay."

"Hi." She only knew she was breathing because she could see it rising in the air. "Funny... running into you like this."

"Cookie, right?"

She could barely make herself nod. Why did this guy make her act this way? She was acting like a complete fool and it made her hate herself. Him too.

"Driving up and down these hills in snow and ice is not going to get you where you want to go."

Cookie wasn't one to ask for guidance from anyone, but in this instance, she was stymied. "What do you think I should do?" She wasn't keen on facing Johnny's ire or his big mouth.

Stanley brushed snow away from the rear of the car to show her a dent about two feet long. Not deep. Damage to the paint was minor. Given what had happened, the car was relatively unscathed. "There's nothing we can do about this today," he said.

Her white boots looked dirty in the snow. She pushed her foot in deeper, making the toe of her boot disappear. Not much snow had accumulated. "It's Johnny's car," she said, kicking up some snow. "He doesn't know I took his car."

"Who's Johnny?"

"My father." Cookie wouldn't look him in the eye.

"You call your father Johnny?"

"When you meet him, you'll understand why. He's just that kind of guy."

'Who said I wanted to meet your father?"

Another man would have left her there and walked home. Stanley was different. Unafraid, he decided to get the car off the street and muscle the Buick back to the North End. "You don't seem banged up to me, but you might want to put on a show for your father. He's going to be mighty pissed you got his car dinged-up. But if he thinks you were in any danger or hurt yourself, he might soften a bit."

"I can play hurt," Cookie offered.

Neither friendly nor phony, Stanley's smile was the same he had given her before, like he knew something about Cookie she did not yet know about herself.

"Let's get out of this place," he said, going over to the passenger side of the Buick and yanking open the door. "It's just pushed in, not much. It can be banged out. Lucky for you, you weren't going faster."

Cookie climbed in the passenger side. Having Stanley shoulder the burden made her feel safe, and at the same time, she cringed at the thought of giving up her independence, even for the length of a car ride.

The Buick crept at a low motorized ebb on Linden Street, until it reached Poplar Street, where Yonkers High School stood as strong as a fort. With its Spanish-style architecture, you could see why kids called it The Alamo. The school's three modest copper belfries looked greener than usual on the snow-covered rooftop.

Stanley took a roundabout way to the North End to avoid as many hills as he could. By the time they reached the intersection between Elm Street and Palisade Avenue, the snow stopped. The sky in the west over the river grew brighter. The sun might have been threatening to poke out from behind a bank of clouds.

"Some storm," he said. "Didn't last long."

The Amakassin Club sat on the left, looking like a big old home instead of a social club with an outdoor swimming pool and tennis courts. Left dormant for the winter months and covered with snow and ice, the club looked small and unused, a leftover from a grander era when Yonkers was called *the city of gracious living*.

"Think I'm going to get paid for this?"

Cookie wasn't sure what he meant.

"My car," he said. "The damage to my car. Does your father have insurance?"

Stanley wasn't much for making small talk, so when he did say something, Cookie listened to him intently. She hated him for having this hold over her. She wanted to do all of the talking, but once again her words failed her.

"I'll leave it to you to tell him what happened. Then I'll come and see him."

"For what?" she said, inching closer to him.

"Money. To fix my car."

"I'm sorry," she said and meant it.

"Forget about it. Shit happens."

Maybe we can help each other, she wanted to say but didn't. She hated the way this guy made her feel, like a tongue-twisted teeny-bopper. How she hated him! Liked him too! And this was the problem. What do next, and if she should do anything at all. Her body temperature rose, and she felt like tearing her coat off. Other clothes too. She was thinking after he dropped her off, he might kiss her.

They were passing St. Paul's Episcopal Church, where Palisade Avenue had begun a gradual descent. The sun appeared to be moving at the same speed as the Buick. The rush of clouds breaking apart and forming new shapes created the illusion that any moment the sun would burst through and take over the entire sky.

"Come winter, driving up and down these hills is hell. You're really better off to walk." He checked out her feet. "But I see you've got your go-go boots on."

"Glad you noticed." She kept giving him little coy smiles to practice the art of seduction and flex her feminine wiles. She stared at his profile, almost sighing out loud. She kept tilting her head to the side, peering at him, pouting, pressing her lips together to moisten them. If he had noticed what she was doing, he didn't let on and talked about hills.

"Within the whole grand scheme of the larger world out there, the hills of Yonkers are small mounds when compared to the steep hills of San Francisco, Seattle or Duluth, Minnesota. Even Fitchburg, Massachusetts, has steeper hills than Yonkers."

Cookie wanted him to think she was impressed. "You've been to all those places?"

"Only San Francisco," Stanley said. "I was based there before I went to Vietnam."

"What was that like?" Cookie asked.

"A hill in Oklahoma is not the same as a hill in Colorado close to the Rockies," he said. It was obvious he did not want to answer her question. "The farthest south I've been to is Florida. Everything's flat. And I can't stand the humidity. It feels like Vietnam."

Cookie folded her arms across her chest and drew them in tight. "You don't talk like a Yonkers guy!"

"I'm not a Yonkers guy. I'm only here a short time. Then I'm on my way."

"Are you going away to college?" she asked him.

"I've already graduated," he said. "That's how I ended up in Vietnam. I didn't have any deferments left. I was going to get drafted anyway."

She meant to tell him to take a left at the light, but there was no need. He seemed to know how to get her home. He turned onto Roberts Lane and slowed, looking for a place to park. "I'm not taking the hill." He meant Arden Place, a modest slope blanketed with snow; its surface was crusted with ice and showed no signs of tire treads. Not one car had tried to take the hill.

Stanley parked the Buick in a tight spot on Rock Lane. They both got out of the car and stood in the middle of the road. Glare from the sun made it hard to see. Faceted chunks of ice and fine white crystals sparkled on sidewalks, roads, lawns, cars, and on the tops of garbage cans. Icicles beginning to thaw dripped large noisy drops of water from electric power lines, gutters and the eaves below roof lines. The sky had broken into uneven patches of a brilliant blue. Her ordinary neighborhood had been transformed into a place of cold beauty.

"You live in a nice place," Stanley said.

Cookie laughed. Stanley didn't see what was so funny. She was reminded of the differences between the *tree 'hood* of Nodine Hill and the *North End* of North Yonkers. Here, people had homes with front yards, back yards, and color TVs, and thought of themselves as middle-class. People in the North End were as working-class as the folks who lived on Nodine Hill, only they had amassed enough savings to pay for a down payment to buy a home. Owning a home or renting divided the working-class into two and created an uneasy coexistence, one of unbridled tension.

Her face felt warm, but she knew the warmth did not come from the sun; the flush consumed her every time she talked to Stanley.

She thought he would walk her home, but he had other ideas. He handed the car keys to her. "This is as far as I go."

Turning away from him, she didn't know what to say or what to do. "I'd like to hear about Vietnam."

"I don't think so."

"Why?"

"I don't want to talk about it."

"Want to meet Johnny?"

"Some other time." Stanley put his hands in his pockets and smiled. "You're on your own. I have a feeling you'll handle it fine."

Preparing herself for a kiss, she moved close to him and picked up his scent. Light sweat, damp cotton and the base notes of woods, moss, fall leaves turning into soil, fresh earth, the depths of clear undercurrents in the river, and something else she could not define. She only knew the fragrance of him possessed her. She wanted to move closer to him and did until she looked up and stood still, mesmerized. She stared into his eyes, hoping he would draw her closer. Her mouth became so dry she lost the ability to soften her lips.

He caught her gaze and did not turn away. "Can I have your number?"

She fumbled in her hemp sack where she had stowed many pens. Her hands were shaking so hard, she fumbled to find one. Just one.

Stanley pulled out a piece of graph paper folded into a square and handed it to her. He produced a pen from a pocket inside of his parka. She scrawled her phone number and accidentally dropped her sack in the snow. He picked it up, brushed it off, handed it to her and smiled. She gave him the paper and he stuck it in his pocket.

"Thanks. After you talk to Johnny, we can get together so I can get my car fixed. I know a good auto body shop, so it won't cost too much."

She moved so close to him, she practically stood on his feet. She drew herself up a bit, expecting he would kiss her, but he didn't. She thought he was being polite and wanted to wait until they were alone. Anyone could see them and there were voices on the street.

A few people walked down Arden Place. Cookie reckoned the Super Bowl was over. Any minute, Johnny might find his keys gone, or he might have fallen asleep on the couch in the same spot where she last saw him. A man dressed in a full-length racoon overcoat came doddering down the hill, holding onto the arm of a woman clad in a skinny white parka. The man took large flat steps in his snowshoes.

Leaving tracks but no footprints, clomping down the hill, and crunching the crust of ice on top of the snow, the man called out, "Cookie!" The woman scrambled to keep up with him and kept squeezing his arm, holding onto him, to stop herself from falling.

As he got closer to Cookie, she saw it was Louie Santamassino. "Fran asked me to get her to the bus stop, so she can make it to The Square. Would you help me?" He practically pushed the woman into Cookie.

Debbie Ochiogrosso bared her teeth as if she meant to bite Cookie and exploded into a string of obscenities. "Fuck you, Stanley! Jesus, Stanley, I never thought I'd see you here. What the fuck, Stanley, what are you doing with a twelve-year-old?!" Debbie's voice was shrill and did not let up.

From the look on Stanley's face, he was not thrilled to see Debbie.

Nor was she happy to see him. "Fuck, Stanley! It's like you tossed me away without ever saying goodbye. Well, fuck you too!"

"I don't understand what's going on!" Louie bobbed his face and uprooted his head as much as he could, but Stanley was tall, and Louie couldn't crane his neck that high. "What did you do to her? What is she talking about?"

"He dumped me," Debbie said.

"Wouldn't be the first time," Cookie muttered under her breath, but Debbie heard her.

"Fuck you, bitch!"

"Debbie, don't talk like that in front of mixed company or I'll tell your mother and get your mouth washed out with soap!" Louie searched Cookie's face for a clue. "What did he do to her?"

Then he asked Stanley, "Did you break up with her?"

Louie waved his hands as if he had hit his limit. "On second thought, forget I asked anything. I don't want to get involved in no personal shit."

"He just stopped calling me," Debbie seethed.

Stanley said, looking embarrassed. "Right after the wedding when I took you home, we talked."

"Then I gotta find you here, on my own block, slinking around with a twelve-year-old. Imagine that!"

"I'm not twelve." Cookie felt the nasty dark part of her brain kick in. She was on the verge of punching Debbie.

"I know you're not twelve! You little slut!"

Louie threw his hands up in the air. His fur gloves matched his coat. "Will someone tell me what's going on? If this is a fight between two broads, I don't need to know. I'm done. I'm outta here."

Louie practically pushed Debbie toward Stanley. "Here sweetheart, he can get you to the bus stop."

"Maybe you should help her," he said to Stanley. It was an order, not a request. "Be real nice about it and get her out of here, so she can get to work. She just needs to take the bus to The Square."

Stanley put up his hands to show he had no intention of protesting. "Come on." He offered his arm to Debbie.

Cookie did not know what emotions were churning. Things had gotten out of control so quickly. Heat seared her face and she was certain she had turned red. She was embarrassed to witness Stanley being a gentleman to Debbie at Louie's insistence.

Debbie squealed at Stanley, "I'm not touching you!" Then her eyes shot venom at Cookie. "He's my boyfriend, not yours!"

"Come on, Honey, give the guy a break," Louie said. "He's just going to get you to The Square. Okay? Is there something wrong with that?"

Cookie stood there, immobilized by the disaster of the situation. Louie poked her in the arm. "I've been wanting to talk to you. I see Herman's got a big bruise on his mouth. No one hit him or nothing. That's all I want to know. If someone hit him, then I gotta take care of that."

"I didn't know." Cookie was burning up. Now she felt doubly bad. She had not made the effort to hang out with Herman. So consumed with Stanley, her life was falling apart. She wasn't normal. She wasn't acting like herself.

Louie motioned to Stanley, who was backing up gradually, ready to walk away. Debbie watched every move Louie made.

Louie asked Cookie, "What the hell you are you doing with this guy?"

"Do I have to spell it out!" Debbie shrieked. "All he wants to do is probably ball her!" She slapped Stanley in the shoulder.

Both Stanley and Louie winced. "Jesus, do you have to talk like that!" Louie said. "You've got such a dirty mouth, I'm going to have to talk to your mother. I don't want to do that, but you give me no choice."

Stanley didn't say goodbye to Cookie and never bothered to look back. Cookie didn't know if she would ever see him again. She walked with Louie up the hill. Every step he took made a loud crunch, clearing a path in the road like an icebreaker. Even from a block away, she heard Debbie's vicious snipe accusing Stanley of hooking up with jailbait. "You're my boyfriend, not hers!"

Debbie threatened to report Stanley to the police, the principal of Cookie's school, the parish priest Father Dunn, and the mother superior of the unwed mothers' home, where she had been a repeat visitor. And for good measure, she would tell Johnny Colangelo but not bother with crazy Kitty. "You do know her mother's crazy!" She made a big point of telling Stanley, "Cookie's as crazy as her mother."

It was too cruel to think about. Nothing could be worse than being labeled sick and crazy like her mother. Cookie felt like she had gone into shock. In one day, she had made too many mistakes to count.

Louie waved his hand, shrugging off Debbie. "Don't listen to her. She exaggerates everything just like her mother."

Cookie had not seen Fran Ochiogrosso in weeks. As a matter of fact, the last time Cookie saw her, the red-headed hag had gone out of her way to avoid her.

The cold air took its toll on Louie; he huffed going up the hill and had a hard time talking. "Herman looks like he got punched in the mouth."

Cookie had no idea what had happened to Herman's mouth.

"I haven't seen Herman as much since school began," she told Louie, but it was a big fat lie. Stanley had turned her life upside down, inside out, and made her feel weak in the knees, light in her head, and mixed up in her heart.

A loyal protector of the people he cared about, once Louie made up his mind about someone, he looked out for them for life. And he had never stopped caring about Cookie and Herman. "I hope Herman's okay," Louie called to her.

Cookie gave him the thumbs up. He seemed good with her response and watched her until she reached the top step of her house.

Just before she pushed open the front door, Louie reminded her again to talk to Herman. "Let me know what's going on."

She closed the door behind her, dreading what would come next. She didn't know what she was going to tell Johnny. As far as Johnny was concerned, she had never left the house. He was on the couch watching Super Bowl highlights. He told Cookie the Dallas Cowboys had stomped on the Miami Dolphins, 24 to 3.

Seventeen

Secrets of the Heart

Johnny's face turned crimson when Cookie told him about her mishap with his Buick. The change in his coloring made his hair appear to spring into tighter rows of kink. He didn't say anything. The only thing worse than Johnny's foolish talk was when he grew quiet and looked thoughtful. He could be thinking. Or not. Johnny's blue eyes misted over, and he took sweet measures of time forming words.

He appeared to be visibly upset, concerned about his daughter's welfare. "You're sure you're not hurt or nothing? I mean sometimes you can be in a car wreck and not know you're hurt, but you've got a concussion. Sure you don't want me to take you to the doctor? Or to the hospital? I can take you to the hospital. Sure you don't got a concussion?"

Cookie closed her eyes with grim certainty. The only thing causing a concussion was the out-of-control, blood-boiling passion and rage she felt for Stanley de Falco.

She assured Johnny she was okay and mentioned Stanley would need to get his car fixed. "He's a good guy," she said. "I think you'll like him."

Johnny squinted his eyes as though he thought he had

been hearing things. It was so unlike his daughter to make glowing remarks about anyone, especially a guy.

She sat on an avocado-colored Naugahyde stool in the living room and wound her hair around her fingers to make impromptu kielbasa curls. Cookie wasn't one to fidget, but playing with her hair had become habitual. Constantly on the verge of being coquettish, flirty, and unconsciously practicing come-hither expressions, she had to catch herself, and tell herself *enough is enough* and *stop*, until she came back to her senses. She had lost sight of the girl who fluctuated between being a hippie and a gangster. Instead, she had turned into a full-fledged Italian girl, hot to trot, hot pants, half out of her mind with lust and overly enthralled with a muscle-bound blond guy, who was, much to her disgust, a half-Italian, half-Polish Yonkers guy, and a baby killer to boot.

"You'll like Stanley," she told Johnny again. "He's a really good guy."

Johnny may have been dense in many respects, but he could see something radical had changed in his daughter. Cookie watched Johnny appraise her body. He rarely touched her to demonstrate affection. Hugs, pats and kisses were uncharacteristic for him. Her body had changed, and he looked alarmed. She looked more like a woman than a kid. *The kid. That kid is alright. She's a pisser*, Johnny used to say, but no more; Cookie had grown up. He picked up on Cookie's understated description of how Stanley had come into the picture.

Johnny puffed up his chest, gathering courage to rise to the occasion of being the father of an Italian girl. He lit a Tarreyton and said, "Tell this Stanley fellow to come and see me."

Spewing smoke through his nose, he eyed her suspiciously. "This Stanley guy, he's not taking advantage of you or nothing? He's not being fresh with you?"

Cookie gave him a small smile and shook her head. She wished Stanley would get fresh.

"Does he have his own car?" Johnny popped himself on his forehead. "Of course, he has his own car! You asked me to help fix it. You hit the car on the ice."

He looked at her with a harder line of suspicion and squinted his eyes so tight, they seemed to shut. "Sure you're not bullshitting me or nothing?"

"You're my father. I wouldn't lie to you."

Johnny was flattered. He smiled and looked happy. Cookie and Johnny were friends again.

"I've been thinking about this kissing thing," Johnny said. "A kiss is never enough to send a guy to jail. Kissing is not really touching somebody. Know what I mean?"

Cookie lit a Marlboro and tossed her match into the same ashtray being used by Johnny.

"Do you have to smoke so much? It's not good for you to smoke so much. It will stain your teeth. Ask your mother. That's why she doesn't smoke. Look at her teeth. She may be crazy, but her teeth are as white as porcelain."

She eyed her father with contempt but was smart enough not to say anything. As soon as Johnny paid to get Stanley's car fixed, she would find another way of dealing with her father. She didn't tell him as much, but in her mind, he was a *dead man walking*, sentenced to death row, waiting to die.

"I also see you've been using my tape recorder."

Cookie nodded slowly but offered no context as to why she made not-so-secret tapes of the inner rumblings of her turbulent Italian girl mind.

"Keep it. Keep it," he said. "I'm all done with this music stuff in the city. I only play in nightclubs now or for weddings and parties. You can use it whenever you want."

Jettisoning an extra-long stream of smoke, she thought snidely to herself, *He's letting me do what I was going to do anyway. Nice!*

Johnny sat up on the couch and looked at her with earnest, pleading eyes. "You do know enough to keep this little thing with Joanie to yourself and not talk to nobody, especially your mother, about it?" For emphasis, he added, "Especially not your mother."

Cookie gave him a smug smile and winked. She meant to appear conspiratorial, but in her heart, she was intent on killing him. He was stupid enough to spell out why he was being magnanimous about overlooking her indiscretions; so, she would forget about his. "Deal," she said.

The next words Cookie uttered into her tape recorder focused on Stanley.

Kissing is lightly touching your lips on another person's lips. Pressing my lips against the guy's lips. Slightly parting my mouth until I feel his mouth, opening slowly to receive my tongue and I receive his. Then we tangle our tongues amid our hot breath, intertwined in desire, probing deeper and deeper still. I want him, and he wants me. Together we are a sodden mass of locked lips, tethered tongues, and quivering bodies steeping together in everlasting bliss. I love you with all of my heart, Stanley.

Eighteen

Kissing. Ouch!

Cookie walked down Ashburton Avenue on a bitterly cold day. The full sun did little to warm her heart. She had purposefully gotten off the bus close to the Café Trento, so she could nonchalantly walk by to see if Stanley happened to be around. No such luck. She did notice Bertha, though, standing behind the pastry counter shelves, sliding in an enormous tray stacked high with loaves of bread. From behind the tower of bread, Bertha did not see her. Cookie did not stop to say hello. She knew her interest in befriending Bertha was a ruse to get close to Stanley. Feeling a little guilty, she decided to genuinely open her heart to her and promised herself she'd stop by the bakery on the way home.

This 'hood, teeming with heroin addicts, close to notorious housing projects with cracked walls and peeling paint, had alleys reeking of urine in the summer. Winter too. Only the stench didn't make you gag once the weather got cold. On Jones Place in front of a worn grey, wooden three-story walk-up, a group of black boys stood looking at her. They looked away, then glanced back in a game of check, checkmate. They wanted to know who she was and if they should talk to her.

As scary as these guys tried to look, they weren't as nearly as terrifying as Fangs, the nun who had beaten Cookie to a pulp. The beating had happened so long ago, it might as well have never happened at all. Memory tricks you into getting over bad things. These boys might have looked scary, but they were poor, not gangsters making money through small-time drug trafficking, pimping hookers, petty theft, money laundering and contract killings.

Most of the boys stood behind a chain link fence in a vacant lot. Some of them were into music and if it had been summer, they'd have had a boom box blasting. In the throes of numb-chilling cold, the guys kept moving, jumping around to stay warm. Two boys stood guard, keeping watch on the other side of the fence. One boy with a large bushy 'fro and a fierce beard leered at Cookie but didn't say anything. The other guy had a short sculpted 'fro, forming a tight skullcap around his head. Exhaling cold air through his punched-in stub of a nose, he recognized Cookie and nodded to the other guy, *she's okay*. He knew she was friends with Mabel Kerry. Herman too. And in this 'hood, friendship meant a lot.

Herman lived with his grandmother on Ashburton Avenue in a newly painted, fire engine red, three-story building. Cookie had arrived in time to see Mabel Kerry walking from the corner of Ritters Lane to Ashburton. Reenie Ruggiero carried a large bundle wrapped in brown paper and tied with a string. Just as they got to the door of their apartment building, Herman held open the door for them. Reenie handed the bundle to Mabel, but Herman took it. Even from a distance, Cookie could see something had happened to his mouth. As she grew closer, Herman's mouth looked too stiff to smile.

"Your mouth?" Cookie hugged him and looked into his eyes.

His eyes crinkled, shooting her a smile.

"Now he has a fine story he's going to tell just the way it happened." Mabel led them through the lobby toward her apartment. The place looked much different than it had in the past. Clean and bright, the woodwork was a lighter color. Treads and spindles on the steps and the bannister gleamed with varnish. Cookie tried to give the rickety bannister her usual shake, but it held firm.

There was little hesitancy between laughter, hugs and kisses, soulful words, *you're my friend forever, how've you been, man, I missed you.*

Inside the apartment, Mabel Kerry set her bundle on an overstuffed armchair in front of a massive bookcase and pushed the door shut. "I was just coming back from the laundromat and who should I see?"

Reenie hugged Cookie again. "I've been missing you, Honky. *The Heart's* not the same without you."

"*The Heart's* not the same with you," she said, giving Reenie a push.

"I'm not missing you, if that's what you think. Hate that *Heart!*"

Only well-behaved Catholic girls spoke highly of *The Heart*, but Cookie and Reenie were having none of the propaganda. As far as they were concerned, *The Heart* sucked.

Cookie noticed Reenie's dark hair was parted in the middle and had gone straight. Cookie figured the dry, cold air made Reenie's hair lose its curl. It was unusual because even in the dead of winter, Reenie took great lengths to kink and curl her hair.

"*The Heart's* a strange name for a school that doesn't have a soul," Herman offered.

"Not true. They've got me." Reenie shoved Cookie back. "I'm more soul than *The Heart* can take."

Cookie reached forward to touch Reenie's hair. "What's with the straight hair?"

Reenie shrugged like she didn't know what Cookie meant.

"Sure, you weren't in a fight?" Cookie asked Herman.

"Man, you're just full of questions!" Reenie shoved Cookie again. "We've got a fight going on here."

Herman looked like he wished he could smile. A zigzag of black stitches pinched the top of his mouth. More stitches ran diagonally from under his nose down to the corner of his mouth. His mouth looked swollen, but the gap between his upper lip and nose was gone.

"Does it hurt?"

"It did."

"What happened?"

"Remember Mr. DeSutter?"

Cookie nodded. She remembered him from the Happy House in Ghetto Square. Mr. DeSutter had given Cookie a Steuben glass owl for free. The owl now sat in Mabel's bookcase. Cookie was distracted by the many books. The building's hallway had been renovated, but Mabel's apartment, and especially her bookcase, had stayed the same. Cookie wanted to find the owl. Her eyes scanned the books, rows of classic titles. Soon she spotted the tiny glass owl in front of a dusty-blue, hardbound version of Tolstoy's *Anna Karenina*. The owl made her feel as though life was coming full circle.

Aside from his holiday job at Happy House, Mr. DeSutter taught music at Gorton High School. "Your music teacher?" Cookie nodded absentmindedly. Fascinated by the owl, she remembered the slight defect making it worthless to sell as a Steuben collectible. The glass owl had a small crack in its eye. Yet it was valuable to Cookie and Herman and reminded them of the hyper talented, but tragic, Blind Owl Alan Wilson.

Mabel had unwrapped her parcel and pressed the brown paper flat as if she meant to save it and put it away somewhere she'd remember, so she could use it again. "Mr. DeSutter found Herman a surgeon who fixed his mouth for free."

"The doctor did it for free," Herman said. "All because of Mr. DeSutter."

"We couldn't have afforded it," Mabel said, as she unpacked pants and shirts from the neat stack of clothing.

Every garment looked starched and had been creased and pressed into flat squares of cloth. "Even when Herman was a baby, his mother couldn't afford it. Herman's not a baby anymore. Now it costs even more."

"Why did you do it? Why now?"

"Really want to know? You think it's because of what you said?"

Cookie nodded, clutching her stomach. She felt sick over hurting her friend for no good reason.

"And it is partly because of you," Herman told her. "It got me to thinking."

"I'm so sorry," Cookie said.

Mabel had an armful of pressed clothes. "Sometimes it's best to hear the truth from people we love."

Herman nodded. "I'm tired of people staring at me all the time. Even after they get to know me, then they think they can stare longer and harder."

"Thought you didn't notice me staring so much," Reenie quipped.

"Reenie, just because Herman's a guy, he does have feelings, you know."

Herman rolled his eyes at Cookie and shook his head. "Man, you're cold. You too, Reenie."

His laughter made his eyes shine. "My mouth will never be perfect, but at least it will be better than what it was before."

Cookie was determined to get to the bottom of why Herman had decided to fix his harelip. "Why now?"

"I want to be able to kiss somebody someday," he told Cookie. Then, he looked at both girls. "This is a big thing for me because of things I'm going through."

"It's because of what I said, isn't it?" Cookie felt terrible. She had been rude and insensitive to Herman. "I'm so sorry."

"Me too," Reenie said. "I should have thought more about what I was saying to you."

"Hurts my mouth to think about it now. Kissing. Ouch!"

"I'm still trying to figure it out." Cookie was too embarrassed to say she wanted to learn how to kiss.

"Not me," Reenie said, clearing her throat excuse me, "I have a boyfriend."

"And get this," Herman whispered in Cookie's ear, "he's white."

"No, sir!"

"White."

"He is that." Mabel smiled. "She's finally starting to understand not all white people are bad. We're all human," she sighed. "There's hope for all us all. You just have to believe."

"He's too white." Reenie tucked her hair behind her ear. Her curls had been ironed as flat as a cotton sheet.

"I swear your hair looks like it's been to the laundromat." Cookie laughed.

Their rhythm, an easy way of being together and not having to say a thing, or sometimes listening to one another as though they were listening to their own hearts; all of this fell back into place. It was as if the three of them had never been apart. The separation of time had not made them distant from one another; they were as solid as ever.

Mabel divided the pile of laundry into two. Pants on the bottom, cotton underpants, t-shirts, and socks on top. Cookie came up by her side, probing her eyes to make a connection without having to say anything. She wanted to talk but did not know where to begin. She knew Herman and Reenie had gone into the kitchen and were getting something to eat. She heard the oven door slam shut, a refrigerator door opening, then closing, the clink of glasses, the clatter of a plate being set on a countertop. All of these sounds were of comfort to her because she knew for the moment, she was alone with Mabel.

What she had to say was a secret she could only share with the one person who would understand. She struggled to find the right words. Hesitation skipped in her voice. She tried. Not one word. Mabel put her hand on Cookie's head and kept it there, then drew her close in a motherly hug. At one time, the thought of anyone hugging Cookie made her cringe. A hug from Mabel was the only affection Cookie had ever experienced. Affection and care did not come from her parents, or anyone. Once she felt the warmth and love from Mabel, she knew now what had been missing from her life.

"It's about your words." Mabel's eyes appeared round and huge, magnified by her glasses.

Cookie spoke slowly. "My words have not come back. As much as I try, I cannot write, not even a sentence. Not even a word or two."

"Don't try to force it," Mabel said. "Just trust your words are truly in your heart. We never lose what we hold close to our hearts. Your words are in your heart, Cookie, and when the right time comes, you will find them there."

When Mabel left to put the laundry away, Reenie told Cookie how Mabel inspired their landlord to put some money into the building to fix it up. Mabel was nice about it. She never said things were falling apart or talked about the leak in the roof messing up Reenie's apartment on the third floor. She never mentioned the infestation of roaches and mice. She never complained.

Mabel found where the landlord lived and began visiting him once a week, bringing him books to read and day-old bread and pastries she bought on sale from Bertha Sokól at the Café Trento. Turns out, the landlord's wife was sick from emphysema and had to use an oxygen tank. Mabel became friends with her, too. Soon the landlord took renewed interest in his apartment building. He asked her what needed to be done in the building. The landlord went out of his way to ask her how he could help.

More than a former schoolteacher and a librarian, Mabel Kerry was getting to be known as a formidable presence, the Saint of South Yonkers. "A real saint," Reenie said. Not a fake saint who's been conjured up to sell indulgences and religious tchotchkes to make money for the Catholic church. Cookie called the impact Mabel had the halo effect. Black & white, rich, poor, or working-class, a person might be meaner than the dickens, but once she had her way with them, they became good to the quick, and so happy about it, she'd have them smiling from one end of Yonkers to the other.

Nineteen

Valentine's Day, 1972

Johnny's Buick had been in and out of the shop and looked as good as new. Cookie thought it was odd Stanley had never called about getting his car fixed. If Stanley had called her at home, there was no way to tell. Kitty rarely answered the phone, and if perchance she did, her conversation would be colorful and fun, sort of like talking to an energetic, very bright toddler.

Since Kitty had come home from the nuthouse, she was reasonably well-behaved and had taken a renewed interest in photography. She dug out an old Brownie camera and at the end of the day would throw open the window in Cookie's bedroom to take photos of sunsets.

This window had profound history in the Colangelo family. Once during a heated battle, Kitty had thrown herself out on the clothesline to get away from Johnny, and he had to reel her in like a fish.

Cookie had jumped from the window to escape from her bedroom to get to Woodstock.

And Donny used the window as an escape hatch to sneak out in the middle of the night and roam the neighborhood.

Clotheslines were symbolic of the working-class culture of Yonkers. It didn't matter if you owned a washing machine or a washboard to scrub clothes by hand; a mob mentality prevailed and a commonly held belief said you had to have a clothesline. Everyone had ropes suspended from windows to walls, posts, trees and utility poles. Clothes dryers tended to be expensive and were still relatively novel. Neighbors in well-to-do 'hoods, who could afford a dryer, found clotheslines to be aesthetically unpleasant, a sure sign of squawking low-class squalor.

But for the Colangelo family, the clothesline was much more than a practical necessity; it was an exit strategy, a way out, a sentiment as certain as the song *We Gotta Get Out Of This Place*.

So far, Johnny was the only member of the Colangelo family who had not made an escape via the clothesline. He had always managed to leave through the front door.

"Look at these. Look at these, Cookie. I took every single one myself." Kitty laid out at least twenty photos on top of the dining room table draped with a patterned yellow plastic tablecloth. The photos were arranged in sequential rows showing the minute-by-minute last vestiges of the sun dropping into the New Jersey horizon.

Kitty's hair was lightly teased in a soigné pageboy with sweeping bangs falling softly against both sides of her face. Her lips were manicured in the splendid *stop red* shade of lipstick by Elizabeth Arden.

"See that fiery burst!" Kitty said in a breathy voice, clasping her hands to her chest. "The ball of fire is my favorite! I'm going to put them into this frame and give them to Johnny for Valentine's Day."

Poor Johnny, Cookie thought. He paid the Nepperhan Avenue Pharmacy so much money for Kitty's medication. Now he was paying the pharmacy to have her color photos developed. But Kitty's latest obsession was a good one. At least she had stopped stalking the parish priest, Father Dunn, and no longer thought the bells of Christ the King Church were impregnating her.

"They're beautiful, Kitty." Her mother looked so pleased that Cookie took the moment to find out if Stanley had called. "I've been expecting a phone call."

"I don't answer the phone, and neither should you." Kitty's pupils dilated to inky-looking, dime-sized dots. "Oh no, don't answer the phone. It might be the neighbors calling and I don't want to burn up in hell with one of them."

Despite Kitty's stance of sanity, she would never stop thinking her neighbors were gossiping about her. And maybe they were. Cookie nodded politely and suppressed the desire to be a smart aleck. Growing up with a mother like Kitty had taught her to exercise self-restraint. "Great, Kitty. Your photos are great. You should be very proud of yourself. Johnny will love them, I'm sure."

"I think so too." Kitty took the scissors and began snipping the white border from a photo, chuckling to herself. "Don't need a frame when it's going into a frame." She took the trimmed photo and squeezed Elmer's glue to the back of the first photo and mounted it on a flat white matboard. "They taught me this in the nuthouse." Her smile was innocent and sincere. "And I'm really having a good time with it."

For a Monday it was very odd for Johnny's car to be parked in front of the house. "Know where Johnny is?" Cookie asked.

Kitty searched Cookie's face. "Somebody picked him up to take him to the Italian Club. He took the day off to play music. The music makes him happy. I think it does because he's doing it all the time." She took the scissors to another photo and snipped away.

"Donny went with him," Kitty offered. "She took my Brownie, too. Little Rascal. Your sister's a little rascal. She had no right taking my Brownie."

Cookie kept an eye on the blades of Kitty's scissors, sharp and shiny. "Who came by to pick him up? Was it Millie?"

"How the hell should I know!" Kitty shot back. "Do I look like his mother or something?" Cookie noticed her mother's hands shaking. Something had caused her to become agitated.

Johnny's right arm in his office, Millie Mangano, clearly worshipped him, but he'd say mean things about Millie behind her back, like *she's as large as a Mack truck*! He didn't mean it; saying rude things was just his way. Johnny made no secret he detested big women. *Look at the fat ass on her*, he'd say.

Cookie wasn't even sure if Millie Mangano drove a car. In the past, Cookie had only seen Millie walking on the street or riding on a bus.

Kitty became immersed in her project and stopped talking. She didn't seem to notice Cookie. Suspicious about Johnny's whereabouts, Cookie slipped away from her mother. Music gigs were unusual on Monday, and it was unlikely Johnny had taken off a Monday from his day job as a liquor salesman. The only thing unusual about this particular Monday....today happened to be Valentine's Day.

One more reason why Cookie thought of Stanley. She'd like to give him a big kiss...for starters. In the past few weeks, she had scoured the streets, looking for him, staking out all of the places she had seen him: The Café Trento, the Kennedy Marina, and the streets of Nodine Hill. Perpetually on the prowl, she made regular visits, sometimes twice a day, to the same place. She had not yet gone to the Midget Bar.

Although the Midget Bar was a likely place to find Stanley, the prospect of going there alone unnerved her. She didn't want Stanley to think she was chasing him.... even though she was. She was an Italian girl, and Italian girls never chase guys. Italian girls put themselves in the right place at the right time, so they can be chased by the right guy.

She dressed in a silky, too-short red mini-skirt and a low-cut top full of bright colored flowers and birds with sleeves expanding into wide bell bottom shapes practically covering her hands. She thought the birds on her shirt looked like the

Catholic images of holy ghosts, née holy spirit, except they were blue, green and yellow, not nearly as subdued as the sketches of holy spirit birds she had seen in religious books. The brightly colored birds brought attention to the rise of her breasts being pushed up in a half-cup, underwire bra. A push-up bra! Ha-Ha! She spritzed Kitty's My Sin in the crevice between her breasts and referred to it as my décolletage.

The road conditions, sunny, a bit on the warm side with no chance of ice or snow, were perfect to take Johnny's car for a joy ride. She lit a Marlboro and flicked the match into the street. Groves of crocuses shot up in the area where the Sumac trees once stood. Sprigs, stalks and buds were on the verge of bloom. She had not seen crocuses there before and thought some caring person had planted bulbs to make up for the murder of the Sumac trees.

She missed the trees Johnny had chopped down in a horrific act of violence. And she missed her Owl Bowl, nestled within the low, tangled gnarl of the Sumac trees. The Owl Bowl had been a natural cave formed by clumps of bent, tangled branches and circular thicket. It was not a real cave but a secret place for Cookie to burrow into the brush and hide from the world. She came to this secret hiding place to think about things. But now it was gone along with the Sumac trees. One more loss in a string of many.

Her other secret place, the Owl Hole, was hidden below the Calvary Baptist Church steps. She had no reason to go there. Not now. It was best left untouched. She cherished the memory of the times spent there with Herman and Reenie, when they confided thoughts and feelings too tender to bare to the world. Down below in this hidden place is where they had learned the courage it takes to show one's own heart. Now her heart had opened in a new and different way for a man whose name and image rose to her mind every day, and who she thought she loved to the extent she forgot about all others. Everyone and everything else in the world had taken a back seat and was put on hold indefinitely because she had fallen in love with a man who hardly knew she existed.

But she did exist, and she was going to make him belong to her.

Looking through her newfound lens of the world, she only had eyes for Stanley. Even the Owl Hole, as sacred as it was, had been discarded from her life.

Lost in thought, she almost missed the spectacle of Fran Ochiogrosso charging up the hill, carrying an enormous grocery bag. She gripped the bag from underneath with two hands to prevent the bag from bursting open. She freed one hand to give Cookie a wave.

"Some trip to the store," Fran said. "I had to buy a lot of groceries so I could make a special dinner tonight. It's Valentine's Day. Doing anything special?"

Cookie expected to be pumped for gossip, but surprisingly Fran picked up her pace. "How's school going?" Fran called out, but her back had already been turned away from Cookie. She had quickly moved on, not really wanting to talk about anything.

From a distance, Fran called to her, "Isn't that skirt a little too short?"

Cookie spent more time playing hooky from school than she did going to class. She didn't know what her grades were and didn't care. To her way of thinking, her deal with Johnny meant she had a permanent get-out-of-jail-free card. She could do anything she wanted to do. She stubbed out her Marlboro, got into Johnny's Buick and stepped on the gas. She wanted to get away from here as quickly as she could.

She cruised the tree 'hood of Nodine Hill, looking for him. Stanley seemed to have made himself conspicuously absent or missing in action, MIA—funny considering he had been in combat in Vietnam. Trees might have been everywhere at one time, but none were left. Few signs of greenery, gardens or growth pocked the streets. Sprocket-shapes of crabgrass sprung up in between concrete cracks. This tree 'hood did not live up to its name.

She pulled to the side of the road and parked close to the intersection on the corner of Oak and Elm Street. This part of the 'hood had its own strip of storefronts: Kaplan's Market, Rabinow's Hardware, Rocco's Pizza, Silverman's Shoe Repair, DeLashios bakery, Joe the barber, and a novelty store named Gippers that sold dirty magazines. A small sign in Gippers window read *must be 18 years old or accompanied by an adult.*

Just about to give up, she found him walking alone on Oak Street, heading in the direction of the Midget Bar. Sun shone on his long blond braid, making it glisten like the tail of a comet. In her new lens of the world, Stanley had taken on a halo effect, the same as Mabel Kerry. It was warm, hardly cold enough to offer someone a ride. She drove up alongside the sidewalk and beeped the horn once. Stanley did not notice her.

She beeped the horn again and waved but didn't get his attention. Completely focused on his own world within, he was in a place where he could not be reached. She drove a car-length away from him. Then, she changed her mind and thought it would be best if he did not see her. Instead, she would see where he headed and nonchalantly show up. It became obvious he was not going far. When it seemed like he would climb the hill of Maple Street, he took a quick detour right into the Midget Bar. The bar's windows were blacked out, making it impossible to see inside.

She did not want to be so obvious in her pursuit by following him into the Midget Bar, but now she had no choice. She pulled into a wide-open space on Oak Street. She checked herself in the rearview mirror and dabbed on lip gloss. She pouted in the mirror and blew herself a kiss. She felt like an idiot, and at the same time, she knew what she had to do. A lump had formed in her throat. She was scared, and at the same time, she willed herself to feel fearless, a contradiction for sure, but at least she knew what she wanted.

Just for the record, her highest ambition was to make Stanley fall in love with her.

It took a minute to adjust to the lack of light in the Midget Bar. She had left the street in daylight and entered a cave ensconced in perpetual darkness, where time stood still. Jimmy the Midget greeted her with a lavish smile as if he meant to say *the pleasure is all mine*. "Cookie, right? Great name!" He had remembered her. Cookie was flattered, but she figured Jimmy only had to meet someone once; he never forgot anyone.

"What can I get you?"

"What have you got on tap?" Cookie thought she sounded grown-up but felt clumsy and awkward. She tried not to be obvious about searching for Stanley but turned her head every which way as if she was tightening a tourniquet.

"Schaefer?" Jimmy asked her.

Cookie nodded.

"You got it." Jimmy climbed on top of a Dellwood Dairy milk crate to reach the tap. He kept his eye on her the whole time while he poured. "Where do you live?"

"North end."

"What are you doing around here?"

Cookie knew people rarely strayed outside of their own 'hood. She had to come up with some reason for being in Nodine Hill.

"I'm visiting a friend," she told him. "Bertha Sokól? Know her?"

"Stanley." Even in the dark, Cookie could see Jimmy's coy smile. Cookie felt transparent under Jimmy's scrutiny. He had a gift. He could see through anyone. "Bertha's son is right over there," he said, pointing toward the back of the bar.

Jimmy hopped off of the crate and held the mug steady without spilling a drop. He set it in front of Cookie, winked and nodded toward the back of the bar. From the corner of her eye, she saw Stanley sitting at a small table in the same place he always sat next to the jukebox. She debated whether she should go over and sit with him or stay at the bar, hoping he would notice her and stop by to say hello, or at least talk to her about having his car fixed.

"Pay me later." Jimmy smiled. "It's Valentine's Day."

Cookie took the beer, trying not to spill any. Foam crested to the top like a turbulent sea. She walked gingerly toward Stanley, trying not to upset the beer and wet her bell bottom shirt sleeves. She cursed herself for wearing such a whimsical shirt.

Stanley scanned her body, from the birds on her shirt down to her bare legs, and squinted as if he had made a complicated assessment.

He asked, "How old are you?"

"Nineteen," Cookie reminded him.

"Going on fourteen, I'll bet."

"Sixteen," she said, setting her beer on the table.

Stanley acted like he didn't believe her and folded his arms. "I'm not planning to stay long. As soon as it gets crowded, I'm out of here."

Cookie sat down at the table and immediately became aware of how far her poplin skirt could rise. Stanley must have noticed, and he had indeed turned away. He wasn't being polite. Her age was coming between them. No coat or sweater to drape across her lap, she dressed—like a full-fledged Italian girl—to show all she's got. Cookie knew she looked good and she liked bothering Stanley. She was getting to him and loving the feeling.

She sat, pulling her chair closer to him. Side by side, every so often she felt her arm graze alongside his. "How's your mother?"

Cookie thought it was best to learn more about Bertha. "I had some of her cooking. She fed me supper one night."

Stanley seemed surprised. "She could make a meal out of anything. When I was a kid, she made soup from chicken necks and backs, and oxtails. She used to save up, scrimping a few quarters so we could have sauerkraut and kielbasa on Sunday. Most people wouldn't eat the stuff she makes. They'd gag on the smell."

"Most people are stupid." Cookie giggled. "Especially in Yonkers."

"Don't let Jimmy hear you talking that way. He'll kick you out of here. He loves Yonkers. So do a lot of the people who come here."

Cookie meant to remind him she had taken an oath. As soon as she turned seventeen, she was out of Yonkers. But if she told him, then he'd know for sure she was not nineteen.

Every move she made would have to be calculated to get what she wanted from Stanley. She pulled her chair a little closer. This time her leg touched his leg. Every time he said something, which wasn't too often, she gave him a knowing nod, dreamy eye contact and her mouth parted slightly—she let him know he was the most desirable man in the world and how much she liked him without being a total slut about it.

"I like your mother." Cookie gazed at him, then cast her eyes downward as a show of feminine submission. She could not believe she was doing such a thing and began to argue with herself, but it did not stop her from crossing and uncrossing her legs so he could take a gander along the entire expanse of her smooth, shapely thighs. She tightened her chest in a slow contraction to heave her breasts upward, almost in his face. It helped to smile a lot too.

Stanley's arms were crossed, and he sat straight in his chair. He stared at her with amazement; he could not believe the full effect of her coquettish act.

Shaking her head, she brushed her hair back, gazing at him with a serene smile. "Your mother works so hard at everything." Then she leaned forward and whispered, "But if you got her a washing machine, I think she'd really like that. It would make her life a lot easier."

Stanley winced and turned away. The notion seemed to make Stanley sad. "My mother has never traveled beyond the United States. Other than her childhood in Poland, she has not been to other parts of Europe. Between her work at the bakery and her volunteer work at the library, her path is narrow. Her only world is Yonkers."

"Your mother told me about her violin. And how she doesn't play it no more. How come?"

Visibly embarrassed, Stanley said, "You ask a lot of questions."

"That's how I learn things," Cookie said.

"My mother's not always well. She suffers from bursitis in her knees and elbows. Every so often a painful rash, psoriasis, flares up. She's from Nowy Targ in Poland. Ever hear of it?"

Cookie nodded as though she had heard of Nowy Targ, but she hadn't.

"Everyone else in her family died in the death camps not far from where they were born and grew up. She was the only blood and bones left of the Sokól family."

"How did she survive?"

"I'm not sure. She has an awe-inspiring presence and a steely will." He paused and looked at her. "Sort of like you."

If she wanted to get to him, she needed to stop talking about his mother, but what else could she talk about? "What have you got going on tonight?" she asked. "Anything special?"

Stanley shook his head but didn't say anything.

Cookie nodded and touched his hand. His hand felt powerful and much larger than her own. He didn't pull his hand away, but he didn't take her hand either. She resorted to talking about his mother again.

"She seems lonely. Do you ever spend any time with her?"

"She smokes. I tell her to quit. Smoking's not good for her, but she doesn't listen."

The mention of cigarettes made Cookie crave a Marlboro, but right now it seemed like a bad idea. She'd also love to smoke a joint right now. She wouldn't mind taking one of Kitty's ludes, anything to take off the edge of the tension between her and Stanley. She considered throwing herself into his lap but didn't know how he'd react and didn't want to wind up on the floor.

"My mother has a hard time getting up and down the stairs."

"Your mother? She's tough. I've seen her working at the bakery and going up hills like nobody's business."

The bar was getting busy. Standing room only, people were beginning to move toward the tables in the back room where Cookie and Stanley were sitting.

Stanley pulled his hand away from Cookie, breaking the intimacy she had foisted between them.

"You're not touching your beer."

Cookie pushed her glass forward. "I don't like beer. Want it?"

"I'll buy you glass of wine," he offered. He didn't ask her why she had ordered beer in the first place, and it made her feel like a grown woman. She had the right to change her mind any time she felt like it.

"Sure," she said. She didn't drink wine or beer. And it would not have made any difference. She was with Stanley and drunk on him.

"Why aren't you keen on the usual flirty bar talk?" Cookie asked, fluttering her eyes in what she thought to be a sultry reflex action.

"I don't flirt," Stanley said. "But obviously you do."

Stanley rocked back on his chair, then bounded forward and stood up. She thought he'd play *We Gotta Get Out Of This Place*, but he didn't. He stood over the jukebox and lost sight of what he was doing. He didn't seem to be looking at anything in particular. He looked remote, drifting in a place only he could imagine. Finally, he dropped a coin in the slot.

The song *White Room* by Cream played. He put his hands in his pockets and leaned against the jukebox. His eyes roved around the bar. He could have been searching for someone, but he didn't focus on anyone. No one could capture his attention. A guy in perpetual search, he was distracted by everything and nothing. He circled back to the table, as if it might be a good thing to do.

"This is my last song," he said. "Then I'm out of here." Stanley sat, moving in closer to Cookie's side. It seemed to be a sure way to avoid looking her in the eye. "My mother was poor when she came here from Poland. She met my father here. He was Italian. My father died a long time ago. So, for the most part, it's always been the two of us. And she's had a hard life."

Stanley stopped talking and touched her hand. "I can't believe I'm saying this to a sixteen-year-old."

Cookie reached out and touched his hand again. "Going on nineteen."

"Might be fourteen. In Yonkers, you can never tell a girl's age, and I'm not asking for trouble, at least not more than I'm used to."

Stanley looked on the verge of getting up again. "I'm going to be leaving soon. It's starting to get too busy for me."

Except for Stanley, Cookie hadn't noticed anything in the bar. She realized he had not bought her a glass of wine as he had said he would. "Thanks for talking to me. I learn a lot when I talk to you."

She pushed a small black & white composition notebook in front of him and handed him a fountain pen. "Can I have your number?"

He thumbed through a few pages. All blank. He scribbled in the notebook and handed it to her. "I'm trying to get used to talking. Most people don't want to listen to what I have to say.... Because of what I've been through... including my mother. It would only pain her to know. I'm all she has, and she wouldn't want to know how close she came to losing me."

Stanley's body leaned closer as though he meant to cover her body. "Or maybe she has lost me," he said. "I don't know. I'm still trying to figure everything out."

The way he spoke to her struck a powerful chord. "This is why I like being with you," she said. "I haven't been in a war, but I've been through my own private hell when no one cares. And no one listens."

"All you need is one person to listen." Stanley pressed the side of his face closer to her. Cookie thought he would turn his face to kiss her, but he didn't.

They both stood up together and faced each other. Stanley rocked back and forth on his heels. He meant to say something but stopped himself. He brushed her arm, motioning her to leave with him. Only too happy to oblige him, she didn't know where they were going and didn't care. She could still feel the touch of his hand. His body so close made her feel like a bare tree stripped of its bark and limbs, leaving only roots. They pushed through the crowd, turning to the side, stopping to let people pass and make their way up to the bar. Every so often, someone acknowledged Stanley and said hello or gave him a slap on the back, but no one stopped to talk to him. Jimmy gave Stanley a smile and a nod. "Way to go, Stanley," he said. "Happy Valentine's Day."

Twenty

Fire Traps

Cookie had not bothered to ask Stanley about why he had not talked to Johnny about getting his car fixed. She didn't want to turn the conversation into something he obviously didn't care about. Or maybe he had forgotten. The one thing she found to be consistent about Stanley was his ability to completely zone out. Drugs didn't seem to be the cause of his strange behavior, and he was a far cry from her great grandfather, Tiny Ten Pint. During the entire time they were in the bar, he had sipped one beer. And he didn't touch her beer even after she offered it to him. She sensed there was pain there, but he kept his emotions under control.

Outside in front of the Midget Bar, it was not clear what would happen next. She craned her neck toward the sky to see if she could find a shooting star as an omen portending what this moment was meant to be for the both of them. She swore she could pick up his scent on her face, but he had not kissed her. He had not embraced her. She wasn't too sure what he thought about her. He took an athletic posture poised for flight, ready to go somewhere, but not necessarily with Cookie, or with anyone.

Her eyes wandered across Oak Street to a white wood-frame walkup. A black fire escape protruded like a cage from the second and third floors, marring the view from the windows. Whoever lived there had to feel like they were living inside a prison. Next door, a white wood-frame walkup was identical in size and structure, but it did not have a fire escape.

Cookie tended to notice exits, especially after she had fled her own home through her bedroom window via a clothesline.

Stanley lived with his mother at 98 Oak Street in a building identical to two other walkups. No fire escapes. The buildings could go up in flames like tinder boxes, a flash fire of dry wood and peeling paint. People would have no way to get out. Fire traps.

"That's where I live right now," Stanley said, pointing to the top floor. Lights were on in the front windows facing the street.

Cookie nodded. "I've been there."

"It's better than the five-story walkup where we used to live in the Bronx."

Cookie asked him to go out for pizza and amazingly he said yes.

"Rocco's Pizza?" she asked.

He shook his head, "Let's get off Nodine."

"Not too far." Cookie didn't want to leave Johnny's Buick. The last thing she wanted to do was to have another accident with his car. She walked fast to keep up with Stanley. She told him, "You seem interested in hanging out with me for a while."

Stanley showed a different side of himself, and smiled as though he was vulnerable, trying to get used to being with her, not wanting to leave, and torn about staying. She had touched him in some way, and it was clear that he wanted to be with her.

They headed in the direction of Park Hill, the Italian neighborhood of Yonkers. He kept his hands in the pockets of his jacket, like he was concealing his heart. In the course of his measure to protect himself, he moved his hands rhythmically in and out. But each time he pulled his hands out, they were empty, and he seemed to want to open up and relax into the heat of his own body. His closely held hands seemed to keep him calm and from doing anything physical with her. He wanted to get close and at the same time he blocked himself, drawing a line, keeping distance.

They both heard a woman's scream coming from Poplar Street. The first scream echoed on the road and into the harsh concrete tenement stoops. The second scream did not stop but blended into a staccato stream of obscenity. "Boring! You're so fucking boring, Stanley! How fucking boring can you be to talk to this girl who's still wearing training pants! No one does that anymore! There is no such thing as a real guy who dates jailbait! You've thrown me over for that fucking little underage trollop! Fuck! I mean do you know how it feels to get dumped on Valentine's Day!"

Stanley told Cookie, "I don't know why she's here."

Debbie Ochiogrosso confronted him with the swift fury of a head-on collision. No one stood a chance of surviving. Hands on hips, blond hair swaying, Debbie's mouth contorted into a frenzy of rage. Cookie became fearful of what she would do to Stanley. Skinny and pale, undernourished looking, sickly, a bag of bones, Debbie did not appear to be a threat. But Cookie had plenty of experience with raging crazy women and it wasn't pretty. She wanted to run for cover, and at the same time she wanted to kill Debbie.

Then the attack came. Debbie lunged at Stanley and tried to punch him in the face, but he saw it coming and was quick on his feet and moved. The punch landed on his chest. He put his hands up to fend off her attacks. She flailed at him, screaming and punching, throwing her whole body at him in one long battery of assault, punching, kicking; she used her head to butt him like a bull and thrusted her hips to ram against him. Her skirt rose up to her waist exposing the black line of her underpants. This was no wrestling match. Stanley did all he could to block her blows. The anger she hurled from her body was frightful but not as bad as the nastiness spewing from her mouth.

"We fucked and you act like it's nothing!"

Even under the yellow film of streetlight, Cookie could see Stanley blush and nod. "Debbie, that was months ago. I'm sorry."

"Now you're out with this little slut!"

"We talked about this," Stanley said. "I'm not ready to go steady with you or anyone right now."

"It was more than a one-night stand to me! But not to you! You fucking used me! Fuck! I mean I don't know how you could do this to me!"

Cookie felt like a third wheel stuck in the mud, a bad scenario where someone was going to get hurt. "I'm going home," she told Stanley.

"Shut the fuck up!" Debbie lunged toward Cookie. "I said to shut the fuck up!"

Cookie braced herself for attack. She knew what she would do if Debbie laid one finger on her. Cookie expected Stanley would take Debbie by the arms and hold her off, but he stood immobilized, afraid to touch her. Debbie scared him to death.

"You fucking little bitch!" Debbie threw a chaotic, aimless punch, landing on Cookie's shoulder.

Everything came back in Cookie's mind, the things she did not want to experience or ever think about, going all the way back to grade school when the nun Fangs had brutally beaten her. No one was going to harm her now.

Debbie came at her again, this time ready to claw her eyes out. She had long fingernails and seemed bent on gouging Cookie's face. Cookie catapulted herself off the ground, heaving her legs high into the air and kicked Debbie squarely in the stomach. The force of the blow made Debbie crumple to the ground, gasping for air, unable to breath. Cookie had knocked the wind out of her stomach. Debbie's eyes watered the same as an injured sparrow. Pathetically weak and stupid, a strange creature, less than a real woman, with a craven soul, she was no match for Cookie. Debbie's breath came back in shallow spurts and small fits. Cookie had every intention of kicking her but stopped. Her white hot rage went to a place she could not define. She only knew Debbie was no longer a threat and too weak for Cookie to want to hurt her.

But all bets were off if Debbie touched her. "If you ever fucking touch me again, I'll kill you," Cookie told her, and she wasn't kidding.

She felt for sure Debbie was done with her. Stanley too.

Cookie was mad at Stanley for not breaking up the fight and protecting her. "Why didn't you do anything?" she asked him.

"Yeah, Stanley. Why didn't you do something?" Debbie sat crouched on the road in fetal position, rocking her body as though she had an infant cradled in her lap.

Stanley's voice was calm. "I can't take any violence. None. I can't go there," he said. "Because if I go there, I don't know what I will do."

"Crazy Vietnam Vet," Debbie spat. "Loser! You didn't even win the war! That's why we're still there because of fucking guys like you! You lost the fucking war! And killed babies! You killed babies! Little, tiny, beautiful babies!"

Stanley stood hard like stone, staring, unblinking and cold.

A crowd had formed on the street, but no one said anything, not even Jimmy. Someone's dog began barking; a big black dog ran on the sidewalk in front of a chain link fence. The curtains in the window behind a fire escape opened like a hole in the wall. Someone was peering out but not seeing too much because the thick black bars of the fire escape got in the way.

Soon everyone would be talking about what had happened tonight. Stanley, Debbie and Cookie, a love triangle gone wrong. Except Stanley didn't know he was in love. Cookie knew she was in love but didn't know what to do about it. And Debbie didn't love anyone, not even herself.

Stanley helped Debbie up from the ground and steadied her to her feet.

"Don't touch me!" she screamed at him. He let go and left her there wobbling on her red, four-inch platform shoes.

"There are crazy women everywhere," Cookie said. "And I need to be out of here."

"You're the fucking crazy woman," Debbie yelled.

Cookie put her hand up telling her to stop. "Don't. I'm warning you. Just one warning."

"Fuck," Debbie sighed. She got Cookie's message.

Debbie sure knew how to say fuck a lot. Most Italian girls knew how to use plain English, but there was something tough and fearless about exclaiming fuck. It made the point. Sort of a Yonkers thing.

As much as Cookie wanted to be with Stanley, the fight with Debbie made her go into shock. She had succumbed to a mysterious illness. Exhilarating but scary, violence freed her inner demons. She enjoyed the adrenaline but loathed the aftermath that forced her to keep reliving Debbie's assault on her body and her senses. She saw herself as her own victor and her own savior but not without paying a high price. Reliving the incident over and over tore her up.

She became aware of Bertha on the street, standing there, watching. Cookie waved. Bertha's stern expression did not soften.

"How'd you get here?" Bertha asked. "Take the bus?"

"I'll give you a ride home," Stanley offered.

"I've got Johnny's car." Cookie wanted to check to see if she was bleeding in some unimaginable way. The violence made her think that even though she had not been physically wounded, her heart had been hurt in a way her words could not describe. Her words. Her lost words. She did not know if her words would ever come back.

"I keep losing things," she told Bertha.

"We all lose things because we all have things to lose,"

Bertha said. "Tie a knot around your finger. That will help."

Tonight, Bertha looked haggard and sad. She wore a faded pink cotton house dress with a chunky knit sweater thrown over her shoulders. "I was doing the wash and heard the trouble out here," she said. Her rough, swollen fingers clutched the sweater at her breastbone to keep it closed. "If you tie a string around your finger, you'll have something good to remind you not to lose things."

The notion of loss made Stanley uncomfortable. He was doing all he could to stay there after the onslaught of Hurricane Debbie. Cookie could feel the sudden uptick in his energy and detected he was on the verge of running off.

Bertha went on. "And then we keep going because no matter what, we can't give up. We have to live the best we can."

No one seemed to know where Debbie had gone. Cookie suspected she had gone inside of the Midget Bar to pick up a new guy. Debbie might have been sweet on Stanley, but he had never been the only one.

Stanley walked Cookie back to where the Buick was parked. He didn't have much to say. Quiet. Intense. Focused. No one word described him. He opened the door to the Buick so she could get in. "I'll take a rain check on the pizza," he said. She didn't know if he really meant it or if he was trying to be nice, especially after she had been assaulted by his crazy ex-girlfriend.

Cookie got behind the wheel of the car and rolled down the windows to wake herself from the numbness of shock. As she drove away, in her rear-view mirror, she saw someone climbing a fire escape. She stopped the car, idling, to see what was going on.

Across the street from Stanley's tenement, Debbie straddled the second floor of the fire escape, climbing, getting ready to jump. A few people were trying to talk her down. One red platform shoe dangled on the edge of the ladder. Taking one step at a time, she paused in between each metal rung long enough to shriek *fuck* and cry. Cookie gunned the gas to get the hell out of there.

The road home to the North End seemed longer than usual. Halfway home, she realized she had lost her hemp sack. One more casualty. Nothing in her life had ever been stable. Then one day, mysteriously, she met a man who changed her life, making it even more unbearable. She had lost more than her words. She had turned into a loser. There is nothing worse than being the Valentine who got left behind.

Twenty-one

Hit or Miss

On a raw Wednesday in March, spine-piercing wind flung stinging ice pellets too small to be deemed hail. Debbie was with Fran in front of Morsemere Market *Down The End*, waiting for the Number 2 bus. The sunglasses and the kerchief tied under Debbie's chin did not disguise her scowl. Her plaster cast hung in a sling on the outside of her woolen cape. Having to lug a plaster cast was the same as having a yearbook. Everyone was forced to write something soppy or clever. Her cast was covered with signatures, slogans and peace symbols in many colors of ink.

In her fall from the second story of the fire escape, Debbie was lucky enough to only break her right arm. The simple fracture required her to wear a white plaster cast for five weeks. Debbie was bitterly unhappy about her mishap. Cookie heard Fran and Debbie talking. Debbie whined to Fran, asking her to check her eye makeup. Her broken arm made it impossible to apply mascara.

Although she had made peace with Fran and had sufficiently intimidated Debbie, Cookie stood on the far side of the corner so they would not see her. She didn't want to have a run-in with Debbie or Fran. The only encounter she would have would be with Stanley. In a radical departure from having to chase him or stalk him around town, Stanley had called Cookie. He wanted to see her!

Although Cookie was miffed at the way Stanley had been passive and non-committal during Debbie's assaults, she took him at his word when he talked about not triggering his own surefire path to violence. The war had done that to him, she told herself, and she issued him the same type of get-out-of-jail-free card that Johnny had awarded to her. One more way of saying, Stanley had donned the halo effect and could do no wrong.

To avoid the two women, Cookie thought about going into Morsemere Market, but every time she went in, the store's manager, Leo DeMarco, stalked her. On numerous occasions, he had tried to feel her up. With nails bitten to the quick, his fingers were monstrously large and pink. He had a huge swollen belly, a balding pate, and every time he laid eyes on Cookie, he broke into a profuse sweat, a panic attack triggered by lust.

Forced to brave the cold, Cookie moved in a loose jog-in-place. As much as she tried to be low-key and invisible, the two women had seen her!

She heard Fran say, "I want to talk to you, Cookie Colangelo."

Normally, she didn't pray, but now she was willing to do anything. Please make the bus come soon! Her jog picked up speed and carried her close to the edge of the sidewalk on the corner of Palisade and Roberts Avenue.

Fran wasn't mean or sarcastic. "I wanted to see how you're doing," she said.

Unlike Fran and Debbie, Cookie was not waiting for the bus. The corner is where she had told Stanley to meet her. She had no way of changing the plans they had made and worried the bus would not get here before he showed up!

Debbie gave her mother a dirty look. "I don't want to talk to you! Fucking ever!"

"Watch that mouth, or I'll wash it out with soap," Fran said. "Debbie's sorry for what she did. Aren't you, Debbie?"

"No, I'm not!" Debbie jerked her cast against her hip in irritation.

Cookie played out different scenarios in her head. The bus would come early; he would come late. The bus came on time; he'd forget to show up. No show. She prayed for a no-show.

Fran lit a Kent 100 and exhaled smoke through her mouth and nose. "How's your mother?"

"How about lighting a cigarette for me! Think it's easy for me lighting my own cigarettes!" Debbie swung her cast in front to hold the cigarette.

Fran lit it for her but did not look happy about taking orders from Debbie and turned her attention to Cookie. "I thought I saw your mother last week. She's such a beautiful girl. It's really a shame."

Cookie shrugged. Fran had gone back to being herself again. For the past few months, she had been uninterested in the Colangelos and actually seemed happy for a change.

"Waiting for the bus?"

"For a ride." Cookie wanted to tell Stanley to meet her somewhere else, but there was no way to contact him on short notice. She knew this situation could turn into a complete disaster.

The more Cookie thought about it, the bus would be late. Road conditions were getting slick. People filled the streets. It was safer to take the bus. She expected to see his car, but it never showed up. The bus still had not come.

She immediately recognized him by the way he walked—lean, efficient and purposeful. His car was nowhere in sight. Cookie wished she could have warned him. He was walking across Palisade Avenue, wearing an army fatigue jacket, the genuine article, not the imitation version sold at Korvettes. If she had seen him earlier, she would have run ahead to meet him, but it was too late. Debbie had already spotted him.

"I'm pregnant, you fucking asshole!" Debbie came in close and blew smoke in his face.

Stanley closed his eyes to avert her smoke and shook his head. He seemed perplexed and didn't say anything.

"What are you trying to do? Deny that we went out together! That we had sex! In the back of your stupid car!"

"That's not how to get him back." Fran nudged Debbie. "You'll never get him back if you talk that way." She tilted her head and spoke in a low tone. "Try being nice to him. You'll get more flies with honey than with vinegar."

"I'm sure it's yours." Debbie narrowed her eyes and tightened her lips. 'It's yours," she alleged. "I'm positive."

"It's just not possible." Stanley shook his head. He was outraged, but he never lost his cool. He looked at Debbie and offered no apology. "I'm not as dumb as I look," he said.

"You're dumber than you look!" Debbie threw her cigarette to the ground and stomped on the butt as though she was squashing a bug. "Liar! Fucking liar!"

This time Stanley did look apologetic. "I'm very sorry about what happened between us, but it was in September. Do the math. You don't look six months pregnant."

"She carries small," Fran offered, positioning herself like a referee in between them. "She hardly shows until the end."

"I have nothing more to say." Stanley motioned to Cookie to walk away with him.

"You shouldn't be with a girl that young!" Fran shouted. "Cookie, I'm going to have a talk with your father!"

"Fucking liar!" Debbie yelled.

Fran and Debbie might have had more to say, but their voices waned under the rumble of the fast-approaching Number 2 bus. Neither Stanley nor Cookie turned around to see if both women got onto the bus.

It was troubling to think of Stanley as being the father of Debbie's baby. He was clearly upset as they walked toward his car parked in the lot behind the bank on Roberts Avenue.

Stanley held open the car door for Cookie and she got in.

He rolled down his window in the car. "The smell of cigarettes makes me sick."

Cookie thought it was not a good time to light a Marlboro and wondered how she'd quell her craving for one. He didn't dare take his eyes off the road to look at her. Cookie could only see his profile. "It couldn't be mine. I haven't gone out with her since last October. That night I saw you crawling on the ground looking for your earring... we had come home from a wedding. I broke up with her. She was so mad that she threw her bouquet onto the road and hit me. That was the last time I went out with her."

"It's her fourth pregnancy," Cookie told him.

"I can't undo what I did," he said. "But there's no going back now."

The early evening light, bluish and damp, came in through the car windows. They rode in silence. The steady but intermittent sweep of the windshield wipers grated against the glass. The rain had tapered to fine mist.

A few minutes later, he said, "She's not my type."

What's your type, Cookie wanted to ask. She'd also love to light up a Marlboro but didn't.

He turned off the windshield wipers and turned the radio on, which was tuned in to a station playing a song by Loretta Lynn. Cookie didn't know the name of the song and didn't care. She wasn't a fan of country and western music but liked listening to the emotional twang of love gone wrong.

They went to the Midget Bar where everyone knew him and let his darkness settle. Cookie ordered a rum & coke and he ordered his lone beer. White light from the jukebox illuminated the top of their table. Neil Young's newly released song *Heart of Gold* spilled into the bar. Stanley's beer, pale and golden, sat mostly untouched. Cookie wanted Stanley with all of her heart, but she had one misgiving about him—he had hooked up with Debbie. Other than this one small detail, no matter how hard she tried, she couldn't find anything wrong with him.

Out of the blue, he said, "Sometimes, we don't see the things that are right in front of us and it takes years to figure it out."

Cookie felt as though he was talking more to himself than to her.

Plenty of couples made out in the dark cave of the Midget Bar. Cookie had made every effort to woo Stanley. Hair in Juliet curls, a shirt as low-cut and a skirt as short as the ones favored by Gina Lollobrigida, she had primped, fussed and gussied herself up to gain Stanley's affection. She polished her lips vamp red and licked them until they glistened. But it was a no-go. Maybe, he didn't see her in a sexual way. She left her hand on the table, hoping he might touch her. She moved her chair alongside his and sat close so she could press her leg against his leg. The hair on his arms tickled her arms. Every time he moved, she felt energy as powerful as electricity run though her body, giving her a little thrill in her heart. She picked up his warm scent from his neck, his shoulder and under his arm, firing her up, a wanton sensation for which she held no shame. And why should she? She wanted this man and was going to get him.

But he was extraordinarily dense and remote, which she attributed in part to his ethnicity—Johnny would have called him a dumb Polack. While she swooned seductively, always aggressively moving toward him, he seemed to be caught unaware. Intentional or not, he never let his eyes linger long on her breasts or legs. She had no way of knowing if his eyes feasted on her plucky bottom. He didn't flirt or lean in for a kiss. With every passing moment, he grew increasingly somber.

He talked about tragedy. A Danish airliner had crashed a world away in Oman. The plane had hit a mountain, killing 112 people. The unexpected disaster fascinated him. At any given moment, bombs dropped from the sky and rained wrath on the young, the old, and the innocent. There was no rhyme or reason to the pattern of whose life was taken and whose life was spared.

He spoke of the bodies he had seen wrecked and damaged by artillery. Men and women with stumps for legs. Arms blown off. Guts spilling like angry red snakes. Torsos with no limbs, no head. Some who had lived and wished they had died. Cookie could have seen this conversation as a warning sign—Stanley was a dangerous and dark man. But the exhilaration of seeing him, being with him, close enough to touch him, if only slightly, won over any trepidation she had to flee the situation.

Then, as if he had out-gloomed even himself, his banter turned light and switched to fun.

He folded his arms, grazing her arm, not so accidentally. His movement became so subtle he had to know the best way to touch a woman was to make her feel his desire, his heat, his hungry eyes devouring her whole and still unable to get enough.

He shot her a smile full of mischief. "I'll bet while I was getting my ass shot at, you were out there protesting the war."

"The war is wrong," Cookie said. "We shouldn't be in Vietnam."

"Thinking that way doesn't do me a lot of good." Stanley turned around in his chair, scanning the back room where they sat at the table, and up front, the bar. Jimmy wasn't there. Another woman who didn't have to stand on milk crates poured beer. Stanley's eyes fastened for a moment on the woman but did not rest in any one spot on her body. "Jimmy's aunt," he said. "She's not a midget and very pretty."

Cookie was miffed. When will he notice how pretty I am? Instead, Cookie chanted, "Hell no, we won't go. Remember?"

He was somewhat amused, a little annoyed; he looked at her as though he didn't know what to say.

"It's an anti-war slogan. One of many." Cookie smiled at him. As she crossed her legs in her chair, she saw him sneak a glance at her skirt rising up. Then he turned away, pretending he had not noticed. She knew she had pretty legs, shapely Betty Grable legs.

"Someone asked me the other day what my favorite fast food was when I was growing up. I never had fast food. My mother made everything from scratch. She made food from the bones butchers throw away."

"No way! That's amazing!" Cookie decided to use a different strategy. She looked longingly into Stanley's eyes and hung on to every word he said, treating him as though he was the most amazing and enlightened man in the world.

"My mother cooked every day and kept a pot going on the stove. When my father was alive, we sat down at the kitchen table and ate together like a family every night."

Cookie didn't know whether she hated him or loved him for having a normal family. She did not tell him about her family. How she learned to cook so she could feed herself and Donny on the days Johnny was gone and Kitty was having a spell. How she'd grown up too fast and never had a childhood at all. Sexually, though, she had been stonewalled into remaining a child. Kissing, making out, doing the things coming naturally from one thing leading to another, all of this eluded her. She wanted to have sex with him in a way no other woman had. Her body would do the work. She would love him to death. She saw no reason to confess the truth about her life, or what she really wanted from him. He had eyes. The most amazing blue eyes ever. Couldn't he see what she wanted? She let her hand drop down and rest on his thigh.

Stanley chuckled so hard she thought he had lost all interest in her. She didn't ask him what he found funny. He didn't seem to be making fun of her, but maybe he was. She pulled her hand away from his leg. If he didn't stop laughing, then she was going to get up and walk away from the damn table.

"What's so funny?" she asked.

"My mother always asks, 'What's so funny?' Except she has a heavy Polish accent, so she says, *'Vhat's so funny?'*"

"*Vhat's so funny, Stanley?*" He stood up and sauntered to the jukebox where he dropped a quarter into the slot and casually scanned the menu to see what he wanted to play. He turned around toward Cookie and smiled, "Anything you'd like to hear?" She shook her head and turned away from looking at his body pressed up against the jukebox.

"Sure?" he asked again. This time she didn't even look at him and quietly chewed her gum, not even going for a pop or two. The days of cracking gum were gone. Gum only kept her from craving a Marlboro.

Riders on the Storm by the Doors began to play. Stanley's hips moved in tempo with the song. As sinuous and as limber as Jim Morrison, his torso, arms and shoulders were muscular and sculpted with exacting proportion. He wasn't the kind of man who scrutinized himself in the mirror or agonized over what he would wear. He looked good in everything or made everything look good.

When he returned to the table, he moved his chair, so he could sit across from her. Now he could see her reaction to the things he talked about.

"There are some things I've come to know about my childhood. My parents never owned their own house. Never had a car. Never went away on vacation. My father died when I was eight, shortly after we moved to Yonkers. We were poor. I used to ride a bike around the hill. A second-hand bike I fixed up. The gears and the handlebars were rusty. We didn't have a television until I was twelve. We still have the same one. It's black & white."

There were moments like this when she wanted to escape, but deep down inside, she knew her time with Stanley was a passage in her life inevitably bound to happen. "I'm not sure what you're getting at," she told him.

"I guess I'm giving you a hard lesson about reality." He took a deep indrawn breath, as though he was about to say something uncomfortable but important. "My family's poor.

We were poor before my father died. Had he lived, things might have been different. I didn't have the money to pay someone off to get out of going to Vietnam."

In Cookie's estimation, Stanley was not a strong candidate to be a victim. He was too good looking, strong and smart. "Maybe it was your destiny to go there," she said.

Stanley was taken aback. "Most of us didn't want to be there. Rich boys got out of the draft. Poor, working-class, black, white and brown—we didn't have a choice. War is a rich man's game fought on the backs of guys like me."

Honestly, she did not know why he was talking this way. Nobody was rich in Yonkers. Nobody knew anybody rich. It was taken for granted everyone was middle-class or poor. Cookie took a clumsy sip of her rum & coke, sending fizz up her nose. She eyed him warily. "You could have left the country and gone to Canada."

The smile Stanley gave her was not unkind, but it did signal his impatience with her. "I was all my mother had left. What would she have done if I went to Canada and couldn't come back? What would she have done if I didn't come back from Vietnam? Think about that next time you sing your anti-war chant."

"I can see why no one wants to talk to you," Cookie said.

"I don't want to talk to most people. I want them to leave me alone."

Cookie looked up at him. Her lips parted slightly, and she fixed her gaze firmly on his face. "I find it easy to talk to you."

Quiet for a moment. Thoughtful. It took effort for him to form his words. "I find it easy to talk to you too," he said. As much as he professed this one small connection to her—talking was as far as it would go.

"I've learned something important about you." He set her hemp sack on the table. "You have two sets of I.D.," he said. "One's fake."

Cookie didn't bother to reach for her bag and left it on

the table. She knew a barrier had come between them. She could tell he was getting ready to leave. Sometimes he sat at the same table in the back of the Midget Bar and nursed his beer for hours. Then as soon as he was getting ready go home, he drank his beer in two gulps—his ritual. She had learned his real purpose of wanting to see her—to return her bag. He picked up the hemp sack from the table and placed it on her lap. He told her he didn't like to look inside of ladies' purses, but he had to make sure it did belong to her. And it was a good thing too. If Jimmy the Midget had found the bag and looked inside, he'd never let her into the bar again, until she turned eighteen. Jimmy wouldn't want to risk losing his license or get shut down. "I know how old you are," Stanley told her.

Twenty-two

Shrunken Peach

Cookie sat by the edge of the river and let her hair fall forward to almost skim the top of the water. She could see her hazy reflection and felt the sun kiss her cheeks. The weather was changing. Bursts of warm days came more often now than the days of cold temperatures just hovering above freezing. She had hoped to see Stanley hanging around the Kennedy Marina. No such luck. He didn't mope much. He always seemed to be on a mission. Maybe being in Vietnam had given him a sense of purpose.

Her hands rested on her bare thighs. She had taken to wearing the shortest skirts possible, hoping it would magnify his attraction and eventually wear him down. So far it had not. He noticed alright, but always managed to turn away as if he embarrassed himself by thinking of her sexually. You know the way men think about taking advantage of a girl? Even if the girl is only too willing or easy, a total slut, guys always think of themselves as being the aggressor, a man of action, the man in charge of the situation.

She tried calling Stanley at home, but when Bertha answered, she always sounded cross and said the same thing:

He's not here and I don't know where he is. Maybe you should do your schoolwork. Cookie gripped a black & white composition book. It was a new notebook with fresh blank pages, nothing torn out, and nothing written except for Stanley's phone number.

A group of boys tracked her movement by the river's edge, but no one moved in her direction. She didn't stare too hard to see if she knew anyone. They were hanging out, too cool to pay her much mind. A girl had to earn their attention, especially when a whole group of them clustered together, croaking like frogs catching flies. She wanted to be with a boy, but she sure as hell didn't want to be with one of them. Lifers, loafers and losers. They were Yonkers boys.

"What are you wearing? A push-up bra? It's about time you grew breasts big enough to push up!"

Toni Ferlinghetti called out from the window of Arky's jeep. "Oh my God, I can't believe it. Look at you with that skirt! You're just asking for it!"

She climbed down out of the jeep and slammed the door shut. She wore navy and red cork platform sandals and shirtwaist stove pants designed to be as vivid and as weird as a bad acid trip. With variations of amoeba designs in coral and many shades of blue, each pant leg flared open around her ankles. The thick cork soles of her platform shoes squeaked with each step she took and made tread marks on the damp earth.

"With all these guys around here, someone's going to nail you but good."

Cookie laughed. "Are you jealous?" she asked, sarcastically.

"Give me a break!" Toni rolled her eyes.

Hardly held captive by a scant bra, Toni's breasts jutted through a transparent coral blouse. She put her hands on her hips. "And all I can say is, it's about time that you think about hooking up with somebody. I think you're the only girl I know who's still a virgin."

Left behind at the wheel of the jeep, Arky yelled, "Hey, where are you going?"

Three other cars were parked on the bank of the river, but Cookie had not paid much attention. If she got too close, she was bound to stumble upon a couple going at it hard, and it would make her feel pretty crummy about not getting Stanley to do the same thing with her.

Toni turned to gaze across the smoky blue haze of water. "Why are you sitting here all by yourself?"

Cookie brushed her hand through tall grass, accidentally hitting clumps of earth, damp and swamp-like at their roots. "I'm just sitting here thinking."

"Thinking!" Toni laughed. As she walked toward her, the breeze from the river blew through her hair, which had returned to its red-tinted raven glory. Her hair looked spectacular in its natural color.

"I turned sixteen," Toni said, "and you know what that means? It's time to start finding the right guy. I don't want to wake up and be eighteen without prospects for a guy to marry and have to get desperate all of a sudden."

Cookie burst out laughing. She couldn't help herself. She was worrying about finding a guy she liked enough to want to kiss, and Toni had gotten herself all worked up over who she would marry.

"He's gotta be rich," Toni said.

"Got that." Cookie smiled.

"Real rich," Toni emphasized.

"Don't you care if he's good looking?" Cookie laughed so hard she started getting hiccups.

"That too. But rich is at the top of my list."

"Good luck finding a rich guy in Yonkers."

"I don't see what's so funny. Maybe you can clue me in. Rich guys do exist. You just have to know where to find them."

"Did you ever ask Arky about his financial position? Maybe his family has money and we don't know it."

Arky had been listening. He perked up, waving long enough to take his hands off the wheel of the jeep, giving

Cookie a good-natured smile. He cranked up the radio playing the Allman Brothers' *Ain't Wastin Time No More*. The band's *Eat a Peach* album had been released in February. Arky began banging on the steering wheel like he was playing the drums. The song had been written about the dead Allman brother, Duane. Arky knew every word by heart. The image of a peach from the album cover flitted through Cookie's mind like an unwelcome fly. So sick of being told what was hot and what was not, what song to listen to and what record to buy, she'd like to shrink the damn peach down to its pit.

Then she started laughing again. "I can't believe you're thinking about who you're going to marry."

"Honestly, Cookie, you're just too weird and whacked out like your mother. You think by now you'd stop acting like a misfit and get yourself a real boyfriend, someone to make out with and take you out to a show at Loew's Cinema. Instead, you got yourself a reputation for always being up to no good. No one's ever going to marry you."

Cookie backed away from Toni. She was too dumb to talk to and too dumb to argue with.

"Don't you think you'll get married some day?" Toni's question was a grand indictment. "Look at you! You're all sexed up with nowhere to go!"

She swept her hands through the air. "Aren't you thinking about who you might marry? Don't you even have an idea of how much money he'll have? I mean, like, money is really important, especially when you don't got any. You could get stuck in the poorhouse!"

Toni was talking in her face; Cookie could smell the sugary scent of chewing gum on her breath. Toni kept talking about finding a rich guy to marry.

Cookie shut her out and had an epiphany. She realized her own brain functioned with the wisdom of a forty-year-old woman, who had already lived a full life. She was the diametric opposite of Toni Ferlinghetti, who looked twenty-five but had the emotional maturity of a child with special needs. She was doomed to behave perpetually twelve. Forever. No growing up for this girl, *unh unh unh unhhhhh*. Toni was going to stay twelve.

"Haven't you done *it*? You know what I mean, the inny-outy thing?"

"Why do you even care?"

"Come on," Toni said, elbowing her, giving her the knowing look of Italian girl sisterhood. "Come on, you can tell me. If you can't tell me, who can you tell?"

Cookie looked at her with wide open eyes. She hoped to sound earnest, sincere. "I'm kind of stuck on kissing."

"I knew it!" Toni got right in her face and began pointing. "That confirms my worst suspicions! I just knew it!"

Cookie swatted Toni's hand away and looked directly into her eyes. "The problem with you, Toni, is you don't care how dumb you are. You think you only have to be good looking. You think being good looking is all it takes to get by in life."

"I'm going to be brutally honest with you, Cookie."

"Aren't you always?"

"You know, I always speak my mind."

"What mind?" Cookie smiled.

Toni erupted into an explosion of Yonkers white noise.

"Everyone knows about you and that Stanley character! People are starting to talk! First, you're with that black boy all the time! The one with the deformed mouth! Except, I heard he got his mouth fixed and you don't hang out so much no more. Now you're out there following that Stanley guy around like a hound dog. He is hunky, but he's also nuts. All of those guys who come back from Vietnam are disturbed. Can't you see he doesn't want to be bothered with the likes of you! And if he did, it'd be even worse for you. Think about it. He's a whacked-out Vietnam Vet and too old for you!"

Midway through Toni's tirade, Cookie had stopped looking into her eyes. She found her attention riveted to the ground surrounding Toni's feet. Staring long and hard, she began to devise a plan. She admired Toni's blouse, orangey-pink, salmon, coral, not sure of the exact color, and her cork platform sandals were definitely navy and red. Toni had good taste. But another more imminent part of Cookie traced the distance to the water. She bobbed her head cleanly, a jungle cat judging the distance to jump an antelope to rip out its heart. She estimated the deed could be done in one swift move.

"We're just friends." Cookie meant Stanley.

Toni thought she meant her friendship with Cookie. "Are we? You still haven't made me a fake I.D. card so I can get into clubs in the city. Manhattan!! That's the only place I'm going to find a rich guy! You call this friendship!"

Cookie found sometimes she didn't even know it, but she was thinking something through. She was setting forth an unconscious road map for the future. Strategy. Cunning. Guile. A course of action was evolving. It was not sheer impulsiveness—being impulsive is something you can't see coming. It just happens in the blink of an eye. Cookie meant to be cold, calculating, and deliberate. She saw what would happen and worked it all out in her mind. She chose not to stop herself. Why should she tell herself to stop when she had nothing to gain by remaining passive, mute, a good girl. From past experience, Cookie knew good girls finish last. Being bad, coupled with being very smart, was the highest form of good. And she aspired to be in high places.

"You think you're so smart, but you're really not!" Toni placed her hands on her hips, a pose portending the first musical phrase of a war dance.

Athletic, strong legs, Cookie had a distinct advantage. Toni, on the other hand, stood on flimsy stilts, unstable, off-balance.

In the strong sun the water smelled like fish rotting on a bed of creosote. The river never smelled so good and so bad. Cookie pushed Toni into the river. Toni never saw it coming. She splashed into the shallow water with the crumbling thud of a cinder block. If you don't mind garbage and foul waste, it wasn't dangerous. Toni fishtailed in between piles of bloated trash bags, hunks of pink insulation stuffing, bricks of Styrofoam, green tube piping, half of a commercial metal garage door, and a random collection of junk food wrappers. A small black pool glazed the top her shoes, leaving an oily rainbow sheen.

Toni had it coming. Not too long ago, Toni had pushed Cookie into the Sprain Brook Reservoir and nearly drowned her. Arky had pulled Cookie out and saved her life. He was there now for Toni too. Still mouthing the lyrics to *Ain't Wastin Time No More*, he ran to the river's edge. In a flash with his arm extended as long as the line on a fishing pole, he began dragging Toni back in. She grabbed onto his hand, pulling like dead weight, and cried out, "Gross!"

Twenty-three

Hot Pants

Every time she called Stanley at home, he wasn't there. Bertha always said the same thing: He's not here and I don't know where he is. Maybe you should go to school and stop worrying about my son. Word had gotten out. Rumors spread as fast as the fire in Cookie's heart. Cookie had stopped going to school and was truant. Everyone except Johnny and Kitty seemed to know she was on the verge of getting kicked out of school and becoming a juvenile delinquent. Sister Mary Eau Claire, the principal of her school, had to have called her home by now, but since Kitty never answered the phone and Johnny rarely came home, her parents were in the dark.

The month of April 1972 was one of the coldest on record. Temperatures hovered in the forties during the day, and by nightfall cold dampness had seeped into everyone's bones. Then on the first truly warm day, Wednesday, April 19, 1972, the temperature rose into the eighties. What had once been a small patch of woods next to Cookie's house had become overtaken with tall grass, purple-headed thistle and milkweed bursting open in pink and orange. Every battlefield has its own beauty. New life had sprung out of war, atrocity and death. The trunks of the slain Sumac trees had not decayed and turned into mulch. The surviving roots in the ground stored energy from when the trees had been alive. Sprouts reappeared, and shiny green blades of new growth emerged. The cool, dark woods had been transformed into a sunlit meadow full of monarch butterflies and birds.

This was the Yonkers Johnny had talked about when he said he didn't know where he was living. *Am I in a city or a suburb or the country? With all of these goddamn Sumac trees, I might as well be in the sticks. YONKERS, Yonkers*, he had bellowed.

Cookie thought snidely, "Well, Johnny, the Sumac trees are back."

She made a note to herself to tell Stanley about the return of the Sumac trees. She thought it might cheer him up and make him see how out of the stench of death comes new life, a victory as sweet as the early bloom of daffodils.

The unexpected warmth of this April day made her feel like taking her clothes off. She walked around her house wearing her new pink bikini with white shoelace strings fastening eyelets in the bra and both sides of the bottom. And when she grew tired of doing nothing, she put on a pair of short jean shorts over her bikini bottom and walked *Down the End*. She took her transistor radio out of her hemp sack and put the earphone into her ears. Preferring to keep personal matters to herself, she didn't want anyone to hear the music she played. She made it a habit to hold her own secrets close to her heart.

The radio played *The First Time Ever I Saw Your Face* by Roberta Flack. Cookie felt so sad. She thought of Stanley and wondered where he was and what he was doing right now. The warm air felt like a balm to her skin. Delicate drops of sweat trickled between her breasts and left a fine necklace of dew. She sat on the ground amid young green fronds, inhaling the fragrance of plants on the verge of bearing flowers. Every April had a day or two like this, when the temperature soared to the heights of summer. Too tender to be deemed buds, leaves on young plants were unprepared for the heat and quivered in the sun from the sudden warmth.

She became aware of the admiring glances from guys passing her on the street and the honks from cars on the road. All of the attention was a fine affirmation of her nubile beauty, unblemished white skin, smooth thighs, long hair, parted in the middle, framing her pretty face. She tightened her features into a bored but bemused expression. Although she attracted hordes of guys, she didn't fully understand what made them so obnoxious, or why she was not the least bit interested in any one of them. The catcalls would come and go in a choir of rogue male voices, ranging in pitch from squeaks to tones as low as a trombone. None of them got her attention. None of them mattered. Not one look of admiration had come from Stanley de Falco.

Everyone was hooking up. Most girls might act as though they were seeking casual hookups, with no strings attached, but the reality was they were intent on sinking their claws into a steady boyfriend. One who would eventually marry them. What used to be a boyfriend-seeking ritual was actually an early mating dance. Yonkers girls married way too young. Some of them got knocked up on purpose so they had to get married.

Cookie didn't want to hook up with a Yonkers boy. She didn't want a boyfriend. Having a Yonkers boyfriend would stand in her way of getting out of here. She didn't want to have sex with no strings attached. She didn't want to go all the way and be labeled as a slut. She didn't want to end up like the jackass slut Joanie and have to put up with the likes of Johnny Colangelo. She didn't know what to do.

She threw her head back, tossing her hair, as though she cared about little in life. These days her passion for fairness and the desire to make the world a better or more noble place no longer interested her. Her body had taken control of her heart, mind and soul. She felt numb and completely mystified by what had happened to her.

It wasn't like Herman Lynch to call. In all of the time they had known one another, until today, they had never talked by phone. He must have found her number in the phone book. Cookie was lucky enough to intercept the call before Kitty got to the phone first and hung up on the first ring. When Kitty was tooting (having a spell), she often said the phone had been hot-wired by the Pope and seven of his nine saints so that it would explode and give her a cauliflower ear.

The relationship Herman had with Cookie was marked by jubilation and surprise. The physical distance between them was ten minutes but they were worlds apart. Herman's home was not ghetto, but he lived close to the projects, far from the North End, a mimicry of the unspoken boundaries separating black & white. They ran into each other because they always seemed to be going to the same place at the same time. Some mystical preordained notion made it so they were always meant to be together.

And as much as she loved Herman Lynch, she was disappointed to hear his voice on the phone instead of Stanley's. She had been waiting for Stanley to call for some time, but he never did.

When she met Herman at the Owl Hole, Cookie could immediately tell something was wrong. His arms had always fallen loosely at his side as though any moment he would use them to spur his body into a dance. On this day, his arms were folded, and he was unusually quiet. The newly stitched flesh above his lip was lighter in color than the rest of his cocoa brown skin. He lit a Marlboro, dropped the match on the concrete slab and stubbed it out. He wasn't wearing Hush Puppies but sporting red Converse high tops. Smoke no longer poured from the hole in between his mouth and nose. He smoked like everyone else now. She had to look hard to see the fine scar on his face. The gaping hole above his lips had been sealed.

"You look good," Cookie told him. "How does it feel?"

Herman blew a smoke ring above his head and beamed her a smile. "I'm trying to get used to it. People still make fun of me, though. I guess they always will. Now it's just for different reasons."

"There's no understanding why people have to try to make someone feel bad so they can feel good. Never understood that." From the ground, Cookie picked up a thin, dried tree branch and dug a line in the soft earth. She meant to write Stanley, but stopped short of tracing a word beyond the letter S.

"No one makes fun of me when I dance," Herman said.

"And why would they?" Cookie twirled around on the concrete landing and set her foot against the bottom step. "You're a natural," she said. "There's no denying talent. And I bet it feels good to have your mouth stitched up tight."

"The hardest part is getting used to people not staring at me all the time. Now they just look at me, but there's no curiosity or pity."

"I still pity you, Herman, for putting up with the likes of me." Cookie laughed and reached to take Herman's Marlboro. He handed it to her and grinned.

She took a long drag and handed the Marlboro back to him. "Did I hurt your feelings when I talked about kissing?"

"Kissing." Herman chuckled. He looked a tad embarrassed and turned away. "It got me to thinking, that's all."

"I was wrong," Cookie said. "Real wrong. Talk about being rude and insensitive." She climbed a few steps, then bounded down in short, even hops. "That's me, the bull in the china shop."

"Forget it," Herman said.

But she didn't feel convinced that it was a small matter to him. Something deeper was going on with Herman. He had developed a new habit of not looking her in the eye.

"I don't know what to do," she told Herman. "All I think about is kissing and sex...I don't know what's wrong with me."

"There's nothing wrong with you," Herman said. "You're just growing up." His smile brightened and she could see his teeth all shiny and white. Smoking had done him no harm. "And from what I've seen of you, and I've seen a lot, you tend to be pretty extreme about everything you do." He stopped, hesitating; he meant to say something more.

"Go on," Cookie said. "I don't mean to interrupt you."

"I go out to see my friends," Herman said. "But none of them live here. They're in the city. How about you? What's going on with you?"

"These days, I'm not doing much." Cookie laughed. "And I feel like I think too much."

"Ditto." Herman smiled and handed the cigarette back to her. "You're a late bloomer. Me too. We bloom later and last longer."

They both laughed and rushed to embrace. "So true." She slapped him five and sought his eyes, finding comfort. There was no hurt or anger in his response. He seemed okay with what had passed between them.

"Hope you don't mind me calling," he said. "I've been worried about you."

She could feel Herman's eyes passing from her short shorts up to her bathing suit top, but he wasn't looking at her like he found her to be sexy. His appraisal of her body was frank but appreciative and coolly restrained. Maybe she had piqued his curiosity, but much to her dismay, he looked into the distance over the top of her head, distracted and daydreaming.

"Damn it, Herman, how do I look?"

Herman's eyes grew huge. "Hot." He grinned.

"It's not doing me much good." Cookie put her hands on her hips. "I attract all the wrong guys."

"Going swimming?" he asked, stretching the expanse of his new upper lip.

Cookie shook her head and let go of a long belch of smoke. "I'm just hot."

"You're looking good, Cookie. All the guys must be chasing you."

She handed Herman the Marlboro. He took a quick hit, like he was toking a joint and handed it right back to her.

She held onto the cigarette, carelessly flicking ashes. "Except the one guy I want. He's not chasing me."

"Not that Stanley guy! He's good looking, but too old for you, Cookie!" Herman pulled his arms in a tighter grip around his own body and it was strange to see. Herman had a habit of always lengthening his limbs as far as he could stretch. Now he had become a prisoner of what he wanted to say. "You go out with a guy like that and you're just headed for trouble. Either he'll break your heart or get you pregnant. Maybe both. What's worse, he might wind up wanting to marry you!"

"So not true. I'm not marrying anyone!"

"I saw you looking at those wedding cakes at the Café Trento!"

"I was killing time." She eyed the Marlboro, wishing she had never taken up smoking. Stanley hated cigarettes.

Herman leaned forward and raised his voice. "I thought you wanted to make something of your life! Be somebody!"

"I do!" She dropped what remained of the Marlboro butt and let it smolder on the ground.

"Now you want to settle for some stupid Yonkers guy and stay here for the rest of your life!"

"You've got me married to him and I haven't even kissed him!"

"Girl, what's gotten into you? You're better than that!"

"He's different," Cookie said. "Real different. He's not a typical Yonkers guy. He's smart."

Herman gave her a cheap guffaw, pretended to take her comments to heart by clutching his chest. "Then what's he doing here?"

She responded to him in a gale of keening laughter. "Swear to God. He's really not dumb."

"I'll believe it when I see it." A slant of sun crossed Herman's green eyes and made them look speckled with brown and gold. "Not to change the subject, but I heard you pushed Toni Ferlinghetti into the river."

"Word gets around fast." Cookie climbed two steps and turned around to look at Herman. "Toni had it coming. I never talked about what she did to me. She almost drowned me once at the Sprain Brook Reservoir. After all the things she's done to me, I can't believe she's gone blabbing about what I did to her. The nerve!"

Herman took a deep breath and sighed. His body spun in a slow turn, lifting his face to the sky, then he turned toward the direction of North Broadway, where cars could be heard but not seen. Quiet, thoughtful, he seemed intent on choosing his words carefully. "I do need to talk to you about something important."

"Like what?"

"I've been hearing other things too." Herman's eyes sought the sky and he touched a new leaf sprouting on a vine curled around the railing. "I heard you're not going to school."

Cookie took a vow of silence as impenetrable as stone. She closed her eyes and could see her stone, grey and hard; the granite would not crack. She thought: *I love a wall where they have not left one stone. The gaps between the stones mean we find another form of hardness there. Set the wall. Keep the wall. Boulders have fallen. We do not need the wall! Old stone!*

She opened her eyes, took her stick and drew a line in the ground, a wall between her and Herman. "This is my line," she said. "Don't cross it."

"Cookie, I'm really worried!"

"I don't need to go to school no more." She glared at Herman. "Any more," she added as a second thought. "I meant I don't need to go to school any more."

Herman stood straight and returned her hard glare. "What about my grandmother? She went out on the limb for you to get you into that school. What are you going to say to her?"

She gave him a vague shrug.

"Cookie, you're not even tracking what I'm saying to you. You're throwing it all away. I don't know what's with you! Is it all on account of this Stanley guy? Or is something else going on?"

"Please just drop it," Cookie implored him.

"Cookie, I've got to tell you something important." He took a deep breath, holding onto the railing for support.

"You might get kicked out of school," he said. "What will you do if you get kicked out of this school? You won't be able to get in anywhere! Then what?"

She could not believe Herman. It was unthinkable she'd get kicked out of school. How could she be in trouble? It wasn't *The Heart*, where Mr. DC was out to get her. At her new school she was invisible. No one even knew she existed.

"No, I won't get kicked out. I'll go back tomorrow and work it out. I swear."

"Promise?"

"Promise." Cookie crossed her heart. "Cross my heart, so hope to die."

She felt ashamed for not considering Herman or his grandmother. She gave Herman a heartfelt hug goodbye to make him feel good, and to make her feel innocent from any wrongdoing. But she knew, in her own private world, nothing mattered except for her deep-rooted oath to lose her innocence. To lose one's innocence, then it must have been there in the first place. For Cookie, innocence was not so grand anyway. She could not remember if she had ever been innocent. She had always been suspicious of losing what she had, even if she had not wanted it in the first place. She had lost her innocence a long time ago. The only remaining thread involved her sexual innocence. Stanley.

Only he could do what she could not do with anyone else. She left Herman with a mournful plea to get together again soon, but it was just talk. Her only aim had to do with Stanley.

She needed to find him, to get in front of him, and to make him want her as much as she wanted him.

Twenty-four

Struck by Lightning

Cookie stumbled like a drunk woman, using her hands to part the brush, bramble and weeds clogging the path back home. By the time she reached the verdant knoll where the Sumacs once stood, she was burning up inside. Her arms and legs blushed and dampened with perspiration. Her cheeks felt too hot to touch. Sore, hot and dizzy, she had the symptoms of fever. Every waking moment, she didn't know if her body raged out of control, gushing hormones, or her brain wreaked havoc. Nothing she had learned in books or pictures had prepared her for the sweeping attacks of heat, assailing every part of her body, upsetting her thoughts, dreams and ambitions. Her obsession with Stanley de Falco had ruined her life. Is this what it was like to be a teenager in love? There, she finally admitted it to herself: she was in love.

If this is what it means to be a teenager in love, then it had to stop! She would make it stop!

Although her inner turmoil was formidable, it paled when compared to the sobbing and screaming coming from her house. Two women were shouting. Donny cried out in small childish spurts and sobs. Their shrill screams brought Cookie back to her senses. Wondering what the hell was going on, she ran into the backyard. Through the sliding glass door, she saw them making a terrible fuss.

Donny sat at the table, her face red and swollen. She looked like she had cried so much she had run out of tears. Kitty and Grandmother Delia vied to vent the most offensive shriek. A winner could not be declared.

Cookie slid open the door and walked in. Donny immediately began to hiccup. No stranger to sniffling, Donny wiped tears from her eyes and her runny nose with both hands. The screaming came to a halt the moment Kitty and Delia turned their heads and eyed Cookie with contemptuous, stony glares. Cookie's intrusion was akin to taking a bucket of cold water and dumping it on their own private fire. The three of them were like the witches of Macbeth stirring the cauldron; and they hated Cookie's interruption more than they hated the horrible event causing their grief. Donny let go of a blood curdling whoop. Both women gave Donny a harsh look of warning meant to end the episode. There would be no further screaming.

Other than their emotional bloodletting, there were no signs of bodily harm, unless you count the cavalcade of torn photographs and stiff negatives, flung to the floor as if they had been slain in battle.

Donny sat at the table with her knees pulled up to her chest in a tight ball. Eyes squeezed shut, she would not look at Cookie. The dining table was littered with photos, some torn to bits, others ripped in half; two yellow photo processing drugstore envelopes had been crushed.

"What's going on?" Cookie asked.

No one answered her directly. She had walked into a family crisis of unimaginable gravity. It was shocking to think Delia had taken the Number 2 bus from the corner of Herriot and South Broadway all the way to the North End. She had not made this visit in years. Delia avoided the Colangelos, especially her daughter who had earned a well-deserved reputation for being certifiably insane.

On the Murphy side of the family it was okay to be crazy, but it was quite another matter to have been committed to the nuthouse and kept there longer than overnight. An overnight stay in the nuthouse could mean you just had a bad day. Indefinite incarceration meant there had been an official diagnosis made by medical doctors prescribing drugs, straitjackets, and shock therapy. Schizophrenic Kitty née Murphy Colangelo had brought shame to bear on the family.

The Irish wear shame like a comfortable woolen cloak. They swear shame gives them permission to take to the drink. All other emotions, conditions and maladies festering under the skin must be borne with alacrity as though it is an honor like original sin bestowed by the angels and God. If cheerfulness is not possible, then one must keep a stiff upper lip so as not to offend either God or the devil.

No one does shame better than the Irish. But of all the Irish in the world, Grandmother Delia O'Toole had woven shame into the art form of an intricate tapestry. Sitting in Kitty's favorite armchair, she used her bare stockinged feet to massage her calves, staving off her loss of circulation.

"I have restless legs," she said with a slight smile, softening like a curl. "Restless leg syndrome, they call it."

Today Delia's eyes looked bright and as blue as Donny's. She wore a pale blue felt hat that had the pillbox style of a modern Easter bonnet. Cookie noticed that Delia had not taken off her coat, which was pale blue like her bonnet. Yet her shoes had been scattered several feet apart, appearing as though they had been hurriedly kicked off.

"Your mother didn't mean to break nothing," Delia said. "Everything fell on the floor accidentally. Didn't it, Donny?"

Donny slowly shook her head yes and shrugged. "Kitty's clumsy sometimes."

Cookie had not immediately noticed the damage, mostly picture frames, vases and drinking glasses. A few choice items had been flung to the floor, but the breakage was not catastrophic. Cookie's feet padded gingerly along the floor, one foot in front of the other to avoid a few shards of broken glass. She moved slowly toward the women and examined the photos on the table: mostly sunsets, light on red glass, reflections of sunlight filtering through trees, and close-up shots of autumn leaves.

Cookie wasn't certain how to assess the situation and decided not to take any chances. From past experience, she knew both women could explode into physical violence. Donny sat on a chair looking lumpish, barely breathing, in shock but still alive.

"Like hello," Cookie said. "Will someone tell me what's going on?"

Donny scrunched her face and shook her head no. Delia pressed her hand over her mouth and looked pensive. She needed time to think about what she should say.

"I took pictures and they came out good." Donny did not look pleased with herself.

"Your father's been horsing around with another woman." Delia's voice was mournful. "We have the evidence. He will have to pay the piper."

Kitty's smile turned serene. "Johnny's been squeezing whiskey glasses again," she said.

Delia gave Cookie a knowing look. "You know the story of Tiny Ten Pint, don't you?"

"Remember what happened to Tiny Ten Pint?" Kitty's comment came in a deliberate voice, an indictment. "Someone will die."

"That means I'll die," Donny whined. "Like Josephine and Mary."

"Stop saying that," Delia shouted. "You have no right to talk that way about my sisters."

"I don't want to die," Donny protested.

"You're not going to die! Never!" Delia pulled out a brown plastic powder compact, pouted at herself in the mirror, and freshened her lipstick, making her lips dewy pink. "So help me, God, you'll never die. Stop talking like that."

"Jesus, Mary and Joseph," Kitty said. "Do you have to talk like that, Ma?"

This time Donny looked at her from the corner of her eye as if she was guilty of making a feeble attempt to watch a peep show. "I took lots of pictures of Daddy," she told Cookie.

Shrieking came with the fury of rolling thunder in the distance. Outside, the weather had changed, and Kitty began to sob. Delia kept saying, "Keep it down. Keep it down, I said. All of the neighbors will hear you. Why do you have to draw so much attention to yourself!"

Donny pushed a picture toward Cookie. A man and a woman looked like they were laughing. Cookie immediately recognized Johnny...with the blond woman...Joanie.

Donny spoke up. "I took pictures with the Brownie. Johnny made me go with them to babysit."

"Who's them?" Cookie asked.

"You know who I mean, Cookie. Daddy and Joanie. She has little kids. I went with them to Tibbets to watch her kids, so Daddy and Joanie could stay by themselves on the blanket."

Tibbets Brook Park in the Lincoln Park section of Yonkers was famous for its public swimming pool. The park also had hiking trails, picnic tables and hidden places to loll beneath the canopies of trees. Cookie could not believe Johnny was hanging out in the woods when he much preferred his life in the city.

Donny leaned forward and said to Cookie, "They kissed. I saw them kissing."

"He has no right to do this! I've never even looked at another man," Kitty wailed. "And he's always accusing me of cheating on him. It's not fair."

"He says those things because he's guilty," Delia said. "It's because he cheats on you!" Delia stamped her foot on the floor so hard it sounded like she wore a boot. Cookie half expected her to stand up and launch into a clog dance.

"They were kissing," Donny insisted. "I told them to stop it, but they didn't."

"You didn't have to say that," Cookie snapped.

Kitty sank into a dining room chair. Miserable and disheveled looking, surprisingly she spoke in an even-keeled voice and sounded sane. "I don't know what to do. I've been a good wife. I don't know what he wants. All these Italian guys are the same. They want the Madonna at home and the whores on the street."

Cookie saw her sobbing again and felt sorry for her mother. She felt compelled to rally and defend her. She patted Kitty on the cheek. "You're still my Kitty. You'll always be my Kitty."

Even though fresh tears filled her mother's eyes, she smiled. "I know, I'm your Kitty."

Cookie had never seen Delia exude a powerful emotion other than the lowest ebb of melancholy. She bore sadness in the most mundane way possible. "Johnny should not have done this to your mother," she said, her voice flat and sanctimonious. "He's got that Italian in him that makes him hot blooded."

Cookie had lost track of time. She didn't think it was late enough to lose light in the sky, but it had grown dark outside. Thunder grew louder. Flashes of blue could be seen through the windows. A storm was fast approaching.

"I'm going to kill Johnny," Cookie said.

Delia shrugged and nodded as though killing Johnny wasn't a bad idea and offered counsel to Kitty. "Whatever you do, don't take to the drink. You'll wind up like Tiny Ten Pint."

The two women became calm, as though they had been sedated from the same prescription drug. The mention of Tiny Ten Pint had an effect on them. He took to the drink because he was grief-stricken after little Mary and baby Josephine died in the Great Influenza. Before little Mary died, she used to stand in the front window of their tenement on Jackson Street and wait every night for her father to come home. After she died, he could not bear to come home at night to see the window empty. Tynan O'Toole became *Tiny Ten Pint*, forevermore.

Delia told a dispirited-sounding tale involving a lightning strike from the past. She had spun this same yarn for as long as anyone could remember. Many years ago, Tynan O'Toole was called Tiny Ten Pint due to the vast quantities of beer and whiskey, commonly called boilermakers, shots of whiskey backed with beer, that he consumed. A binge drinker, Tiny disappeared for months at a time, becoming a fixture in Irish bars in parts unknown. After his usual three-month long binge, he returned home as a sober gentleman who disdained all forms of the drink.

One unfortunate night, after Tiny returned to the family home on Jackson Street, he suffered a relapse. Sitting outside on the back stoop, he helped himself to beer chased with two-ounce shots of cheap whiskey. He seemed to be rearing up to leave home to go on another long binge when a summer thunderstorm rolled in. The skies to the west above the river darkened. Large drops of rain began to fall, and the wind kicked up. But there was no reason for Tiny Ten Pint to leave the back stoop. The porch overhang protected him from the rain and the churning wind. Even as the rain grew heavy and the skies poured wrath from the heavens, he stayed put on the stoop.

He was having a helluva time drinking and muttering cheap invectives about Edith P. Welty, who was the mayor in 1949. Mrs. Welty, a 61-year-old grandmother, became the first woman Mayor of Yonkers and served for one year. In a narrow political race, she had been chosen to serve out the unexpired term of Curtiss E. Frank, who had resigned as mayor for reasons unknown.

Tiny Ten Pint didn't let his mutterings get too ribald. He had always been known as a happy drunk. Then the unexpected happened. From behind the dark clouds, a bolt of lightning struck. The strike was so powerful that it knocked Tiny's beer stein from his hand. Followed by a horrific thunderclap, the house shook with enough force to knock off framed photos from the walls. While Tiny's large beer stein was made from an undefined metal, no one could be sure if the bolt had struck his stein or the gutter spouts. One thing was certain, Tiny suffered permanent nerve damage in his right hand, making it impossible for him to clench a fist or hold a beer stein. Never again did Tiny Ten Pint take to the drink. Some people in South Yonkers claimed it was nothing short of a miracle.

Delia massaged her calves with her feet in the tempo of a sad song about how love comes and goes. "You're going to have to do something to keep your husband home at night," she told Kitty.

"Come on, Ma, no one can keep an Italian guy home at night."

"You can be the first," Delia said with the hint of a cocky smile.

The room became illuminated with a flash of blue, causing the overhead light to flicker. In the distance, thunder struck. The storm had moved closer.

"Tiny Ten Pint is back." Delia stood, picking up her feet, and marched in place. The movement of her bare stockinged feet was deft and delicate to avoid the shattered glass.

"It's just a spring storm," Cookie told her.

"Some storm," Donny said, drawing herself into a tighter ball as if that would protect her from the wind and the rain.

"It's more than a storm," Delia said. "It's a sure sign from God."

The lightning strikes came frequently, and the wind picked up, rattling the metal downspouts against the house.

They could hear the rain spattering on the roof, and grew still for a moment, listening to the booming thunder while they watched the terrible crackling flashes in the picture window. The wind howled, and a loud crash hit the side of the house. No one moved to see what had hit the house. Donny put her hands over her ears. Delia closed her eyes and might have been praying. Kitty held composure, smiling sweetly. With all the things in this world Kitty had reason to be scared of, the storm was a hapless non-event with no purpose under the sun other than to bring water to the earth.

Cookie went to the window and saw a metal garbage toppled over and blown up against the house. Gutters and downspouts had overflowed, leaving an avalanche of water to fall from the awnings. They watched sheets of water pouring from the roof and listened to the drum and rumble of thunder. This angry outpour of rain brought silence to them, but it had not brought them peace.

Delia spoke first. "Reminds me of what happened years ago."

"Stop it, Ma," Kitty said. "Donny doesn't like it when you talk that way. I don't want to hear no more talk of dead babies."

"Josephine and Mary. Josephine and Mary. There I said it five times," Cookie grumbled. "What do I have to do to get my point across?"

Delia's eyes glinted a broad flat flash, like sheet lightning. "How about by being quiet for a change?"

Cookie clapped her hands to applaud her grandmother and was greeted by a thunderclap so loud it shook the house, sounding like the sky had cracked in half.

Donny stuck her tongue out at Cookie. "That's what you get for talking about dead babies."

Cookie was annoyed with her grandmother's woeful tale of Tiny Ten Pint. She refused to settle for the fate and the misery of winding up like them! She was going to go places, see the world, and become famous. Maybe rich too. She wasn't so sure about the rich part yet, but she knew for sure she was going to see the world.

"Look at you. Look at the both of you! Like, I'm not going to be like you!" Cookie yelled. "I'm so outta here."

Delia sighed. "Being disrespectful will get you nowhere."

Kitty eyed her daughter with fresh scorn, but spoke to Delia, "Oh, Ma, there she is going on again with her big plans."

"I know. I know," Delia said. "She'll find out what it means to be too big for her britches."

Both women had no clue what Cookie meant. She didn't have the patience to explain it to them, and even if she had, they were incapable of seeing the world beyond their own narrow ken—eight blocks between Getty Square and South Yonkers.

Delia laughed and looked at her granddaughter like she was a fool or playing a practical joke. "Okay, have it your way," she said, with her voice too soft to be sincere.

"And you," Cookie said to her mother, "you married the wrong man. He's all wrong for you. Can't you see the awful way he treats you! And treats us! He's not capable of being a good husband or father to anyone. Johnny's a lying, rotten bastard!"

It didn't matter how he got there or exactly at what point he had walked into the house, but Johnny stood there, and he had to have heard what Cookie had said. His curly hair had gone flat and dripped water onto his large face, but he showed no indication of wanting to rebuke his daughter. Standing there soaked, Johnny was a sorry sight. His complexion usually straddled between beefy red and swarthy, but at this moment the color had drained from his face. Something had scared him to death. He had been caught in the rain. His khaki work pants and a short sleeve shirt were waterlogged and plastered to his body.

Cookie did not know where her father had come from. He could not have gotten this wet coming from his car to the house. She had never seen her father in such an awkward position. This was his home, and yet he looked like he felt out of place, as though he did not belong here. His blue eyes were rimmed with red and not from the drink. His eyes met his wife's eyes. Her eyes grew moist, but she did not cry.

Delia stood as stiff and as implacable as a steel subway stanchion. "I have nothing to say to you," she told Johnny. "And I will be going home…as soon as the rain stops."

"Come on, I'll drive you," Johnny offered. "As soon as the rain stops, we'll go."

Delia frowned at him. "Maybe another time when I can stomach sitting in the same car with you."

"I'm not going anywhere with you ever again," Donny chimed in.

Cookie squared off, faced her father and said, "I'm so disappointed in you that I can no longer call you my father."

If Johnny meant to collapse to the floor, he stopped himself and let his head hang in shame. He knew he was outnumbered. "Oh Madone. Oh Jesus. I swear I think I almost got struck by lightning."

"Serves you right," Delia snapped.

No one commented on the passing storm. The drum of thunder rolled low, a sure sign the storm had passed as quickly as it had come. Blue flashes of light didn't come as often. The rain could no longer be heard. Tired and broken like an old dog, Johnny had not lifted his head to look at anyone. If he had worn a hat, it would have stayed sodden in his hands for an unimaginable span of time.

Twenty-five

The Good Nun

Whether it was lightning or something else, Johnny Colangelo had indeed been struck. For the first time, he became more grown up and started acting like a father. Cookie had been raising herself and on her own for so long. Having Johnny around all the time made her life difficult and took some getting used to. Johnny bought Donny her own camera, a small instamatic Kodak. Everyone expected Kitty to fall apart, but the opposite happened. She and Johnny started going on dates again. Every Sunday afternoon, they got into his car and went for a drive in the country. Kitty dressed up in silk stockings, garters, short skirts and satin camisoles with plunging necklines she had rescued from a keepsake chest filled with mothballs. She threw cashmere sweaters over her shoulders with the panache of a carefree teenage girl.

And Johnny began to speak highly of trees. All trees. Even the Sumac trees that were growing back. The earlier attempt to destroy them had only led to a less than certain death, and the earth encouraged them to return from the dead to live once again.

Stanley de Falco disappeared from Yonkers. No one knew where he had gone. If Bertha Sokól knew, she wasn't telling.

Cookie called Stanley at home, but Bertha always said the same thing: *He's not here and I don't know where he's gone. Maybe you should go to school and stop chasing my son. The best thing to do would be to let him chase you. If he likes you, he'll call you.*

Cookie knew what she had felt pass between them had to be real. And yet, she had seen time and time again how she could feel something so incredible, with verve and certainty, but it turned out to only be wishful thinking, a pipe dream, pure fantasy, a delusion—Tiny Ten Pint on a binge or Kitty Colangelo having a spell. She had willed a relationship with Stanley de Falco to be real. If you believe something long enough, you believe it's true. This was the primary life lesson she had learned since she had turned fifteen. So far, being fifteen was the worst thing to have happened to her! And she didn't know why being fifteen sucked worse than being fourteen or thirteen, or twelve!

At the end of the school year, Cookie had been summoned to the principal's office. She was facing expulsion. The June sky felt heavy with ozone. Thick with humidity, car exhaust and city soot, dense air yellowed to the same shade as the clouds. An inert mass clung to the city, making everyone feel oily, sticky, dirty, hot and tired. Clearing the air would take nothing short of a big storm moving in.

Sister Mary Eau Claire ushered Cookie into her office. "Come in, come in, come in." She gesticulated with her hands to make sure Cookie sat in the chair closest to Mabel Kerry.

Cookie sat in her designated chair and smiled weakly at Mabel. She loved her and felt great embarrassment for letting her down. This was the last place in the world where she wanted to be—watching Mabel examine her face and gestures for signs of madness, or drugs, or both.

Sister Mary Eau Claire smiled at Cookie and Mabel. "I guess I should tell you we're not here today under the most pleasant circumstances."

Mabel nodded to the nun and turned to Cookie. "There seems to be a problem with your attendance. Do you mind my asking what you do with your time, if you're not going to school?"

Cookie hit a dead end and blanked. She didn't know. "I'm not sure," she told them.

And she wasn't lying. She was in a fog, the fugue-like state, neither reality nor a dream. Hovering somewhere in between the real and unreal, in a suspended state of consciousness, her mind was a static pool held in reserve for the moment when she would see the man who made her body respond in ways she had not known until now. Cookie had lost a lot of things, but she had not lost the desire to kiss, and to kiss him in particular. Her fugue-like state had not been caused due to mind-altering drugs. If it had, it would have been easy to come down from a drug-induced high. She was in a place where her words could not be written. She only heard music, symphonic and classical, interrupted by loud discordant bursts of the song *A Hole to Hide In* by the heavy metal band *Foghat*.

She had the sneaking suspicion if she broke the hold Stanley held over her, she would be able to write again, get out of Yonkers, and reclaim her persona of unabashed cockiness. Cookie Colangelo was a brave warrior goddamnit, but this guy made her feel feeble and weak, reducing her to a trembling mess of a girl.

The two women watched her carefully. They were trying to understand what the hell was wrong with her. She tried to give them something to go on and threw them a bone. "Sometimes, I stay up late so I can go out. Then I can't get up in the morning. So, I sleep in. Other than that, I'm not really sure."

Sister Mary eyed the pack of Marlboros spilling out of her hemp sack and asked, "Are you taking drugs?"

"No more than usual," Cookie said.

Sister Mary closed her eyes and shook her head. In all of her years as a principal, she thought she had heard everything. Cookie's matter of fact admission of casual drug use as the normal activity of all fifteen-year-old girls was too much to bear. "No more than usual," she repeated to let it sink in. "And exactly how much is the usual?"

Cookie shrugged and looked Sister Mary in the eye. "I'm not trying to evade your question, Sister. On second thought, drugs are not on my mind. I'm just not interested in drugs no more."

"Any more," Mabel corrected her.

"Are you depressed?" the nun asked.

Cookie shook her head. "Not that I know of."

She didn't have anything to say. She was bottoming out. Nowhere to go. She stared at her feet and noticed that much to her horror she was wearing two different shoes! She had spent the entire day wearing mismatched shoes, one brown, the other blue, but did not notice until now.

"What a horror!" She immediately retracted her feet, turning them inward into a pigeon-toe stance. "It's nothing," Cookie said sheepishly.

"Come again?" Sister Mary turtled her head forward. The skin on her face was as smooth and as red as a baby's bottom made warm from the bath. "Are you okay? Has anything changed in your life?"

"Why are you being so nice to me?" Cookie yelled suddenly. Her outburst was so abrupt it even took Cookie by surprise. "You're not normal for a nun!"

Sister Mary's face registered shock. Mabel's too. Discipline, wisdom and perhaps a touch of compassion forestalled her from boxing Cookie's ears.

Mabel looked vexed. "That's quite unusual for you! Why are you so angry, Cookie?"

"I don't know." Cookie glowered. She crossed and uncrossed her legs, feeling stickiness and a tingling sensation lurking under her rising skirt. "Or maybe I do know...."

Her voice grew faint but never left her. Both women hung on to her every word. Even though she had lost her words, something was still working in her favor.

She had an instant understanding of herself, the world, what was wrong with her and everyone. "It's hugely embarrassing to me."

"Many things are embarrassing, but we get through it." Sister Mary shifted her upper body over the surface of her desk, spreading open her white tunic. Wing-like, the white broadcloth enlarged her facial presence to the visage of a raptor preparing to take flight. Unlike many nuns, Sister Mary did not wear glasses. Her eyes were remarkably blue and intensely fixed on Cookie. "I've done things that I'm embarrassed of," the nun said without an air of apology. "I'm human and bound to make mistakes..."

"Yes," Mabel agreed. "We all have."

"It's original sin," Sister Mary said.

"That's why it's important to believe in God," Mabel said.

Sister Mary nodded in agreement. "Whatever is bothering you, Cookie, can be no worse than things I've heard a half a dozen times. I might have even done them myself."

Turning away, Cookie toyed with a velvet choker she had taken to wearing around her neck. She felt it chiseled her profile in repose to bear romantic resemblance to a cameo. "I'm too embarrassed to say," she mumbled.

"Come, come," Mabel said. 'It's okay to share."

"We're here to help," Sister Mary said.

Cookie cocked her head, so she could hear better. Surely, she was hearing things. This nun was crazy. She said she wanted to help. It was unthinkable a nun could be so kind. Cookie considered what would happen if she told her the truth.

"It's okay, Cookie," Mabel reassured her.

Sister Mary crossed her arms, closed her eyes briefly and nodded that it was okay, Cookie should go ahead.

"I don't know...." Cookie hesitated.

"Come now. What is it?" the nun persisted. "If you can't tell us, who can you tell?"

Mabel said, "It's a burden to carry a secret, alone, with no one to listen."

"We're willing to listen," Sister Mary said.

Cookie blurted out and gushed, "I'm in love!" Astonished at what she had said, she turned beet red and lowered her head.

"Well I'll be...," Mrs. Kerry said.

"That explains everything," the nun said. "I didn't want to go there, but guess what? Here we are. So be it. We have a starting point. Something to go on."

"I guess," Cookie mumbled.

"Are you pregnant?"

"No."

"Has he met your parents?"

Cookie looked at Mabel. "Have you told her about my parents?"

Mabel nodded. "Everyone knows about your parents."

Sister Mary got right to the point. "How far along have you gone with this boy?"

Cookie was being asked about the one thing she wanted to do with all of her heart and soul, and her ears burned. "He doesn't even know I love him. I wish he did, but he doesn't seem interested."

The nun proclaimed, "Then it's infatuation!"

"A passing fancy." Mabel looked jubilant. "And a flash in the pan."

Sister Mary agreed. "Here today, gone tomorrow."

"No, it's real. I think about him, morning, noon and night. I think about him every waking moment and in my dreams. I think about the things he's said, and I wonder if he feels about me the same way I feel about him."

Realizing she had not been breathing, Cookie stopped talking for a moment until she caught her breath. "I'm in love." Cookie looked at both women for their reaction. "Have you ever been in love? Do you know what I'm talking about?"

Sister Mary smiled weakly as though she had a big headache coming on. She turned to Mabel and discreetly said, "She's lovesick."

"It's puppy love," Mabel said.

"No, it's not," Cookie protested. "Most guys leave me cold. I can't stand them."

Sister Mary raised her eyebrows with renewed interest. "Are your urges different? How shall I say..."

"Do you like girls?" Mabel asked.

Their prying eyes left ugly red welts on her heart. Cookie bristled in her skin as though she was being rubbed raw. "I can't stand guys my own age. I can't imagine kissing them. I can't imagine wanting to do anything with them. Especially that! Has a guy ever touched you this way? That you love him so much, you'd do anything for him? Anything?"

Cookie had no desire to keep her legs permanently crossed. She set both her feet on the ground, solid, legs apart slightly, so when and if Stanley showed up, she could bring it on. Easily. For Stanley, she would do anything. She was a slut on call. His slut.

Both women looked at each other as though they were indeed sisters in hurt. Mabel cleared her throat and stiffened up in the chair. A pained expression crossed her brown eyes. "It's not something I want to talk about. I haven't thought about Chester in years. He's gone now. So, what's the point?" She shrugged. "I have no need to live through that time again."

"Tell me about it, sometime," said Sister Mary. Her cheeks flushed with spidery red veins, showing all of the symptoms of a heat rash coming on.

But it wasn't a rash. It was the recollection of lust from days past. Sister Mary leaned forward and gave Mabel a slow, wry smile. "There isn't a woman alive who has not experienced the little bump between her thighs wanting to run rampant and burst into pride to rush ramshod right into the object of her affections."

"Mmm mmmm mmm. I remember," Mabel said.

Stunned, Cookie enunciated every word. "Oh My God."

Both women shifted uncomfortably in their seats.

Sister Mary went on. "Women do not want to talk about these desires, emotions and urges unless it's imminent, about to happen with the guy they want to have."

Silence came. The fog of fugue. Unreasonable sounding musical notes. Cookie forgot what time she had arrived here. She heard a tick-tock sound, looked for a clock and found two. A ceramic wall clock sitting on the nun's desk was mounted in a heavy wooden picture frame and looked to be a relic from the 1950s. Another clock, round and rimmed in aluminum, was mounted to the wall. Its face had greyed with age; bold black hands set the time at 3:15. The wallpaper face of the clock behind the glass bore faint yellow streaks, as if water had once dripped into its works. She didn't know which clock made the tick-tock and studied them both. The larger wall clock made a faint click when the second hand moved to the next minute. The ceramic clock did all of the ticking. Cookie thought it would drive her mad if she had to listen to the sound of clocks all day.

Mabel's face was full of sadness and her eyes welled with tears. "There isn't a woman alive who has not had a broken heart."

"But you get over it and live to tell." Sister Mary looked on the verge of giving Cookie a hug, but she had second thoughts and stayed firm in her seat. "Yes, you do move on. And you, young lady, need to move on."

Cookie was certain Sister Mary did have a tale to tell. With lust the nun eyed the pack of Marlboros spilling out of Cookie's hemp sack.

"I used to smoke Marlboro," the nun said. "Two packs a day. I quit cold turkey the day I entered the convent. If that's all you're doing, then it's not so bad."

Cookie smiled at Sister Mary, the same way she smiled at Kitty when she was having a spell, or at Donny because she was too young to know any better. Cookie had a strong desire to protect the nun from harm because the nun was courageous in a way she did not need to be. The church kept a roof over her head for life and fed her three square meals a day. The nun didn't have to do too much of anything to qualify for sainthood. All she had to do was suit up in her habit and show up every day. It was a fait accompli.

Mabel's laugh was heartfelt, sincere and almost disruptive because Cookie had gone off into the deep recesses of her mind to think about the life of the nun.

"I always told you, Cookie, that you remind me of Herman's mother, my Annie. Annie Cole. She had ambition and wanted to make something of her life, but she got mixed up with the wrong boy—it ended up killing her."

"A bad man can take you down." Sister Mary looked grim. "Not every woman can survive being with the wrong man."

"I don't think you understand. Stanley's not a bad guy."

"Oh, but we do understand," the nun said.

"You love him, but he's not loving you back." Mabel shrugged. "That's doesn't mean he's bad, but it doesn't make him good either."

"It doesn't matter," Cookie said. "He's gone. No one knows where he is."

They looked at each other and nodded frankly. Everything would work out after all. They talked about disappointment, love, and heartbreak, as though Cookie wasn't there.

"The heart can fully heal, but it never ever forgets." The tone of Mabel's voice rang like a cantata rising above the dropping air pressure.

The room had darkened; outside storm clouds had covered the sun. In the distance, thunder rolled its own song, having little to do with the women who had assembled in the room, but instead spoke of some deep foreboding of what would come next. A timid knock announced someone standing outside Sister Mary's office. Sister Mary was used to being interrupted this way. All day long, people lined up outside of her door.

Sister Mary rose from her desk and greeted the young girl with the shiny cap of hair, Carole Zukowski, who was beautiful minus her rotten teeth. Sister Mary smiled at Carol. As soon as Sister Mary stood, Cookie picked up the nun's scent, clean laundry, soap and freshly starched linen. There was no breeze flapping in from the open window. Sister Mary had moved the air by virtue of her flowing black & white habit. No matter how foul a nun could be, there was something special about the way they always smelled so clean. Mabel Kerry was busily jotting notes in a small brown leather-bound notebook on pages as thick as parchment.

Flashes began outside the window, sending sugary waves of air working hard to trickle through the dense humid mass. A storm of great magnitude, capable of making the air feel clean again, seemed to be on its way. Handing the nun a flat white envelope, the girl smiled, exclaiming, "Thank you, Sister Mary."

Cookie noticed the girl now had a set of teeth. She didn't stay long. Whatever business that had needed to be done had easily taken place. This time when the girl smiled again, saying goodbye, her new teeth slipped. White, even, and gleaming, she wore dentures, passing for a full set of teeth.

On the way out of Sister Mary's office, Carole Zukowski almost bumped into Johnny Colangelo. Johnny smiled at the girl like he thought she was pretty. Sweating profusely, Johnny mumbled a confused apology; he didn't expect to scope out a pretty girl at Cookie's school. Two wet patches had settled in the underarm areas of his blue cotton shirt. Other than the sweaty bulges under his arms, Johnny looked crisp and well put together. He wanted to make a good impression on the nun and Mrs. Kerry. Cookie could smell his Old Spice; he had even put on deodorant.

"Speak of the devil," Mabel said. She gave Johnny the biggest smile she could muster.

Just as everyone was getting resettled into their seats, a horrendously loud burst of rain dumped from the sky. The storm happened so suddenly, it was as though the heavens poured open to lend a touch of divine support to the mission set forth by Mabel and the nun. Thunder took full force. Every flash of lightning was quickly backed by a thunder clap the same way boilermakers are pints of beer backed with a whiskey chaser.

Johnny grimaced every time another boom of thunder filled the room. He didn't like torrential rain, lightning or thunder. Johnny rarely spoke about Korea, but once said he had spent the night in a foxhole while the earth exploded with lightning and thunder and rain, snow and hail. He admitted he had prayed that night. He said the *Hail Mary*. Other prayers too. He had been scared of getting struck by lightning, a bullet, a shell, or a grenade. Since then, storm clouds followed him everywhere.

Despite the quick influx of a big storm and a new rush of air blowing through the open window, the conversation thickened with Johnny's acknowledgements and Sister Mary's welcome notes. Mabel chirped praises for his fatherly concern and told him she was proud of him. Johnny did his best not to do or say anything. Cookie had to hand it to her father. Sometimes, he detected when he was really in over his head and the best thing to do was to shut up. No matter how loutish Johnny could be, there was something endearing about hearing his earnest voice revealing he really wanted to do the right thing for his daughter.

The nun spoke about love. Everything in the world must come to resemble love. Love is the only truth to illustrate the divine law of God in action. And while love comes in many shades of grey, from the sweat of intertwined lovers, to the insolence and loneliness of Narcissus preening upon his own reflection in the water, in the end, only love underscores and emboldens the truth of the world. There were other forms of love too. The love a newborn infant extends to its mother in its babyish wobbly gaze, searching for her lubricious scent, otherwise known as her nipple, is more than a quest for milk. There is also the all-encompassing love one has for every living thing on the planet, including ants, slugs and moths.

Blessing himself twice, Johnny chimed in, "The earth, the moon, sun and stars, everything in the universe is eclipsed by this place called heaven, where eternal love triumphantly reigns in the form of God the father, God the son, and God the holy spirit."

Sister Mary nodded and rolled her eyes. "Okay. I'm so glad you get it."

Mabel smiled. "There are other forms of love too, but let's not get overly complicated."

Cookie covered her hands over her eyes. As far as she could tell, she was listening to some really good bullshit. The test of good bullshit is it always resonates as the truth. Cookie could tell Johnny knew it was bullshit too. He gave his daughter a too cute smile, a knowing nod, a wink, and handed a sealed envelope to Sister Mary Eau Claire. The nun did not have to open the envelope to count the money. The deal had already been done. Staying in school meant Cookie had to promise to read books over the summer! Cookie had not lost her words, the women insisted. Her words were misplaced, but soon after spending the summer reading, her words would again be found, and this Stanley character would be forgotten. Hard as it was to believe, there was such a thing as a good nun. It was rare—not everyone encountered a nun who was good, but it does happen.

Twenty-six

Tripping and Kissing

On Tuesday, July 4th, 1972, Cookie felt restless. Herman Lynch and Reenie Ruggiero were nowhere to be found, which did not bode well for Cookie. When she was hell bent on being a wild child, her two closest friends tended to provide a ballast for her baser instincts. The Beatles' song *Day Tripper* had been released in 1965, and although Cookie had only been nine years old at the time, she never forgot the song and forever associated it with her own sentiment about LSD. She believed she was very much a *Day Tripper* in the full complexity of the term's meaning—a part-time hippie imbibing in casual and intermittent use of hallucinogens. Hardly hard core, but not entirely innocent either, Cookie sought a thrill to commemorate the summer. She dropped a full tab of orange sunshine and went to Playland in Rye.

She would have taken Johnny's Buick, but knew it would not be wise to drive on acid. Her trip started out on a fairly pleasant note. Arky Lovato, who had long ago abandoned any sign of promise, was at the helm of his jeep, bouncing in his seat. The windows were permanently rolled down. Luckily the doors were on, otherwise Cookie might have been inclined to jump out.

Arky was not her date. He had not grown in stature from being a doofus. Once again, he was a designated driver and nothing more. They had gone everywhere together. Playland. Woodstock. It had been nearly three years since they had gone to Woodstock and Arky was still looking to get laid by squiring under-age girls around town. He spent most of his time at the beck and call of Toni Ferlinghetti. The only reason why Arky was free to take Cookie to Playland that night was because Toni and Fern had gone on vacation to the Jersey shore.

As soon as Toni left town, he let himself go. His hygiene told a short tale of bizarre personal neglect. His fingers were stained from nicotine, yellow teeth, a middle-aged paunch of a belly, and a face looking as though he rarely washed—forget shaving. Okay, he was not a hunk. He didn't smell too good either and his clothes reeked of a long day festering in the hot sun. His stringy brown hair had grown longer than two summers ago and ran down to the middle of his back.

Storm clouds were moving in. A storm could come from nowhere this time of year. The heavy humidity in the air made Cookie's face feel like it was getting mopped with a damp washcloth. Her hair curled in unexpected places around her forehead, behind her ears and along the nape of her neck. Tuning into the stations on the radio, Arky turned up the volume, and kept hitting pockets of static, one more indication the atmosphere was electrically charged. Black clouds brewed in the east, where an orange glow lit up the sky.

Arky found a song he liked. Cookie shouted above the road noise and sang the lyrics to the song *American Pie* by Don McLean. She knew she couldn't sing well, and Arky made a big point of telling her so, but she paid him no mind.

"Drive faster, Arky! Hurry boy, it's waiting there for you!"

"I never thought I'd meet a girl like you," Arky crooned. "Yonkers girl."

Cookie couldn't tell what he was talking about and frowned. She was so not into him, but it did not stop him from trying to get into her pants. Dropping acid allowed her to keep her distance from him and still have fun.

Among variations of LSD, orange sunshine tended to be stronger than yellow sunshine, purple haze, window pane, white lightning or LSD-25 because it was cut with so much speed. Speed caused hallucinations to come in rapid succession and appear to be more powerful. Thought to be pure, LSD-25 had no speed and was a popular cocktail for the Timothy Leary crowd, who were far too old, rich and sophisticated to mix with Yonkers girls.

Once they arrived in the parking lot at Playland, they ran into a different problem. No spaces were open on this last night of the long weekend. Arky traveled to the outer lanes of the lot. Every time he thought he saw a spot, it turned out to have been taken by a small car and he yelled, "Damn!"

The jeep spun in circles around the circular greenbelt. A rotund-shaped flower garden sat in the center like a pink bull's eye. Cookie thought she saw an arrow shoot through the air and land spear-like, dead center in the midst of the pink flowers tinged brown, blooming beyond their prime. She heard noise too, a subtle whir in the air, gyrating like a comet or a shooting star. Insects began hissing in short abrupt clicks. Crickets, cicadas and June bugs appeared over her head in rounds of stubby brown meteoroids. With so much light in the horizon, stars could not be seen. Robins, sparrows and blue jays prowled the greenbelt for worms, but there were no signs of an owl. Her acid was beginning to kick in.

The jeep popped in the air and came down to the ground, making heavy, clanking thuds. Cookie could not be sure if he was doing a wheelie or ran up against a curb. He asked her, "Why did I let you talk me into this?"

Because you're so dumb, she thought, but didn't mention this to Arky.

Cookie became fixated on the profile of his nose where three warts appeared. Even in her drug-induced state, she recognized he was driving erratically. The warts she could take if indeed they were real, but she could not accept he would put her in harm's way. She folded her arms across her chest to protect herself and yelled at him, "Slow down!"

They took a quick loop around the beach area before idling near the main entrance to the amusement park. Cookie watched him as he stopped the car momentarily to put it into reverse.

"Sure you know what you're doing?" She felt a small lump rising in her throat as a metallic taste filled her mouth. She had not eaten for hours and wasn't hungry, a far cry from how she felt whenever she walked into the Café Trento. Her stomach had seized up. For the uninitiated, this is how you feel when acid is first starting to kick in. Some people claim it's because acid is cut with strychnine, also known as rat poison. Her chest felt fluttery, as if she had ingested a small dose of helium from a balloon. She had begun to hallucinate but wasn't quite speeding. Soon the rush would come.

"I'm going for the beach," he said. "It's late. No one's going to notice one more car on the beach."

Arky was right. Other cars were parked on the beach, facing the water. As they drove up onto a bank of sand, the sun was setting, but enough light remained in the sky to see the water. The first flashes of lightning flickered like blue neon. A small cloud rose from the hood of the jeep and curled around the front bumper, where the hands on his plastic clock were frozen at six o'clock. The beach was filthy, littered with garbage; mounds of cigarette butts, crushed beer cans, plastic bags, a rusted hubcap, tampons and condoms washed up on the shore. As the tide ran out, a new curving swath of debris settled on the sand.

She heard whistles and loudspeakers commanding the last few stragglers to get off the beach. She wasn't sure if what she heard was real. Even as the acid started to kick in, she knew they didn't allow anyone to stay on the beach at night, and she didn't see anyone who might be thinking about taking a late-night swim. She did feel the first few drops of rain and thought the storm would pass and blow out to the Long Island Sound.

Cookie felt like she was flying along the coastline. By staying close to the edge of the water, she was so into the rhythm of the gentle tide, an ebb and flow belonging only to her. The water enticed her to take off her shoes. She waded through the water, skipping over the tide as it came in. She loved the feel of the cool rush of water until she almost stepped on a hypodermic needle.

She didn't know where Arky had gone but heard him say, "Why don't we walk faster? I think it's going to rain!"

The sky lit up with sheet lightning, but Cookie did not know if a real storm was brewing. "Why don't we just fly?" She jumped up in the air to show him how high she could go and landed on the ground on one bent knee.

A flock of sea gulls were swarming the beach and getting away from the impending storm. Raiding the trash to see if anything was ripe for the picking, the birds began to glow phosphorous white and lit up like lightning bugs. Their faces grew fierce and their wings flapped incessantly, resembling slender silver blades of steel. Then they soared like planes into the night sky, making a whooshing sound and the echo of a timber log drum. Sticks on the ground turned into wooden mallets beating the timber drum in slow, steady notes. She wanted to play the drum, but by the time she reached for the mallets they were gone. Warm resonance echoed around her and tapped against her ears, but she could not see the drum. She crouched close to the ground of a gravel path. She rubbed the gravel with her hands in tune to the rhythm she heard in her head, but the drum was nowhere to be found.

She contemplated the pebbles on the ground, while she continued along the gravel path that began widening into a walkway. The pebbles came to life as miniature cars and sped in a figure eight pattern of bright colored circles the same size as the circles on a plastic mat in the game *Twister*. On the ground, more cars joined the fracas, speeding faster and faster, until a superhighway was born. The cars lit up as bright as streetlamps, traveling sideways, upside down, forward and backward, barely missing one another, never crashing, beeping their horns, flashing their lights along the blacktop, and trapped as prisoners within the fluorescent white lines of a vast network of intersecting roads. In her mind, she stood in the center of the New York State Thruway and could see the cars driving toward her, about to run over her; she jumped in the air to stay out of their way. A single bolt of lightning struck the center point of the highway. Cars exploded into a billowing plume of grey smoke until everything vanished leaving a smoldering pile of black rubble.

She had lost her shoes, but her feet hardly felt a thing. She grew proud of her expanding size. No longer small, her body enlarged into the shape of a sudden riptide overtaking the beach and moving inland to cover the amusement park. Feeling so full of herself, she thought she would disappear into her own self-made flood of water and drown. She wanted to cry and didn't want to cry. She was in awe and curious about the next thing she would see or hear.

She thought Arky was calling her. She didn't know where he had gone or if he was there at all, and it did not matter. Hardly feeling a thing, her feet spirited her forward in proud prancing goose steps, arcing high into the air. She might never have to feel a thing again.

"The storm's coming," Arky yelled. "They're going to close the dragon coaster!"

Even as she gripped a railing and climbed the steps to the wooden platform, she had no idea of how she had gotten there. She also did not know if what she saw and heard was real or a hallucination.

"The coaster's still running," Arky said.

She stood behind a pagoda-shaped ticket gate under an

iridescent dome-light. A stubby brown wooden pillar carved with a chart to measure height bore a luminescent line, and it was written in red, *You Must Be Four Feet*.

"I'd say I'm at least five feet," she told Arky.

"You're over five feet." He guided her into a seat for two. "The storm's moving fast. Can't tell if it's moving on or settling here," Arky said in a frantic voice. He had a wild look in his eyes; he was scared but found it thrilling anyway.

A metal pole came down and clamped into place to hold them in their seats. The metal clink sounded final. There was no way of turning back and no way out. The back of the seat in front of her read *Remain Seated At All Times*. These words of warning glowed yellow and grew into small squirming worms. She reached to touch the worms because they looked velvety, but she could not feel them, and they wriggled away.

The small train of open cars creaked up a wooden track, struggling to make it to the top of a hill, its wheels sticking on the track, clacking and groaning with the drag of shooting sparks from the friction of metal on metal. A flash of lightning turned the sky blue.

"Up the hill, down the hill. Up the hill, down the hill," she chanted.

She gripped Arky's arm and clung to his sleeve. He didn't seem to mind at all. He gave her hand a squeeze and did not let go. Fork lightning cracked open the dark sky in the distance.

"I can't wait to get to the top."

"Me either," Arky said, squeezing her hand tighter, causing the nail of her index finger to dig into her middle finger. "Your pupils are the size of dimes," he told her.

"Oh yeah." Cookie wasn't feeling a thing.

A Ferris wheel lit with red lights began spinning into her face. Was she going to meet it up there, high in the air? Forked lightning bolts lit up the sky behind the Ferris wheel. The small train of cars continued to climb up the track. Clickety-clack. Clackety-clack. She heard rhymes popping up from children's books and felt herself disappearing into the *Little Engine That Could*. At the top of the first wooden hill on the track, they stopped for a brief pause to enjoy the pinnacle of being on top of the world. The last trace of grey-pink light spread across the Long Island Sound. Dark clouds clustered overhead in a sky rapidly being pierced by successive waves of flashes of lightning.

"So scary! Not real. Not real," Cookie kept saying. "It's not real."

"Like hell!" Arky yelled. "And if lightning hits this ride, we're toast!"

Suddenly the car lurched forward, careening down the track, hitting a sharp unexpected dip, jolting the car up into the air and increasing the momentum, speeding down, down, down. Arky yelled at the top of his lungs, "Whoa, Nellie!"

"Don't be like that," Cookie screamed. She removed her hand from his grip and pressed her head against the guard rail. The dank scent of the Sound flooded her mind with the image of schools of silver fish swimming upstream in between reams of lightning bolts.

The train approached another peak, straddling the precipice in a raucous rocking motion. Arky continued to yell with the same intensity, "Whoa, Nellie, don't look down. Whatever you do, don't look down."

The force of the momentum made them both veer sharply forward. Cookie tried to stand up, but Arky shoved her back down in her seat. Steady streaks of lightning turned his face blue. The train hurled itself sharply to the left and sped with greater intensity, throwing her head back. Then as the train lurched forward with even greater speed to take a smaller hill, her head fell forward. Climbing around the bank, the train threw the cars to the right, then to the left, while the track groaned of rickety wood and the clack of the metal track. Full speed ahead, the train went directly into the mouth of the dragon.

Arky screamed like a girl, "Whoa, Nellie!"

The dragon's body was actually a tunnel, blocking light and air from the open night sky. The motorized roar of the dragon echoed in the tunnel, and the eyes in its terrible head surged with electricity, lighting up in red. Cookie was sure it spat fire and singed the tops of her hands as she held onto the guard rail for dear life. She could not see her hands at all, but she could feel them, hot and tired from trying to hold onto the rail. Until they came out of the tunnel, she thought for sure her hands had burned black.

The train hurled along the track, wrapping around in an S-curve, then turning back on itself. Again, her head lurched forward. As the train emerged out of the tunnel into a straightaway, her body pitched against the guard rail. She saw the lights of small boats out on the Sound, people on the ground striking matches to light cigarettes, and the large pagoda-shaped dome of light hanging above the gate. The strange mixture of creosote and hot metal flooded her senses and melded into the pervasive scent of burning leaves. She reached for her face, thinking if she did not hold on to her nose it would fall off. Then she screamed. She was sure if she stopped pressing her nose, it would break off of her face and fall into her hand. She was forever doomed to carry her nose in her hand.

No one seemed to mind her scream. Screaming was not out-of-the-ordinary on the Dragon Coaster. Leaning to the right, the train climbed a wooden peak, violently surged downward, ramming the train full throttle against the track in a final run, and returned to the platform where they had first boarded.

"This is what love feels like!" Cookie squealed.

Arky's final word, "Damn," squeaked a whole octave lower than his earlier screams of "Whoa!"

The ride on the Dragon Coaster lasted just over a minute, but Cookie could not stop hearing the clackety-clack of chains, wood and the metal track banging inside of her head for the rest of the night. And she was not sure if she had been on the roller coaster at all or if she had stood on the ground the whole time. Overcome by the strangest notion, she could not be sure of where she was, or what she had done, and felt like exploding from the inside out.

She put her hands over her ears and yelled, "Get me out of here!"

Arky hugged her close to his side and led her toward the beach, where she felt coarse sand beneath her feet and rain pelting the top of her head. The lightning had subsided, but thunder shook in the distance. An engine. Heavy artillery. From every direction, she was being hailed by bullets and bolts of lightning. She put up her hands and saw they were covered with water. It was raining pretty hard.

On the beach by the jeep, she saw a sea gull who looked at her, and she could swear he called her name. His head grew large, round, and the down of his feathers turned from white to brown. His eyes grew immense, not blinking. He was unfixed in his beliefs, neither good nor bad, a mixture of both probably, and he stared at her, but not in a good way. The bird folded and spread his wings as though he meant to be wholly confrontational.

"Go home," the bird told her. It smiled, but its stare did not waver. The gull had become a genuine owl.

She closed her eyes and could feel her hair getting drenched but could still see the vivid image of the owl as he tried to kiss her. She felt his sharp beak stab her bottom lip and make a small bruise. The taste of metal flooded her mouth. Her lower lip might be bleeding. The bird's breath was hot, sour, and wet. His beak sought her upper lip and drew it close to his mouth to chew in an agitated gnawing motion. Yes, the bird was hungry, angry, and he seemed intent on eating her lip. His oily-scented wings wrapped around her body and drew her close to his stubbly feathered breast.

Then the bird's tongue probed into her mouth, searching for her tongue. He drew forth her tongue with the force of a suction cup. His mouth tasted like stale tobacco and bird pellets. There was nothing subtle about this owl. She could feel his wings rub up against her breast and his talons pressed into the back seat of her pants. She shrank away from the bird and opened her eyes. Through the rain, she no longer saw the owl.

Arky Lovato grinned at her. "What's the matter?"

"Gross!" She spat, trying to erase any trace of him. She saw his dripping wet face.

"You don't know how to kiss, do you?" Arky laughed. He had scored a victory over her and wickedness flickered in his dark eyes.

"Kissing! That was not kissing!" She wiped her mouth with the edge of her sleeve.

"What's the matter?" he asked again.

"Forget about it, Arky! It's just not going to happen! You're like my brother."

He smirked, taking it all in stride. "You really don't know how to kiss," he said.

She could not believe this doofus told her she did not know how to kiss! The nerve! Being told she did not know how to kiss rattled her more than dropping acid, the ride on the Dragon Coaster, or the storm.

She could handle whatever was going down. She was so sick of the world telling her a heap of lies for no good reason other than to make her think a certain way about things. She wasn't going to get sucked into someone else's game.

The owl told her to go home. "Get the hell out of there. Now!"

Arky helped her get into the jeep and checked to make sure she was secure in her seat. He got into the jeep, but he didn't say anything to her. He had made his big play, and while he did not get what he wanted, it did not mean he would not try again. He turned on the radio and cranked the volume of the Rolling Stones' hit pop song *Brown Sugar*.

Was she there or not? In the jeep, she looked down at her feet and saw she had lost her shoes. But she had a habit of losing her shoes. And her feet were black and caked with dirt; she had a few cuts, a blister, but she did not feel a thing.

She pulled a ballpoint pen out of her hemp sack to jot a note, but the pen took on new dimensions and began to wriggle. Soon it slid out of her hand and dropped to the ground. The pen had turned into a slender garden snake and slithered away from her. So much for dropping acid as a prompt to write.

She never suffered from a shortage of experiencing good thrills. A strong hit of acid was far preferable to bad marijuana, even if it ended up making her dotty and daft like her mother, who was indeed schizophrenic, and regrettably so. And in this moment when she recognized what she had done, she felt a horrible wave of guilt overwhelm her and shake her to the core of her being. Here she was, dropping acid, and inducing the same symptoms afflicting Kitty. Only her mother did not choose to be schizophrenic and suffered from a biochemical malfunction of her brain—a real disease. Her mother had no way to stop her own bad trip. What she had learned from her trip to Playland had little to do with drugs, and less to do with her mother, but had everything to do with kissing. She made an oath to herself as surely as she heard one final crack of thunder. Never again would some guy tell her she did not know how to kiss.

Twenty-seven

Spin the Bottle

She didn't need a bottle or a group of participants to play spin the bottle. She made herself the bottle and pointed herself in whatever direction where a guy caught her fancy. She threw her head back to toss her hair in the sun, knowing it caught honey highlights. She clamped down both hands on her breasts; she meant to plump them. Mostly, she enjoyed feeling as loose as lazy large raindrops falling to the earth one at a time. Her lungs filled with the crisp air cleansed from the rain. She was free to do whatever she wanted. She heard a bird chirp, then fly up into the branches of the willow tree and thought for sure she could feel the aftermath of its wings flapping. She wondered if it was an owl and knew if it was, the owl would approve.

She soon found out it was not hard to nab partners willing to partake in kissing. Darrell Ricci would be her first. She scouted him below on the grassy knoll, spread out on a blanket under a willow tree that shielded him from direct sunlight. Cookie watched him closely while she took a deep breath and made her way across the upper bank of Lennon Park. She slowly walked toward him, stopping every now and then to turn on her heels in a spin intended to show her curves from all angles.

Darrell wore a thin cotton tank top, an Italian boy muscle shirt. She could see his black curly hair poking from under his arms, making him look manly. She'd like to tug on his hair. But first she wanted to kiss him. A corner of the blanket had a lump concealing his belongings. Could have been his shoes, cigarettes and matches, illicit drugs other than marijuana, and beer; it really didn't matter what had formed the lump. She sat down on the blanket and looked up at the boughs of the willow tree quivering with leaves.

She touched Darrell lightly on the hand. His face bore traces of dark peach fuzz too soft to shave. She grew bolder still and pressed her finger against his right cheek. She could tell this was going to be a silent conversation. He didn't have to lean far to reach her lips. She waited for him, expecting his mouth to open to receive her tongue. Ah! The French Kiss! Slightly parting her lips and opening her mouth worked like a charm. While Cookie had not had the chance to practice her skill, kissing came naturally.

Sexual awakening begins with a kiss. They locked lips, linked tongues, ebbing and flowing, parting and closing, searching and seeking. One kiss led to the next, and another. Kissing him, she let herself go, and she lost herself, eventually losing track of time. His breath came as heavy and as steady as a heartbeat. No dribble and drab had spilled onto her chin.

While his hands briskly explored her body, she tried to imagine him to be Stanley. She felt ardent about the task at hand, but when she looked into his eyes, there was a distinct absence of heat. She considered him to be an efficient kisser, but dull. She did not feel anything other than her mouth growing a bit dry and her lips becoming numb. Even when his kisses traveled along the ridge of her neck, she felt each kiss to be a separate standalone event without momentum and lacking the rise of feverish desire. While she was not experienced, she felt certain kissing was not supposed to make you feel like yawning. Soon his hands fumbled under her midriff shirt and made a short climb toward her breasts—this is when she pulled away from him. Kissing was one thing. Getting felt up was quite another.

"What's the matter?" he asked her. She had nothing to say to him but did soon come to learn guys always asked this same question when the girl wanted to stop. She liked Darrell but not enough to stay. This was her game, not his.

She rose to stand and looked down at him as if to say, you're a nice guy but so Yonkers. In all of the time they had spent together, he hadn't even opened his mouth except to kiss! Thank God, she didn't have to talk to him. By the time he caught on that she meant to leave, he revealed the contents of the lump under the blanket and pulled out a can of Ballantine. He offered to share it with her, but she didn't care for alcohol and especially disliked beer.

Her interlude with Darrell could have been the end of her outdoor make-out sessions, but it marked the first of many to come. Soon she advanced into other neighborhoods and embarked on a kissing spree.

The sign read: *Untermyer Park, Parks Department, the City of Yonkers*. She entered the grounds from its southern border and crossed onto the footpath toward the caretaker's cottage. Home to bevies of feral cats, the barn-like wooden building was falling down. Splintered rafters and cracked shingles had been left on the ground where the wind had carried them. A few of the more daring cats watched her. Flicking their tails like snakes, beautiful and wild, they ambled along the pebbled path with their long sleek backs shining in the summer sun. The cats carried themselves with the preternatural pride of witches practicing black magic. This was their place and they were allowing her to pass. Fickle by nature, they looked bored but could just as easily have exploded into violence: lunging, spitting and hissing. She enjoyed watching the cats watch her. Every time she moved, the cats moved along with her in a sinuous, syncopated dance creeping along the winding footpath. Soon they stopped following her and stayed behind, twitching their tails like they were sad to see her go. She missed the cats and the excitement of not knowing if they were her companions or enemies.

The smooth grey stone wall bordering the front of the park swarmed with raggedy haired guys who were dressed in tattered blue jeans. Braless girls wearing skimpy summer tops milled about aimlessly, but Cookie paid them no mind. She scanned the grey stone wall, cruising for the juiciest low-hanging fruit. In an instant, she scoped out Crazy Dave and scored eye contact with him. Brash and perpetually stoned, Crazy Dave bore a striking resemblance to David Crosby of Crosby, Stills and Nash. He was toking on a joint, but when he caught sight of her, he squinted hard and held his breath to get the full effect of the hit.

"How are you, doll?" Crazy Dave winked. He had a sweet spot for her despite her age.

Cookie walked up to him and smiled. "How's it going?" She took a hit from his joint without asking him and blew the smoke right into his face.

Too stoned to show surprise, Crazy Dave reached for her hand, giving it a long lingering kiss. The two exchanged conspiratorial smiles, as though this was the first flush of sexual awakening for the both of them. He jumped up on top of the wall and offered his hand to pull her to the top. Arm in arm, they strolled through the great lawn toward the walled garden, where the narrow vertical pool lacked enough water to cool one's body in a slow swim.

Originally, the Indo-Persian walled garden had been designed to replicate paradise on earth, but the pool had fallen into dereliction and decay. That summer, the park was kept alive by kids scoring drugs, getting stoned and playing music like runaway renegades from rock 'n' roll bands.

Cookie sat on the pool's ledge, removed her sandals and placed her feet in shallow water as tepid as the humid air. Crazy Dave, who often talked too much, fell silent. Cookie kept things sweet and simple. Taking the lead, she pulled on his arm to make him sit beside her. It occurred to her she didn't know his age and didn't care. He came to sit in a graceless plop, casting his legs astride like he meant to mount a horse. For a young man, he was terribly stiff and inflexible. Cookie hoped his lips were pliable and limber, and he was not a world champion at drooling. She also hoped he was stiff where it counted—and she did not mean kissing.

Without asking him, she took another hit from his joint, pushed her face into his and pressed him for a kiss. She opened her mouth to release the plume of smoke into his mouth. She tried to pretend Crazy Dave was Stanley, but his bushy moustache got in the way. His mouth tasted bitter and smelled like burnt leaves. Though blond, he was no stand-in for Stanley de Falco. Crazy Dave's broad face and lack of bone structure caused his eyelids to droop toward the center of his rather flat nose. He lacked Stanley's strong angles, linear charm and sculpted torso. Strong as a Neanderthal and slightly stooped, Crazy Dave, though not bad looking, was nothing special.

She felt his face coming in closer, but he opened his mouth too wide to take her lips. She thought of offering him something larger than her mouth but quickly decided against it. Bold moves were not meant to be thrown away on him. Her mouth opened, waiting for his tongue, and when it came, she flicked it with her own tongue. The way he approached kissing was lazy. His tongue seemed flaccid, and his eyes kept having trouble focusing. He used his tongue like a large rubber scoop; it felt excessive in her mouth and overwhelmed her lips. And she felt a spot of wetness growing on her chin. From all she had inferred about kissing, wetness was supposed to seep elsewhere and not all over her mouth. He was very bad at kissing, a wet kisser. She drew her face away from his mouth.

"What's the matter?" Crazy Dave asked.

Not subtle about his desire to take this as far as he could go, Crazy Dave hatched an alternative approach. Even though the kissing had stopped, his two hands had become many permutations on the verge of directing air traffic in the sky and doing a handstand at the same time. Not to be blind-sided, she moved farther away from him. She had no intention of moving to the realm beyond kissing. She retreated onto the pool's ledge among a row of weather-beaten pots holding rusty colored coleus plants.

Calling her "really cute," he stretched out on the lawn next to the pool. Unfurling every inch of his body, he slowly lifted his face toward the sun and began to drift away. Drowsy, he had trouble keeping his eyes open. Crazy Dave going adrift was very different from Stanley popping out of the present and into a war zone in his mind. Crazy Dave was stoned on pot. Stanley de Falco had been shell-shocked from combat.

Every time Cookie got herself into an uncomfortable situation, she immediately sought a way out. But there was no need to find an exit here. Within a few minutes, Crazy Dave had fallen fast asleep and began to snore.

If Crazy Dave was a wet kissing stoner and Darrell Ricci was ho-hum boring, then Tommy Parrello made Cookie scream. Without a doubt, good looking, wiry-haired, brown-eyed Italian guy Tommy Parrello exhibited pride in his sexual prowess, strutting *Down the End* wearing his tight jeans, Italian boy muscle shirt, and brown Frye cowboy boots like he could take any woman he wanted. Through the years, Cookie had made no secret she didn't like Tommy, but he had been rumored to be the best kisser in the North End. Out of the seventeen guys Toni Ferlinghetti had kissed, she gave him the highest rating of all, a nine.

Cookie wasn't looking to necessarily hook up with Tommy Parrello. She knew lots of other guys would be there tonight because it was so damn hot nobody could sleep in sweat-soaked sheets. Running into Tommy would be fine. She was curious to experience a higher form of kissing, even if it meant she had to kiss one more frog, a major frog. She had not forgotten how bad Tommy had been to Herman Lynch, trying to beat him up, saying mean and nasty things about him.

She dipped her finger into Yardley Pot o' Gloss and dabbed enough to make her lips gleam. From Roberts Avenue, she entered the parking lot behind the bank. Coming in from this side street gave her the advantage of scoping out the turf instead of making a grand entrance from Palisade Avenue.

Layla by Derek and the Dominoes blared from the open window of an orange VW bug parked on the street. A gang of twenty or thirty guys moved through the parking lot, making their own high voltage action: putting out tons of male energy, sitting on the hoods of cars and leaning against walls; standing, walking and sprinting through the lot; laughing, kidding each other, and talking trash. So many guys were hanging out on this hot summer night that no one guy stood out in the crowd. Cookie stared at the dozen guys sandwiched together against the sidewall of the Barber Shop and finally managed to recognize Jay Marcello, Reenie Ruggiero's brother Billy Dee, and Tommy Parrello.

Word on the street said Billy Dee had taken to shooting smack. Poor Reenie; Cookie wondered if she knew her brother had gone beyond dealing drugs and had gotten himself hooked. With his shaved head, Jay Marcello looked out of place among all of the longhairs. Jay's body had the shape of a compact trash can. His disproportionately long arms swung away from his squat body, and his hands were so massive they looked like they could crush someone's head with the strength of a vise grip.

On this summer night, with yellow air thicker than dirty steam, Tommy cocked his head at the approach of Cookie Colangelo. It's not as though he wanted to listen to what she had to say. As soon as she had stopped looking twelve, she had caught his eye, but he wasn't pleased about her chummy pal Herman Lynch. No matter how hot the temperature rose, you could hear the staccato click of Tommy's heels. He wore his boots year-round and had broken them in the same way he had broken in girls in the North End. He looked at girls like they were horses, assessing their lineage and body type: Thoroughbred, Clydesdale, Arabian, Appaloosa, Draft Horse, or maybe just a pony.

As a city stud accustomed to riding in buses, subways and in the back of beater cars, it was unlikely Tommy knew how to ride a real horse. Nonetheless, he eyed Cookie like she was a wild Mustang who needed to be broken. Walking the sidelines of the shadows along the low guard rail marking the front barrier strip of the parking lot, she fancied herself to be tough, glamorous and sexy in her silk midriff halter top and low-slung bell bottoms. She thought being naked under her jeans and halter top accentuated her delicious curves. Swathed in Heaven Scent perfume, she meant to have every guy in this lot on their knees by the end of the night, like the woman Eric Clapton sang about in *Layla*.

It could have happened the way Cookie had wanted it to play out, but realistically these guys were too unhinged and macho to get rattled over a cute chick. Tommy had his cool guy gaze down pat. He gave her a nod—he recognized her and at the same time, he could care less how fine she looked—his way of saying maybe he might be interested, maybe not. She put her hands in her pockets and turned around on her heels to face him. Looking him in the eye, she tossed her hair, parted her lips slightly, put her leg up on the guard rail close to where he stood and turned her attention to Billy Dee. Instinctively, Cookie knew she controlled the situation. It was always about the tease.

You'd never know Billy Dee was Reenie's brother. Blunt blond hair parted left like a helmet—pegged Billy Dee. Fair and blue-eyed in stark contrast to Reenie's dark hair, skin and eyes, they looked more like litter mates than biological brother and sister.

So strung out, Billy Dee hardly knew Cookie stood there watching him. He knelt on the ground between the two parked cars, concentrating on turning up the flame of his lighter under a bent metal spoon, cooking his works, getting ready to shoot up. Cookie didn't like heroin, thinking of it as a slow death wish. She remembered how Herman's mother had died and the sadness and grief left behind with Herman. She didn't feel shock or fear over seeing Billy Dee so wasted. She just didn't want to watch anyone die. Her feelings must have registered on her face.

Tommy shook his head and admonished Cookie with his finger. "Just leave him alone," he said. "Don't try talking to him. And don't rat him out to Reenie."

"He's cool." Jay Marcello nodded appreciatively. "He's got good dope. It's all about trust," he said.

"It's always about trust," Tommy said, glaring at Cookie. "Can you dig it?"

For sure, Jay Marcello, Billy Dee and Tommy Parrello were *Down the End* and up to no good. They didn't pay much mind to Cookie hanging around on the outer fringe of where they stood, but they didn't do much to welcome her into their group either. If she stood there long enough, she would automatically be part of their gang. But no one would notice if she left, and no one would care. Cookie didn't know how long it would take to get their interest but found she could run a marathon holding a sultry pose, shifting her hips every so often, licking her lips, sending them a hungry, girlish invitation to kiss.

Billy Dee finally spoke to her. His blond hair soaked the sheen of amber crime light. "What do you want?" he slurred.

"I just want to be one of the guys and hang out," Cookie said.

All the guys scoffed except a glassy-eyed Billy Dee, but they weren't mean enough to laugh outright. Besides, Cookie had it going on.

A smoky haze had collected around the bright crime lights, illuminating some sections of the parking lot. The muggy summer night captured cumulus-shaped clouds of smoke. Two cars sat parked away from the strobe of amber light. Car lights had been turned off so the people inside could not be seen. Too low to hear distinct words, intimate whispers drifted into the night. Dark shapes moved inside the parked cars, appearing as the silhouettes of limbs and hair, arms slung over shoulders and legs splayed over heads. Music from one car played the summer's hottest release *All the Young Dudes* by Mott the Hoople.

Cool guys bunched into troops, holding down the fort to stave off the moment when they would come under siege. Clustering in tight huddles made them strong enough to withstand onslaught from a pack of she-wolf Italian girls. The guys were intimidating to a one-off girl going at it alone, like Cookie. They looked askance at lone girls. It was a pack animal thing. They had a bad attitude: what have you got for me that I should want to bother with you?

Noreen DiOreo and Jimmy Lalla were going at it hard. Both had chin-length blond hair. Her arms up around his neck. His eyes cold and stony. His arms hung casually as if he could care less about the hookup. He opened the car door to his lemon-colored 1970 Fiat 124 Wagon. Seats slid down. Noreen squatting over Jimmy outstretched on the bottom. Rolling one on top of the other in frenetic toss of shifting bodies and yellow hair. It was late at night in August *Down the End* and so damn hot.

Cookie wandered back to the northern edge of the lot. Amber light glowed between the two parked cars and on Billy Dee scrunched up on the ground with a needle in his arm and a tight band of clothesline coming untied from around his bicep. Billy Dee had injected directly into his vein, mainlining smack. Not caring much about passing out, his head flopped forward. Jay Marcello's one rolled-up pant leg showed marks, dimples and small cuts on his flesh. Under the lights, his leg looked like he had scars from the chicken pox.

Only Tommy was left standing. "I'm not into that shit," he told Cookie. "Sometimes they mix it up with speed. Speedballing's a rush. If you want to try it, let me know."

Cookie hesitated, thinking she might try it once. Tommy picked up on her cue and walked over to her. He touched her on the cheek, caught in an unexpected gentle gesture. Cookie thought to herself, *Am I sure I want to kiss this guy?*

She didn't ask the question again. She didn't have to pucker up or spend time anticipating his first move. Already there, inside her mouth, his tongue spiraled with the speed of a power drill. If Crazy Dave had used his tongue like a scoop, then by comparison Tommy Parrello had mastered advanced technique. He relied heavily on using his tongue with the precision of a pool player. Every stroke he took landed his cue ball into the corner pocket. Alternating pressure as strong as steel and as soft as velvet, his tongue caressed the inside of her mouth, and touched her lips with featherlight curiosity. Linkage locked their two tongues together like twine.

Being with a good kisser made her feel like it could be love. She liked kissing him so much. She opened her eyes and looked at him, wondering if she could ever fall in love with him. He opened his eyes too, but his look was flat and non-committal.

He drew her closer and began using his tongue like a pincer. His mouth became a vacuum, yanking and pulling on her tongue with athletic strength. The more she pulled away from him, the harder he yanked on her tongue. Lizard-like, his tongue darted lancing blows, skewering the inside of her mouth. She hardly had time to respond. She didn't know how to break away because she could not figure out if she liked what he was doing. Then it became apparent—he did not want her to keep up with him and could care less about her response. He was the guy, and in charge.

His mouth turned into a plunger intent on swallowing her tongue. He would not let go. And it began to hurt. Not hurting in an off-the-Richter-scale way. It hurt like a guy sucking hard on your neck to give you a hickey. And you had to wear a turtleneck or a scarf around your neck for a week to cover the mark. She cried out in a muffled whimper, but he did not ease up, and yanked harder. After the blood-thumping pummeling of her mouth, she ripped herself free from his embrace. Wondering if he had taken her tongue and swallowed it whole, she clasped her hands around her neck and wiggled her wounded tongue. It was still intact, but sore and numb. Looking surprised, Tommy held his hands up and asked, "What's the matter?"

Twenty-eight

The Dumbwaiter

Cookie's tongue had been sprained from her interlude with Tommy Parrello. She tried sucking red and orange twin popsicles, but only time would heal her tongue. It took three days to physically recover. When it came to kissing, most guys did not know what they were doing. She attributed this lack of finesse to being young. Some guys had plenty of experience but never got any better. Later, she would learn this new-found truth about kissing held fast throughout life. Most men were not good at kissing. Just horrible! Bad kissers! After sulking about her sprained tongue and the inevitability of running into one more bad kisser, she got over it.

On the third day of her recuperation, she threw off her damp sheets, thrusted her sweaty body out of bed, and looked out the window. A mid-morning sun hung in a creamy blue sky.

Her tongue felt good enough to lick an ice cream cone. Where off to next? Who else could she kiss? The summer had been ripe with possibility, but she felt down on her luck.

She took quick pitter-patter steps out of the house. Intentionally quiet, she needed to avoid Kitty and Donny, especially Donny. Her parents were upstairs in the bedroom, sleeping in. She grabbed Johnny's car keys to take his Buick for a joy ride.

Buttery yellow light bathed the streets and the trees swollen with lush green leaves. Morning sunlight filtered between yards and alleyways, occasionally flashing in her eyes and pinging off the chrome of the car. She drove south on Broadway, heading to Ghetto Square. Turning on the radio, she blasted Foghat's heavy metal hit *I just want to make love to you*. She cranked the volume even higher and rolled down all of the windows. She imagined her car to be a convertible with its top down. The air had not cooled during the previous night and bore the mild aroma of the river heating in a stew of fish and crab grass. The day promised to be another scorcher.

If Johnny came looking for her, he'd find a flinty-eyed, wild haired chick, a siren, a ravishing temptress unparalleled in her raw lust and carnal sexuality.

"I'm not trying to be sexy," Cookie told herself. "It's just my way of expressing myself when I move. If I like someone who is a little crazy but coming from a good place, it's cool. I think my mistakes are sexy because it means I'm used to making a big mess. And man, I am making a big mess!"

She sloppily parked the car on Nepperhan Avenue close to the corner intersecting with South Broadway. When she got out of the car and checked her parking job, she saw that the back of the Buick had fishtailed onto the road. Not willing to put Johnny's car at risk, she got back into the car and tried again. Now aligned in its rightful spot, the Buick would stay safe from getting dinged.

Totally self-absorbed and fanciful, she told herself she was a wild thing, very beautiful, extremely clever, and she would love to do something sexy and dangerous. The next guy she saw on the street, whether she knew him or not, she was just going to go up to him and kiss him!

She could not imagine anything more daring than going up to an unsuspecting guy and kissing him. The guy would never see it coming! She had never heard of any girl doing such a thing! Outrageous! Audacious! She would be an urban legend!

Cookie pulled out a Marlboro and lit up. Leaning against the library's retaining wall, she waited patiently for her quarry. She would surprise him and make him her captive. Not a victim. What guy in his right mind would not want a sexy girl to come up to him and kiss him out of the blue? It was winning the jackpot, without having entered a contest.

The street in front of the Yonkers Carnegie Library was mostly deserted. A few cars drove by, but not one slowed, and no one parked. Across the street, an elderly woman pushed a stroller-style shopping cart resembling a walker and tottered into the Finast grocery market.

Distant movement caught her eye. At the top of Nepperhan Avenue, a guy slowly made his way down the hill. Even in the distance, Cookie could see he carried books, and was probably heading for the library. She turned away from the hill to face the street. She didn't want her captive guy to see her first. No one else approached the library aside from the guy coming down the hill. While she waited, she felt impatient and closed her eyes. If a different guy approached first, he would be the one. First come, first served. She made the rules. This was her game. She couldn't wait to spring on the guy and say, "Surprise!"

"Cookie Colangelo?"

Even better! The guy knew her! Cookie spun on her heels, pivoting in a circle to zoom in on her quarry. What she found stopped her in her tracks.

Mike Trapani gave her a sheepish smile. "How are you doing? Long time, no see."

Cookie eyed him with great consternation. She put her hand up, a preemptive move to block a pass, and said, "Don't even think about it."

Somehow, he figured he had caught her off guard. His smile opened up and grew huge. He shook his head and scoffed,

"You always were weird. You're a really cute girl, but nutso. Crazy," he emphasized.

So much for kissing the first unsuspecting guy passing by. Mike Trapani's pants were slung low on his hips below his belly. The last time she had seen him, he had already developed plumber's crack and plaque coated his teeth. Nothing had changed. If anything, his belly had grown bigger, and the plaque on his teeth had mellowed to the texture of Cheetos.

With great pride, he told her, "I'm going to Saunders now. I'm going into business with my father. Don't need these books no more. I'm learning mostly everything on the job."

"Nice," Cookie said.

"Told you I was going to be a plumber. Well, I'm doing it!" Eyeing her with curiosity, he said, "Heard you got kicked out of *The Heart*. What are you doing now?" He leaned in and whispered, "What are you doing, hanging out down here? What are you looking to do? Pick up them darkies?"

Cookie stepped back from him and exhaled a long plume of smoke. She eyed him through the smoke and considered decking him, but he had weight on his side. She could deploy the surprise element—smack him and run. She pondered the stakes, quickly losing interest, and decided running into him was the price she had to pay for being a wild thing. She wasn't going to kiss some strange guy anyway. It was pure speculation. A wild girl's fantasy. She knew how to entertain herself, sort of like playing charades.

She heard Mike Trapani laughing as he walked away. Heaving himself up the front steps to the library took enormous effort. He called down to her in jest, "Just wondering how you're doing, that's all."

Cookie didn't need an excuse to go to the library. She planned to check out a novel she had found at school and had started to read before summer began. As soon as she pulled open the heavy door, cool air rushed at her from the inner sanctum of the library. On the main floor, rotary blades whirred at high speed on two tall standing fans. Although the library didn't have air conditioning, the two monstrous fans kept the rooms cool. Massive amounts of marble decking the floors and steps helped to make this Yonkers landmark one of the few places to get relief from the summer heat.

Mabel was working at the circulation desk. She took an armful of books from Mike Trapani and set them on top of a stack piling up on the circular mahogany desk. "See you around, Cookie," Mike said, winking at her, making smooching noises and laughing at her as he rushed out. "Kiss, kiss," he mouthed. Exerting too much force on the main door, he made it swing behind him as he left.

Shuddering, she closed her eyes.

"I never expected to see you so soon," Mabel said, kidding her. She knew Cookie was a constant fixture. Letting her glasses drop from her nose and dangle from a chain, she leaned over the desk and told Cookie in a hushed voice that Reenie was upstairs reading to little kids during story hour.

"I'm keeping her by my side this summer, so she stays out of trouble." Mabel smiled. "She'll be done in an hour if you want to wait. Is there something special I can help you with or are you just browsing?"

Cookie's voice automatically softened around Mabel. "*The Winds of War* by Herman Wouk. Do you have it?"

"I'll check. I had two copies. It's been very popular," Mabel told her. "Be right back." She came out from behind the desk and went to the rows of shelves on the left where new releases were on display.

Cookie felt embarrassed to ask for a particular book. Next thing she knew, Mabel would start asking her about it to prompt topics for discussion. Mabel wasn't wrong to ask. The problem lay within Cookie. She felt inward and solitary, as though she did not want to share her innermost thoughts with anyone, not even with Mabel whom she adored. The feelings she experienced were somehow rooted in why she had lost her words.

Cookie raced up the marble steps to the children's room on the second floor. Reenie sat in the middle of a circle of very young children, kindergarteners or first graders. In the midst of reading a romantic story—*Sleeping Beauty*, Reenie looked up and smiled. Cookie stuck her tongue out at Reenie, meaning to be funny, not to distract her. She knew Reenie would have to exert self-restraint to not stick her tongue out in return. Cookie gave her an exuberant wave, whisked out of the room and back down to the main floor.

Mabel came up to her and said both copies of the book had been checked out, but she would put one on reserve for Cookie. She recommended *War and Remembrance*, but Cookie told her she had already read it.

Cookie had an insatiable craving to immerse herself in a long, sprawling epic, full of heroic women, and a few good men, braving the travails of war. And it had nothing to do with Stanley.

Mabel smiled at her as though she wanted to reach forward and give her a big, quick hug, but the propriety of the job kept her behind the desk.

"I have something I've always wanted to ask you."

Mabel's curiosity was piqued. "Yes, what is it?"

Cookie whispered, "It's about the nuns. Sister Mary Eau Claire...."

"Do you want to go somewhere and talk privately?"

"No," Cookie burbled. "It's not a big deal. I just wondered... Are they really cloistered?"

"Yes, of course, they cannot leave the convent or school without getting special permission." Mabel nodded her head slightly. "Why do you ask?"

"Do they really have a dumbwaiter that brings groceries into the convent?"

"As far as I know, they do, but come to think of it, I've never seen it."

Cookie drew her hands together and pointed her fingers down to the ground and said, "Righto."

Mabel gave her a funny look; Cookie was being her usual self. "You never cease to amaze me. Some of the questions you ask are very unusual and I never know what's going on." She laughed lightheartedly.

"Gotta go!" Cookie had not lost the desire to be a wild thing. Too impatient to wait around for Reenie, she ran out of the library, headed straight toward the Buick, hopped in, started the ignition and hit the gas to get out of there as fast as possible. She didn't know why she had to move so fast. She only knew she'd get excited over something and have to act on it, quick as a bunny.

She took a different way home and wound up on Palisade Avenue, passing the Schlobohm Projects, also known as "Slow Bomb." She remembered when she used to ride the bus through these streets and took the time to think about why poor black people had been shoved behind a high wrought iron fence to keep them in a ghetto. No yards, front or back, no trees, plants or flowers, tiny cubicle apartments etched in concrete cinder blocks held people as though they were prisoners in a death camp. Driving by made it seem less real, like a bad dream from which she could awaken. She could get out of here and never have to think about it again.

But what about them? People were left behind, unfortunate casualties, victims of war. The lucky ones had dreams and clawed their way out.

Taking an impromptu side trip to her school on a summer day was a wild hair, purely impulsive. She thought she would do a bit of sleuthing around the grounds to see what sorts of trouble she could stir up. She easily parked the Buick on Park Avenue in front of Blessed Sacrament Academy. Officially closed for the summer months, the school didn't offer a summer program, and the grounds were deserted. She tried the front door of the school. All chrome and glass with sharp angles and walls, the building had the irregular look of bland 1960s architecture.

Tall maple trees bordered the grassy area to the south of the school. Beyond, a twelve-foot retaining wall, constructed from uneven blocks of granite, had been heavily mortared with concrete. This wall ran the expanse of the entire block, creating a hidden compound enclosing its bucolic grounds, a chapel large enough to be a church, and the actual convent— home to the Sacramentine nuns. The wall ended on Park Avenue, a flat plane on the bottom of the hill where it met Ashburton Avenue, the new dividing line between the blacks & whites. It's where the ghetto began.

The wall annoyed her and would never stop her. To this day, Cookie does not know why she had this reaction, but she scaled the wall. She was intent on finding out if the nuns did have a dumbwaiter. Also, if she got inside of the school, she could steal I.D. cards and sell them to underage girls who needed fake I.D. to get into bars and dance clubs. If she got really lucky, she could snag *The Winds of War* and take it home with her.

Closer to the convent, the wall was lower in height by four feet. With force from her legs, she catapulted her upper body upward to straddle the top and hurled herself over the wall. On the other side, the splendid lawn had been kept green and immaculate. A water sprinkler sat in the middle of the lawn, making a melodic hissing sound, rotating its axis to evenly disperse water. She crept along the inner sanctuary. Gobs of geraniums and petunias bordered the grounds. In the shaded area under the maple trees, royal blue lobelia overflowed in flower beds, and rows of impatiens grew abundantly in red, pink, yellow and white.

She scouted another entrance to the school. She knew the nuns often used a secret passageway from the convent to the school. Because they were cloistered, they shielded themselves from the prying eyes of the public. She roamed the lawn nonchalantly, acting as though she had a right to be there. A narrow alley led to the side door of the convent.

Following the alley to the door led her to a dimly lit overpass that connected the convent to the back entrance of the school. She walked toward the side of the convent and detected a familiar scent, making her regret leaving her hemp sack in the car. Someone nearby was smoking a cigarette.

Buttressed by a low granite wall, a yellow and tan brick outhouse-sized building protruded from behind the convent. She wondered what was inside of this building. It did not appear to be connected to the convent or the school. She walked gingerly, not to avoid making noise so much, but to maintain her self-concocted aura of secrecy. Padding across the grass made no noise. Cookie followed the rounded corner of this small brick building, opening into a lovely meadow filled with the fragrant multitude of white and deeply rose-colored Oriental lilies. Despite the heady fragrance of the lilies, the scent of cigarette smoke hung heavy in the air and made her crave a Marlboro.

Deeper into the grounds of the convent, she spied a small freight elevator built-into the exterior wall. The dumbwaiter! It was true! She had heard about this elevator but thought it was an urban rumor, adding to the great litany of the many tales of terror often told about nuns. The dumbwaiter transported groceries and sundry items to the upper floors of the convent, making it possible for the nuns to remain otherworldly, separate from the maddening crowd, never having to deal with delivery men.

Fascinated by the dumbwaiter, Cookie feasted her eyes on the contents set on the platform. Someone had left six or seven grocery bags, ready to be lifted to the upper floors of the convent. The smell of cigarette smoke grew stronger and more enticing. Cookie figured a delivery guy had dropped off the groceries and then stopped to take a smoke break. She walked forward to examine the bags and thought fleetingly of peeking at some of the contents, maybe even stealing them! It was just a whim, a mad impulse, pure mischief, a possible prank, not necessarily leading her to take any sort of action. Her eyes followed the path beyond the dumbwaiter. Ensnared by two overgrown honeysuckle bushes, and there for no reason known to God or to man, a black and white mirage with a smooth, blushing face sat huddled over a cigarette. Smoking! When the nun saw Cookie, she gasped and turned deep red. Then for some strange and mysterious reason, Sister Mary Eau Claire giggled like a naughty girl and said, "You caught me!"

Twenty-nine

Kissing Again

Cookie willed herself to feel fearless about walking into the Midget Bar alone and late at night. Most of the other bars around town had shut. A few stayed open after hours, serving drinks, but it was done secretly to foil the suspicion of the Yonkers Police. Jimmy had his hands in the bar's sink, washing glasses. He held one up to the dim yellow light close to the tap and dried it with a towel. The moment he saw Cookie, he flashed his signature smile, greeting her as though she had never left. She didn't recognize anyone sitting on the bar stools except for Pinky O'Hearn, whom she regarded with singular curiosity because of his red hair. Cookie sat down on a bar stool next to Pinky and gave him a furtive smile, as though she had a secret to tell, and she did—she considered kissing him. So far, she had not made out with a redhead.

She hardly knew Pinky and had only seen him from afar. Up close, she was astonished to see his eyelashes were eerily pale, glowing in the dark under the dense effect of the black light. She didn't think he'd respond, but he held up his beer mug and eyed her playfully through the glass. "Want to share?"

Cookie took a sip of his beer, pretending she didn't mind the bitter aftertaste. On the road to becoming an indiscriminate kisser, she felt sultry sitting in the bar. Beads of moisture trickled in between her breasts. She wore a skimpy white midriff halter top, knowing the black light made the white fabric transparent. To any onlooker, she appeared to be sitting naked from the waist up. Cookie wore the shortest short-shorts, cut-offs. The backs of her thighs were laid bare on top of the leatherette bar stool. Sweat skimmed the skin on the backs of her leg, making her flesh stick slightly to the seat. The surface of the wooden bar counter had a waxy glaze, the cumulative effect of too much spilled beer. If the place had air conditioning, then it wasn't working properly. She placed her hand on Pinky's freckled arm; his skin felt warm and moist.

"I thought you were taken." Pinky winked.

She could smell his hot breath, reeking of beer. His tongue had thickened, making it difficult for him to talk.

"Everyone knows you're sweet on Stanley de Falco," he whispered in her ear, tickling her. "And I don't want to get into a fight with him. He's bigger than I am."

Cookie was a bit taken aback and suddenly pissed off. "You know what, Pinky, everyone's bigger than you are."

"Except...," Pinky raised his glass to toast Jimmy, "Jimmy. Here's to Jimmy."

Jimmy slammed a glass mug on the counter, sending a small wave of beer crashing over the top and onto the surface of the bar. "What are you doing with this loser?" he playfully asked Cookie.

Cookie put her face up to Pinky, pouting, parting her lips, expecting a kiss. Pinky was bashful. He grinned at her and turned his head as though he didn't know what to do.

Jimmy caught the action. "Come on, Pinky, she's real cute! What does a girl got to do to get your attention?" Jimmy grinned at Cookie. "Dump this loser. If you want to come with me, sweetheart, just say so. Anytime. I'm here for you."

Pinky seemed to be thinking about what to do. Rocking on his stool, he put his arm around the small of Cookie's back, and gave her a passing rub, once or twice, as if he meant to polish his shoes. Then he became distracted and stopped. Cookie's face came closer. Her lips were inches away from his. His face had a mischievous leer. Cookie decided Pinky was the worst kind of bad boy; he boasted about wanting to do something reckless or risky but did not know what to do when given a half a chance. He had been drinking far too much for too long.

She lost interest in Pinky; he was not worth her effort. Bodies pressed up against the bar. The crowd hammered together all the way to the back room. White go-go boots and sandals gleamed on the sticky floor. The pounding percussive thump of Argent's *Hold Your Head Up* blared from the jukebox. Cookie felt the back of her white halter top loosen. When she reached for it, Pinky grinned and sloppily rubbed her back. She arched her body with the supple curve of a feline and felt for the ends of her halter. Pulling the loose ties together, trying to turn them into a knot, she felt another set of hands and quickly shrugged them off.

"Let me help you with that."

She didn't expect to see Stanley de Falco standing beside her at the bar. He didn't say anything, not even hello. He tied her top tight, adding a double knot.

He didn't bother to notice women looking at him as he walked to the back of the bar. Women slowed as they passed him, primping and smiling. Some played with their rings or bracelets, others flipped their hair. One girl took two front chunks of ultra-long bangs and pulled these pieces taut to her chin to measure the length of her hair. He didn't notice the woman who unbuttoned the tiny eyelets on her blouse to show off her breasts, or the woman who plunged her hands deep into the pockets of her hip huggers to pull them down to the top line, exposing her pubic bone.

A blond neon apparition who had returned to the Midget

Bar from parts unknown, Stanley de Falco took his favorite table, close to the jukebox in the back of the room, where he could observe everyone, but not have to talk to anyone.

Pinky was oblivious to Stanley. He chugged the last of his beer and asked Jimmy for another. The midget plunked down a full mug in front of him. The temperature in the bar had risen to be as hot as an old furnace about to overheat. Cookie dropped off the bar stool to find Stanley. The astonishment of seeing him appear from nowhere sent a jolt to her heart and shocked her senses. Partially adrift, sleepwalking, yet fully engaged in the moment, she was at the same time wholly unconscious and floating. She could not remember how she had arrived here or what she had been thinking about. She had no idea what she was doing or how long it would take to find him. Her body took over and led her to where she needed to go.

Passing shaggy heads in a sea of faded bell bottom blue jeans, Cookie battled her way to the back of the room. Twice someone stepped on her foot, but it was accidental. The floor was sticky with spilled beer. A messy line of women stood close to the bathroom door. A warning rippled through the line, telling all the girls to take napkins from the bar. The bathroom stall had run out of toilet paper. Every time the door opened and shut, a squalid heap of sodden paper dragged along the floor. Bodies tumbled in and out. So many people were drunk or stoned, or both.

By the time Cookie reached Stanley's table, she could feel a swarm of eyes buzzing around her. Without waiting for his nod, she sat across from him. Stanley had been there all along, watching the massive build-up of bodies coming into the Midget Bar to take one last dive into debauchery before the long crawl home. Stanley had long ago staked out his own turf. His beer mug was half full.

He leaned forward to make a comment only Cookie could hear. "Do you know that you can see through your top? Black light makes white see through."

"Huh? Black light makes white see through?"

She got the picture and smiled without apology. She also noticed Stanley intentionally avoiding looking at her breasts. It annoyed her and at the same time it made her love him madly. She also couldn't get the line *Black light makes white see through* out of her head and committed it to memory, so she could share it with Herman and Mabel. Black light makes white see through was a metaphor. Mabel would hoot for days. Maybe Cookie would write about it someday, if she ever got her words back.

Cookie smoothed her hair back, tucking it all behind one ear, then she shook her head forward, letting her hair fall free. Her arms reached in the air until she leaned back in her chair to show him the undulation and undercurve of her breasts. Flexing her legs out, shuttering in and out in scissor kicks, she didn't know what she was doing; it came naturally. Italian girl bravata.

She didn't know Pinky had been on her heels until he found an empty chair at another table and abruptly pushed it up to the one where Cookie sat with Stanley. He slapped his mug down hard, spilling beer, leaving a small wet stain. Cookie thought Pinky O'Hearn was heading down the same path as her great grandfather Tiny Ten Pint. For anyone Irish, a weakness for the drink was the same as original sin, a punishable offense only God or the Devil could reckon with.

Stanley did not want to talk to Pinky. He folded his arms, making his back ramrod, closing himself off to the world. Pinky should have been pissed. He was obviously being rebuffed, but he was too drunk to notice or care. He put his hand out to bump fists with Stanley as a sign of camaraderie and respect.

"Glad you made it back from Nam," Pinky said.

"Me too, man."

Their two fists didn't touch long. Stanley retreated first. Folding his arms again, he looked uncomfortable. Cookie found herself offering comfort. She stretched slowly to his side, moving her arms and legs gracefully in her chair. Her legs crossed and uncrossed, becoming open and letting him know that her body was responding to him as if it had a rhythm of its own. She moved her leg close to his chair, then closer to his leg, and patted his arm, but he didn't seem to notice.

"I'm next," Pinky said. "They're going to make me go to Vietnam. I can feel it in my bones."

"Pinky," Stanley said, shaking his head. "Pinky," he said again, "there's no way you could get sent to Vietnam. Not now. Unless you want to go."

"Not true," Pinky yelled, slurring his words, "they're going to get me!"

"Nixon announced no more draftees would go to Vietnam. That was months ago," Stanley told him.

"But he lies," Cookie said.

"There are still guys going there, but they're volunteers," Stanley said. "They've volunteered to go."

"No matter how much you try to tell me that, Stanley, I don't believe you," Pinky said, pointing his finger. "I don't believe you!"

"Never let the facts get in the way of a good story," Stanley said.

Pinky looked angry. Shaking his head, he said, "My brother Kevin. Should not have happened. He was only twenty, man. That should not have happened!"

Stanley nodded and closed his eyes. Cookie watched him carefully. He didn't want to talk to Pinky about the war but was too polite to get up and leave.

Pinky's voice tremored. "Every day, I think he's coming home. I forget for a minute that he's dead. But he is dead. He's dead," he said again as if he was trying to make himself believe. "He's never going to come home again."

Pinky wiped tears from his eyes. Stanley couldn't stand to see him crying and moved his chair back a few inches.

No longer sitting straight, Stanley's legs were in motion; he sought a chance to escape.

"Got a smoke?" Pinky asked. His wet lips glistened in the dark. His mouth hung open and took on the look of a panting dog.

Stanley shook his head. "In Vietnam, they gave us free cigarettes. Never smoked."

Cookie rummaged through her hemp sack for her Marlboros. She pulled out a pack, flipped open the top and offered one to Pinky, then struck a match for him. As he leaned forward to catch the flame, a spark of light illuminated Pinky's face wet with sweat, tears, and beer.

Blowing the match out, slurring his words, he said, "Sometimes, I think they made a mistake and it was someone else who got killed. That Kevin's really alive and some other poor bastard's the one who got killed."

Pinky gulped from his beer. Getting sloppy, he found it hard to juggle the beer and his cigarette. He let go of his beer long enough to use the bottom of his cotton t-shirt to wipe away the wet spot on his chin. "It's not fair that some guys got killed and others didn't."

"You want to talk about fair?" Stanley shook his head and closed his eyes. "I'll tell you all about fair. How about all of the guys who got out of it? Every time I see a guy around my age, I wonder how he got out of going. One guy I know had five deferments. Another guy bragged that his father paid off a Senator. Every one of those guys who didn't go sent another guy in his place and chances are the guy who got killed took a bullet for the guy who got out of going."

Stanley looked angry now. "I don't want to talk about this," he said. "Maybe some other time. But not now. It's just not the right time."

"Mistaken identity," Pinky said. "Does that ever happen?"

Stanley nodded. "Sure, that can happen." He reached and pulled his dog tags to the outside of his shirt where they dangled and caught a scant flash of light. "That's why we wear dog tags, so when we're blown to pieces, they can tell who we once were." He tucked his dog tags back under his shirt, glanced at his watch, and then his beer, but didn't touch it.

"I don't know of anyone who got out of going," Cookie said. "They say when a guy's been in combat, he's never the same again. Like Johnny. My father never talks about it."

"What are you doing with her?" Pinky nodded toward Cookie. "I mean why is she here when it's just us guys talking?"

Stanley moved toward Cookie, put his mouth up to her ear, and whispered. "Don't stay. It's going to get ugly, I can tell."

Cookie looked at him but didn't move to leave. Stanley didn't force the issue. As much as she didn't show fear, she understood she ought to be afraid because a change had come over Pinky. His eyes turned dark and the tears were gone. Something else simmered beneath his pain. His voice hissed with the kind of slow-churning violence that was about to explode. "If it was some other guy who died instead of my brother, then I'd feel bad for the poor bastard that died. But if I had to, I'd kill that guy myself, with my own hands, if that's what it would take to make Kevin alive again! I'd do anything, man!"

Stanley put his hand up, signaling him to take a time out, but Pinky didn't listen. He was spiraling downward and could not be stopped.

"I bet you saw lots of guys getting blown up!" Pinky dropped his cigarette and stomped it on the floor.

Stanley didn't bother to nod. He might have been focused on keeping his cool.

"You were there! Why did it have to be my brother?!"

"Sorry, buddy." Stanley gave him a squeeze on his shoulder. More than offering comfort, he was reining him in.

"Do you know why? Tell me why!" Even in the black light, Pinky's face seemed to have turned a deeper red. Crazed with the mind-numbing effect of cheap beer, hatred seethed through his every pore. "Commie bastards," he yelled, slamming his fists on the table.

"Hey, buddy, I said I'm sorry."

"You were there, Stanley! Why did it have to be Kevin?"

"I don't know," Stanley said. "I'm not God."

"Or the devil," Cookie added.

Pinky lowered his voice to a malevolent drunken hush. "Tell me something, Stanley. It's a question I've been meaning to ask you. Why didn't you get killed?"

Stanley looked like he had been punched in the stomach. For an instant, Cookie thought he would grab Pinky by the neck, or punch him, anything to make him shut up. Instead Stanley flinched, turned his head away and withdrew from what was happening. He drifted to a vacant place and said nothing.

"Did you hear me?" Pinky yelled. "You're here and Kevin's dead! Why? That's all I want to know! Why?"

Cookie took Stanley by his arm and prodded him to stand. "Let's go," she told him.

Stanley listened to her and rose to his feet, but the look in his eyes was faraway. He had gone to a place within where no one else could go.

Pinky staggered to his feet, knocking into the table and his chair. He looked like he was ready to start swinging his fists. Stanley prodded him to get out of his way. Pinky didn't fight him. He was as helpless as an infant on the verge of spitting up on his mother's shoulder.

"Someday it's going to be me," Pinky said, slumping back into his chair. "I'm next."

"We're all next," Stanley said. "Some of us just don't know it."

Cookie hardly remembered how she jostled herself through the bar with Stanley. He walked ahead of her and had the advantage of mass and muscle to clear a path. No matter how drunk or stoned people were, they stepped out of his way.

As they pushed open the door and stepped onto the rutted sidewalk of Oak Street, a steamy curtain of air met them more than halfway, covering their bodies and soaking into their pores. In the heat, she felt like she had just stepped out of a bath. Her skin felt lush and her hair curled without doing anything to it. She knew she looked good, hot and loose, and hoped Stanley noticed the same thing.

Stanley grinned, then stared at her through his dark lashes. "I'm sorry about Pinky. I wanted to kill him."

"Why didn't you?" She never thought of herself as a clingy kind of girl, and yet, she took his arm and held onto it.

He told her Pinky's mother had died while Kevin was in Vietnam. The long-suffering Irish mother, Mrs. O'Hearn, didn't want her son to know she was sick and made them promise when she died, they wouldn't tell Kevin until he came home. She never lived long enough to find out that her son got killed. Kevin never knew his mother had died. Pinky had answered the one letter Kevin had sent to their mother. Pinky could not shake the awful guilt—for the letters he wrote pretending to be their mother, but Kevin never wrote back, even after sending him stamps. Pinky had been mad at Kevin for not writing back.

"But then Kevin got killed." Stanley stopped for a minute. He was stunned by what had happened to him and looked Cookie in the eye. "I also didn't hit him because Jimmy would never put up with it. Then I'd have nowhere to go. The way my mother smokes, I can't stand being home."

Cookie threw herself toward him in an embrace and felt the steady beating of his heart. Her sudden movement had pushed his left hand to press against her bare thigh. She took hold of his arm and pulled it to wrap around her waist. She was going to give Stanley the greatest kiss he had ever known. She thought if she was destined to writhe all night in sweat-drenched sheets, she didn't need to do it alone. This hot summer night, more humid than most, had become the end note after an intensely long hot summer. She held on to Stanley fiercely and picked up the salty scent of his sweat. She closed her eyes and lifted her head to meet his. Between Stanley and the heat of the night, she wanted to open up naturally and give freely of herself. She wanted to take him somewhere but didn't know a good place to go. She did not know he had already made up his mind about her. He told her he had made other plans.

Thirty

Love Minus One

Yonkers had two types of summer rainstorms. Some storms gave full vent to the humidity. Rain fell to the earth, making the air hotter, and heavier with water, so you could take a dirty bath just by walking outdoors. In other storms, the wind and the rain cleansed the air, leaving blue skies and a full sun. In the aftermath, a purifying light from the sky touched upon on every living thing and made the mighty Hudson River sparkle. Any memory of feeling muggy could easily be forgotten. Only a big storm could clear the air.

The day before, a torrential downpour cleansed the city after ten straight days of stifling humidity. Cookie fled into the depths of the Owl Hole and sank into despair. This place had always been her refuge, where she found the answers to life's mysteries. Her kissing spree had not brought her happiness. In her darkest moment, she fancied herself as indomitable as an owl. Self-contained, beautiful to observe, and driven to survive, an owl did not need love to soar through the sky. The owl remained alone, untouched and aloof, only to spread its wings and fly west along the river.

She sat on the bottom step of the Owl Hole and opened

her black & white notebook. The smooth stone floor felt refreshingly cool and slightly damp. Other than to write book reports for school, it had been months since she had taken a pen into her hand to write a poem born of her own creative expression. She thought she would write about Stanley. He wasn't an ordinary guy. Something deeper was going on that she had yet to come to understand or embrace. Stanley de Falco gave her life meaning, but she did not know why.

Familiar sounds came from above; no voices, no whispering, only shoes scuffed through blade-like reeds and spiny branches to clear a path. Concealed by thorny bushes and tall crops of horsetail made lush by the August heat, a newcomer would not easily get through the thicket to reach the Owl Hole. Strong muscular legs snapped twigs and stomped bramble to the ground. Feet floated down the steps soft and cloud-like. The moment she recognized his footsteps, she felt grateful and began to smile.

Her smile felt small compared to the way Herman Lynch opened up and smiled at her. His mouth would never be perfect in the classic sense, but the irregular line of his upper lip curled with superior prowess, making him look immortal and invincible. Like the Greek god Apollo, he was wiry in repose, powerful on the move, and quicksilver on his feet. He was the boxer who never lost a bout and the baseball player who did a long slide home. The new power and raw strength of his body had come from months of devoted dance training.

He bounded down beside her and placed his hand on her knee. "How's my Cookie girl doing?"

"God, Herman," she said, embracing him, "you're my best friend, but I never see you no more."

"Any more." Herman grinned. "Don't let my grandmother hear you talking that way. She'll tan your hide."

Herman stood up and walked to the center of the concrete landing. He looked toward the top of the steps. "Reenie said she might show." He scuffed the top of his shoe against the step, bending his arch and toes, then stretching out his foot. "Don't know for sure what's going on with her, but I think she's having a hard time. Might even be in trouble for all I know. She's always on the run and never has time to stop and talk."

Cookie didn't know if she should mention Billy Dee and thought she'd wait until Reenie got there. "Is it a guy thing? I mean her hair has gone straight. She's not looking like herself."

"Might be," Herman said. "I've seen her boyfriend around. He's whitey, alright, and drives a blue Corvette. Don't know how a young guy can come into a car like that unless he comes from money." Herman worked on his other foot and stretched his leg up on the railing in a full extension. "Speaking of guys... Are you still mooning over that Stanley guy?"

Cookie laughed. "I'm confused. Real confused. He confuses me. I don't know what's going on."

"Heard you're not going to get kicked out of school any more." Herman leaned in and emphasized saying "any more," for good measure. "You hear what I'm saying to you?"

"That's news to me. No one told me anything," Cookie said. "Why am I always the last to know?"

"So, what have you been doing with yourself? I never see you around."

"I'm working on my kissing." Cookie delivered her news with a deadpan expression. "I've been making the rounds."

Herman clutched his chest. "You, Cookie! What are you talking about? What are you doing that for? You've never cared about that stuff!"

Herman referred to the days when she straddled between being a gangster and a hippie, but those days were gone. Cookie didn't know how to tell Herman that she had entered a new phase in her life: siren, wild child, and queen of the night, hell bent on being the sexiest woman alive. She stood up and put her hands on her hips, about to do a pelvic tilt and swiveled toward him. Then she eyed him seductively until their eyes met in chilling silence. "How about giving your new lip a workout?"

Herman stared at her, completely at a loss for what to say. He didn't know what to do. He tried to talk but ended up shaking his head. He put his hands up in front as a barrier to protect himself. "I don't think so."

Cookie came up to him and took his hand and drew herself close to him and looked into his eyes. "Come on, I'll show you. It takes practice."

"Practice?"

"Practice."

"I don't know." Herman didn't seem convinced.

"Like this." Cookie leaned her face close to his and thought they were about the same height, almost, judging Herman to be a few inches taller, and kissed him, a tight peck square on his lips. She saved her deft open-mouth move for later. His mouth tasted as tart as an orange, yet warm like salted honey. He didn't recoil from her, but stiffened up, uncertain about what to do. He tried closing his eyes, kissed her back, a quick friendly peck, then stopped.

"I don't think so." Herman withdrew his face from hers, looking upset.

Cookie felt upset too and put her hands on her hips. "Is it because I'm white?"

"No!" Herman looked indignant at the suggestion. "Color is not it at all!" He put his hands in his pockets and moved away from the steps. "You are so rude! Since when am I prejudiced?! I'm surprised to hear you say that! After all of the time we've spent together and everything we've been through!"

"Then, what's the big deal? I'm confused. It's play acting, that's all! Just silliness."

"Nah, I don't want to do it, unless it's the real thing."

"I thought we're friends," Cookie insisted. "Not just friends! We're best friends!"

"Not that way! Not like that, Cookie. I'm not going to be

kissing you and pretending that's what I want to do. Not with you! I've never thought of you that way!"

"We're always going to be friends."

"Cookie, you know I love you. But...." Herman jumped up the step and looked back at her. "I'm not into it, Cookie. I'm different. Don't ask me how. I don't know. I don't know how to tell you anything other than what I'm telling you right now."

Cookie stood still and stopped breathing. She felt horrible. "I'm sorry. Really, I don't know what else to say."

"This is the worst possible time to do something like this to me!" He started up the steps. "Not now. I have nothing to say right now."

Up the steps, she pursued him to make a point. "Got it," she said. "I didn't mean to offend you. I'm just trying to forget about Stanley."

"I got that," he said. "Man, oh man, I got that," he exclaimed. "Wow, this is not cool at all. I can't believe you!"

All the way up the steps, Herman kept saying, "Wow, this is so not right. I don't know what's gotten into you. Ever since that Stanley guy showed up, you've been acting crazy."

"This has nothing to do with Stanley," Cookie insisted. She didn't know what to make of Herman and listened to him carrying on, rolling her eyes when he wasn't looking.

In case Reenie showed up, they stayed by the edge of sidewalk on the corner of North Broadway and Roberts Lane. No longer being swallowed up by Cookie in the Owl Hole, Herman didn't seem so uncomfortable now.

Cookie lit a Marlboro to bide her time. "I'm sorry," she told Herman. "I didn't mean to upset you."

"I don't know what's going on with you," Herman said, staring at her. "It's just good if we don't go there again and stay away from things that aren't going to be good for either of us."

Cookie could not understand why he had become so oversensitive. She became distracted and looked for Reenie. Light traffic on Broadway, the few cars cruising by looked familiar. Cookie expected to see her neighbors. Everybody knew everyone else's business. The North End was a giant grousing fest where gossip spread like the plague. It made her think of Fran Ochiogrosso, who made it her job to know every little thing about everyone.

She handed her cigarette to Herman and he took a drag. "We've always shared everything," she said. "I didn't think the kissing thing would be such a big deal. I was just joking around."

"Look," Herman said, "can we just drop it?"

Cookie thought Herman had gotten mighty thin-skinned and she found herself saying all the wrong things to him. She wondered if Reenie knew her brother Billy Dee had become a real junkie, mainlining, making it easy to OD and die. It had been months since Cookie had connected with her to bare their hearts in a tough girl sort of way.

Herman handed the cigarette back to Cookie. She held onto it but didn't take a drag. She was losing her desire to smoke and thought about tossing her Marlboros. Might have had something to do with Stanley. Might not. Maybe she ought to smoke her brains out.

A Mercedes Benz stopped at the traffic light, but there were still no signs of Reenie. Cookie remembered the days when she and Reenie had sung the words to *Mercedes Benz*, the last song ever recorded by Janis Joplin.

Louie Santamassino owned the only Mercedes Benz in the North End. The car headed toward Cookie's block. Louie caught sight of Cookie and Herman and beeped the horn, saying hello. He slowed to stop at the corner and rolled down the window. He told Herman he looked good, without mentioning Herman's harelip. With a nod, and his hand motioning thumbs up, Louie let them know he still had their backs. Cookie didn't know why he would be going to her block. She and Herman stood in cautious silence, each prompting the other to say something polite, while they waited for Reenie. If Reenie's plans had changed, she had no way to let them know. Eventually, they gave up, stopped waiting, and headed *Down the End.*

Thirty-one

We Saw Nothing

Hedy frowned at them when they walked into her luncheonette. Everyone in the North End called the place John's Luncheonette. Hedy's husband John was a burly Polish guy who had a Marine Corps shaved head. Known for being contentious, John didn't say much, but when he did, he used fighting words that baited people to spar with him.

Hedy made no secret she did not appreciate Herman coming into her domain. She quickly came toward them and stared but didn't ask if they wanted anything. "I can't serve you," she told Herman. "I'm out of everything and closing for the day!" Her statement was a not-so-polite way of asking them to leave.

"You see, Cookie, I told you so." Herman elbowed Cookie in her arm. "Nothing's changed," he said. "It's still the North End not wanting to serve black people." Herman said the same thing again, this time emphasizing the words colored folk. "They call us colored or worse! I hate this shit, I really do, Cookie. I just don't see as much of it in the city. If you can dance, or you can sing, or you can play music, or you can act, or you're beautiful," he said, grinning, "no one cares what your skin color is, they only see your talent."

Hedy placed her hands on her hips to defend her turf. On the surface, she had made a solid point to keep them out. The luncheonette only had two customers. Oonah sat on the last stool next to Rosie. Both women were small and had matching pixie haircuts, except Oonah had pale skin and blond hair; Rosie looked dark and swarthy, like a Sicilian. Rosie was related to Johnny Colangelo by marriage, his sister Ro-Ro's sister-in-law. Oonah worked at the luncheonette as a breakfast waitress. Oonah and Rosie were inseparable, an item, a pair, best friends.

Hedy became momentarily distracted by a customer who came in to buy the *New York Daily News*. She gave the man a brisk smile, took his money without counting it and put it into her pocket. Another man came in and looked around at the candy section. He, too, picked up a newspaper and also brought two Hershey bars to the front counter. This man didn't have exact change. Hedy rang it up on an old-fashioned cash register. When its cash drawer opened, the sound of money changing hands was confirmed by a *Ca-ching* bell chime.

The luncheonette was obviously open for business, but not open to Cookie and Herman.

"Let's get out of here." Herman nudged her.

"Just a second," Cookie said.

All eyes fastened on Cookie and Herman as though they were monsters or criminals. Hedy stared them down. She might have been named after the movie star, but she was no Hedy Lamar and suffered the misfortune of being shaped like a milk bottle. Her black framed eyeglasses magnified the glassy-eyed rejection she cast upon Cookie and Herman.

Cookie said, "You don't even have a coke?"

"Nope, nothing," Hedy said. Even from behind the magnification of her thick lenses, Hedy's eyes remained beady black dots. "You can leave now."

Hedy gave Cookie a menacing stare, not Herman so much. Instead she gave him quick, nervous side-eye glances. His very presence caused her extreme discomfort.

Cookie did not appreciate Hedy's rudeness and told her so. "You're discriminating against my friend and it's not okay."

"This is my place," Hedy said. "And if I don't want you here, I can make you go."

Cookie locked into a stare-down with Hedy and felt her skin prickle on her back. Perspiration formed above her lip and on the palms of her hands. She felt like Fangs the devil nun had returned incarnate. The humiliation of being treated unfairly flared up with the wrath of an infected boil. She had the distinct feeling her moxie had come back. Then and there, she let Hedy have it.

Herman saw the change coming over her. "No, Cookie, don't! Please don't!" he yelled. "Don't get yourself into trouble over me!"

But it was too late. Cookie shoved Hedy against the front counter and pointed her finger in the woman's face. "Don't you ever, ever treat my friend like that again. Do it again, and I will kick the shit out of you. Got that?!"

Hedy shrank back and sprang for the black dial phone on the wall.

"I saw that," Oonah said.

"No, you didn't," Cookie said.

"You saw nothing," Rosie agreed with Cookie. "You saw nothing," she told Oonah. "We saw nothing," she said to Hedy. As a Sicilian, born and bred in Yonkers, Rosie had a distinct mistrust of the authorities, especially law enforcement, preferring that personal matters got settled quietly at home.

Everyone in the luncheonette stopped talking. Hostility scattered like yesterday's humidity, and while everyone knew it could easily return, for the time being calm prevailed. Hedy bustled behind the counter, serving up cokes to Cookie and Herman, and tucked straws into their glasses. Rosie sat on a stool next to Cookie and asked her how Johnny was doing. Oonah smiled bashfully at Herman. Within seconds, she moved behind the counter to the grill, and started cooking up fried egg sandwiches, for herself, Rosie, and Cookie and Herman. Hedy said she didn't want nothing to eat, clutched her stomach, looking paler by the second, not smiling but not scowling either.

"Man," Herman said, "this place is like a foreign country where civil war's about to break out any second."

Hedy's husband, John, barreled into the luncheonette. "Why is everybody so quiet today? Did the sun do a whack job on your heads?"

John immediately eyed Herman with curiosity. Black, yeah, black, but since Herman sat next to Rosie and Cookie, he had to be okay. If Hedy felt like telling John what had gone on, she had decided to keep it to herself. This was the Yonkers way. If someone tough put you in your place, you stayed there, until you could slink away unnoticed with your tail between your legs.

Thirty-two

The Trouble with Kissing

The sky had turned the color of a scotch bonnet pepper. Although the summer of 1972 had come to a close, stifling humidity and high temperatures persisted throughout September. Cookie had commemorated the second anniversary month of the Blind Owl Alan Wilson's death by descending into the Owl Hole and brooding about all of the things she had lost. Since she had become smitten with kissing, turning it into an ardent, everyday pursuit, her life, as she had known it, had stopped. The trouble with kissing is it can make you exhausted, leaving little room for all of the other things in your life you hold holy and inviolable.

Her relationships had been stretched thin or entirely broken. She hardly knew what to say to Herman Lynch without upsetting him, had not seen Reenie Ruggiero in weeks, and had all but banished her childhood friend Lizzie Lovato and her own sister Donny from her life. She had not talked much to Mabel Kerry since her quick, fiery visit to the library. She didn't know how her mother was faring, whether she was having a spell, nor did she care. If Johnny was still alive, she had not noticed. Ditto Grandmother Delia.

She lived in a fugue, a short interlude or phase, a melody or a musical phrase, where one part interwove with other parts, and repeated like the refrain in a popular love song. When Cookie told Mabel about losing her words, she had said, "You're human. We never lose what we hold close to our hearts. Your words will come back." Bertha advised her to tie a string around her finger. "We all have things to lose." If she had bothered to ask her childhood friend Lizzie Lovato for advice, she would speak of aliens, goblins, wormholes, other dimensions and the Bermuda Triangle.

She did not know when her losing streak would end. In the last year, she had lost her keys, her earrings, her hemp sack, several nickel bags of pot, her shoes, her jeans with the seventeen patches, and her words. She had spent the entire day at school wearing mismatched shoes without ever bothering to look to see if both pairs could be made intact by pairing the right shoe with its mate. Now the time of year had come when the days were growing visibly shorter. Loss followed her everywhere as surely as the sun had begun to shrink in the September sky. And she was sure she had lost her heart for everyone except for Stanley.

Back at school, she went to her classes, or at least most of them, occasionally cutting out early, changing out of her uniform and into sexy street clothes, and wander down to Ashburton Avenue, where she hoped to accidentally bump into Stanley. She had not seen him since the night the drunken Pinky O'Hearn had clashed with him at the Midget Bar. She had purposefully not gone back to the Midget Bar. Stanley should want her, seek her out, chase her, and make his desire be known. Why did she have to make all of the moves, only to have him reject her with no explanation, no apology, nothing.

Stanley de Falco had turned her inside out and ruined her life. Her obsession with him had taken over, and the time had come for it to stop.

Vaulting out of the school building, down Park Avenue, she dragged an oversized blue leatherette tote bag. Heavy with books, the bag did not weigh her down. If anything, the bag added to her momentum as she ran, passing the wall she had once hurdled over into the convent's fragrant garden. She wore impossibly short, white cut-offs, showing not only her legs, but the bottom of her cheeks peeping out from behind. She loved the feeling of bouncing up from the concrete sidewalk as she ran hard with the ambling gait of racehorse. Her sleeveless midriff top stopped in a curve above her navel. Short, spare, skimpy, small, little, tight, low-cut, knit, silk, satin, sateen and see-through is how she best described her summer clothes. She latched onto these clothes, wearing them into the fall on the hot days of September because she never knew when she would run into him.

How could she let a guy ruin her life?

She didn't even know what he did during the day, whether he worked or went to school. She thought of stopping in the Café Trento to see if he might be visiting his mother, but then she would have to deal not only with him but with Bertha too. She walked on Ashburton Avenue away from the bakery, vaguely aware of the appreciative stares from guys on the street. The occasional honking horn reminded her she had not only dressed scantily for Stanley but for every guy she happened to run into. She stopped at a pay phone booth and rummaged in her tote for her change purse. The plastic, oval purse had bell-pepper-shaped red blots, stray dots and hearts. She snapped it open. Her money had dwindled ever since she had stopped dealing drugs.

In the phone booth, she pulled out a dime and called the number she had long ago committed to memory. His number. Bertha's too.

Bertha answered the phone. Cookie had miscalculated, thinking she would not be home and at work. Cookie almost hung up, but when she heard the woman's husky broken

English, sounding worried, repeatedly asking "Who is this?" Cookie spoke up and asked for Stanley.

Surprisingly, this time Bertha did not say the same thing. She said, "He's not here and I don't know where he's gone. He comes and goes like the wind. But I want you to come over. Can you come over and visit me? Come over now. I want to show you something. I have this wonderful thing to show you. When can you come?"

Cookie hopped on the first Number 2 bus heading toward Getty Square. As she boarded the bus, she saw it was standing room only. The bus driver hollered for anyone standing to move toward the back of the bus. She dropped her last quarter and dime into the cash box. Clambering toward the back, the bus threw her, making her unsteady on her feet. She bumped into passengers in seats and those standing, apologizing. The bus had no room to sit and hardly any room to stand. She set her oversized tote bag on the floor in between her legs and stayed in the aisle. She couldn't understand why the bus was so crowded. School had not yet let out for the day. She noticed most of the passengers were older women. She held onto the pole to steady herself, while she pulled her radio out of her bag and plugged in her earphone.

The news blared commentary about Vietnam. The Second Battle of Quang Tri had begun on June 28 and had lasted 81 days, ending September 16th, with the South Vietnamese Army of the Republic of Vietnam defeating the North Vietnamese at the ancient city of Quang Tri, recapturing most of the province. There were talks about setting the date for the last U.S. ground troops to be withdrawn from Vietnam. She wondered if Stanley knew the war would soon be coming to an end. All of those American boys killed for what?

She heard rumbling about a break-in in Washington, D.C., involving five men who attempted to bug the U.S. Democratic National Committee. They had begun referring to the break-in as *Watergate*.

Radio D.J. Cousin Brucie came back on the air and said, "Chime time right now is twenty minutes past noon and the hit song of the week is *Baby Don't Get Hooked on Me* by Mac Davis."

Cookie was so riveted by the song, thinking the lyrics spoke to the present situation she found herself in with Stanley, that she barely felt tugging on her arm. She thought it was an accidental brush, but it wasn't. Stunning blue eyes peered out from under a mass of messy blond corkscrew curls. Donny grinned at her and looked a little apprehensive about getting caught playing hooky from school, but at the same time, she was proud of herself.

"I never thought I'd see you on this bus," Donny said. "The first one broke down, so they got another one. There's nowhere to sit."

"Where are you going?"

"I don't know," she sighed in the weary tone of a cranky older woman. "I'm running away from home." She lifted up a square metal lunchbox emblazoned with pink and yellow psychedelic flowers.

"You can't do that!" Cookie said. "Besides that's my lunchbox!"

"Yes, I can!" Donny shot her defiant look.

"No, you're not," Cookie said. "You're coming with me."

"Am not." Donny crossed her arms tight across her chest.

"Are too!" Cookie grabbed her by the arm to pull her out of her seat.

"Don't treat her like that," an older woman yelled. Cookie could see the woman's teeth, yellow and flat as though they had been purposefully filed to look like horse teeth. The people sitting immediately around Donny were staring, some shaking their heads at the ruckus.

"You're hurting me," Donny protested. "I don't know who she is," she told the onlookers.

"I'm her sister," Cookie yelled.

"Are not," Donny insisted and turned to the onlookers for sympathy. "I never saw this girl before in my life. I think she wants my lunch pail. And she can't have it!"

Cookie was met with stony stares by other passengers, especially the woman with horse teeth, who snorted, "Leave her alone!"

Shocked, Cookie said, "I can't believe you're saying this to me." She stepped back, wobbling as the bus lurched to a hard stop on the corner of Main Street in Getty Square.

"Look at how you're dressed," a woman called out. "Who would want to be seen with you!"

Cookie realized her skimpy top and shorts were a billboard to be a guy magnet but provided little credibility for her as a concerned big sister.

"Okay," Cookie said. She was going to call Donny's bluff. "Have it your way. Be like that. You're on your own, kid."

On second thought, Cookie held out her hand. "This is your very last chance!"

"Why don't you get off the bus," horse teeth said. "Yeah, leave her alone!" someone yelled. A heavyset woman sitting behind Donny stood up and asked, "Is this your sister?"

"No." Donny shook her head.

"Okay, fine!" Cookie felt blood rush to her face. She stared at Donny with disbelief.

"Go away." Donny turned her head and crossed her arms tighter. "I said go away and I mean it."

Cookie pushed her way through the other standing passengers. "Excuse me. Excuse me, please. Get out of my way." She scooted out of the back exit of the bus. Standing on the sidewalk, she watched the bus pull away. In the bus window, Donny gave her a nasty grimace and stuck out her tongue.

"Huh?" Cookie huffed to herself, "that little brat."

As the bus turned onto South Broadway, through the window Donny smiled like an evil munchkin. Cookie watched the bus going south on Broadway, until it was completely of out of view. In a minor state of shock, she walked in a daze. Feeling red-hot shame and anger, she declared herself guilty for not keeping a closer eye on Donny. She tried to sort through what had happened but could not come up with a definitive answer. Soon reason prevailed; she came back to her senses. She knew Donny would not go far with only a lunch pail, and she was only two bus stops away from Grandmother Delia's house. Cookie had indeed been a big sister in absentia, but in the interim, Donny had undoubtedly developed a flair for high drama.

By contrast to her alarming encounter with Donny, riding the Nodine Hill bus was tame. Cookie hardly had time to keep an eye on where she needed to get off. Soon she recognized the green copper belfries of Yonkers High School. Knowing she got off at the next step, she pulled on the bus cord to alert the driver.

The Midget Bar had not yet opened for business. Cookie didn't turn the corner to see if any of the regulars were around. Jimmy lived above the bar on the top floor of the brick building, but she had never been there. Although the Midget Bar was an after-hours joint, Jimmy cooked breakfast for his closest friends in the wee hours of the morning just as the sun came up.

In Stanley's 'hood, she expected that at any moment she could run into him. She felt bad for Bertha. Cookie knew her own intentions were not noble or pure. She was cozying up to Bertha because she was a conduit to Stanley. Awkward and lonely, the Polish woman didn't seem to have many friends.

Cookie walked into the bottom floor of the apartment building. In the poorly lit narrow hall, she buzzed Bertha to let her in. Insufferably hot, the building was an ode to an old tenement, retaining too much heat in the summer, only to completely let go of its warmth in the cruelest way possible during the cold winter months. Drafty, dank, framed from old wood, the building became whatever the weather dictated it should be: a raging sauna or steam bath in the summer and a splintery-blue icebox in the winter. The days and seasons in between were not extreme, neither hot nor cold, but not enough of either to change the level of comfort in the old building.

Climbing the stairs, she picked up the distinct odor of sour cabbage and kitchen grease. Bertha held the door open for her on the top floor. She wore a fading pink checkered house dress and spongy orange slippers.

Her face flushed with pride. "Wait until I show you my surprise," she said. "Come in. Come in."

Once Cookie was in her apartment, Bertha closed the door behind her, looking more than concerned. She clutched her heavy cotton shirt to her chest, as though she was frightened for Cookie. "You will catch a cold walking around like that," she said, padding around Cookie in a tight circle. The tone of her voice was partially stern but tender too. "Doesn't your mother care how you dress? Do you want me to find you some more clothes to wear?"

Cookie shrugged. "It's hot."

"It was much hotter yesterday," Bertha quickly replied. "But I can smell the air. The weather's changing. These days in September are hot and cold or cold and hot. You can't count on much of anything. The sun will go down before you know it and you'll be freezing."

Through the open window, the early afternoon sun threw light like a torch. The harsh light revealed terrible flaws everywhere. The walls had not been painted in years, leaving multiple older layers of paint to cast wavy shadows in between chips, cracks and chunks of missing plaster. Small bubbles of varnish had hardened onto the woodwork and parquet floor. All of these defects seeped like a balm into Cookie's heart and touched her deeply in a way she could not explain. This is the place where Stanley had grown up; he lived here, dreaming about one day leaving this city, the same way she would one day leave too.

"Let me show you my surprise!" Excited as a child, waving both her hands over her head, Bertha squealed with delight. "Over here, look!"

Pushed up against the kitchen sink, a heavy duty washing machine took up so much space on the floor that it was the focal point for the entire apartment. Bertha lifted the lid. "Look inside, it's brand new!"

Bertha bade her to come over. "Look," she said excitedly. "It's new!" She pointed to the agitator basket inside of the machine and pulled it out. "I can do a small load. Look at this," she said, holding up a small white metal basket.

She placed the basket back inside of the machine and touched the soap dispenser. "I can even add fabric softener to make the clothes soft and smell so sweet." She turned the silver knobs, making clicks on an unseen, miniature metal track. "I can set all the different temperatures."

Like a model in a showroom, Bertha stepped to the side of the washing machine, expressing herself with windmill arms. "This is my new washing machine! Isn't it a beauty?!"

"It's beautiful," Cookie agreed. Bertha's enthusiasm was infectious, and it made Cookie happy for her. It also made her a touch sad to think a simple washing machine gave her so much joy.

"If you take off your clothes, I will wash them for you."

Cookie shook her head. "No, I'm fine."

"Are you sure?" Bertha asked. "I will give you something to change into."

"No, it's fine." Cookie looked down at the floor and saw her feet. Scarlet nail polish on her toes made her feet feel luscious and as sexy as the rest of her ensemble. She had dressed to be alluring for Stanley, only to be held captive by his mother and her washing machine.

"Stanley bought me the washing machine," Bertha said, walking to the opposite side of the room. "He surprised me with it. I didn't even know it was going to be delivered." She threw open the window next to the table with a small lamp. She fetched a crumpled maroon pack of Pall Malls and pulled one out. Unfiltered. Strong. "Here," she said, offering Cookie one.

"I have my own." Cookie pulled a pack of Marlboros out of her leatherette school tote. Bertha flicked open a brushed silver lighter to light Cookie's cigarette first. Cookie noticed the lamp on the table had a parched tan shade and its light had been left on.

"The sun's so strong," Cookie told Bertha. "You don't need to have the lamp on," she said, reaching to turn off the switch.

Bertha put her hand on top of the lamp to stop her. "I leave it on anytime I'm home," Bertha said, pushing a round amber glass ashtray toward Cookie. "It's to let Stanley know I'm home. I've done it ever since he was a little boy. He never let me know he was scared of the dark. But I figured it out."

Cookie wondered where Stanley was but didn't ask. She knew Bertha would tell her everything she needed to know about Stanley, but never mention the things she did not need to know.

"He doesn't tell me about when he's scared," Bertha said. "He doesn't even talk about that war. He doesn't tell me things because he thinks it will scare me. Just like when he was a little boy, he'd be scared of thunder and jump into my lap until it was over."

Bertha stopped talking for a minute and became lost in her own thoughts. Stubbing her cigarette out in the ashtray, she didn't look at Cookie. "I don't even know if he likes you," she said. "He doesn't tell me nothing. You don't tell me nothing, but I can tell that you like him."

Bertha's eyes followed Cookie's gaze to the kitchen, where a pink cardboard bakery box sat on the kitchen counter. Tied with a white string, the box had not been opened. How about if I treat you to sfogliatelle or a cannoli?" Bertha asked. "They're both good, but I can never tell which one you like best."

Cookie leaned out the window and looked at the street below. A steady stream of cars sped up Maple Street. The

Nodine Hill bus coughed its throaty engine to make it up the hill. The traffic light at the intersection had not yet turned red. A young boy on a scooter careened across the intersection on Oak Street. Cars slowed as the boy came closer to their lanes. Two other boys about ten, the same age as Donny, were trying to get a stickball game going. The thought of Donny made Cookie cringe.

"Look at that," Bertha said. "A storm's going to come. I can smell it. Look at the clouds."

The worn and beat up wood around the window framed an unsettled sky. A storm could be blowing in from the river or could just as easily blow over. Only the next few hours would tell which way the day would go. Clouds raced in streaks of grey, charcoal and the edge of mottled heather to form distinctly new patterns. The sun still shone even though the clouds took on new shapes and forms. The head of a rhinoceros, the arms of a mighty Greek god, a domed mountain top sloughing off its glaciers, a moon landing like the sandy craters of Death Valley—all of these images melded together in whole round notes, metered tempo, a fugue measuring the distance between time and space, where her words flowed into music, and suddenly she would be able to write again. The day ended with fog but no rain or thunder, and no signs of Stanley.

Thirty-three

Lightning Strikes Twice

A girl's heart can be a small boat gone adrift, about to be shipwrecked, while desperately seeking to set sail in a new direction. Cookie felt like a cat who had watched the caged bird sing for too long. Tapping its tiny clawed feet on the floor of the cage, swinging and singing on its perch, or poking its beak through the fine wire bars, the bird toyed endlessly with her, but ultimately always pulled back, eluding her. She gave up wanting her prey because no matter how hard she tried, she could not get the bird.

Stanley de Falco had made himself too remote and unavailable. She was getting bored. Losing interest.

While her ardor for Stanley had cooled, the temperature outside spiked to eighty-five degrees. Even though it was exceptionally hot for the end of September, the summer really was over, and it was time to stake new ground.

Her paperback version of *The Winds of War* by Herman Wouk contained 1002 pages. As she approached the end of the book, the last page was missing. Gone. Lost. She did not know how the page had been torn from the book. She rationalized her loss by telling herself she knew how the story had ended anyway. She did not have to read the last page. Any time she wanted, she could read another version of the same book. And yet, the missing page haunted her as one more loss among many. Her losing streak continued uninterrupted.

The knocking on the door came so suddenly it boomed like a cannon. Whoever had come to her house had been unable to find the doorbell and resorted to knocking loudly.

"Don't answer the door," Kitty cried out. "I don't want no one in the house."

Kitty looked slightly bug-eyed again, never a good sign. She might be okay in a day or two, or this could be beginning of a long spell.

"Please don't let nobody in," she cried out again.

The knocking grew louder and bolder. The visitor had also located the doorbell; it had a broken chime that pinged a half note. Alternating between knocking and ringing the broken bell, the unanticipated visitor did everything to gain access to the house.

"If you don't answer the door," Kitty said, "they'll just go away."

"Mrs. Colangelo," a man's rough voice called through the door, "it's Father Dunn. I'm looking for your daughter."

Kitty ran away from the door and left Cookie to deal with the priest. Having a priest come to your door was nothing short of a proclamation of death. It could only mean either someone had died, or someone was about to die. Cookie didn't know what she had done, but she was certain of her guilt—it was an innate response in her programming as a bad Catholic girl.

She opened the door to a hostile stranger. Far from being a friendly visitor, Father Dunn looked stern and irritated. He did not want to come calling on the Colangelos and found his predicament to be a grave inconvenience. Cookie returned the sentiment. She had never liked the priest and considered him to be a nasty man, a gruff wiener in a gunny sack. She noticed the priest eyeing her short shorts and low-cut midriff top. She felt like lifting his cassock to see if he wore anything underneath.

Cookie eyed him suspiciously. "What do you want?"

"It's not about you," the priest said. "It's your sister. Is your mother or father home?"

"No," Cookie lied. "You'll have to talk to me."

Built like a bulldog, the priest had a reputation for beating up young boys. He didn't have much of a neck and his eyes blazed with violence, as if he was bent on punching somebody. Never one to mince words, he got right to the point. "Your sister hasn't come to school in a week. Is she sick?"

"She hasn't been to school?" Cookie backed away from the door, still looking at the priest. "Are you sure? The classes are so big, sometimes kids are there, but you don't see them."

"We've tried phoning, but no one ever answers." The priest shook his head. "If she's not sick, I'll have to declare her truant and she could be expelled."

Cookie's response was pure reflex to get rid of the priest. "She's been sick!" Cookie spewed her words emphatically. "She'll be back at school on Monday! Thanks so very much for coming by, Father," she said.

Not even giving him a chance to respond, she slowly closed the door right in his face.

Through the small window of the door, Cookie watched him leave. Instead of walking away from her house, the priest shifted his direction and disappeared into the opening between two overgrown hedges that led to the steps of Fran Ochiogrosso's house. Cookie waited and watched to see what the priest would do next. Fran must not have been home. The priest left Fran's house, walked down the front steps, got into his black Ford Mercury sedan and drove away.

Frantic to learn what had happened to Donny, Cookie rushed down the front steps with her hair flying into her face. She stood on the sidewalk, out of breath. She had not seen her sister since the day she had been on the Number 2 bus, carrying a lunchbox, threatening to run away from home. It had been over a week since she had seen Donny! If anyone knew of Donny's whereabouts, then Fran would know! Cookie had a sneaking suspicion Fran might be harboring Donny, giving her a place to stay, refuge from her insane family. Cookie waited, biding her time, making sure the priest was gone, before making her next move.

She didn't wait long. Fran's screen porch door swung open. Fran wore a large slinky red-hot teddy that barely reached the tops of her swelling thighs and emphasized the full weight of her breasts. A cigarette dangled from her lips while she looked around to see who had come to her door. Someone had come up to her porch without her permission. Like most busybodies, she tended to be fiercely protective about guarding her own privacy and resented the type of intrusion she foisted upon everyone else.

She yelled to someone inside of her house, "Must have been the Fuller Brush man or some kid selling raffle tickets!"

Fran left the door partially open and stood in the doorway keeping watch. Her bright red hair tumbled onto her shoulders in a disheveled mess. Her lightly flushed face matched the crushed orange color of her puffy lips. Fran stubbed out her cigarette on top of the porch railing.

Cookie held her breath and waited until the front door closed. She crept along the retaining wall in front of Fran's fence line so she would not be seen. Pocked with tiny holes too powdery to touch, the wall had worn away in chunks. She reached to climb above the wall so she could see down into the house but could not gain a foothold into the disintegrating concrete. Tiptoeing through a narrow side alley, she arrived at the back of the house. She crept close to the exterior wall, while shadows flitted from within the house, but one form could not be distinguished from another. A partially open window had a makeshift sliding screen to keep bugs out. Cookie hooked her foot into an unblemished crevice of the retaining wall, hoisted herself onto a heap of boulders, and peered in.

Spread out on the floor in the shape of an eagle in midflight, Fran was not alone. Two heads flew about in the folds of Fran's fiery red teddy. Grunting and wheezing and uneven breath accompanied Fran crashing all over her rug and onto the wooden floor. Two people were panting for air.

Fran plucked the man's head from underneath and lifted his face toward her mouth, but his features could not be seen. With the tenacity of a regal cat, she pounced on him, pushing him down to keep him on the floor. She had him splayed on the ground and unzipped his black pants. Making a banging sound, as she forced her legs against his thighs, Fran undid the snaps in her teddy, hiking the red satin above her hips.

In the midst of her frenzy, Fran yanked his pants down to his socks. The man's face swung involuntarily to the side, where his eyes rolled to the back of his head. Overpowered by Fran, the man did not appear to be tall, but he was stocky, with muscular arms and had a hard pot for a belly. His head was all jaw and too large for his body. His eyelids had closed, but it did not hide the single line dash forming the shape of his distinctive mouth. No one in the entire North End had a mouth quite like him.

Louie Santamassino gasped and grunted, breathing hard and fast.

"Gross!" Cookie could not bear to see anymore. Running back to her house, she continued saying, "Gross," while clutching her stomach, churning in knots. Panting for air, Cookie could not believe what she had seen. Then she began laughing uproariously! If she had not seen them with her own eyes, she would not have believed it! As appalling as she found the erotic coupling of two of the most unlikely life forms on the planet, she did not begrudge either of them a chance to find love. If even Fran and Louie could find happiness together, then why couldn't she? Everyone in the world had managed to find love except for Cookie Colangelo.

She found Kitty in the bathroom spritzing her neck with Chanel No. 5. When Cookie told Kitty about Donny being missing, her mother gave her a catatonic nod, neither here nor there, and devoid of terror or concern. She put her hand up to her red mouth as though she meant to blot her lipstick, and exclaimed, "Oh, okay. She'll turn up."

Donny's bedroom door was shut. Cookie pushed against the door, but it kept sticking. The door would open a few inches then slam shut. With all of her might, Cookie pushed, and the door burst open, releasing a barrage of bedding and toys. Booby trapped! A crude pulley and rope system had been rigged from the door to the bedpost. Other than the stench of dirty socks and the sight of mold growing in two cereal bowls, Donny's room showed no signs of life.

Word traveled fast in the North End and was akin to someone standing on top of the hill, using a megaphone to announce Donny Colangelo had gone missing. Everyone began looking for her.

Arky Lovato slowed his jeep at the top of the hill. Pulling up alongside of Cookie, looking alarmed, he said, "She's too young to run away. She's got all of those cute blond curls. I think she went into the woods and someone grabbed her."

"Oh, shut up," Cookie said. "Even if it's true, you don't have to say it."

"Yeah," Toni said springing out of the jeep. "I just know something bad happened to her!" Rushing to Cookie, she hugged her, keening how terrible this must be. Toni's eyes were engorged with concern. Spurred by the drama, she rose to the occasion, hugging Cookie over and over. "You poor kid, you must be in shock. Look at you, you look like you're a mess!"

Cookie didn't budge. "Everything will be okay," she told Toni.

"I'm so sorry for you," Toni kept saying. "Wanna come with us in the jeep and we'll look around for her?" she asked. "Come on, we'll go looking for her. It's better than standing here doing nothing!"

Cookie couldn't understand why Toni had showed up, seeking her friendship. She could have been faking it. With Toni, it was tough to know one way or another. Maybe she was just attracted to the drama.

"She's gone for how long?" Toni shrieked.

"It will be fine," Cookie told her.

It had been months since Cookie had seen Arky's kid sister Lizzie Lovato. She came out of her house and stood on the front porch, sucking her thumb. When the going got tough, sucking her thumb gave Lizzie comfort.

"I think Donny got sucked into a wormhole," Lizzie called over. "She's in another dimension, but she'll be back."

Not knowing whether Lizzie was a genius or a lunatic, Cookie gave her the benefit of the doubt and stared at her hard, deeming her to be a natural wonder to behold.

Lizzie took her thumb out of her mouth and gave a mini-lecture. "Wormholes were predicted by Einstein's theory of relativity. It's a passage through space-time so you can take long journeys across the universe. I'll bet Donny is traveling faster than the speed of light right now and having the time of her life!"

"Weird." Toni stared at Lizzie standing on the porch. Loose rafters under the porch ceiling resembled daggers and swords dangling in the air. The house had not been kept up. Painted the weary red shade of an old barn, the entire house looked ready to collapse during the next gust of wind.

"Oh my God," Toni said under her breath to Arky. "Your sister's sucking her thumb again. "When's she gonna grow up? She is your sister, isn't she? Why don't you tell her to stop sucking her thumb?"

Arky grinned to himself and asked Toni, "Are we going or staying?"

"Going, like right now," Toni told him. "Sure you don't need us to go looking?" she asked Cookie. "Don't mind helping out! You don't seem upset! I don't think you're taking this seriously enough, or maybe you just don't like your sister!"

"What's he doing here?" Toni yelled.

Fran and Louie walked Blackster on the road, calling for Donny. Alongside of Fran, Louie appeared to be much slighter in build. He wore a white cotton muscle boy shirt and the same black trousers Fran had unzipped a short time ago. It made Cookie feel embarrassed to look at the two of them, cooing to one another, flushed in the face from the rush of hot love in the afternoon. Cookie wondered how Louie could see without his eyeglasses. Maybe that explained his attraction to Fran. No matter. He had his seeing-eye dog beside him, and Cookie didn't mean Blackster.

Fran blathered a mile a minute, commenting on everything she saw, including Lizzie Lovato sucking her thumb. "Get that thumb out of your mouth. You look ridiculous. Sucking that thumb at your age! When are you gonna grow up?"

"Good, I'm glad finally somebody said something," Toni yelled from the window of Arky's jeep. "I've been waiting to see if someone would speak up and tell her off!" Toni continued to rant from the jeep as it sped down the hill until she could no longer be heard.

Louie piled Blackster into the back of his car while Fran complained about the dog shedding fur all over the seat. Fran slipped into the front seat, rolled down the window, and hollered after Cookie. "I'm sorry about your sister. She's gotta be around somewhere! We'll keep looking for her and I'll keep praying. God always listens to me."

Donny had disappeared in the past, so Cookie didn't jump to conclusions and assume the worst. Then Grandmother Delia showed up. This was the last straw. Delia dolled herself up, putting on more pink lipstick, without looking into her mirrored compact. She lingered in front of the house, taking lengthy breaks, composed of dramatic pauses and sad little comments, before she climbed the next step. Cookie braced herself for what would come next.

"It's your fault that Donny's gone," Delia said. Her soft,

non-threatening voice didn't detract from the meanness in her cold blue eyes. The old woman's bangs were shorter than usual. Her hair had been freshly cut in a sweet silver pageboy. "You better start praying, because if something happened to Donny, it will be your fault."

"I'm not her mother," Cookie yelled. "Or her father!"

Delia shook her finger at her. "You're the only one in the family that doesn't have a screw loose. Your sister's your responsibility."

Cookie didn't bother arguing with her and broke into a brisk trot through the woods, where the Sumac trees once stood tall and proud. Three stumps showed signs of life. One stump sprouted a new branch, bending in an arc and bearing tender sage-green leaves. The air smelled of humus tinged with car exhaust. North Broadway was not her final destination. She needed to be in the bowels of the Owl Hole to regain her equanimity.

Her legs were getting scratched from the thorny bramble protecting the opening to her secret hideaway. The last remnants of dew had been left by yesterday's blanket of fog. Fine beads of water caught a lance of light from the afternoon sun. The last time Cookie had seen Donny, she looked impish, gamine-faced. The canny street urchin had been tough enough to stand up to Cookie, and if she could stand up to Cookie, then she would have no problem standing up to the world.

As she passed the opening into the Owl Hole, her legs became nicked from where sharp brambles had cut into her skin. She closed her eyes to fend off an attack from a cloud of gnats. Brushing her cheeks and her eyes, the gnats blurred her vision. She kept her lips pressed together, so the nasty little bugs didn't get into her mouth.

As soon as she could see again, the first thing she noticed about the Owl Hole were signs someone else had been there. As she moved in the shadows, the telltale signs of another person became more certain. Junk food wrappers, cardboard cartons, bottles of Yoo-hoo, soda cans, all had been emptied and discarded as garbage. Other items came into view: a blue blanket, two pillows, a portable organ keyboard and a red transistor radio. This sacred place was now being inhabited by someone else. Her Owl Hole had been taken over and trashed.

Propped against the cement retaining wall, Donny stared at Cookie. "I'm getting bored and want to sleep in my own room," she said in a feeble voice. "Will you take me home?"

Cookie lifted her from the ground. It wasn't easy; almost her size, Donny was muscular and dense in her body composition. As they rose to the top of the steps, Donny confessed she had not stayed in the Owl Hole all of the time. During the day, she wandered through the woods in Untermyer Park. By night, she slept in the basement, sometimes playing with the tape recorder, listening to Cookie's secret tapes about kissing.

Johnny Colangelo loitered in front of his own house. The timing could not be worse. He never hung around outside, and actually had a fear of standing still for too long. But Johnny had reason to hang around. Stanley de Falco.

Johnny and Stanley were talking the way boys do sometimes when they don't care about the goings on of girls, especially girls coming and going. Giggling, Donny gave Cookie a yank on her arm, then a nudge, and finally a poking blow to her stomach. Cookie did not feel a thing and thought she should run away.

The red hot flush of a terrible fever came over her. Her mouth grew dry. She started to swallow to get her saliva flowing. Her knees felt weak and rubbery as though her trick knee had returned or her knees were about to knock together. If he gave her the slightest indication of wanting her heart, she would rip it out of her chest and give it to him then and there. She behaved like a stage-struck groupie, and it irked her. Yet she could not help herself.

For the first time since Stanley had come into her life, she pretended she had never seen him before and they were starting all over again. Overwhelmed, terrified, such madness! He rocked her body from inside out.

Johnny did all of the talking. "Oh good, you got her. I knew she wouldn't be far."

He yelled at Donny, "What the hell did you do this for?! The whole frigging city's been out looking for you!" Holding his hand up like he meant to hit Donny, he smacked the air instead. "What have you got to say for yourself?"

Donny snarled at him, "I'm not talking to you and I'm not putting up with the likes of you no more!" As she calmly walked up the steps, she told Johnny, "The problem with you is you know nothing about girls!" Then she lifted her head high and turned her back on him.

Cookie smiled at Stanley, giving him fair warning. "That's Johnny."

"We've met," Stanley told her. "We've been talking about the Sumac trees."

"They're back!" Johnny said. "The goddamn Sumac trees! Stanley, right? Have I got your name right? I don't hear so good sometimes, so I just want to be sure I got your name right. I was in heavy artillery attacks in Korea and don't hear so good sometimes."

"Then why do you play so much music?" Cookie asked him.

"Because I hear it up here, in my head," Johnny said, pointing to his temple. "I've got the ear. The music's in my head. I hear music all the time in my head."

Stanley nodded and relaxed his arms to his side as if he meant to salute him or hit him, maybe both. Johnny had that effect on people.

"Stanley says the Sumac trees aren't poisonous. I didn't know that," Johnny said. "Maybe someone should have told me that before I spent all that time having to cut them down."

Cookie closed her eyes. It was too big a job for her to take Johnny on. She'd just have to take him where she found him. He wasn't mean and he wasn't dumb. He was something else altogether. Once he locked into an opinion, strange or not, he was as immovable as stone.

"Hey, Cookie!" Donny called down from the top landing. She turned around, showing her bottom, wiggling. Seventeen patches. An American flag patched on the seat. Cookie's missing blue jeans. The jeans had been gone a long time. Too much time had passed for Cookie to care. Donny leaned over the porch and began snapping pictures with her instamatic Kodak camera.

"What the hell are you doing with that thing? You're supposed to be taking pictures of nature, not people! Animals and flowers," Johnny yelled to her. "Want me to come in and break it? There she is with the camera again, taking pictures of people, making trouble for everybody!"

Donny puffed her cheeks and puckered up. "Kissy, kissy," she said, smacking her lips. "Now's your chance. Go on and kiss Stanley," she said, mimicking a girlyfalsetto voice.

"Who you talking about, Donny!" Johnny yelled. "You're a real ball buster! You gotta keep giving me a hard time over nothing! That Joan broad."

Johnny shook his head and looked at Stanley, guy-to-guy, trying to gain his sympathy. "She's gotta keep bringing it up and up and up! Again and again!"

Johnny thought Donny was getting kissy-faced over him and the blond woman. He didn't know Donny had been goading Cookie about Stanley. A part of her wanted to apologize for Johnny's ignorance, but she couldn't bring herself to do it.

"Why'd you come here?" Cookie asked Stanley.

Stanley's dark eyelashes fluttered, but he didn't smile. "I've been looking for you," he said. "I've called you at home, but no one ever answers the phone."

"Who is this guy?" Johnny asked. "Don't mind you bringing no one home, but could you ask me first to bring him, the guy, home so I can meet him in person to see if he's okay or not?"

Intending to be polite, Stanley nodded.

Cookie smiled at Stanley. "That's Johnny," she mentioned again.

"I got that," Stanley said.

Stanley touched Cookie on the shoulder. She held her breath. "I have something to show you," he said. He reached into his top shirt pocket and pulled out a slender silver circle. "I think I found your earring," he said, handing it to her. "When I came up the hill, it was buried in a pile of leaves but at that instant it caught light from the sun. It was just a fluke that I happened to see it there."

"I don't know what's going on or what to do," Cookie said. With one deep breath, she gushed, "I just know I want to be where you are."

"Come again," Johnny said. "Are you talking to me or him? And what kind of crazy talk is that?"

It didn't matter if Johnny was there, or not.

She could pick up Stanley's scent in the air, a combination of warm cotton and the light sweat of his body. He held his hand open to her. Whatever indifference he had expressed toward her in the past was gone. She walked over to him and took his hand. In silence, they made their way to a separate space on the sidewalk and stood there, where they were corralled by the warm light of the sun, making a private world for the two of them. Stanley looked at Cookie, as though he wondered what to do next. She felt a space in her heart, hot and hard, but also too soft and fragile to touch. They stood so close together. His arm touched her skin. Small shocks jolted her body like electricity from sheet lightning. White and bright, sheet lightning lit up the sky but never needed to be followed by thunder. She had stopped breathing, but knew she had been struck by lightning, not once but twice.

Thirty-four

Out on a Limb

Stanley told her he'd stay until after her birthday. Cookie felt a lump form in her throat every time she thought about his leaving. The next few weeks of her life compressed into an expanding fugue-like state. The same musical fog she had been experiencing all along rose a whole octave higher now, creating different measures, beats and phrases in an altogether new melody. Her body moved effortlessly, taking her to places where she needed to go: school, *Down the End* or Getty Square shopping for groceries, and the Yonkers Carnegie Library.

After school and at night, she spent every waking moment with him. Sometimes she fell asleep alongside him, tucked into a ball by his side, but he always woke her, picked her up into his lean arms and took her home. He wanted her to sleep in her own bed so her parents wouldn't worry. The matter of her age did not sit well with him.

In those weeks, not always sure of her surroundings, her physical place in this world, she only remembered being with him. She had heard about love. Now she had the time and experience to define what it meant to be in love. Cookie also experienced change she had not bargained for. In the past she had prided herself as being an athlete, a scrappy tomboy, the fastest girl on the block, a great kickball player, and then a cross between a gangster and a hippie. This year she became the siren, a wild child, and queen of the night, hell bent on being the sexiest woman alive. What she had not considered until now, by default, she had also become a woman.

Through a large measure of new musical beats in her changing fugue-like state, she had formed an immaculate bond with the women she held in high esteem: Mabel Kerry, Sister Mary Eau Claire, Bertha Sokól; they all worked a lot harder in life than they needed to. She came to have a tinge of respect for her Grandmother Delia, who occasionally brought zany Irish wisdom to burn between her cold blue eyes. And she felt a resurgence of love for crazy beautiful, crazy smart Kitty, who was crazy enough to teach Cookie to have gumption—to stand up for herself when no one else would.

Cookie mapped a network of places where they could go to be alone. He didn't want to be cooped up indoors in the apartment he shared with his mother. They talked a lot and walked. He finally began to talk to her about some of his experiences in Vietnam. "The walking wounded, guys who served in Nam, have come home. No one knows what to say or how to deal with us," Stanley told her.

Unsettled, a strange disquiet followed him everywhere. He had indeed been wounded in action, but not physically. The damage was to his heart and soul. Most people sensed his woundedness and left him alone. Except some, people like Debbie and Pinky, tried to use Stanley as a punching bag to beat themselves up, not knowing sooner or later, they would knock themselves out. And by that time, Stanley would be gone, out of their lives for good.

Cookie increasingly saw a world divided, not only between black & white, but between rich and poor, the haves and have-nots, and the educated and the clueless. The educated knew how to work the system to get what they wanted out of life.

The clueless, well, they were just done for. Of all the divisions and the polar opposite experiences and extremes separating people, Cookie found the widest gap to be between those boys who had gone to Vietnam and those who had not.

Stanley found Cookie to be funny because she said could no longer listen to the Rolling Stones. Mick Jagger sang about heroin addiction among the rich, the bored and the famous, while boys who really needed morphine screamed in pain and died in Vietnam. Every time *Brown Sugar*, Sister Morphine or *Wild Horses* came on the radio, Cookie turned it off. The things bothering Cookie about Vietnam didn't seem to faze Stanley. Little things, though, ticked him off. Or maybe they weren't so little.

The afternoon they were walking through the great lawn of Untermyer Park, a cop hassled Stanley, goading him, treating him like a vagrant drug dealer or a low-life. "You goddamn long-haired hippie," the cop said.

Cookie remembers Stanley stopping, standing still, not saying anything, his eyes large, roving and seeing bloody carnage.

"Keep moving, keep moving, that's it, you, keep moving on," the cop said as if Stanley was scum.

Cookie remembers Stanley not saying anything to the cop but taking time to think about what he should do, or not do. Cookie knew Stanley well enough to know when he was enraged. "Sir, I fought for my country in Vietnam," he told the cop.

"Well, you didn't do a very good job," the cop said, breathing heavily, with his forehead looking hot and greasy, "because we're losing the war."

Eyes wide open and unblinking, Stanley stood there, hardly breathing or moving. Cookie could feel the heat rise and boil under his skin.

"Move on, move on, keep moving," the cop kept saying.

After they walked on, Stanley told Cookie he wanted to kill the cop. "I wanted to beat his brains out and shit on them."

It was the only time she had seen him angry and she did not know what to say.

"It's my hair," he said. "I'm going to have to cut it off; either that or I'm going to kill someone."

She implored, "I love your hair." She especially loved when their hair tangled together in a thatch of straw and gold. "Please don't cut your hair." But she knew one way or another, it would make no difference. Stanley was going to do whatever he needed to do. More than once, he had been hassled about his hair, and it made him feel foolish. He thought, after what he'd gone through in Vietnam in service to his country, he should be entitled to wear his hair any way he wanted. But things don't always turn out the way we want them to.

The day Cookie and Stanley met Herman Lynch in Trevor Park most of the leaves had fallen to the ground. Two grey stone pillars guarded the entrance to the gothic Trevor mansion housing the Hudson River Museum. Under a trio of fanning elm trees, they sat close to the playing field on two park benches, configured in an L-shape and facing one another. The river loomed in the background like old wallpaper that everyone took for granted and didn't pay much attention to.

Tense introductions were made. Herman was guarded and gave Stanley a nod of recognition, saying he'd already seen him around. Keeping his hands in his pockets, Herman eyed Stanley suspiciously as though he had no good reason for wanting to be with Cookie. He lit a Marlboro and handed it to Cookie, but she didn't take a drag and that bothered Herman. Sharing a Marlboro had always been their thing.

It was just like Herman to dance around, but not waste time and get right to the heart of the matter. Moving as he blurted out the obvious, "Cookie here is like a sister to me. Aren't you a little old for her?"

Cookie felt embarrassed Herman would say such a thing. "Herman," she said, shaking her head and looking to the ground. "Herman, we're just friends."

"Yeah, sure. You expect me to believe that!" Herman looked doubly disappointed in her. He knew she wasn't speaking the truth. "I don't think I want to be here right now listening to this. Why'd you invite me here in the first place?"

"Least you could do is give me a hug, like we're friends again," she told Herman.

"Whatever you do, don't give me a kiss," Herman said, putting his hand up to stop her. "I don't need to practice. I'm not planning to be kissing cousins with you," he said, throwing his hands up in the air, obviously irritated about what had passed between them.

Stanley stood up to face Herman and said, "Sometimes, things happen we don't want to happen, but we're only human. In the end, there always seems to be a way to learn from it."

Herman eyed the top of a mature elm tree where a blue jay sat screeching. Exhaling smoke through his mouth and nose, he seemed to be searching for the right thing to say. The blue jay had company in the tree. Three sparrows flitted from branch to branch, blending in with the bark, almost unseen. Herman was attracted by the screech of blackbirds. His eyes darted two trees over, until he found the birds. Red and yellow on black, the birds flashed brilliant epaulets of color on patches above their wings and emitted a succession of screeching chirps, laying full claim to their turf.

"Some older guys take advantage of young girls," Herman said, gazing into the elm trees. "Like my mother. That's what happened to her. Now she's dead."

"I'm sorry," Stanley said, sitting down on the bench. "I didn't know your mother, but I know your grandmother. She helps my mother sometimes. Practicing her English."

"You know what I don't get is how Cookie's changed since you've been around and I'm not sure it's doing her good. Know what I mean?"

"I know what you mean," Stanley said. "I don't know if I'm good for her either."

"Let me be the judge," Cookie snapped. "You can't be talking about me, trashing me as if I'm not here, and then give me guff about it."

Stanley turned around and faced Herman. "You're the first black guy I've talked to since I've been home."

"What's that supposed to mean?" Herman shot back. "Cookie, you hear what he's saying to me? He's pulling out the colored card, like I'm some kind of uppity nigger."

Stanley blanked out. He was physically standing there, but no longer present in the conversation. He wasn't tracking Cookie or Herman, the park, the trees, the mist in the sky, or the river. He stared into space, not looking at anything in particular, but fixated on something going on inside of his head.

Herman jumped to his feet. Cookie jumped in front of him to stop him from leaving. "I'm really sorry, Herman. He doesn't mean it that way! Please hang out with us for a while so we can talk."

"I'm not going to have some big white dude telling me I'm the first black guy he's talked to since he's been home. There are thousands of black guys in Yonkers and he's telling me I'm the first one! Just what does that mean?"

"I didn't mean it that way. I'm sorry," Stanley spoke slowly, enunciating one word at a time. "Meeting you triggered something I had forgotten, or I'm trying to forget, but now I remember. I think I have to remember. I have no choice but to remember."

Herman looked mystified. "What's he talking about?"

Cookie took Herman by the hand and led him to the park bench. "Just listen," she said.

Herman looked Cookie in the eye the whole time, protesting, but his scowl grew soft and he sat. Slowly, she sat on the bench beside him and tucked her legs under her bottom.

"In Vietnam, everyone was the same," Stanley said. "Black and white and brown, there was no difference unless you ended up in LBJ, that's Long Binh Jail. The guys who ran the jail were older white guys. They didn't like draftees, especially black guys."

"Why should I care about black guys in Vietnam?" Herman asked. "What does that have to do with me? And why are you telling me this? It's not like I'm going to go there! I'm too young and I'm a dancer!"

"No, you're not going to go there," Stanley said. "This war will be over by then." He took a deep breath. "But there will be others."

Stanley's voice softened. "I'm just learning how to talk about it."

A frailty came over him and his face turned to bitter ash, same as the bark on the elm trees. Stanley relaxed, leaning his back into the bench. He looked lost, confused, adrift. His voice became flat; when he spoke, his words tumbled forth one after another, without inflection.

"There was a big storm on top of the hill where I was with Ralph Walker. We were on ambush patrol. Lightning flashed. I could see strikes coming down. We crouched on the ground, practically hugging one another. I had never been that close to another guy, especially a black guy. We were lashed by wind and rain. The thunder was loud. Then the storm stopped. Everything grew very quiet."

"Then we heard the pop of mortars being fired from their tubes. We knew the VC knew where we were. And we had to get out of there fast before the mortars hit. We made a run for it. We were running together. There were explosions as the mortar rounds hit. I threw myself on the ground and started crawling forward on my belly. That's when I knew Ralph was no longer with me."

"Blood blew like a red cloud, spraying everywhere. I didn't know what had hit us or if it had hit me or him or the both of us. I didn't hear him or see him. I ran back and looked for him, but all what was left didn't look like Ralph.

"I started to run blindly, and I haven't stopped since."

Something stirred in Stanley's body; he looked inconsolable, but he no longer looked cut off from himself. "I've never told anyone about this until now." He looked like he would cry but didn't. His eyes stayed fixed beyond the park and toward the river.

Stanley sat on the opposite bench and stared at the ground. Looking stunned, he slowly shook his head and said, "It could have been him or it could have been me. It was totally random. What does being black mean to me? My buddy died, but I lived, and I don't know why."

Herman nodded and didn't say anything. A stubborn tear sprang to his eye but stayed there.

Finally, Stanley said, "It takes time. First there's the shock. You don't want to talk about it, but then you have to."

Herman nodded. "After my mother died, I rumbled around in the middle of a storm—that's when I met Cookie," he said, but he purposefully didn't look at her and turned to face Stanley. "That's why Cookie's so important to me."

"I know," Stanley said.

Herman's gaze shifted toward the grey water of the river. "When something really bad happens, it takes a long time to pound out the fire, and it's never completely gone. It's always there, a small burn coming up when you least expect it."

Stanley nodded. "We're all trapped in a storm. It's worse for some of us than it is for others."

No one said anything, and moments passed, but the time left in silence wasn't awkward. The river had picked up in a swift current and cast a grey reflection onto the great lawn. Herman moved first, and looked at Stanley, nodding as though he understood. Stanley moved toward Herman, slapped him buddy-like on his shoulder, and the two of them punched their fists together.

Cookie watched them and felt herself receding into the background, asking herself, "What have I lost since meeting

Stanley, and what have I gained?" The answer was not about being black or white. She noticed the elms had limbs that looked more like arms than any other type of tree she had seen. These arms prayerfully reached for the sky in a powerful union, a show of hands. The branch of one elm tree held two fiery-orange leaves coming together in the shape of a flag, not to announce a ceasefire, and not to surrender. It was the sign of a hard-earned truce.

Thirty-five

Sweet Sixteen

Her birthday fell on a Tuesday. After school, she had shed her school uniform and stuffed it into her blue leatherette tote. Wearing a rust color, ribbed, long sleeve cotton shirt and matching rust cord pants, she tried to remember how she had bought a top and a bottom the same deep burnished orange color as the leaves on the twin oak trees in front of her school. The changing weather meant chilly days were ahead. She pulled her navy wool school sweater from her bag and put it on. Fall had set in with an unexpected spate of fog and cool drizzle.

It took her ten minutes to walk down Park Avenue to get to Ashburton. The street was unusually crowded with delivery trucks. Smoking streams of exhaust shot into the misty air. She looked forward to satiating her craving for all things sweet by going to the Café Trento.

Bertha worked behind the counter at the bakery. Today she wore a black hair net kept in place with black bobby pins. Her face had reddened from the heat of the kitchen. Flour covered her arms all the way up to her elbows. Her smile came almost too quickly when she saw Cookie. Bertha told her to help herself to whatever she wanted from a tray of cookies still warm from the oven. Cookie eyed a trove of many flavors: anisette, rainbow tricolor, fudge swirled, and almond studded with pine nuts. She took two quick bites from a warm miniature almond biscotti.

"It's your birthday," Bertha said, setting down a tray of Italian cookies. "Take a look here and help yourself to what you want. There's more where they came from. I've been baking all day. I have these too," she said, pushing another tray of round pumpkin cookies coated with orange icing to the front of the pastry case.

She didn't know how Bertha knew it was her birthday, but figured Stanley must have mentioned it to her. Cookie didn't expect to find Stanley here, but he stood in front of the kitchen and looked stunned to see her.

"I'm just settling up some last-minute things with my Mom," he told Cookie. His arms were folded across his chest in a stance making him look more remote than he had ever been in the past.

"Shh! You'll ruin the surprise," Bertha said, whisking a few cookies into a bag and hurling them across the counter to Cookie. "Isn't it the time you get going home?"

Bertha looked upset. Stanley didn't budge from the kitchen to tell her what was wrong. Cookie swallowed, trying not to feel uncomfortable, trying hard to cast away her pride. "Is everything okay?"

"Fine, just fine," Bertha said, scowling so hard she practically lisped. The next time she said, "just fine," and knocked her knee up against the back of the counter. "I'm always fine."

"Fine," Stanley winked. "By the way, Happy Birthday," he said, off-handedly as though he meant to be obligatory.

"Quit your talking or you'll ruin the whole thing," she snapped at Stanley.

Stanley shrugged and his blue eyes turned dark. Whatever

bothered his mother did not prompt him to rescue Cookie from an increasingly uncomfortable situation.

"Go on, take your treats," Bertha bellowed.

"Take them and go home," Stanley said.

Cookie grew more visibly upset. "I'm not..."

Stanley cut her off. "We'll talk some other time."

Cookie couldn't believe it. He gave her the brush off, treating her like she was a child, or a nuisance, or a pet cat he had shoved off of his lap.

"I don't understand...." Cookie tried to say.

"You don't need to understand!" Bertha cut her off. "Don't forget your treats."

Cookie stormed out of the bakery. Outside on Ashburton Avenue, her face stung, burning with embarrassment. She didn't dare turn around to look back at Stanley. She did not know what had come over him. She had just been in this guy's arms...inside of his head...inside all of him, and now he behaved as though he didn't know her. He had gone from hot to cold, the same as an October day made miserable by extreme changes in bad weather. It was one thing for him to be leaving Yonkers and quite another for him to behave as though he hardly knew her. He had shunned her. More than troubling, she found his behavior to be maddening, hurtful, devastating, the most embarrassing thing that had happened to her in a long time. Of all of the things she had lost, the worst loss of all was going from the heights of ecstasy to this bleary, dark place.

Then the day grew worse. With no thunder or lightning to announce its onset, rain cut loose from the grey sky in a loud downpour. No awnings, storefronts, or random places to duck; Cookie was immersed in the sudden squall. Then the wind from the river whipped up, churning a damp chill. She ran through the streets, scrambling to find the nearest bus stop. Up ahead a bus had stopped, letting off passengers. Cookie raced ahead, trying to make the bus. Only one more block to go. But by then the last passenger had boarded, and the doors shut. She ran ahead, trying to get to the back exit of the bus, pounding on the side. But the driver did not see her and soon the bus was out of view. By then, it didn't matter. She was drenched to her skin. Even her hair had plastered to her back. She felt anything but glorified by the event of turning sweet sixteen.

Closer to home, she trudged down Palisade Avenue. Turning the corner onto Morsemere, a car sped through a dirty puddle, splashing her pants. Two sharp wet drops grazed the left side of her face. The sky had turned a dull grey-white, the same color as smoke from the cigarette smoldering in her hand. She dropped her Marlboro on the shiny wet pavement, leaving it to fizzle out on its own.

As quickly as it had started, the rain stopped. Misery happens when you least expect and at the worst possible time. In front of the Calvary Baptist Church on Broadway, Debbie Ochiogrosso stood under a parrot green umbrella as fancy as a parasol. She wore burgundy pedal pushers capped by a brown blouson jacket. Her eyes were stroked with thick eyeliner and fringed with heavy mascara. The palest of pink lipstick rimmed her lips. She looked fresh, dry, and animated talking to a guy who had stopped in a green car. Her umbrella's color almost matched the guy's car, a marine green Oldsmobile.

Stanley and Debbie. Cookie didn't wait to see if they saw her. She didn't need to have a mirror to know she looked like a drowned rat. She didn't wait to see if Debbie got into his car or if they sped away together. She took off and ran the same way she thought Stanley had run after his buddy had gotten killed in Vietnam. She ran to save her life. She had made a fool out of herself by falling for him.

Out of breath, she entered her house through the basement door. Sitting on the bottom of the steps, she tried to cry, but could not bring herself to do so, especially over a guy. How could she have done this to herself? Slowly she climbed the steps, creaked open the wooden door leading into the family room where the lights were off. Nobody home. She had almost turned the corner to head upstairs to the bathroom, when the lights flooded on. Nebulous forms yelling, "Surprise!" emerged from the shadows!

Johnny appeared first. He ran toward Cookie, yelling, "Boy did we have you fooled! Surprise! Surprise!" Behind him, Kitty blew twee chirps and kisses, her breathing husky, singing in harmony, "Happy Birthday, Sweet Sixteen!" Donny held three helium-filled balloons, skulked to the sideline, and waved her hand. "Happy Birthday."

Johnny kept yelling, "We were going to have a party for you, honey, with a live band, music, lots of boys, lots of girls, hanky-panky going on. I booked the Italian American Club and everything."

The Italian American Club on Lockwood Avenue boasted a dining hall, a bar, and a regular restaurant-sized room serving down-home Italian food. Johnny had taken to playing the drums in a band there on the weekends. He also stayed at the club longer than he needed to, all night long, chasing gigs and squeezing whiskey glasses.

"But we didn't know your friends," Kitty said.

Johnny chimed in, "We had to cancel the club."

"No one wanted to come to your party," Donny said. "Cookie, did you hear what I said? No one wanted to come to your party."

"Did you have to say it that way? Do you have to say it like that? You don't have to say nothing," Johnny said. "What your sister meant to say...."

"It's the raccoon-headed bitch's fault," Donny sniped, letting go of the balloons. They floated up to the ceiling in the far corner of the room.

"Donny!" Johnny yelled. "Would you butt out and stop being a tattletale. And you shouldn't talk that way, using a curse word!"

Johnny sat on the couch, his eyes pleading with Cookie. "I asked that friend of yours, Toni, to help me with this. Then last week, at the last minute she tells me she doesn't know none of your friends. Now that you're in different schools, she doesn't know who your friends are. So, I had to cancel the party."

Donny delivered the final blow. "Not even Lizzie wanted to come. She was too busy with her science project!"

A sheet cake sat in a big pink box on the table. The cake had white frosting and swirling red letters spelling Sweet Sixteen, Cookie. She knew where the cake had come from and, much to her horror, realized Stanley must have known about the failed party attempt. Bertha probably made the cake, custom order!

"How could you do this to me?" Cookie swallowed hard, trying to come up with some reasonable explanation why her father would do such a ridiculous thing. He wasn't smart enough to do this to embarrass her. What could possibly be wrong with him?!

"Come on, don't be like that." Johnny looked visibly hurt, like she had wounded his manhood. "I was trying to make things up to you. I know I haven't always been a perfect father. I'm trying to be better."

"He is being better," Kitty piped up. "Aren't you, Johnny? He means well, honey. He is your father. Look, you both have the same jawline."

She put her hand up to her mouth to mask her whisper. "You've got to forgive him for the things he does, he's Italian."

"I can't believe you did this to me! Both of you!" Cookie yelled. "You don't understand what it's like to be a young girl! A teenager!"

Johnny's red face bore a sheepish expression. "You're right," he said. "I don't know what it's like. I was just trying to do the right thing."

Storming off, Cookie yelled, "Well, why don't you just stay the hell out of my life. The way you always have in the past. Things worked better then. I don't need you," she said, slamming the door to her room.

Moments later, a small slip of paper slid in under her door. Happy Birthday, Cookie, Donny had written. Donny also slipped in page 1002, the missing page from Herman Wouk's *The Winds of War*. She picked it up and read it, realizing she had been right—the last page didn't reveal anything she hadn't already known about the story's ending.

She pressed herself up against the door and sat on the floor. What was she going to do? How was she going to go on? Everyone would find out about Johnny's failed attempt to give her a sixteenth birthday party. Such a strange notion! She was so different from most teenage girls, cerebral, deep thinking and bold, a wild thing. How could her father think she would want something as conventional and as boring as a birthday party? Worse yet, he had failed at the execution! A botched birthday party! She wanted to scream at the top of her lungs, but it would call attention to one of the most embarrassing moments of her life. No one had wanted to come to her party! And she didn't even want a party!

Although he had not been invited, Stanley did want to come to her party. He showed up at the front door, knocking loudly until Johnny let him in. From her bedroom, Cookie could distinguish Stanley's calm voice from Johnny's bellicose thunder. She didn't know what was going on but needed to be there. She pulled off her damp clothes and hastily rummaged through her drawers, pulling out short shorts, knit tights, a floppy oversized sweater and stepped into her brown Frye cowboy boots. She tossed her hair, brushing it forward, then throwing it back to regain her natural curling sprawl. Spreading gloss across her lips, she made a wicked pout in the mirror, and darted down the steps.

Johnny stood in the hall looking belligerent, as though any moment he might punch Stanley. "What's an older guy want with my daughter?"

"We're friends," Stanley told him. "Good friends."

"Friends. You better keep it that way!" Johnny turned around and looked at Cookie. "Is what he's telling me the truth?" Then he turned back to Stanley. "There's no monkey business going on that I need to know about to protect my daughter's honor?"

Stanley held out his hand. "You have my word."

"Better be," Johnny said, shaking his head. "Otherwise, I'll have to come looking for you, and it's not going to be pretty." Then he leaned in closer to Stanley, whispering. "There's no such thing as being friends between a guy and a girl. Don't you think I know that?"

Stanley nodded to placate him. "What happened to the party?" he asked.

"There is no party," Cookie said, glowering at her father.

Kitty lit into the room with the zing of a newborn firefly. The moment she laid eyes on Stanley, she smiled, and as she appraised him from head to toe, her smile grew toothy and generous. She circled around him in a seductive walk as though she had never laid eyes on a man before and hungered for his attention. No shame. No pretense. Showing off her finest asset, her ass rocked, rolled and twitched like a deadly weapon. Stanley picked up on her energy and gave her a weak smile. Poor Stanley, he never saw it coming and did not know what to do.

"Oh, shit, no! Look at her go." Johnny saw what was happening to his wife and did his best to break the spell. "Want some cake?" he asked Stanley. "Come on, let's have some birthday cake, everybody! All together, we'll sing Happy Birthday to Cookie."

Cookie nudged her father. "Mind if we have cake some other time?"

"Gotta eat the cake," Johnny said. "It will go bad if we don't eat the cake. I don't want to be left with all that cake."

"It's my birthday," Cookie said, "and I don't want cake."

"We'll come back," Stanley said. Looking Johnny square in the eye, he reached out shaking Johnny's hand. "Promise."

"Those Sumac trees are coming back," he told Stanley. "Are you sure those trees aren't poisonous? I read somewhere they were."

"The trees are different from the plants," Stanley said.

For a while, Johnny stopped talking. A peculiar expression crossed his face. "Are you sure?"

"I'm sure," Stanley said, folding his arms with an air of authority.

"I don't believe it. I don't believe it." Then Johnny stopped fuming. He was thinking about it long and hard and ran his fingers through the hair on the back of his head. "Okay, if you say so. I'm sure then too," he said, throwing his hands up in the air. "What do I know, anyway?"

"Where'd you find this guy?" he asked Cookie. "He seems to know everything."

Making a quick getaway, Cookie flung open the front door. Johnny kept shouting to Kitty. He came up from behind her and pulled her back into the living room to stop her from trailing after Stanley. "He's so good looking. Too good looking," Kitty squealed. "His hair is so long."

Johnny gave her a firm pat on her bottom. "I can't understand why all the guys she brings around are kooky. First, she's got the black kid Herman, now she's got this character. I don't get it. Why can't she find a nice boy her own age? Someone who she could marry someday and get out of my hair." His voice rose high in pitch to make fun of his name. "Stanley!" he called out in a mock femme voice. "Where'd he get a name like that! He must be a Polack! A dumb Polack! But I got to admit, he does seem to know what he's talking about when it comes to those goddamn trees!"

Thirty-six

Last Leaf Hanging On

Two weeks after Cookie's sixteenth birthday, they walked through the woods, stumbling together, entwined by the last band of sun circling around them. Stanley told her he would be leaving soon, heading west to California. He said he was going to work for a while, then apply to graduate school. Cookie wasn't too disappointed at hearing his news and told him so. She had known all along he wasn't a Yonkers kind of guy, only here for a brief passage of time. He said once he had settled, he'd send for Bertha, but doubted she would move.

"She's set in her ways," he said. "She likes her life the way it is. She got used to me being gone when I was in Vietnam."

Cookie smiled mysteriously, as though she could see far into the future. "You never know. You're all she's got."

Deep in the woods in the lower ring of Untermyer Park, Cookie was entranced with the trees, searching for the one tree—home for the owl's nest. So many trees clustered together, forming a canopy, bringing darkness to this unruly, overgrown land. As they descended deeper into the woods, no sunlight remained, not even the slant of sun weaving thick diagonal rays though the trees. While it rained above and everywhere in the city, it did not rain here. The canopy of the trees served the woods as a gigantic umbrella, so sheets of water cascaded directly into the ground on the outer perimeter, drenching the earth, feeding the intricate root systems of the trees far from where they stood.

No one would trek down here into the bowels of old trees unless the light shone strong enough and the makeshift trail could be seen. Even if the sun could not penetrate the woods, there was something remarkable here. Cookie had told Stanley about her discovery of the owl.

Brushing back boughs, he told her about his own experience with an owl. "I heard the owl long before I saw it," he said. "It was upstate New York in a small town named Millerton. Ever hear of it?"

Cookie smiled, shaking her head, nudging closer to him in what appeared to be an accidental misstep, but it wasn't.

If she had gotten too close to Stanley, he didn't mind, and placed his arm around her waist to steady her. Himself too. "I was walking alongside a barn when an owl swooped down. It flew right over me. I could feel the rush of air from its wings. But it never harmed me. I don't think it intended to."

Stanley's eyes darkened, but he had not stopped looking at her. "It was just a barn owl," he said. "It felt funny to have an owl fly so close over the top of my head."

Cookie thought he would lean forward to kiss her, but he didn't. She reached up to kiss him. He touched her on the cheek, and took her by the hand, then they moved on.

This was not a normal forest, but clogged with rigid bent trees, bending trees in the process of wending into an arc to find sun, and gnarled snakes of roots thickened by mossy beds growing on top of bark. Forgotten and neglected, this patch of woods choked on its own lush overgrowth. No one traveled here because no one had a need to be here. Except Cookie. She was driven with pugnacious tenacity to see if the owl still nested here. She wanted to show the owl to Stanley.

"There's something I've been meaning to ask you," he said.

Cookie nodded. She knew whatever he would ask, it would not be to go steady or some such silly thing. His look was soft and vulnerable. She could imagine him someday far into her own future as her erstwhile lover from the past. First love.

Stanley looked directly at her. For once his eyes stayed true to their natural shade of blue, a pure blue, and did not waver with shadows or light. "That night Debbie showed up, she hit you. There was a moment there when I thought you were going to fight, but you didn't, you stopped yourself."

He took a deep breath, as though he had been working hard, trying to figure something out about her. Himself too.

"Why?" he asked. "What made you stop?"

Cookie lowered her head and smiled to herself. She toyed with the idea of telling him a tall tale, something ridiculous and entertaining, but she had too much respect for Stanley to play him for a fool. She remembered the night on Valentine's Day and thought about it. She told him she didn't know why she stopped herself in the midst of punching Debbie. But she knew a deeper measure had come into play, a few beats, the skip of a lyrical phrase, the fugue-like state coming from the first and most intense phase of love, and anger too. As if love and hate can be mixed and matched like the toss of a coin.

"Heads or tails?" she asked.

"I'm not understanding you," he said.

"Debbie reminded me of a small bird," Cookie said. "Defenseless, weak. I couldn't hurt somebody so weak. No matter how pissed I was, I couldn't hurt somebody that scared. She wasn't able to hurt me. I wasn't able to hate her enough to hurt her more than I already had been hurt. It didn't take away what she had done to me."

She didn't have to prove anything. He knew who she was.

Now she understood why he had given her life meaning. She didn't feel so lonely because he asked her such a strange question, the type of question no one else would ever think of asking her. He struck the lost chord she had been trying to find on her own for some time.

Stanley nodded and looked away. He was thinking about something, but it had nothing to do with Cookie. Whatever he was thinking about brought him to another time and place. She pressed up against him.

He took her into his arms and said, "Thank you. Thank you so very much." He kissed her mouth very lightly, skimming the surface of her lips. A lovely kiss, tender, strong and wanting her. His mouth was smooth, warm, and she craved more of him. She could tell he wanted her more than anything. He drew her tight into an embrace and held onto her.

He didn't want to go on, but she did. "What's the matter?" she asked.

"You helped me understand something about myself," he said. "Vietnam. I don't want to talk about it right now, but maybe someday I will."

The trail below where they stood was deceptively steep. It appeared more treacherous because vines, rocks, litter and natural debris had clotted into hammock shapes hanging above and overflowing from the low hanging boughs of trees.

"Here grows an old tree." Cookie laughed. Her face felt hot, making its own brand of light. "You could be a thousand years old today and I would not know. I cannot see your rings or guess whether the thickness of your trunk is meant to be a small wonder or maybe it has no meaning at all. I love you, funny tree. Branches, leaves, and bark tough like worn tire tread, I love all of you."

"Here's an ode to an old tree," Stanley said, kissing her on the top of her head, not moving, in stillness and solitary, he was memorizing the scent of her hair.

"I really can't remember where I found the owl the day I was down here with Herman. Everything looks different."

"The woods are always in a state of flux, always changing," he said, pulling himself erect, then moving toward her.

Only conscious of him in this wooded place where she came to worship stillness, the silence of her heart in the form of plea or a prayer and this dazzling man with his smooth flesh and steady heartbeat, she held onto him as they walked on, and he wrapped his arm around her, pulling her closer to him.

Brown and green spores spiraled upward from mounds in the earth, looking like the round heads of stalagmite crystals. The songs of birds whistled through the trees, sounding different and never singing at the same time. The silence between the songs of the birds spoke its own language.

The earth began to level out, flattening. As they walked, she noticed his legs were impossibly long, twice as long as her legs. She wondered if he could wrap those legs around her head, her body, her heart. Stepping in between the spaces of a labyrinth of gnarled roots, he jumped on top of a fallen tree and held his hand to help her up there beside him. They stood on top of this log and looked back to the path where they had come from. The labyrinth of roots made a subtle movement, evoking a crackling sound. Intertwined like snakes of many sizes, thick fibrous cords covered the earth. In the open patches, green moss lay flat beneath a field of feathery ferns. Green wisps, tendrils and fine hairs kept rhythm, secret movement, soft beats transcending time even though no hint of wind passed through the trees.

"Kiss me," she said impudently. She reached and pulled his head toward her face, giving him a generous kiss. She could tell he liked the way her mouth tasted and wanted more. But he held himself on the outer edge of reserve. She thought he enjoyed being there, hated it too, wrestling with himself, too torn to go one way or the other. He wanted her more than anything, but she was too young.

"I can't do that to you, and I can't do that to me," Stanley told her.

She could see he was really struggling but weakening too. And she knew she would win.

Every tree swayed, slightly bending in different directions; they were drunken trees staggering, about to fall over like Tiny Ten Pint or Pinky O'Hearn. They saw forked trees, forked with the shape of a V, or forked in a U-shape, split down the middle, still growing strong. These forked trees would not give up and die or ever lie to the world. Their strong branches reached toward the sky, paying homage to a merciful god.

"The holiness of trees is as close to the truth as we will ever come to know," Stanley told her.

"You're as close to the truth as I've ever known," Cookie said.

Stanley drew her to the ground beside him. "There are many forms of love," he said. "You owe it to yourself to explore them…to study them all. The ways we love and the ways we don't love. You don't have to do anything you don't want to do."

She wished she could perch herself on a bough, as though it was a ledge on a mountain, where she could see all, everything, the entire world, and no one could see her. She was an owl, a rare bird of prey. And she was not scared of the silence between them. For every moment they did not speak, the air grew warm and the sunlight filtered in between them. His eyes, seeking hers, reached her and drew her to him. She knew he was allowing her to enter his private world, where he had not let anyone else in.

She faced him fully and completely. His mouth widened. He was lying on his back. She sat over him, crimson-faced. She could feel the tops of her own bare legs and his smooth thighs. His hands searched for her body streaming beside him like a current of water coursing from the river. They were close to the river, but it did not belong in this moment, where the light streaming from the trees ignited the fire between them. Lying down, their flesh was prickled by twine, coiling vine, fall leaves, and cushioned by a wooly web of moss for a bed. Light crackled beside them as they stretched and moved. She felt the trees had seen all, experienced all, and knew much more than she would ever know. This is where her heart was, and it is where she came to rest. Their cries were loud like the ones you hear in a song meant to enslave you. A fugue.

A solitary leaf floated to the ground as if it had given up trying to hang on. You are here today for me and I wonder when I shall see you again, Cookie thought to herself, and she meant to mention it to him, but it didn't really matter if she had—she didn't expect for him to reassure her. She'd love to find him again someday in this same way, surrendering to her the way he had never given of himself before. The sun shone on the dilapidated stone footbridge as it lay looming ahead. Two of its old stone stanchion posts had collapsed into a heap of grey stone blocks, rubble, making it impossible to cross the bridge. Surrounded by the ruins of the aqueduct, it was clear they couldn't go on much farther, but they didn't have to. They had already gone as far as they needed to go. Only the trees knew for sure what happened there that day.

Thirty-seven

Kiss and Tell

While they were sitting together, their arms touched, staying there, warm and melding together. Cookie felt his soft cotton sleeve graze the side of her arm. His movement was intentional. He stayed as close to her as possible until the time would come for him to leave. A coarse electricity charged through her body with a ragged edge making her jittery but, at the same time, calm. She thought he had to feel the same magnetic pull but didn't ask him. She didn't need to ask him about how he felt about her. When he looked at her, his eyes had a look she had not seen before. In this moment, she moved her lips toward him and meant to kiss him on his neck, but his lips reached hers first. She did not know how to describe what she felt. She knew he wanted her, but she also knew soon he would leave. Of all the things in life she had experienced so far, knowing he felt so strongly about her was one perfect instance of gratitude. For her entire life she had waited patiently to experience the joy only borne of love. She always would remember this feeling, in this time and place.

First love.

They had come to the Midget Bar together so Stanley could

say goodbye to Jimmy. The bar wasn't crowded tonight and being there felt unhurried. A few regulars at the bar, including Pinky O' Hearn, sloshed down one beer after another. The jukebox played *Nights in White Satin* by the Moody Blues. Sitting at his table, Stanley sipped his beer slowly. Cookie still had not developed a taste for beer. She felt intoxicated though, giddy; Stanley had a powerful effect on her, and she wondered if it would always be this way.

Stanley had picked the song to play. *Nights in White Satin* had been recently re-released and steadily climbed the charts. Cookie would always remember it as the last song they had listened to. He leaned in toward Cookie and touched her silver hoop earring.

He spoke of Jimmy with admiration. "The thing that amazes me the most about Jimmy is he never takes any shit. No one messes with him. He has the most amazing strength I've ever seen in anyone, except for maybe my mother, and you."

He looked Cookie in her eyes for a long time as though he would never let go.

Cookie didn't know quite what he meant. She didn't see herself as strong. She knew she was tough, tough enough to get by, a Yonkers girl.

"Jimmy reminds me of the Vietcong," Stanley said as he watched Jimmy slapping down another mug onto the bar in front of Pinky. "People who don't know him will underestimate his strength, but he's like ten big guys put together and then some."

"That's why we're losing the war in Vietnam," he said. "Our fine leadership underestimated the strength of the Vietcong. And in the end, they're going to beat us."

By the time Saigon fell and the North Vietnamese took over the entire country, Stanley had been long gone from Yonkers, but Cookie later remembered what Stanley had said on their last night together in the Midget Bar and took it to heart. He had been right about what would happen in Vietnam. And he had been right about Cookie.

Tension escalated in the Midget Bar, once Debbie made her way over to talk to Jimmy. While she talked to Jimmy, she kept looking in Stanley's direction. Turned out in studded leather platform heels and a shiny shirt glowing silver in the black light, her hair was teased in a pile on the top of her head, a throwback to the 1960s. And she didn't look pregnant.

Giving Stanley a small wave and a bright white smile, she chewed her gum with a vengeance, but her pops and clicks could not be heard in the noisy bar. She turned her attention toward Cookie and gave her a look like she meant to slash her throat. Debbie said something to Jimmy and Pinky. Both guys glanced back and forth several times toward Stanley and Cookie.

Pinky stumbled out of his bar stool, standing unsteadily for a moment before ambling to the back of the room. He nodded to Stanley to say hello, but completely ignored Cookie. Fumbling for a quarter, he finally managed to get one out of his pocket. Rocking in front of the jukebox, he dropped his coin on the floor twice, almost falling over, trying to pick it up. Stanley shifted uncomfortably in his seat. He placed both of his hands on top of the table and looked at Cookie with concern.

Plugging his coin into the jukebox, Pinky stumbled, turning around to smile at Stanley and Cookie. Just as the music started to play, he gave Stanley the high-five. The song *Go Away Little Girl* by Donny Osmond flooded the bar.

Pinky leaned over to Cookie and laughed. Cookie picked up the nauseatingly strong stench of beer on his breath. "Go away, little girl," he said, leering at Cookie. "Get the message, kid."

"I hate Donny Osmond," Cookie told Stanley.

Stanley reached for her hand. "Let's get out of here," he said.

"What? Did I say something wrong?" Pinky grinned.

Stanley hit him in the shoulder, buddy-like. "See you around, Pinky. Take good care of yourself. Stay out of trouble."

Debbie sprang out from the side of the bar, yelling, "I told Jimmy, she's underage," she said pointing to Cookie. "You have no business being in this bar!"

Cookie looked away to avoid Debbie. There was no use fighting a battle when a prize could not be won. Jimmy swung from behind the bar and planted himself directly in Stanley's path. He screwed up his face and shook his head, giving Debbie the brush-off with his hand.

"Don't pay no attention to her," he told Stanley. "I know the score around here. Who's underage and who's not." Jimmy put his hands on his hips and solidly held himself. Then he threw open his arms to hug Stanley. Grabbing onto his legs, Jimmy did not want to let Stanley go, and pretended to be dragged along the floor by Stanley. Stanley picked him up in the air and hugged him, then swung him back down to the ground, where they locked fists like brothers.

"I'll be back," Stanley told him.

Jimmy nodded and smiled, brushing back a tear. "Stay cool, man," he told him.

When Cookie and Stanley came to the outside of the Midget Bar, something had changed between them. They did not part as they had in the past. She trailed after him until he reached the other side of Oak Street, where normally he would turn and go into the apartment he shared with his mother.

Tonight, she stayed on top of him, and he stayed on top of her. Then, he turned around and looked at her. She reached up and put her hands around his head and drew his face to hers and kissed him on the mouth. His lips were warm, smooth and slightly parting, and he surrendered to a long kiss. The world belonged to them and no one else could come between them.

He pressed his body close and pulled her into his arms and kissed her lips, her face, her neck, fiercely with no thought of ever stopping. It was all too much for him. Her too. Her body trembled, half with excitement, half with anticipation of what would come next. Only aware of the pressure of his lips on hers and her mouth opening to receive him, she knew she had awakened the same thing in him.

Then he just stopped. His movement wasn't just abrupt. He

was intentionally stopping himself. Standing back, he looked at her. "I wish I didn't have to leave," he said, "but if I don't, I will never forgive myself, and you will never forgive me."

He held her. She wanted to do so much more, but there was some great obstacle between the both of them. Her lips were soft, expectant, cheeks flushing with fire. Eyes wide open, arms opening, and their lips coming together. His lips were around her neck, a clasp locking a delicate chain. She wanted to flee into the night to get the goodbye part over and done. She wanted to pretend many days had already passed since he had left and she had not heard from him. She knew she might never hear from him again. Life was more than cruel, it was unkind when there was no need, nothing to gain, nothing to win.

She told him she could save him. He told her, "No one can save anybody. Only you can save yourself."

She closed her eyes to imagine the future. And she thought he would be gone when she opened her eyes, but he was still there and only too willing to leave her with pangs of sorrow, but not regret.

"Caring about you is not the problem," he told her. "You're sixteen and I care too much about you to stay with you. You might not understand that now, but someday you will."

The nippy autumn air made it cold enough to wear a sweater. Not too cold. A slight breeze made the tops of two trees quiver. Leaves fell from trees with the lightness of snow flurries. The weather was changing. Soon winter would come. Not too fast. She wanted to stop time. They walked on Oak Street until very late. Both a little giddy. Sad too. Their happiness coming from just being with someone you really like, and love.

"What am I supposed to do now?" he asked.

"You're supposed to kiss me."

At every corner, he stopped and kissed her. The kiss lasted until a car passed or the light changed. She was crying, smiling too. Stanley brushed the tears off of her cheeks.

"Always remember where you are going and never forget where you've been," he told her. Those were the final words he said and how she remembered him. Whenever she thinks of him, she feels love, tender and hopeful, fraught with the sorrow of loss, and she feels grateful, so grateful for having come to know him, even if it was only for a short time.

So, it ended that night.

Thirty-eight

The Last Note

The day after Stanley left Yonkers, Cookie ran into Lizzie
Lovato, who apologized for not going to her Sweet Sixteen party.
Lizzie stared at Cookie with dreamy eyes as she explained with
great passionate conviction about how a wild dream led to her
discovery in a scientific breakthrough about planets.

"Some planets are called booth planets," she told Cookie.
"Booth planets are girl planets who cooperate with other
heavenly bodies, and because they spend time immersed in
cooperation, they have a heart. Having a heart makes them
move more slowly around the sun, sometimes leaving the solar
system to float indefinitely in an orbit of their own making."

On a cold Friday in November, Cookie was sitting on
the floor, smoking a Marlboro, writing in her black & white
notebook, when Sister Mary Eau Claire found her in the secret
janitor's closet. Located behind the cafeteria's kitchen, the
janitor's closet was Cookie's latest place to hide. Filled with
mops, brooms, buckets, bottles of industrial strength cleaner,
and reams of toilet paper, it wasn't an inviting cubby, but it
gave Cookie great solace and a place to write. And the walls
were blue, so blue.

The nun wore a starchy expression. Then she had a change of heart and smiled. Instead of sentencing her to doom, the nun held up two fingers to her mouth. She was bumming a cigarette. Cookie held open her pack of Marlboros and brushed her cigarettes forward, offering one to Sister Mary. Gleefully, the nun took the cigarette and lit it with the burning head from Cookie's cigarette. A wisp of ash flew into the air and floated to the ground. The casual exchange appeared to be a familiar ritual, one that had been carefully cultivated between them.

"What happened with the guy?" the nun asked, flicking her ash.

"He's gone," Cookie said. Her voice went flat. "He moved to California to go to school." Cookie's voice dropped even lower. "There are plenty of schools in New York. He could have gone to school here."

"Hmmm," Sister Mary intoned. "That happened to me once. I was about to be married, but he had a change of heart."

Cookie didn't know what to say. Sometimes, it was best to listen and let someone share a story. The nun and Cookie stayed in the janitor's closet, smoking. The nun had a funny habit of shaking her cigarette a lot, fidgeting with it, to take more drags than you usually take from a single *ciggie*. She probably craved a cigarette all day long and looked forward to running into Cookie.

The nun didn't talk more about her broken heart. It was plain to Cookie she could feel the nun's hurt and see it in her eyes. She took a long deep drag from the cigarette and stared at her plume rising to form a fine grey cloud above the sink in the janitor's closet. "He did me a favor," the nun said. "In a funny way, it was a gift. I wasn't meant to be his wife. I was meant to be here."

Sometimes, the nun asked her for a second smoke and finished it—all the way to the nub. She wanted to get all of her smoking in, all at once. In another time and place, it would seem strange to think about bonding over Marlboros.

But you can do something bad and bond in a way that leads to something good.

Sister Mary let go of a cumulus cloud of grey smoke and asked, "What are you working on?"

"I'm not sure," Cookie told her. "I'm just writing."

Cookie had been writing about kisses and she dared not show it to anyone.

What would happen when the kissing stopped? Would he become part of my soul and I of his? Kisses are like an angel tapping hello to say I'm here for a while because I think I love you. Hello kisses. Goodbye kisses. Ardent kisses. Lingering kisses. Loving kisses. Long kisses. Kisses so short they feel like the flutter of a bug flying by. As energetic as a hummingbird. A kiss in the moment. A stolen kiss. A secret kiss. The silent kiss. A furtive kiss. An electric kiss. A long and lingering kiss. A lusty kiss is a prelude to a bold sexual advance. A kiss of love. A kiss of sorrow. An angry kiss. A kiss of heat. The heat in a kiss. A kiss can be weaponized and used to hurt someone. A kiss of joy. The kiss can be one of intent—to seal a promise. A kiss embraces two souls.

"Enough of this shit," Cookie said out loud. "It's time to get on with it."

Every time she thought of Stanley, she remembered the way he had made her feel. When she felt sexy or sensuous, she naturally wanted to open up and give, and she thought the feeling comes from being able to receive love and desire. She felt she was sexy because she could say this is who I am, and strut down the street as though she owned the world. This is what I think is sexy. Who doesn't love a girl who can look sexy and be funny at the same time?

She wanted to find out what had become of Stanley and knew the only link would be through big Bertha. She stopped at the Café Trento, but Bertha wasn't there. She worried calling Bertha would be a repeat of the past, when she shunned Cookie and evaded telling her of Stanley's whereabouts.

Cookie had no choice but to call her. Bertha's husky voice panted into the phone as though she was excited. "Come over now," she told Cookie. "There is something I want to show you! You will love it!"

In Bertha's apartment, Cookie's eyes fixed on a pink cardboard box with a shiny gold and black Café Trento label. Bertha opened the box to show her miniature eclairs, cream puffs, and, of course, cannoli and sfogliatelle.

"Take one now and have another one for later," she told Cookie as she balanced the box on one hand.

Cookie reached to take a miniature cannoli and bit into the crisp pastry, waiting for the ooze of sweet ricotta crème to fill her mouth. A tangy bit of citron added bite.

"I cannot eat the pastry," Bertha said. "I have to keep my hands clean so I can show you my surprise. Besides, I eat too much of that stuff anyway."

Bertha did not go far to retrieve a worn black leather case, obviously holding a violin. She pressed her fingers to her sides, wiping them gently along her coarse woolen jumper.

Carefully, she unlatched the case and lifted her violin to show Cookie. "I love the smell of my violin." She placed it gingerly under Cookie's nose. "See how the scent is rich and so sweet. This my violin."

Cooked detected the scent of old lacquered wood and ancient perfume with a hint of something minty like pine needles.

Bertha pulled the violin slowly up to her shoulder and held it there. Swooning. Losing herself. She played the beginning of an uneven song that Cookie recognized but could not remember its name.

Then she stopped and looked at Cookie. "I am not very good. It has been so long since I played. But now that I have my washing machine and Stanley moved away, I am practicing again."

She came close to Cookie and whispered, "Stanley hated the sound of me practicing. Now that he's gone, I'll practice every day."

She took the violin and lovingly returned it to the case. "It will take time for me to get good again. I love the sound of the music. Soon I will play for you."

Then she shrugged as if nothing in the world mattered. "Even when you lose someone you love, you gain something too."

Latching the violin case, she turned to Cookie, and smiled serenely. "You must miss him. I know you like to kiss him. That's how I felt about his father. Such a very long time ago. Still, I remember."

She took a deep breath, sighed, fighting back tears and patted the violin case. "All of the music I have ever played is in here. It is so beautiful that it makes me cry. It reminds me of love. Even when you lose someone you love, you never lose the love. It is always there. A song that you hear until the very last note."

Cookie's cheeks burned. She was sure the temperature in the room had gone up. "Mind if I open the window?" she asked.

"Not at all," Bertha said.

Cookie moved toward the window, but Bertha got there first, jiggling her massive arms while she threw open the window. "Let's have a smoke."

Bertha stood beside the window, lit a cigarette and tossed the match into the night. "It's starting to get cold," she said. "Before you know it, the snow will come."

Cookie joined Bertha at the window and lit her own Marlboro. She shot a stream of smoke into the cold night air. "Have you heard from Stanley?" she asked.

"Stanislas." Bertha nodded. "He's okay. He doesn't tell me much. That's his way." She blew smoke out the window.

Turning to Cookie with smoke still coming out of her nose, she said, "When he was a little boy, he was the same way. He never talked about his feelings. He was hard to reach. Know what I mean? But whenever a storm would come, he'd get scared by the thunder. He hated loud noise and put his hands over his ears, like this," she said, covering her own ears.

"Then he'd jump into my arms and squirm into my lap, and get *very, very* still until the storm was over. As soon as the thunder stopped, he'd go away and pretend like nothing happened. Other than those storms, he never came to me for a hug."

Warmth came to Cookie's cheeks, as if Stanley had unexpectedly stopped by to say hello. Cookie tilted her head toward the window and looked out into the night. As long as she lived, she would never forget him.

"Stanley was never like other boys," Bertha said softly. "He has a big heart, bigger than the whole city of Yonkers."

They drank wine by candlelight. It was unlike any other wine Cookie had tried. Later, Bertha admitted the wine was a cream sherry. As the night wore on, Bertha loosened her woolen jumper and sat at the small table wearing a cotton shift, wide bloomers, and an oversized sweater. She looked lumpy in her underclothes, very much like a woman who was beyond middle age. Prone to suddenly getting very warm, then cool again, Bertha kept taking her sweater on and off. Sometimes, she seemed to be out of breath, especially when she became excited over something.

"The shortest distance between two people is a kiss," Bertha said. "Don't ever forget that."

Cookie had lost a lot of things, but she had not lost the ability and desire to kiss. She entered a new fugue-like state where her words became music and she could write about many things, and especially her experience with Stanley.

Bertha slid the window shut, making a rickety creaking sound. In the reflection of the glass, Cookie saw her own face and noticed her baby fat was melting away, leaving angular lines. Outside under the streetlight a few snow flurries were falling. She hugged Bertha goodbye and went out into the night where she noticed the flurries were few and far between, the kind of big wet flakes that never stick to the ground and always wash away.

The view from the top of Nodine Hill swept down into the heart of Yonkers, straight into the large expanse of the Hudson River. By night, the river became dark, but everyone knew it was there. On Maple Street, she saw her breath rising like steam and dissipating into the clear night. The flurries had stopped, and the wind had subsided. A slight chill in the air sharpened her senses, making the power of her memory more acute. She remembered the first time she had seen Stanley down by the river. The scent in the air had been full of salt, heat and him. Hot enough to take her clothes off, she would have gone in, had the water been clear and fresh. He stood by river's edge looking at her as though he could see through her, and he really liked what he saw.

If we do not find our lovers, we can always dream of them until they become real. She found the passage somewhere and it amused her because she could not pinpoint the origin.

Even though Cookie had regained her words, she found mere words were inadequate to describe what it felt like to be kissed by Stanley. The power of the kiss is one of the strongest forces on earth. Heaven too.

More than anything she wrote about kissing. The bond between the kisser and the kissed conveys a promise.

Kisses can be gentle and reassuring, urgent and pressing, or lusty and all consuming. A kiss nourishes the heart and might actually touch the soul. When a kiss is over, it lingers on the lips with certain warmth and the power of afterglow.

She remembered what Mabel Kerry said about loss. "We never lose what we hold close to our hearts."

Kissing is an experience, ephemeral and in the moment, and when a kiss embraces two souls, time is transcended in a melody or phrase of interwoven parts, creating a whole—a fugue. Every woman on earth experiences this feeling the first time she truly falls in love. While the bond between the kisser and the kissed conveys a promise, sooner or later, and over time, all promises can be broken. Every woman has a first love, the only love, or one love in a string of many. Do you remember your first love? Posing the question runs the risk of raising soreness, a bruise or even opening a wound. First love can be strange, unwanted, vexing and exhilarating. It can be all of these things, but no matter the outcome, first love is never forgotten.

www.ingramcontent.com/pod-product-compliance
Lightning Source LLC
Chambersburg PA
CBHW032135110726

47902CB00003B/588